# The Legend of Oescienne

# The Finding

By Jenna Elizabeth Johnson

THE LEGEND OF OESCIENNE

———

THE FINDING

For more information and to contact the author visit
**www.jennaelizabethjohnson.com**

*For Dad, who instilled in me a deep respect and admiration for Nature and all her endless wonder.*

*For Mom, who taught me to see the good in humanity, and to cherish and strive for that goodness in myself.*

*And for Cate, my one and only sister, who makes me laugh more than anyone else I know.*

# CONTENTS

# The Legend of Oescienne

# The Finding

# -Prologue-

# Evasion

Morning's first light poured into a cramped, dank cave casting strange shadows against its distorted walls. It was a very ordinary cave as caves go, and up until a few days ago it seemed things would remain that way. The cave had sat empty in a cliff above the western sea, left alone to inhale the ocean's salty air and capture the sound of the waves crashing below. Hidden and unseen in a cove only a few knew about, the cave had remained empty for so many years. But that was all about to change.

A piercing beam of light fought its way through a narrow hole in the ceiling of the cavern, breaking into the empty chamber and making the sunlight flooding through its mouth seem dimmer. The ray came to rest upon the pale face of a figure bunched upon the cold, dirty floor like a pile of discarded rags. His eyes were closed in sleep, but the silent expression on his face was far from restful. His dark hair was unkempt and his face appeared almost bloodless. He was as still as death, but his tense features and the grim cut of his mouth confirmed the struggle that only the living possessed.

The man stirred awake and rolled onto his side, sending a scraping and soft groaning sound playing against the curved walls. Wincing and gasping in pain, he clutched his shoulder and dragged himself up into a sitting position. The bright beam of light was now slanted across his profile, illuminating the distinct characteristics of his race. His fine features and narrow, sharply tapered ears proved that he was of elfin descent, but it was his dark hair, pale skin and uncommonly tall stature that revealed him as one of the Aellheian elves of the east.

He blinked his eyes as the waves of pain ebbed and passed, looking blankly around the natural room that he'd been sleeping in. The cave was littered with jagged stalactites and stalagmites, making it resemble the mouth of a yawning dragon. Several conical tunnels were scattered throughout, giving the impression that a giant had pressed its fingers into the small space while it was still a soft cavity of clay, leaving their indentations behind.

The injured elf breathed deeply as he recalled climbing up here only a few days before. He was grateful despite the exhausting effort; at least now he could rest easy. This place was a great secret not known to his pursuers. He closed his eyes and tried to clear his mind. A sharp, metallic taste in his mouth forced him to recall the skirmish he'd had not long ago, the one that had landed him in his current situation. He sighed and rested his head against the wall, listening to the low rumble of the waves outside as he tried to distract himself from the endless sound of dripping water echoing throughout the cave. The smell of saltwater and pine resin, dust and distant fog hung in the air like a delicate feather, reminding him of the thick forest perched on the edge of the cliffs just above his head.

Despite his hot skin and the relatively relaxing rhythm of the crashing waves, the elf felt a cold chill clenching his heart. He ran his fingers through his tangled hair as if this action might comb away the grogginess and pounding headache that seemed to swallow him. He'd been in this place for three days now, or so he thought, and he feared the wound in his shoulder might be infected. He'd cleaned it and treated it with an herbal balm, but it was swollen and throbbing.

For several months he'd managed to evade the Tyrant's men but now it seemed they'd finally caught their prey. He'd gone so far as to enter the land west of the feared Thorbet and Elornn mountains, a place the Crimson King would never go, but it was clear the Tyrant's soldiers thought differently. They'd finally moved in close enough to place an arrow deep in his shoulder just to the left of his heart. Desperate, injured and out of options, he headed farther west towards a land he'd once considered home only to find a familiar place of sanctuary. This particular cave would hide him well, but he also knew that if he died here so would the secrets he carried.

# The Legend of Oescienne – The Finding

The elf trembled again, blinking against the harsh light hitting his face. Whether the shivering was a result of an encroaching fever or from the thought of his world crashing down around him, he couldn't tell. He drew a long, deep breath and carefully pulled a leather-bound journal, a pen and an inkwell out of the saddle bags he'd had the sense to grab before fleeing on foot. He propped himself up against the wall, quietly thanking Ethöes it was smooth, and leaned forward so that one of the empty pages of the journal lit up to a blinding white from the sunbeam pouring through the roof. He thought for a while as he continued to fight off the sickening heat emanating from his shoulder. After several moments of reverie, he dipped his quill into the inkwell and began to write:

*It has been three centuries and more since the world changed, but not much has happened since. Whether that fact bodes good or ill towards the people loyal to the Goddess, I cannot tell. The pages before this tell the story of the world and how Ethöes created all the living and nonliving things that exist upon its surface, of the rise of the god Ciarrohn and Traagien's defeat of him, of the folly of the elves and the creation of the humans and their eventual end. All of the pages before this one hold that story and the secrets of the royal family of Oescienne.*

*Therefore I, the last Magehn of the Tanaan king, will not waste time with the tales of old. What I can tell you, however, is that three hundred years ago the Crimson King cast a terrible curse upon the last race of humans, transforming them into dragons and severing their link to the province of Oescienne. From that point on, the tie between the western*

# Evasion

*province and its rightful sovereigns, the race of humans, was destroyed, setting in motion the Tyrant's first steps in clearing the way for the complete domination of all seven provinces of Ethöes.*

A muffled shout followed by a torrent of angry words brought the Magehn's pen to a stop. His heart quickened its pace and the throbbing in his head and shoulder fell into rhythm with it. The noise came from above, and through the tiny skylight in his cave the elfin man could barely make out the foreign tongue of several of the Tyrant's men. He hoped they wouldn't find his horse, but then he remembered he'd removed its bridle and saddle, encouraging the animal to flee just before he made his way down the narrow trail leading to his hiding place.

Although he couldn't decipher what it was the men said, the Magehn knew that they'd tracked him this far. *How they found the courage to cross the mountains is beyond me,* he thought bitterly. Then he realized it hadn't been courage but fear. Those loyal to the Crimson King may have feared the far western mountains, but they feared their king more.

The elf listened silently as the voices trailed off. When he was certain they had moved on to search for him in some other location, he got back to his work, focusing on finishing while he still could:

*Though the humans are now dragons, and those dragons are now scattered, there is reason yet to hope. The Tyrant still suffers from the wounds inflicted upon him in that final battle with the last Tanaan prince and his people; he still struggles to regain his strength from the effort it took to transform them. Yet no one knows when the Crimson King will regain his former might and attack the remaining provinces. Most believe it is only a matter of time, and time is running short.*

*The last Tanaan prince is now lost. Many claim he is long dead, for wouldn't he have returned to his people and rallied them by now, even in their reptilian forms? Yet I saw his transformation and witnessed his escape within the confusion of the aftermath of the great battle. I believe with all of my heart, though I may not live out my immortal existence as I had once hoped, that a day will come when the Tyrant's curse is lifted and the Tanaan humans will return to rule in Oescienne once again.*

The elf halted his hand, staring down at the stark black marks he'd sketched upon the paper. He was writing in his native language, the language of the Dhonoaran elves, descendents of the Aellheians. He should have felt pride for their development of such a beautiful language, but instead he felt a bitter taste of disgust rise in his throat. So much sorrow, so much pain, destruction and avaricious betrayal had come from his people that it brought him some shame, even though he knew it wasn't his fault.

The Magehn drew a sharp breath as a sudden stab of pain ripped down his arm. He had been about to continue his notation but instead he paused, his jaw clenched, willing the ache to pass. As he waited in agony, he returned his thoughts to the ugly circumstances of his world. Instead of thinking of his ancient elfin ancestors, however, he recalled his own loved ones

# Evasion

harmed or corrupted by the Tyrant King. He thought especially of the one whose trust he'd lost, someone who was still dear to him. Soon he felt another pain, a pain that would never heal. The ache in his shoulder and the ache in his heart mingled, combining to form one great pang of anguish.

The elf took a deep breath, suppressing the distracting memories that were now surfacing in his mind. *I don't have time to tell my own story. I have time only for this . . .* He forced his screaming thoughts to the back of his mind and continued on with what he had started. Beads of sweat broke out on his forehead, but he wrote on:

*I have spent long years mourning my king and my people, but I could not hide from the terrors of this world forever. I came out of my hiding no more than six months ago, and it took the blessed words of hope to make me finally face my fears. I knew the Tyrant searched for me, that he seeks vengeance, even now. He is aware that I hold the secrets of the Tanaan and believes that I know the location of their prince. But I braved his wrath and went forth into the world despite the great danger, for I had received word of something amazing, something extraordinary.*

*Before I was tracked down and wounded by the Tyrant's minions, I had been riding throughout all of Ethöes, spreading this great news, news of an answer to our plight. The Oracles, those that still remain with us, spoke of a miracle promised by Ethöes herself, one that could mean the salvation of our world.*

Pain beyond description flared through the elf's fevered body. He cried out in anguish as his pen dragged across the bottom of the white paper leaving a long, jagged black line. This ache was worse than the ones before, and it struck fear into the Magehn's heart. His eyes watered and his vision became fuzzy as he wondered about the origin of the arrow that had caused this wound. Perhaps it had been poisoned. He felt lightheaded and sensed his mind being pulled in and out of consciousness. Furiously, and with fresh determination, the last Magehn of the Tanaan king began writing as fast as he could, able to produce one more sentence before he knew no more:

*I have done what I can to spread this new prophecy throughout the land, a prophecy about the return of a lasting peace, a prophecy about a lost prince, and a prophecy about a young, pure-blooded human girl born to save us all.*

# - Chapter One -

# A Very Surprising Discovery

Jaax wrinkled his nose as the sound of a chattering bird pulled him from his slumber, but he kept his eyes shut and remained motionless nonetheless. Not that he could've moved much anyway, for the small, fern-laced hollow he'd tucked himself into the night before was just big enough to accommodate his large size, wings and all. He sighed softly, releasing a hot, smoke-tinged breath that forced the damp leaves plastered to the forest floor to peel and curl in protest.

After a few heartbeats he risked a peek, opening one silvery-green dragon's eye to catch a glimpse of the damp, grey morning that congested the forest like a heavy cold. Most dragons had eyes of yellow, orange or red, dominated by a wild intelligence. It was only the Tanaan dragons whose eyes were shaded in the blues, greens and browns of their human ancestors. Jaax shivered at the recollection. A terrible curse had meant the end of the humans in Ethöes, the same curse that had brought about the existence of his particular race of dragons nearly five centuries ago.

Jaax blinked several times as if doing so would remove these dark thoughts from his mind the way tears dislodged grains of sand from one's eyes. And his eyes were quite unique, even for a Tanaan dragon. They shone with a fierce obscurity, as if they'd been tame at one time but had since returned to being wild. Why they had become this way, however, was a mystery known entirely to the soul buried behind them. It was only during this first waking moment that Jaax revealed any clues as to what sorrows and secrets he kept locked away, but that small amount of time was never long enough for anyone to discern the dragon's troubles.

Jaax sighed and continued to listen to the singing bird from earlier. It was a heartsong sparrow, a harbinger of luck, hope and love. The tiny creature trilled on before it was frightened away by something larger foraging for food. *Well*, the dragon thought with an amused smile, *at least it wasn't me this time.*

With his fine musician flown, the dragon lifted his triangular head and gazed more thoroughly at his surroundings. The feathery ferns that brushed against his face acted as a fragile screen between his tiny vale and the outside world and the great, gnarled oaks stretching overhead resembled giant, arthritic hands reaching up out of the earth to grasp at the insubstantial fog. Despite its early morning lethargy, the forest was alive with a variety of scents: cold fog, decaying leaves and the distant tang of a fresh fire being the most prominent. Jaax tilted his head to listen for possible intruders, but all he heard was the drip of condensation gathering and slapping against the leaf-litter below. The Tanaan dragon smiled softly, his eyelids drooping lazily as the cool silence weighed heavily upon him. His initial instincts told him there was no threat here. The instincts that ran deeper, however, told him something else. As the heartsong sparrow had announced earlier, there was change in the air, and not just any change, but a *good* change, one that had led him to this secluded corner of Ethöes to begin with.

Yawning widely, Jaax stretched himself out of his forest bed, snapping twigs and cracking joints as he stood to his full height. The strong scent of earthworms and wild mushrooms filled the space around him as he pressed his weight into the dark, rich soil, and the taste of damp, mossy air filled his mouth and throat as he breathed. Jaax smiled despite himself. He loved the absolute quiet and heavy scents the fog evoked.

The foraging animal from earlier, a towhee, noticed him immediately and twittered energetically as it fled the scene. The dragon grinned again as the bird's distress calls disappeared into the mist. He was used to being feared but he never took it personally. As he shook the cold and sleep from his body his irony scales, rough and glimmering like polished granite, gradually changed from the bland colors of his surroundings to shades of copper, rusty bronze, deep-green and turquoise.

# The Legend of Oescienne – The Finding

Finally fully awake, Jaax at last allowed his mind to consider his long awaited duty, and the letter that had called him to it. He was here on the bank of the Saem River to retrieve a young child, a newborn baby to be exact, and, according to what the correspondence had claimed, the only one of her kind. It was a very odd task for such a large dragon, but there was a chance that this child held the fate of the world in her tiny hands.

Jaax felt a rippling shiver pass under his tough skin as he considered what all of this meant. *A baby girl,* he thought in wonderment mixed with skepticism, *found inside a hollow, yet very much alive shell of an ancient oak tree in northern Oescienne.* The familiarity of it all made his great heart quicken with anticipation and even fear. *The words of the Oracles . . .* Jaax tried to bite back that enticing thought, but it was no use. This had been his purpose all along, to find her and protect her the day she was born. He realized that if this child truly was what the message claimed her to be, then there was good reason for the sudden flare of his once dormant emotions. Yet he still doubted, for he had been disappointed too many times before.

After one last lingering glance at his campsite, Jaax set his jaw in determination and spread his enormous wings. He beat them once and leaped into the gray sky, forcing the thick mist to dance in small eddies and the tree branches to whip around in protest. Once he'd climbed high enough, he noted the fog sagging like a heavy blanket between the two ranges forming

# A Very Surprising Discovery

the Saem Valley. He glided soundlessly over the gray-white ocean of clouds below him, counting the miles as they passed and narrowing his pale eyes against the brilliant sun.

The dragon's final destination was a place called Crie, a place as unassuming as a newborn infant. It was a small, secluded village on the river bank just a few miles east of where he'd slept. The location was ideal, set against the southern Saem Hills on the flat land that rested just above the calm tributary.

He knew this village well and the elves who lived there: they were descendants of the Woedehn elves, a race that still resided in the great forests of Hrunah to the east. Some of them had traveled to this part of the world after the rise of the Crimson King, hoping to relocate beyond his grasp. A great number of them, Jaax recalled, were actually Nesnan or Resai, the mixed-blood descendents of elf and human unions from long before the Tyrant transformed them. Though not immortal, they had inherited from their elfin ancestors at least some of their longevity. Many of these people were hundreds of years old but appeared rather youthful.

While he soared over the treetops, Jaax passed the time by picturing the townspeople he knew from his past meetings with them. He saw in his mind's eye a gentle folk, secretive and simple in their ways, yet lively and sociable when the mood called for celebration. Like their Woedehn kin, the elves of Crie were short in stature but not petite and delicate like so many of the other races of their kind. They never quailed from hard work and were always eager to take on a good challenge. Whether that task be something as risky as driving a rabid dremmen wolf from their village or something as simple as removing a stubborn turnip from their garden, it didn't matter.

As he drew nearer to his destination, Jaax drifted below the fog line once more, flying low over the outskirts of the sleepy village. Many communities like this small colony were thought to be hiding in sheltered valleys and on mountaintops all throughout Ethöes, but Jaax was only aware of a handful of them. He scanned the settlement quickly, counting the stubby, stone-and-adobe houses as they darted by. They looked remarkably like rounded cones with a thatching of reeds or small twigs for roofing. Some of them were several rooms large and gave the impression of a group of gumdrops being pressed firmly together. A single road twined through the village and the randomly placed dwellings like a brown snake searching out mice in a harvested field. Most of the stone huts had small gardens and fenced-in yards to grow kitchen herbs and to hold small livestock.

Smoke from early morning fires curled sluggishly above the earthen houses, their roofs dusted white with the crystalline frost of this uncommonly temperate winter. From what Jaax could judge, the elves had only been up long enough to light the fires in their hearths. He cast his eyes towards the center of the sprawling town and from his lofty view he spied a low burning bonfire ringed in by great, round stones. The coal-choked blaze looked like it had been burning for quite some time. Red-tinged smoke still rose and blended with the white mist above, signaling that this fire stood for more than just the celebration of the Solstice that had passed just over a week ago.

The dragon grinned as the cool winter air whipped around him. He knew these elves would be preparing breakfast for the whole town in anticipation of their rare visitor. *It's been so long since they've seen dragons grace the skies . . .* he thought with a heavy heart. He secretly blessed the low cloud cover, for it masked the tainted smoke of the bonfire which, on a clear day, would point out a forbidden celebration.

Jaax grimaced. He knew that this ancient tribe still remembered the time when the Crimson King first came into power, putting an end to their carefree way of life. No longer could they take part in the festivals they once cherished unless willing to risk enslavement or even death. Even now, nearly five centuries later, the people of Crie feared the Tyrant King. To them the threat of Cierryon was as real as it ever was and many of the villagers had to sacrifice much of their tradition to avoid discovery by the Tyrant's minions. One of these sacrifices had been the large bonfires that were a central part of their ancient customs. On holidays and special occasions, the blazes were fed sacred plants and herbs, staining the smoke to a specific color. This was a sure sign of an outlawed festival, one not tolerated by the king.

# The Legend of Oescienne – The Finding

This fear had kept them cautious for centuries, but today was different, today they had good reason to be joyous for the first time in ages. They had a real reason to celebrate and the thick, low clouds offered some protection from a curious gaze that might otherwise notice a large plume of ruddy smoke. *Fear not this day, elves of Crie,* Jaax thought with an optimistic grin as he glided in low to graze the conical tops of firs and spruce. *If you have truly found what you claim, then today is the dawn of a new era, an era that will bring a lasting peace to Ethöes.*

Jaax swooped in between two ancient sycamores, standing bare for the winter. He came to rest just beyond the border of the settlement, beating his great wings and balancing his long tail to soften his heavy landing. He swiveled his thorny head, his keen eyes scanning his surroundings, his steamy breath puffing in the crisp air. The valley was a palette of cool colors this time of year with the frigid wilderness set against the wide and deep Saem River. Sycamores, oaks, aspen and a few conifers grew between the steep hills. Although the aspens and sycamores had lost their leaves, their white mottled trunks looked quite beautiful standing against the cool grey sky and sharp granite stones that protruded from the earth like giant, jagged teeth.

The great reptile looked out over the Saem River, moving slowly past the small islands like liquid ice. He wondered when a lasting snow would fall, but was grateful it wasn't any colder. Once his survey was through, he turned and walked east along the river's edge, following the scent of roasting meat and smoke. As he approached Crie, the villagers cautiously poked their heads out of their houses, their eyes growing wide with delight when they recognized their rare visitor.

One of these curious townsfolk spotted the dragon just on the edge of town and shouted jovially, "Raejaaxorix! You've come at last!"

The Resai man came rushing out of his squat home with a wide smile on his face. He was tanned and wrinkled with fading brown hair that stuck out at a hundred odd angles. He wore a simple white, long-sleeved tunic, worn russet pants and a pair of scuffed clogs. "For such a large creature you sure make a quiet entrance!" he continued in his cheerful, melodic voice, olive eyes twinkling brightly.

This time the dragon Raejaaxorix gave a full smile, revealing a line of white daggers. He loosened his stiff gait and answered, "I hear you've found an infant, Aydehn, probably Nesnan, maybe even Resai or full-blooded elf, but it can't possibly be what you claim it to be."

"Ah," replied Aydehn with a grin and a shake of his finger, "you never change Jaax, always straight to business and never time for too much small talk."

"I just can't justify wasted time." Jaax gave the old elfin man a tired smirk.

"Ha-ha! Right you are! Come, you must tell us news from the outside world, we're dying to hear anything, and you must have something to eat, yes?"

Jaax allowed himself to be led away by the small crowd of interested people that had gathered. He didn't mind their stares and whispers. In fact, he was glad for the company and couldn't blame these people for enjoying a chance to be hospitable. The discovery of this child could mean good news for them too, and perhaps the years of living their lives in secret might finally come to an end.

Following a meal of roasted deer and a detailed discussion of the state of Oescienne and its surrounding lands, the elves took Jaax to where they'd found the infant. The group climbed deep into the boulder-strewn hills, skirting around a jagged hillock and up a granite-laced canyon. The narrow gullies, crowded trees, and giant slabs of stone made movement through this forest cumbersome. If Jaax had been an old dragon, moving across this terrain would have proven difficult, but his lean frame and powerful build aided him much as he followed the people of Crie deeper into the hills. Instinctively, he peered around every corner, smelling the air carefully, a habit he'd developed as a result of his elusive lifestyle.

When the entire party finally crested the steep rise, Jaax paused and gazed in wonder at the great tree spreading its thick canopy from one side of the expansive hilltop to the other. It was an ancient oak, magnificent and gnarled, its several knobby limbs twisting and grasping for the sky. The giant tree was hollow as a shell but strongly attached to the ground due to several knotty roots plunging deep into the heart of the earth. The heartwood of the oak had been burned out in a firestorm ages ago and now all that was left was an empty area large enough to accommodate him and the drove of elves.

"Do you know this tree, Racjaax?" asked Aydehn quietly. His tone was more serious now, his face turning grave as he clasped his hands together in anticipation.

"Yes, yes I do," Jaax answered in similar tones as he focused his silver-green eyes on the full beauty of the tree. "It's Ethöes' first oak, the Sacred Oak. I knew it was located in this part of Oescienne, but I wasn't aware it was so near Crie."

"Aye," answered the Resai man in an anxious whisper, his eyes wide with feeling, "this is why our ancestors came to rest here when they fled the east. They knew this was Ethöes' Oak, and the oak of all trees! The most sacred! They found themselves quite blessed when they happened upon it, and they knew then that the Goddess would keep them safe here. It has become a sacred place to us, and it is here that we give thanks to the Goddess."

Jaax looked around inside of the hollow tree, ignoring the silent and inquisitive stares pouring over him. There was a charred pit in the center for a fire, perhaps to be lit on the Solstice and the Equinox. He sniffed at the air again, this time trying hard to detect any aroma that might reveal the secret to this place. It smelled of old smoke, dust and ancient forest, but nothing unusual or even unique drifted on the air, not even the smallest trace of magic.

"There was no mother?" Jaax asked suddenly, turning his keen eyes on the group that had accompanied him.

Aydehn nodded somberly, his voice sounding dry, "We found her here, completely naked and only a few hours old, according to our midwives." When Jaax adopted a pensive look, the Resai man added, "That must be significant, inside the Sacred Oak?"

"We didn't see anything out of the ordinary, no markings, nothing on the ground around her," continued one of the village elders, a wizened old woman leaning on a crooked cane with a voice like an irritated frog. "She was just here. In fact, it's a miracle that someone happened by. Luckily the Solsticetide had just passed, or else we would generally not come out this way, for weeks sometimes."

Jaax puzzled this over. A female child seemingly born from the earth itself; yes, this did sound similar to what the Oracles had promised. And there was the Sacred Oak, a connection to Ethöes herself. There was only one more thing to prove, and the Tanaan dragon didn't see that as likely, despite what the message he received had claimed. It was all probably coincidence anyhow, coincidences happened all the time and he'd definitely been alive long enough to know that.

Nevertheless, he couldn't help but wonder: could this girl really be human?

Jaax sighed as he thought about the strange circumstances. Over the years he'd gone on mission after mission, receiving word of a human child having been found. He'd been to what seemed like every province of Ethöes, as far north as the Baer Mountains in Rhohwynd and as far south as the Soahna Flatlands and all the other places in between. He'd seen hundreds of infants, all being proclaimed as the one the Oracles had promised, but none of them had been human. Some of these children had even been boys, in which case Jaax became angry. It was clearly foretold that the human child would be a girl. Half the time he thought these people only wanted to see a dragon, a rare sight in Ethöes these days.

"Where's the child now?" queried Jaax, leaving his thoughts for later.

"She's with my wife, Thenya," Aydehn answered. "Shall we go and get her?"

"Yes." Jaax dropped his distracted gaze and looked at the elderly Resai man standing below him. "I'll see her now and decide if she's better off with Hroombra or better off left here with you."

Jaax followed the elves back to the village, reflecting in silence the entire journey back. He was thinking about what had been prophesied, although his better judgment told him not to. He'd waited so many years, long years, longer than his patience should have had to endure. Could the Oracles have spoken truth and could the search finally be over? *Now's not the time to ask yourself these questions*, he thought in self-chastisement, *they're all counting on your final say. Let's hope that this time the child really is the one.*

The young dragon sighed, scorching the icy air as he exhaled. The Oracles' claim had been faulty and vague, that was undeniable. When has an Oracle ever been absolutely clear about the future anyway? But right now he needed to focus on what was best for this child if she wasn't the one he sought.

Thenya stepped out of her small hut as the party approached Crie. Jaax looked up at her as she drew near and saw a tangled look of reluctance, joy and sorrow on her wrinkled face. Like her husband, Thenya was short and sturdy. She wore her salted chestnut hair in a tight bun, but several wisps had come loose and now framed her head like a halo. Her eyes were a light hazel color, and her slightly pointed ears appeared to be tucked back into her hair. She wore a dark blue dress dusted with flour and a stained white apron. In her arms she carried a bundle of multi-colored cloth that could've been a load of dirty laundry headed for the washboards. Jaax froze when he saw the bundle squirm.

Thenya slowly approached the towering dragon and pulled back a violet-blue cloth revealing a tiny face, two bright blue eyes and quite a lot of golden-blond hair. Jaax's heart caught in his throat: *blue eyes.*

# A Very Surprising Discovery

"When was this child found exactly?" he asked, perhaps a little too harshly.

"A few days after the Solsticetide, about a week ago." Aydehn's response from beside him was both startled and automatic.

"And you're positive she was newborn the day you found her?" Jaax was finding it hard to wait for his friend's answers. His mind was beginning to hum, mingling with the buzzing of the curious voices of the onlookers.

"Oh yes, absolutely sure, only a few hours or so."

Jaax's head was no longer humming but spinning. *Blue eyes!*

"Your children Aydehn, they're born with eyes white except the pupils, is this not true?" he continued in that rough voice.

"Why of course, any race containing elf blood or dwarf blood is born with white eyes and then the color comes in later. In fact, the only known race to be born with blue eyes is . . ."

"Human," Jaax cut him off. "And not just part human, full-blooded human. A pure-blooded human, unbelievable! Impossible!"

His voice was now a hiss, almost inaudible over the growing clamor of the shifting and murmuring throng. Jaax was astounded. He knew he'd hoped for this, for centuries he had, but he'd never expected this day to come after so many long years of disappointment. How could a human, a race that's been extinct for five hundred years, end up inside an oak tree in a tiny village in northern Oescienne? Could the Oracles, then, be telling the truth? Had Ethöes not forsaken them after all? Jaax took in a deep breath and released it on a long, heated sigh.

"Well, Aydehn, I'll definitely be taking this child off your hands." His words carried over the crowd, suddenly hushed by the return of the dragon's strong voice. "Don't worry, she'll be well protected," he added after seeing Thenya's tearful eyes. "I'll take her to the Korli dragon Hroombramantu in Oescienne. She'll be well secluded and protected there, so Ethöes willing, the Crimson King will never find her."

Reluctantly, Thenya handed over the infant with shaking hands. She had known this day would come, but her composure proved that she hadn't expected it so soon.

"What do you call her?" Jaax's voice was suddenly soft, full of understanding for what Thenya was giving up.

"We haven't thought of any proper human names since we know none," Thenya answered in a trembling voice, her eyes fixed upon the infant's small, round face. "But we call her Drísíhn, *Little Oak*."

"Then that shall be her elfin name." Jaax nodded courteously.

"What shall we call her as a human, if she ever comes back this way?" Thenya asked, looking up at the great dragon with clear and hopeful eyes.

# A Very Surprising Discovery

Jaax paused, turning back to face the inquiring village, all of whom had now gathered around the strange scene. The bonfire behind them still breathed out its tainted smoke, now more of an orange hue than the red he had seen earlier that morning. The hungry bleats of goats and clucks of chickens sounded in the near distance, but every last townsperson was silent, their eyes trained upon the dragon gazing so intently upon the tiny infant.

Jaax's mind was still reeling from what he'd learned this day, but he forced the shock and excitement away as he tried to answer Thenya's plea. He had once known a human name, a girl's name, and he allowed his memory to wander back to the time when human names were still known.

"Jahrraneh," he replied quietly after a long pause, then out loud for all to hear, "'All's Hope'. But I think she'll be called 'Jahrra'."

"Then Jahrra Drísíhn we shall call her," Aydehn replied quietly, smiling as he placed a gentle hand on his wife's shoulder.

Jaax watched as the tiny child was strapped to him by some of the less timid villagers. He purposely kept his gaze away from Thenya, for she had drawn away when little Jahrra had been taken from her. The dragon sought the eyes of the baby, surprised to find her watching him as well. She gazed back up with what looked like wide, blue amazement and began to laugh.

"Now, would you look at that, she likes you Raejaax!" Thenya exclaimed, showing a bright smile in an attempt to hide her tears.

*Well,* thought the dragon, recalling the songbird that had sung for him that morning, *what do you know? Two for two.*

Thenya shooed the young villagers away and finished wrapping the baby securely to Jaax's neck. When she was finished, he turned to leave, but stopped short.

"What is it?" asked Aydehn.

"I need something to give her when she asks from where she came," he replied, brow furrowed.

"Here," Thenya reached into a large pocket in her skirt and pulled out a closed fist, "take this." She opened her hand to reveal a single acorn. "It's from the Sacred Oak. In fact, we found it right next to little Drísíhn, next to Jahrra." The woman dropped her eyes and swallowed before going on, "It is winter; there should be no fruit on the trees, yet Ethöes must have wanted her to have it. Perhaps she can plant it one day."

"Yes," replied Jaax calmly, "that'll do just fine."

Thenya tucked the fat acorn into the bundle that was Jahrra and patted it affectionately.

"Take care of her Raejaaxorix. Don't let any harm come to her," Thenya whispered solemnly. "My sister Thedhia awaits your arrival this very evening in the hills above Arlei. You do remember how to get there?"

# A Very Surprising Discovery

Jaax looked at the woman with his piercing eyes and nodded. "Of course, I remember it well."

Thenya closed her own eyes and bowed her head as if finally letting go of her own heart.

With a last glance around and with a small grin that he hoped would bring peace of mind to the elves and their kin, Jaax lifted off the ground with one beat of his mighty wings and climbed into the living mist, the tiny, helpless Jahrra strapped securely to him.

# -Chapter Two-

# Hroombramantu

From his relatively low altitude Jaax could see the entire landscape spreading out before him like a patchwork quilt. His two day journey had been pleasant, especially since Jahrra had given him little trouble. They had soared easily over the Great Thronn Wilderness, camping on the hillside beside Thedhia's tiny stone cabin the night before. The elfin woman had fussed and clucked over Jahrra, feeding her and cleaning her once she had peeled her away from Jaax's scaly hide. But when she tried to take the baby in for the night, the young dragon interjected.

"She stays with me," he said in a voice stern enough to make a giant redwood tremble.

Thedhia objected weakly but backed down when the dragon gave her one of his deadly glares. She had stalked back to her cabin dejectedly only to return in the morning, her mood much improved, to bid them farewell. Now they were far south of Arlei, closing in on the secret part of Oescienne that was protected by two giant mountain chains. Jaax breathed in the wild air and grinned, the pleasure of being in this place coursing through his blood like the wind flowing over his scales.

The Elornn Range and the Thorbet Mountains together looked like a huge, purple-spiked serpent wrapped in a wide arc, beginning and ending on the shore. To the west was an unobstructed coastline with a delicate ribbon of golden-cream sand stretching for several miles beside the deep expanse of sapphire -water.

A crop of rippling sand dunes, grooved farmlands, rich valleys, thick forests and rolling hills dotted the earth in a perfectly random pattern. The Raenyan and Oorn Rivers in the north and south were a brilliant contrast against the varied landscape; the sun's reflection blazing upon their glassy surfaces like a flame burning angrily along a fuse.

Jaax grinned when he spotted his destination, a great hill that sloped upward from the east and ended as a dramatic drop at its western-most point. The flat hill itself was covered mostly by a dark forest the locals called the Wreing Florenn, but the rest of it was covered in open fields and small wood copses. This obvious landmark was simply called the Great Sloping Hill, and this was where the dragon Hroombramantu awaited the arrival of the infant Jahrra.

Jaax soared over the Elornn Foothills, descending a little to get a closer view of the land below. He frightened a flock of sheep and sent them bleating and scattering in terror as he swept over the rolling fields of the Raenyan Valley. They looked a lot like oversized cotton balls being blasted by a gust of wind, and he couldn't help but chuckle lightly as he passed.

Jaax climbed once more to glide over a collection of tall hills but realized he was getting too carried away when he felt Jahrra stir against his neck and then begin to cry. He straightened himself out and fell into an easier drift and breathed deeply when he felt the baby settle comfortably against him again.

The edge of the Great Sloping Hill crept nearer, and after flying over the first few miles of its western edge, Jaax espied Hroombramantu waiting below, looking like a gray statue in the late afternoon light. The old dragon sat with a patience that only comes with age, barely moving his head to watch the descent of the much younger Jaax. He waited in front of a tiny little cottage which, when Jaax got a closer look, was actually situated on a small farm surrounded by orchard trees wedged between the house and the dark woods behind it.

Jaax missed, however, the soft smile on the other dragon's face as he watched him land gingerly upon the narrow dirt path trailing away from the small house. Jaax beat his wings vigorously, sending up clouds of dust and stray leaves. Once confident he'd done a good job of the landing, he turned and looked at the Korli dragon sitting only a few dozen yards away, smiling wryly.

# Hroombramantu

The old dragon slowly rose and clambered towards the younger one, betraying the evidence of arthritis in his ailing joints.

"Raejaaxorix, it's been so long since I've seen you," Hroombramantu remarked in a deep, worn voice.

Despite the obvious struggle in his steps, he didn't appear feeble or delicate.

"Master Hroombra, it's good to see you out of your crumbled castle," Jaax commented, trying to mask the weariness in his own words with dry humor.

Hroombra chuckled and shook his great head. He looked different from the younger, stronger Jaax. He was a palette of blues and grays and had a great crest atop his head which was surrounded by sagging skin, both a sign of age and a trademark of the Korli race of dragons. His eyes looked like cool chunks of amber, full of wisdom and centuries of experience, and a few saber-like teeth protruded from his lower jaw to rest against his cheek.

As daunting as this dragon's appearance may have seemed, his eyes betrayed his kind soul, one that was slow to anger. His wings, great flaps of gray skin, showed the signs of many a battle fought hard and looked like they no longer could lift his stocky frame off the ground.

"Yes, well, I do get out as much as I can these days, especially this day," Hroombra said, answering Jaax's earlier comment. Then he added more lightly, "So, where is this human child you are supposed to have found?"

"Right here." Jaax shifted his wings with a quick smile, revealing the sleeping baby nestled just in front of his shoulder.

"Isn't that a wonder," replied Hroombra quietly, smiling widely and exposing many more jagged teeth.

"So this must be her new home now. . ." Jaax said, ignoring the shining admiration in the older dragon's voice. He was looking past Hroombra towards the old cottage.

"Oh yes, it belongs to a kind old Nesnan couple. They just lost their only child, one born in their later years," Hroombra explained, still gazing lovingly at Jahrra. "This young one will bring some comfort and love back into their lives and they'll be sure to return the favor."

"What sort of people are they?" Jaax inquired, shifting his wings casually against his back. "How do they make their living?"

"Their names are Abdhe and Lynhi," Hroombra began. "They are poor farmers who moved here from the plains of Torinn long ago during a severe drought. They bought this small patch of earth and have managed to grow a good grove of fruit trees which they depend on for most of their income. They tend a small family garden and raise some livestock, selling their homemade crafts at the markets at the annual festivals."

Hroombra finished his reply with the tone of someone who was speaking of something very honorable.

"That's good to hear," Jaax answered after some time. "I believe she'll be absolutely safe here. These people, if they are truly as you describe them, will be able to teach her the foundations of life."

Jaax seemed suddenly distracted and shot a quick glance towards the setting sun on the horizon. The old dragon picked up on the gesture like it was second nature to him. "Already anxious to be off are we?" he said dully with a sad smile.

Jaax pretended not to hear the slight note of disappointment in Hroombra's tone, but failed to hide the sudden impatience in his own. "If she's the final part of the prophecy then I have much work to do, you know that."

"I only hoped you might stay a few days until the little one got settled," Hroombra said firmly.

The younger dragon quickly jumped on the defensive. "Gets settled? She's an infant! What could a dragon do to help her settle in?" Jaax released a short, frustrated breath, "Hroombra, I can't waste any more time, I must be off to Felldreim today if I'm to make any headway securing our allies."

Jaax snapped his jaw shut and furrowed his brow. He hadn't meant to sound so harsh, but he was tired from the journey and he was anxious to rally support against the Tyrant.

After a short while, he collected himself and began again, this time speaking slowly but obdurately, "The human child has finally been found Hroombra, this changes everything. I won't let petty sentiments get in the way of a plan five hundred years in the making. I've brought her safely to you and her new family. I hardly think she'll care what I do from now on. She doesn't even know me, she's only a baby!"

Jaax turned to go, but Hroombra attempted to reach the younger dragon one last time. "I can't stop you from being who you are Jaax, but someday I hope you can pause and put your past grievances second and your life first. She's the one Jaax, the one the whole world has been waiting for, and you're just going to leave her here without a second glance? She could be the one to make everything the way it once was . . ."

The old dragon finished his speech quietly, allowing his mind to wander onto times long past.

After gazing at Jaax with trouble eyes, Hroombra continued in a much more solemn tone, "Go if you must, but all I ask is that you check in on the child's progress as often as possible."

"Don't worry," Jaax replied firmly, "I will. Her progress is imperative to everything."

The younger dragon turned and began walking to the end of the drive, the dipping sun casting a long shadow in his wake.

"What's her name?" Hroombra called, just before the Tanaan dragon spread his great wings before taking off.

"Jahrra Drísíhn," he answered, and was gone in one mighty thrust of his wings.

# Hroombramantu

The air swirled about the Korli dragon and stirred a few leaves around on the ground. Hroombra watched as Jaax's dragon shape became nothing more than an emerald blur against the sun-gilded sky. He inhaled a great breath and blew out a stream of smoke, then considered the squirming bundle below him.

"Jahrra, huh?" Hroombra's old reptilian face smiled down at the young human one. "A new hope you are, a new hope you are indeed."

Hroombra turned his weary gaze to the eccentric stone cabin that slumped at the end of the dusty road. He saw that Abdhe and Lynhi had quietly crept out of their home and were now standing calmly on the doorstep, remaining perfectly still as if petrified to move lest they provoke him to attack. A great smile cut across Hroombra's furrowed face and the two figures relaxed a little.

Abdhe stood to the left of his wife. He was a tallish, worn looking Nesnan man, but not as tall as the humans Hroombra could barely remember. He wore faded gray pants that stopped at mid-calf, a dirty white shirt and a deep red, patched vest. His hair was gray and wiry and he had a weathered look about him. Lynhi, the woman who stood to his left, was a few inches shorter than him and wore a faded yellow skirt and a brown shirt. Her hair was ginger streaked with white and pulled loosely back into a braid.

# The Legend of Oescienne – The Finding

How wonderfully ordinary they looked, Hroombra thought. He could almost feel their joy and anticipation, their fear and apprehension, their hopes and dreams for this vulnerable girl. It hung in the air like the night chill clung to the early morning, reluctant to release its grip. He had spoken to them about this undertaking many years ago, for he had always counted on them to care for the child when she was found, if she was found in their lifetime. He'd explained everything to them then and he trusted them beyond anyone else he knew in Oescienne.

The young Jahrra cried as Hroombra gently lifted her sling in his teeth and carried her towards the cottage. "Don't worry small one," he said rather awkwardly, trying not to let the sling fall, "he'll be back to visit you, he hasn't left you for good."

This didn't seem to comfort the baby, and it didn't comfort Hroombra either. He hoped Jaax would keep his word, but he had known the Tanaan dragon his entire life and knew how unpredictable he could be during difficult times. *He can't help it,* Hroombra mused, *his life has been harder than most.* The weathered old reptile sighed, a sigh that revealed his inner thoughts. *Now I have another young one to worry about.*

Although this day was no different than any other winter day, it felt new, clean and strangely calm. Hroombra didn't know what the future held, even though his life experiences had given him some insight. All he knew was that Jahrra was safe for now and that it was his responsibility to look after her until her fate called.

Hroombra left little Jahrra with Abdhe and Lynhi that evening, knowing she was in good hands. They promised to raise her as their own, a poor Nesnan girl growing up in a quiet, sleepy land where the Crimson King's deadly force hadn't yet reached. They promised to send her to school with the other children of Oescienne and they promised to give Hroombra free rein over extra lessons with her. They promised to love her and care for her, to teach her some good in this cruel world. And they promised, as hard as it was for them to do so, to part with her when the time came for her to face her destiny.

These promises, along with all that had already happened, truly gave Hroombra something to look forward to. She would be safe here, and growing up as one of the Nesnan elves would keep her away from the curiosity of prying eyes. They looked enough like humans with their rounded ears and taller frame; Hroombra only hoped that Jahrra would look enough like them as well.

*Yes,* he thought with a heavy yet hopeful heart, *this is where she'll be most safe.*

What Hroombra didn't know, however, was that the arrival of this tiny, rather inconspicuous infant had already drawn someone's attention, and as he greeted the happy new parents of the baby Jahrra, two glowing eyes were watching from the edge of the dark forest.

❀ ❀ ❀

When Jaax descended upon the Sloping Hill earlier that afternoon, something strange and wild had stirred deep within the shadowed forest. The eyes of a peculiar being, eyes so much like an animal's, opened ever so slightly to reveal a smoldering within. Its soul had been awakened, realizing that something familiar and something important had entered this part of Oescienne.

The creature lay absolutely still, contemplating the spirits of the two new life forms inside the boundaries of this province on the forgotten edge of the world. The larger essence was a familiar one; there was no doubt about it. *But how do I know this soul?* the being wondered. For years, maybe even centuries, the curious creature had lived in this feared forest, sensing the ebb and flow of the life around it, but never before had its core been stirred so violently.

The creature spent only a few more minutes trying to grasp some memory imbedded deep within, but with no luck. The younger spirit it now sensed, an infant, was different and new. Her life force was strong and enduring and there was something unusual about this one that differed from all of the others living in Oescienne.

Unable to discern who the young new comer was and unsure of whom the larger one might be, the creature rose from its lair deep within the Wreing Florenn. As quickly and quietly as possible it began following the source of the spirits the way a hound follows the scent of a deer.

*Hurry,* thought the creature guided only by its intuition, *for the large one is fading and it will soon be gone.* The being covered the ground rather smoothly, not making a sound against the dead, damp leaves stuck to the muddy forest floor. A rare smile crept across its face; a silent appreciation for the rain that had fallen a few days ago making the ground damp and quiet underfoot.

Finally the aura of the familiar, larger spirit grew stronger, and just as the creature peered around the last tree on the edge of the forest its gaze fell upon something shocking.

"Impossible!" it rasped, speaking aloud for the first time in many years.

The sound of the creature's own voice startled it, forcing it behind the nearest tree for fear of being heard or seen. Finally, it braved exposure and peeked out across the small, fallow field and towards the front of a little stone cottage. The house was small and the bare trees in the orchard behind it blocked the view like a gray lattice screen.

Frustrated and irritated at the hindrance, the creature slinked northward seeking a better view of the two dragons standing in front of the house. The older dragon was easily recognizable. His presence in Oescienne had become as comfortable and familiar as an old scar. Oh yes, it was easy to spy on him from the forest, as long as one stayed as far away as possible to avoid detection.

The creature narrowed its eyes in perusal, now recognizing the younger dragon as the other presence it had felt. The being knew this dragon, knew him well. But where had he been since the last time . . . ? *Never mind that,* thought the creature bitterly, *he's here and he's found something very important, very important indeed.*

Just as the Tanaan dragon turned away for flight, the creature caught a glimpse of the powerful spirit it had sensed before. It looked like a Nesnan child, an infant, wrapped in a bundle of colorful cloth. The creature's eyes glittered and crackled in slight confusion as a cold wave of disappointment poured over it. *What could he possibly have a child for? And why does her life force feel so important?*

A sudden blast of strong wind caused by the dragon's passing overhead made the creature cower once again. This was no place to stand and think about what it had just witnessed, so it quickly ducked behind a large eucalyptus tree and drifted like a semi-solid smoke back into the heart of the trees, muttering to itself the entire way.

As Jaax soared over the Wreing Florenn in the last light of day, his long shadow skittering across the tops of the dark trees, the creature crept over the forest floor with, for the first time in many, many years a glimmer of anticipation. *I don't know what that dragon was doing with an infant, but I intend to find out. And why would an infant's spirit call so strongly to me?* it wondered. *I may not know now, but I have all the time in Ethöes to find out.*

With a flicker of determined patience, the creature disappeared into the depths of the woods to do what it did best, to wait.

# -Chapter Three-

# Dreams, Dragons, and Making Friends

The mist was always the same, low to the ground but rising quickly as if being brushed up by some mighty, undetectable breeze. He was always there too, a figure shrouded in an emerald, cowled cloak. His behavior seemed restless this time but the only way to tell for sure would be to look at his face. Unfortunately, it was hidden beneath his shadowy hood like always. The stranger stepped forward, slowly cresting the top of the small knoll that marked the boundary of the forest and the small orchard. Sometimes he seemed cautious, sometimes he seemed amused, but he always kept silent, at least that is how Jahrra always perceived him.

As the man stood gazing down at her under the shadow of his cloak, Jahrra could almost feel his eyes locking with hers. She'd always wondered if this strange man was young or old, brutal or kind, dark or fair, but he'd never shown his identity, not once. She wondered if he had black hair or blonde like hers.

She even wondered, with delight, if he was an elf, like the brave elves in the stories her father and Master Hroombra told her. In fact, the only thing she did know about him was that he was tall, much taller than her father and that he never said a single word to her.

Jahrra looked up once more at the stranger hoping to see something of his identity. But he bowed his head ever so slightly, causing Jahrra to wake with a start.

"Jahrra dear, time to get up, breakfast is ready!"

Lynhi stepped into the room a few moments later and looked down at the young girl in slight bewilderment. "Oh my, did you have another bad dream?"

"Oh no, Nida, I was just startled awake is all!" Jahrra replied through a yawn. She often called her mother Nida and her father Pada. She'd been calling them this for as long as . . . *As long as I've had that dream. Since forever,* she thought.

The dream of the tall stranger had been frightening at first, but when it started recurring Jahrra became less and less fearful of her enigmatic visitor. She couldn't remember the first time it had come to her; all she knew was that every now and then while she slept she would end up in a misty orchard all alone except for her imaginary companion.

"Don't linger too long, your food will get cold and you'll miss the wagon to Master Hroombra's," Lynhi called over her shoulder on her way back downstairs.

# The Legend of Oescienne – The Finding

"Master Hroombra!" Jahrra squeaked as she leaped out of bed.

She always enjoyed visiting Hroombra at the Castle Guard Ruin on the edge of the Great Sloping Hill. Once a week she met with the dragon to learn all about Oescienne and the stories of old. He told her tales of real elves, the ones who can perform magic and live forever. He also told her stories of the Tulle people and dwarves who lived outside of the boundaries of Oescienne.

When she was at Master Hroombra's Jahrra heard stories of all the strange and wonderful creatures of Ethöes, including all the other dragons of the world. The stories about the dragon Raejaaxorix were Jahrra's favorite. She would sit in wide-eyed wonder, her ears prickling to hear more about the noble dragon that fought against the terrifying beasts and menacing bands of raiders roaming the countryside terrorizing the weak and the innocent.

Hroombra reveled in telling Jahrra these stories but he never mentioned the fact that the Tanaan dragon had a role in her life. He still feared the younger dragon wouldn't keep his promise about checking in on the girl. For now, Hroombra found solace in his decision by telling Jahrra stories of Jaax from years ago, before he became as embittered as he now was.

Six years had passed since the younger dragon had brought Jahrra to her foster parents, and he hadn't been back since. Hroombra had received word from him on several occasions; a letter or two informing the older dragon of his various diplomatic activities, but not once had he mentioned a possible visit to Oescienne. Hroombra didn't let it get him down, however. Jaax was known for avoiding emotional situations and this one was no different. He would come around in his own time.

Hroombra expected that Jaax would receive quite a surprise when he eventually returned. Jahrra was no longer an infant and she'd grown to be quite a handful. She was always climbing trees, splashing over creeks and running through fields. She was constantly exploring and having a great time: building forts from piles of pruned branches her father had created, gathering wildflowers to spruce up the kitchen, or bringing in lizards and other crawling things she insisted were her friends, keeping her frustrated and repulsed mother constantly on edge.

Lynhi never knew if she might find some strange caterpillar on the kitchen table or reach her hand into the dirty laundry to find a family of snails living there. Soon, however, Jahrra would be starting school with the rest of the local children. Despite the fact that Lynhi was looking forward to fewer encounters with unidentifiable bugs and reptiles, she and Abdhe were anxious about the approaching school season.

They worried mostly about Jahrra's interaction with the other children; she'd only ever known them and Hroombra. The isolation of their orchard, the fact that no other youngsters lived close by and the lack of time and finances to visit town more often had forced Jahrra to grow up with the farm animals as her friends. They made good companions, but they couldn't teach her about living in the great world that existed beyond her home.

Another of her parents' concerns was the girl's stubborn personality. They feared she wouldn't listen to her schoolmasters and might cause trouble with her peers once her classes began. She was bright and very eager to learn, but mostly only what Hroombra was willing to teach her.

When Abdhe and Lynhi approached the elderly dragon with their concern he simply replied, "Life itself is an ongoing school lesson. She'll be fine. It may be rough at first, but she'll learn when to ask questions and when it's time to listen. Don't worry so much, she isn't as misplaced as you think she is."

Hroombra's reassurance calmed them a little, but they still had their doubts. They thought that perhaps her human characteristics might stand out among the mostly Resai group.

Nevertheless, Hroombra assured them that no one would ever guess she was full-blooded human.

"The others have never even seen a human. They wouldn't know what one looks like. Even if some of their parents have seen humans before, it's been so long since there were any in Ethöes, I doubt they'll notice."

Abdhe and Lynhi knew that Jahrra had to grow up thinking she was a Nesnan elf for her own safety, but being a Nesnan in an elite Resai school wouldn't be easy. There had always been great debate over those who found themselves in the middle of these two races, whether they were Resai or Nesnan, and whether they could prove it with family records. Many feuds were fought and many grudges set, simply over something as silly as who was more elfish than the next person.

It had become a status war and Hroombra, Lynhi and Abdhe hoped that Jahrra wouldn't get caught up in the middle of it. What Abdhe and Lynhi knew, however, was that above everything else Jahrra's true identity must be kept secret. But for now, the only thing they need be concerned about was getting Jahrra to her first day of school on time.

Jahrra traipsed downstairs into the kitchen of the small cabin breathing in the rich aromas of bacon, eggs and fried potatoes. These scents along with the anticipation of another great story of dragons and unicorns and other mystical creatures from Hroombra had finally coaxed her out of bed. Her hair looked like a tangled haystack and her eyes were gritty but she was now fully awake. She took a deep breath and thought a little about the dream of the hooded figure still lingering in her mind. She often wondered if he could be someone she'd once known or someone who existed in real life. *Maybe he's my true father coming to visit me in my dreams!* she mused before forgetting it altogether.

This thought often made her feel guilty, so she dashed it aside immediately if it ever pushed itself to the front of her mind. Jahrra knew that she was adopted. Abdhe and Lynhi had told her that her true mother and father died when she was just a baby. She loved them both very much but always wondered what her real parents had been like.

Jahrra sighed and rubbed the sleep out of her eyes and shuffled across the rough stone floor and down the stairs to meet breakfast. She would think about her dream later when there weren't so many smells distracting her nose and stomach. She entered the tiny kitchen to find her mother working over the food on the stove. Her father was sitting at their little dining table, smoking his pipe and fidgeting with a tool.

"What're you doing Pada?" Jahrra asked through a yawn.

"I'm just fixing my ball peen hammer. Look, the metal part has loosened from the wood."

Abdhe lowered the tool so she could see. He wore his usual brown work pants, white shirt and faded vest. His age-roughened face was covered in stubble and his feathery light hair floated around his head as if it wasn't attached to anything.

His eyes were fixed on the hammer in intense concentration. "I'm trying to attach a metal strip to keep it in place."

He had such old hands, Jahrra thought, but they were experienced hands. They had made so many things grow and had created so many wonderful objects that they'd become tools themselves.

# Dreams, Dragons, and Making Friends

"Alright, breakfast is ready. Jahrra! You're not dressed! Go get dressed while I make your plate," Lynhi scolded in a terse voice as she scraped some eggs onto a chipped plate.

Jahrra scuffled back upstairs in a disgruntled manner. She hated having to change clothes all the time, *and* she was hungry. Once back in her room, she quickly pulled on her new school uniform, a plain white shirt and a blue plaid jumper. Jahrra cringed as she pulled the jumper over her head, *Yuck!* she thought, *I hate dresses!*

Her mother had insisted that it was more of a long shirt and not a dress at all but Jahrra wasn't fooled. She could sniff out a dress if it were buried in the back of an immense closet jammed with clothes. Unfortunately, it had to be worn to her new school. The only way that Lynhi convinced Jahrra to wear it at all was by threatening to keep her from attending Hroombra's lessons. Jahrra would do anything to keep visiting Hroombra, even wear a pudgy, itchy, bulky *dress*.

Jahrra quickly pulled on her long socks over her bare feet, squirming as she tried to move in the restrictive uniform. She didn't usually wear anything so formal but was always running about in long pants and shirts that were too big for her, her hair streaming wildly behind her like golden silk.

Jahrra yanked at her collar as she scurried back downstairs as fast as she could, anticipating potatoes and eggs. The sun was poking its fingers through the trees in the east when she finally sat down to a plate of steaming food. The little bit of fog that lingered on the edge of the woods was slowly creeping away and the golden sunlight pierced through the cool autumn air like a hot knife through butter.

"Hroombra tells us that he'll be taking you to your first day of school." Lynhi began the conversation somewhat cautiously, setting down her half-eaten toast. "In fact, he's told us that he's sure there'll be at least fifteen other students in your class. You'll get to meet other children from around Oescienne, how does that sound?"

Jahrra sat poking at her bacon with her fork. She didn't like the idea of sharing Hroombra with anyone else but she answered her mother nonetheless, "Good I suppose."

"Just good? I think it'll be great for you to meet someone else your own age. You'll make friends and play games and learn so much more. Aren't you looking forward to it?"

Jahrra thought about this for a while and then figured it would be nice to see what other children were like. She nodded with a small smile and got back to breakfast. Lynhi in turn looked at her husband who gave her a quick she's-going-to-be-just-fine look before returning to his work.

Jahrra finished her breakfast and dumped the plate into the hot, soapy water waiting in the sink. She grabbed the thick wool sweater her mother had knitted for her, pulled on her mud-crusted boots and ran out the front door, jamming it shut behind her.

"Now be careful, and mind your manners! And be sure to keep your shoes on the entire day!" Lynhi shouted after her, following her halfway to the closed door.

Abdhe chuckled behind her.

"What?" she asked in a snappish manner, turning to glare at him with her hands on her hips.

Abdhe smiled, thinking amusedly of how much his wife sometimes reminded him of a spirited child stuck in an older woman's body.

"You worry too much. If she makes a few mistakes the first day, it's not the end of the world. We're all entitled to some mistakes when we're first learning."

When Lynhi continued to glare down at him with her lips pursed in slight annoyance he took a wearied breath and continued, "She isn't the only one going to her first day of school you know. The other children are facing the same fear that she is. Relax, she'll be fine."

Lynhi eased a little and moved to gaze out the front window.

"I hope you're right," she said as she watched their young daughter skip down the path.

Abdhe simply smiled and chortled and shook his head as he fidgeted some more with the hammer that refused to cooperate with him.

As Lynhi peered out the window like a mother bear eyeing her cub, Jahrra sprinted to the end of the rocky path that led to the main road. She eventually stopped to catch her breath and glance back at the little stone cabin. It looked the same way it did six years ago when she first arrived here; nothing had changed but perhaps a little growth on the trees in the orchard and a little more moss on the roof.

The small, two-storied structure was the image of home to Jahrra. She simply adored the way that none of the stones in the walls were smooth, but rather they were rough and jagged like they'd been chipped off of some huge rock by a giant's pick. The tiny house always smelled of earthly things like old smoke, dried lavender, soil, leather and eucalyptus oil. Sometimes it would smell of the wildflowers she or her mother collected in the spring and summer and every night and every morning it held the aroma of home cooking. Jahrra could always count on that.

The first sound of rickety cart wheels in the distance caused the young girl to jump out of her reverie and release a small yelp of fright. Once she saw that it was only the mail cart creeping up over the hill in the distance however, she grinned in relief. The mail cart always picked Jahrra up on the days she met with Hroombra and it was always driven by Mr. Dharedth the mail carrier. The mailman was a kind soul, not grumpy like most letter carriers in town. He was big and jovial with brown hair, brown eyes and a full beard, one that he was quite proud of.

Jahrra would ask him about it sometimes since her father didn't grow a beard.

"How do you get your hair to grow on your face like that?"

"Well, Little Jahrra," Dharedth would say cheerfully, "it takes time, patience and the ability to keep oneself groomed."

Jahrra would sit on the wooden seat next to the mail carrier and ponder this question on their drives to the Castle Guard Ruin.

"I think I'll try to grow one myself," she would answer after spending some time lost in thought.

Dharedth then laughed warmly, telling Jahrra not to try too hard. He didn't think a beard would look too becoming on a young girl. Jahrra would smile up at the middle-aged Nesnan man, one of the few people she talked to besides Hroombra and her parents.

As Jahrra made a mental list of all the questions she'd be asking her new classmates, the wobbly old hay wagon she'd heard only minutes ago pulled up and stopped in front of her drive. The mail cart, a retired hay wagon now full of stuffed canvas bags, was pulled by a fat, tired looking dapple-red horse that sagged sluggishly as soon as the cart stopped moving. Jahrra beamed as Mr. Dharedth gave a gapped-tooth smile above his bristly beard, his form partially blocking the two other children that were already sitting in the cart.

Jahrra's heart caught in her throat when she saw them. She had no idea she'd be meeting her new classmates so soon and she suddenly lost the gumption she'd felt earlier. On a normal morning Jahrra would skip up to the cart and hop on, but today she approached warily, keeping her head low and her eyes veiled.

Dharedth rested his arm on his knee, one hand loosely holding the reins and smiled down at Jahrra.

"What's the problem Little Jahrra? Don' you feel well today?"

His brow furrowed with concern and his smile began to fade.

"Um . . ." was all Jahrra could muster as she started to turn pink.

"Well, cheer up! You have some classmates here who're headed to school just like you. Why don' you introduce yourselves?"

The mailman turned to the two children sitting behind him. They looked as timid as mice but luckily Dharedth was patient and knew how children could be shy when meeting others for the first time. Jahrra braved a glance up at them: a boy and a girl about her age sitting in the back of the cart. They both had very dark hair and green, slightly slanted eyes. Their uniforms were the same as Jahrra's but instead of looking hand-sewn like her own the girl's jumper and the boy's vest and pants had most likely come from a tailor. Jahrra quickly returned her gaze to the ground and continued to stand in silence, pushing the loose soil around with her toe.

# Dreams, Dragons, and Making Friends

"Oh, for goodness sake!" Dharedth exclaimed, chuckling in amusement, "How'll you three last in a classroom full of children if you can' even introduce yourselves here?"

Finally, the girl in the cart spoke.

"Hello," she said in a quiet yet friendly voice, "my name is Gieaun and this is my brother Scede."

Jahrra could now see that the girl named Gieaun had cool green eyes and her brother Scede had a little bit of brown mixed in his own. They both, however, had black hair that reminded Jahrra of the shining, silky feathers of a rooster's tail. Jahrra gave them a genial grin back.

The girl was all smiles now that the ice was broken but the boy seemed much more bashful than even Jahrra. Jahrra took a deep breath and introduced herself to the siblings and then, after a questioning glance to Dharedth, jumped up into the wagon.

On the ride to the Castle Guard Ruin Jahrra learned that Gieaun and Scede lived about three miles down the road from her on a ranch.

"Wood's End Ranch," Gieaun piped more confidently now that the cart had started moving once again.

Their parents raised sheep and horses and even traded with merchants outside of Oescienne. Scede, it turned out, was seven months older than her and Gieaun was four months younger.

Jahrra began asking the two siblings questions of her own, such as: "What's it like where you live?" and "What type of tree do you like to climb the most?"

Gieaun was happy to answer these questions having many for Jahrra herself. Scede nodded every now and again, still reluctant to speak.

"He's really shy," Gieaun whispered knowingly. "We'll be lucky if he talks at all today!"

The ride to Hroombra's went by much quicker with two other children to talk to along the way, even if one of them only listened. Before they knew it the group reached the remains of an old stone building perched near the edge of the bluff. A narrow but long dirt path ran from the road to the crumbling stone structure.

Once Jahrra, Gieaun and Scede were out of the cart and the mailman was well on his way, the three children walked slowly up the small path gazing around in wary interest as they did. Jahrra naturally led the way, having been to this place many times before. It didn't take them long to traverse the trail and at its end they found themselves standing on a wide patch of earth free of the tangled field grass but littered with weathered stones.

"What *is* this place?" asked Gieaun in a small voice as they stood in the ancient courtyard.

"This is the Castle Guard Ruin. It's where Master Hroombra lives," Jahrra said knowingly.

"Oh," Gieaun answered simply, a little too frightened to question any further.

"I wonder where all the other students are?" Jahrra inquired aloud as she crossed over a circular area that was about ten feet in diameter. She had always imagined a great tree might have once grown here, guarding the building that used to be.

The three children gazed up at the stone wall looming before them. It was quite large and continued around to the other side of the building. The roof, one built of poles and large wooden slats, looked much newer than the ancient stone. In one corner there stood a large circular tower, easily twenty feet tall, with a conical roof of wood. A few windows, looking like empty rectangular eyes, stared at them from just below the tower's peak. The entire building backed up into a tiny hillock that dropped off at the edge of the bluff on the opposite end.

Jahrra, having seen the Ruin a hundred odd times, shuffled over to sit down on the stone steps in front of the doorway.

"I guess we should wait here until everyone else arrives. I wonder where Master Hroombra is."

"Who's Master Hroombra?" Gieaun asked, dusting off a place to sit next to her.

"Oh just wait, you'll love him!" the other girl replied.

She neglected to tell her friend that Hroombra was a dragon, but Jahrra had grown so used to him that she hadn't even thought that perhaps Gieaun and Scede had never seen one before.

The two girls continued to chat while Scede walked around the old courtyard, kicking stones and drawing in the sand. After several minutes of loitering around the edge of the Ruin, Scede gave up and sat down next to the girls.

Gieaun and Jahrra were so busy talking about their summer adventures that they hardly noticed Scede stiffening next to them. Something was moving from behind where they sat and he was the first one to notice. It sounded like something rather large, something much larger than an animal or an adult shifting around inside the old building.

Scede elbowed his sister and the two girls stopped talking immediately, looking in the direction where the disturbance was coming from. The children glanced at each other and quickly scuttled behind the massive boulders bordering the steps.

Finally, after what seemed like an eternity, a great beast stuck its head out from around the far corner of the Ruin. Jahrra had to resist the urge to burst out laughing. She'd been so caught up in her conversation with Gieaun that she'd allowed herself to think that anything dangerous could be lurking around the Castle Guard Ruin.

The terrifying monster was none other than the dragon Hroombra, easily the size of her little cottage if not bigger, and he was peering between the edge of the wall and the curve of the tower on the northern end of the building. Gieaun and Scede looked terrified but Jahrra broke into a bright smile, her blue eyes shining with mirth.

Hroombramantu inhaled deeply, looking very old as the morning light cut deep shadows into his wrinkled hide. Jahrra wondered if he knew that the children were there because she was getting the impression he was trying to sniff them out. She was almost tempted to sneak up on him and surprise him but another glance at her new friends told her that maybe she should introduce them to her mentor a little more gently. It was obvious from their terrified expressions that they'd never seen a dragon before. Well, at least a friendly one.

Hroombra stopped sniffing abruptly and turned to look directly at Jahrra. Her grin widened and she skipped towards the looming reptile not at all fearful or cautious of him. Gieaun and Scede simply looked on in horror.

"Young Jahrra?" Hroombra sounded quite confused indeed. "What are you doing skulking around in the shadows?"

"I was going to sneak up on you but I thought that if I *actually* frightened you and caused you to shout my new friends might faint!"

Jahrra giggled cheerfully, hoping that Gieaun and Scede would see now that Hroombra was harmless. When she looked in their direction, however, she noticed that they still crouched behind the stone rubble.

Hroombra smiled and spoke, "It seems you've been distracted with the task of making friends. It's alright children, you can come out. I won't eat you." The voice was deep, soft, kind and definitely not hostile. "Come on. I assure you no harm will befall you."

Hroombra's speech wasn't coaxing but patient, proving that he'd dealt with many terrified children before. Jahrra immediately stood up taller and told her friends that she'd known Hroombra her whole life and that he was a wonderful storyteller.

"Come now, everyone out in the open!" the great dragon said once more, "My name is Hroombramantu for those of you who don't already know, and you can call me Master Hroombra. Now what should I call you?"

By this time Gieaun and Scede had mustered enough courage to crawl out reluctantly from their rock barriers. "I-I'm Gieaun," answered the girl in a voice that could have belonged to a mouse.

"And you?" Hroombra nodded towards her brother.

"Scede," Gieaun put in, her voice still small but audible. "He's, my, my brother. He doesn't say much. He's shy."

Now that Gieaun had spoken and realized she wouldn't be swallowed after all, she became a little more confident.

"Well, Gieaun and Scede, it's nice to meet you two. But we must get moving. The day won't wait," Hroombra said.

"We're not staying here?" Jahrra asked in surprise.

"No."

"What about the others?"

"They'll meet us in town."

"Town?"

Hroombra smiled at his small pupil's incessant questions. Most schoolmasters would've grown impatient by now but not Hroombra. He took a small breath and answered, "In Aldehren, where the schoolhouse is."

"Why can't we stay here?" Jahrra pressed, becoming slightly upset.

"Oh, no Jahrra, you must go to school and be taught by a teacher of your own kind. A dragon may be a good tutor for you on occasion, but it's not for most children," Hroombra said seriously.

Jahrra stood with her brow furrowed. *What's wrong with having a dragon as a teacher?* she wondered to herself.

"Well then, shall we get going? It'll take quite a while to get to the schoolhouse. Unfortunately I'm not as young as I used to be or else we could fly there. We'll have to make do with walking."

Jahrra, Gieaun and Scede looked up at Hroombra in disbelief. *Walk?! All the way to town?* Jahrra thought with horror. She was certain it would take her more than a day to walk to town.

Hroombra realized what they were all thinking and smiled once more. "Don't worry! You three can ride on my back. We'll arrive faster that way."

Jahrra's expression of disbelief turned to one of enthusiasm and even Scede and Gieaun brightened as they imagined riding atop a dragon. Jahrra scuttled over to the decrepit stone staircase that flanked the doorway into the Ruin. She smiled at her friends confidently as she climbed the stairs and came level with Hroombra's thorny back.

Gieaun and Scede watched in awe as she grabbed a hold of one of Hroombra's worn spikes and hauled herself onto his cool, rough back. Once she gained her balance and breath Jahrra beamed down at her friends. "The trick," she breathed, "is sitting between the spikes."

Hroombra turned his great head, almost knocking Jahrra off balance, and grinned down at the two timorous children that stood before him.

"Now it's your turn."

Scede reluctantly climbed the steps, swallowed and took a deep breath. Jahrra thought he looked a little like a kitten determined to make a big jump. He grabbed the bony spike just behind Jahrra and pulled himself up with excessive force, almost throwing himself clear over Hroombra's back. His sister was next, releasing a tiny squeak as she pulled herself up. Finally the three of them were perched precariously upon the great dragon's back, looking a lot like stranded sailors lying across the keel of a capsized boat.

Hroombra turned his great head to view the children once more and chuckled at the sight.

"I promise to walk slowly," he said, "but it may take some getting used to."

And with that the great reptile left the ruined building behind, crossing the wide field and heading north along the old road that twisted down the side of the Great Sloping Hill.

# -Chapter Four-

# Surviving the First Day of School

Hroombra's ambling trek down the twisting dirt road was both soothing and refreshing to the anxious children. The road itself was wide and smooth like a great lazy snake creeping through the autumn-dried fields. The view of the farmlands and distant ocean from the bluff's edge was off to their left but Jahrra had trouble seeing past the few trees that grew on the brink, even from the height of a dragon's back. Instead she turned her sights to the looming Wreing Florenn on the other side of the road, looking like a sleeping monster basking in the early morning light.

Jahrra felt Scede shift behind her to get a better look at the landscape surrounding them. Once he was finally settled she relaxed a bit and breathed in the scent of fresh morning dew, smiling inwardly as the group crossed the Danu Creek. The bridge that spanned this small waterway was wide and made of heavy logs, creaking irritably as Hroombra set his weight to it.

"Have no fear," he said, shocking the children into an attentive posture, "it'll hold."

Jahrra had no doubt that it would but when she glanced back at Gieaun and Scede she could tell they hadn't been so sure. Between the creaks and groans of the old bridge Jahrra heard the bubbling of the shallow water below. She was sure that if it wasn't for Hroombra's deep breathing, the noisy complaints of the bridge and the anxious sounds coming from Gieaun and Scede every now and then behind her, she would've been able to hear the water trickling over the bluff's edge several yards away.

Gieaun and Scede released two small sighs of relief when Hroombra finally stepped back onto solid ground. Jahrra sighed too, but not out of concern. The cool morning air felt wonderfully refreshing as it coated her lungs, leaving the distinct taste of fire smoke behind. She smiled dreamily, leaning into Hroombra's vast, soft neck and listened to his deep, strong heartbeat.

It wasn't long, however, before Jahrra was pulled away from her relaxed pose. The view from the road was beginning to shift and she could now see the fields far below, their dark furrows of earth dressed in the rich colors of early autumn's ripening crops. Jahrra and her new friends now passed the time searching for the slivers of white dunes and glinting sea peeking between the trunks of tall trees, pointing and gasping at the delightful sight.

Hroombra chuckled and picked up his lumbering pace forcing Jahrra, Gieaun and Scede to grasp for his spikes to keep from sliding off. He gently ruffled his leathery wings before folding them back up again as they resumed their light flapping sound as they brushed against his flanks.

About halfway down the winding road, Jahrra saw something that took complete control of her attention. "Oh, Master Hroombra! What's this place again?" she squealed as she pointed at two degraded stone towers tucked into the woods to their right.

They resembled the tower at the Castle Guard Ruin but besides the dead ivy and forest debris piled against them, they looked relatively undamaged.

"Those two turrets once marked the entrance to the great castle of Oescienne. Very long ago there was a bridge spanning between the tops of them with a massive gate at their base. Anyone wishing to visit the king or queen would have to enter through that strong gate. This way the king's soldiers could make sure no one wishing harm upon their majesties entered the castle grounds."

Jahrra looked on in wonder, trying hard to picture every last detail her mentor described. Behind her she could sense Gieaun and Scede leaning forward to get a better look and she imagined they too were trying to picture it.

Hroombra continued on as the children listened, "The entire castle was once surrounded by a great wall. There was another much larger tower just on the other side of this road, on that small hill there."

Hroombra nodded to a smaller path leading down to a hillock jutting off the western side of the road. Jahrra couldn't see a tower; all she could see was a small grove of trees with a ring of weathered stone resembling a fire pit and the bare earth within it.

"What happened to the king and queen?" Gieaun queried in a meek voice.

Hroombra turned his great head, a troubled look etched on his creased face. "That, my child, is a story for another time, but not for today."

Although Hroombra had used a gentle voice the hint of sorrow lingering within it caused Gieaun to hunch down like a scolded dog. Jahrra realized with mild irritation that they wouldn't be visiting the castle ruin today. She slumped a little and like Gieaun, she wondered what had happened to the king of Oescienne. *If there was a castle and people to guard it, how could there no longer be a king?* Jahrra shook her head, trying her best to be content with the sights around her as they continued on down the hill and into the farmland. She would have to find out the answers to her questions another day.

The trip to Aldehren, which would have taken an hour in a cart, took twice as long with Hroombra's slow pace. The children didn't mind, however; they used this time to get to know their carrier and it wasn't every day one got to take a ride on a dragon's back. Gieaun got up the courage to ask Hroombra if he could breathe fire and he happily demonstrated this by breathing a stream of deep red flame that seemed to split the air. The children clapped in delight and even Scede smiled and joined in.

When they finally reached the bottom of the hill Hroombra promptly turned northwest taking the road with a sign that read *Aldehren, Hassett Town* and *Toria Town*. The fields that stood between the Great Sloping Hill and Aldehren were practically deserted but the few people that were out on this fine morning stopped to watch curiously, or cautiously, as the huge dragon carrying three young children passed by.

Jahrra thought they looked like rag dolls bent over their fields, nurturing the delicate plants that stood stark and helpless in the chill air. Some of the farmers leaned against shovels and rakes in order to give their aching backs a rest. Jahrra waved hesitantly but the people just continued to stare like living statues, probably too far away to have seen the gesture. Their tiny crude stone houses littered the flatlands like large boulders overgrown with sod. If it hadn't been for the narrow tendrils of smoke curling from their green roofs, or the glint of the sun reflecting off their minute windows, Jahrra would've dismissed the huts as eroding piles of rocks.

Jahrra sighed and turned her attention back to Hroombra's stories, failing to notice the other farmers coming out of their houses to see the rare sight of a dragon walking through their fields. These people had seen Hroombra before, of course, and they even remembered seeing a large dragon flying overhead some five or six years ago. It was an uncommon sight to see a dragon and was well worth a break in their important work to stop and take a look, even though they knew this particular dragon lived atop the flat hill looming above them.

The three children were so caught up in Hroombra's stories that they hardly noticed the miles ticking by. The next time Jahrra bothered to take in her surroundings she realized just how far they'd traveled. The vast farmlands were tapering off and a few small hills, looking like nodules covered in tawny velvet, rose up around them. A few small clumps of scattered woodlands spread out like a great, patchy quilt of green, red and gold, and the flat farmland was beginning to dip and climb into rolling fields.

Hroombra rounded the last small grouping of hillocks and finally the town of Aldehren tumbled into view. Jahrra clutched tightly to the spike she'd been hanging onto as Gieaun and Scede craned forward to get a better look. The low, primitive cabins of the fields had been replaced by sturdy houses built of cultivated stone with smaller, fenced-in yards surrounding them. In the distance Jahrra heard the buzz of society and soon Hroombra's large claws were clicking against smooth cobblestones instead of digging into soft earth.

The empty street quickly became dotted with people scurrying about on their morning business. As soon as they saw the giant reptile ambling down the center of the road, however, they froze on the spot and gaped with fear and awe. Jahrra found it funny how Hroombra left a wake of silence behind him as they made their way deeper and deeper into the heart of the city.

Several small children, too young yet to go to school, clung to their mothers' skirts, eyeing the great dragon warily. Jahrra, Gieaun and Scede waved merrily, encouraging several of them to smile and trot cautiously after them only to be discouraged by their chastising parents.

"Master Hroombra," Jahrra said quietly so that only the old dragon could hear, "why's everyone staring and getting out of the way like that?"

Hroombra took a while to answer but finally he turned his head slightly and said, "Because they never see dragons, Jahrra. I come into town seldom and I'm the only dragon in Oescienne."

"Why are there no other dragons in Oescienne?" Jahrra pressed, wondering to herself why she'd never asked him this before.

Again, Hroombra paused before answering, "The complete answer to that question is something not ready for such young ears to hear."

Jahrra squished up her face, revealing a small dimple on her left cheek. When Hroombra used that phrase it meant he wouldn't be telling her the whole answer. *Why do adults always have to be so secretive?* she wondered in frustration.

Jahrra forgot about her ire when Hroombra began talking once again, "I will tell you this however: the world is a large place with many people and many different ideas, and one of those ideas is that dragons are troublesome creatures. People hear stories and fear we might burn down their village or eat their livestock. Most dragons don't do this but too many people believe the tales they are told. Most of my kind now live in secret places where we can be at peace, but not all of us. Does this answer your question?"

*No,* Jahrra thought ruefully even as she signaled her compliance, *at least not all the way.* She wondered why people believed the stories about dragons being dangerous but she withheld any other inquiries. When Hroombra ended an explanation with another question she knew he was finished with the topic.

Jahrra soon forgot about the distracted and disapproving townspeople. She was dazzled by the shops with their crooked hanging signs and intricate window displays. The stores had everything for sale from professionally tailored dresses and suits to garden tools and small wagons. Every so often she'd catch a glimpse of a grungy, gritty alley and just as soon as it appeared it disappeared once again. She was always amazed that buildings could be built so close together and wondered what it would be like to live so near to one's neighbors.

Jahrra breathed a sigh of relief and leaned into Hroombra's great neck for comfort, closing her eyes and allowing her other senses to take over. The sun felt like a warm fire as it beat down upon her face creating quite a contrast compared to Hroombra's cool, scaly skin. She heard the clinking of harnesses, the clucking of chickens, the bleating of sheep and goats and the snorting of horses. She listened to the shouts of more children running away from the dragon walking down the street and she even heard the chinking of the blacksmith's shop several blocks away.

Familiar smells of smoke and manure filled the air and the clean swish of a horse's tail nearby finally convinced Jahrra to open her eyes. The scene had changed; there were no longer crowded stone and wooden houses surrounding them but a few compact cottages propped up between small groves of young redwood trees. They'd left the main road and were now on one of the more narrow paths leading away from the center of town.

Jahrra blinked and glanced over her shoulder. Gieaun and Scede looked distracted by the stables on the left but directly behind them Jahrra saw life returning to normal on the main road. The people who'd been avoiding Hroombra quickly filled in the space he had created, leaving behind no evidence that three children riding a dragon had ever passed through.

# Surviving the First Day of School

The lane Hroombra took rose gently, twining between the redwoods that dappled the path in shade. Soon the dull red walls of a stone cabin pushed their way through the ruddy brown and deep green of the trees. The cabin was rather large and Jahrra noticed that it had a steep sloping roof, a towering chimney, and great dust coated windows. Oak and laurel trees gathered in the gully around the schoolhouse like chilled campers hunched around a fire and several large chunks of granite littered the yard.

"Well, children," Hroombra said, sounding slightly out of breath, "welcome to your schoolhouse."

Hroombra stopped just outside the front of the building and allowed the children to slide off of his back. Once on solid ground the three of them gazed around in wonderment. Although the structure was built amongst trees, there was a small hollow and a tiny meadow on one side of the yard. To the building's right, in another small clearing, Jahrra spotted tables and benches. The whole scene had a musty and shaded atmosphere, but Jahrra smiled brightly anyway, feeling for the first time that she might truly enjoy school.

"It looks like we're the first ones here," Hroombra commented casually, taking in the dormant scene.

The schoolyard was vacant and the road below was deserted, but soon the emptiness was disrupted by the sound of a horse and carriage drifting up the main road. The children and dragon looked in the direction of the faint clatter and saw a very clean and beautiful yolk-colored carriage emerging over the small incline of the road. This cart was much nicer than the hay wagon Jahrra always took to the Castle Guard Ruin. It was obviously a well-maintained family vehicle and was drawn by two matching snowy horses fitted with intricately carved leather harnesses.

Once the carriage pulled up to the path in front of the schoolhouse, Jahrra found herself gaping in surprise. Now that the horses were closer she saw that their harnesses were encrusted with tiny, yellow rhinestones. Gieaun and Scede shifted behind her and she turned her head to see what had caught their attention. Right behind the first carriage were four or five more exactly like the first, also drawn by two white horses.

The lead carriage came to a complete stop and a young footman hopped down and opened the door, completing his task flawlessly despite the shocked look he flashed towards Hroombra.

A matching girl and boy, both with hazelnut brown hair and clear, brown eyes, stepped out of the carriage. They were shortly followed by a dozen or so other children. The twins, for there was no mistaking that fact, wore the same uniform that Jahrra, Gieaun and Scede wore but theirs looked to be made of silk and satin.

Jahrra could only imagine that these children came from a palace and she hoped, with a small thrill that they might even be pure elves. Their ears looked pointed at the end, and they had an air of richness and importance floating about them. As she stood there gaping in wonder, the other carriages unloaded more blue and white clad students of various ages.

Despite their intimidating appearance however, Jahrra was glad to see the other children and couldn't wait to introduce herself. She'd gotten along so well with Gieaun and Scede that she figured it would be wonderful to make friends with all the new students, especially if these children were really true elves. She quickly ran over to greet them, Gieaun close behind and Scede trailing back.

Before Jahrra could say anything at all, however, the brown haired girl looked up from fussing with her uniform and let out a blood-curdling scream. Jahrra froze and felt her heart jump into her throat. *What's the matter?* she thought as she stood staring at the girl in confusion. Only, the girl didn't seem to notice Jahrra; she was standing with her eyes fixed on something just over her shoulder.

Jahrra turned to look and then realized what had caused the girl to scream: Hroombra. Hroombra stood back, still as stone and blending in with the gray shadows of the trees. Jahrra almost laughed. How could these children not have noticed Hroombra before now?

"A dragon! We have a dragon teaching us? This can't be right!" the girl shouted, sounding half outraged, half frightened.

Jahrra was taken aback and quickly jumped to Hroombra's defense.

"He- he's Master Hroombra and he teaches me once a week," she faltered. "He only wanted to bring us to school on the first day."

The girl finally noticed Jahrra and looked her up and down, sneering rudely. "When did they start letting *Nesnans* in to study with the Resai?"

The hazelnut haired boy sniggered along with most of the other children. Jahrra inched away, feeling the full blast of the girl's acidic tone. She had thought school would be an exciting adventure where she'd make new friends, but it seemed she was making enemies before class even begun and she didn't even know why. By now all of the other children had started murmuring and backing away from the dragon and the three children that had come with it. Jahrra looked back at Gieaun and Scede for support but they only let their eyes drop, moving away charily from the crowd of upset students.

"He won't hurt you!" Jahrra blurted out desperately.

But the girl who'd screamed and the boy standing next to her started shaking their heads in disgust and began gathering the other children together as far away from Hroombra as they could. Jahrra stood on the pathway feeling like the only person in the world. *Why doesn't Master Hroombra just tell them he won't hurt them like he did with Gieaun and Scede?* she thought, feeling smaller and smaller as so many wary pairs of eyes darted between her and the towering reptile standing behind her.

"We don't make friends with people who know dragons." The girl whispered haughtily to her friends, "My mother and father told me that dragons sometimes eat children."

Jahrra was shocked to hear such things. Hroombra would never hurt anybody!

The old dragon sighed and shook his great head, shocking Jahrra back into the present. He'd been listening and watching the children the whole time and he knew there was nothing he could do to make this easier for Jahrra except to leave her and hope her classmates would find a way to put aside their differences.

"I'd best leave you now Jahrra," he said quietly for only her to hear. "I fear I'm causing you harm by being here."

Jahrra whipped around, terrified at the thought of Hroombra leaving her alone with this horrible group.

"Master Hroombra! Don't leave!" she pleaded, running frantically after him.

Hroombra stopped and turned around to speak to her, "Jahrra, I can't explain why those children say what they say but you must stay and learn to be patient with them. You'll be alright. You have Gieaun and Scede. Try not to let the others get you down, just focus on your lessons and know that your family awaits you back at home."

Hroombra gave Jahrra one last encouraging grin then turned to leave. Jahrra watched him go, fresh tears beginning in her eyes. The twin brother and sister took another besmirching look at Jahrra and then the girl glanced at Gieaun and Scede and said, "You know, you still have a chance to be *our* friends. But you can't talk to *her* anymore."

The girl finished her speech with a jerk of her head in Jahrra's direction. Jahrra hadn't even heard what the girl had said; she was still trying hard not to cry. Gieaun just crossed her arms and stuck her chin in the air, a gesture that contained more gall than Jahrra had seen from the timid girl all day.

"We don't want to be your friends," was Gieaun's reply. "We like Jahrra *and* Master Hroombra."

The awful girl just glowered and said, "Fine, you can't be part of our club then."

The other children seemed too reluctant to defy this girl so they just stood there, looking between her and Jahrra. A malicious glare from the mean girl quickly made up their minds and they all stayed right where they were, except for the older children who tapered off on their own, eager to talk about the huge dragon who'd brought three first year students to school.

Gieaun and Scede walked over to Jahrra and put their arms around her shoulders.

"Don't listen to them," Gieaun murmured encouragingly. "We've met them before in town. Their names are Ellysian and Eydeth. They're twins and their father is richer than anyone else in Oescienne. They think they're better than everyone else so they'll treat you badly. Just ignore them."

What Gieaun said comforted Jahrra and even though Scede still wasn't talking, his comforting gesture was nice just the same.

The small group of the youngest children waited a while longer for their teacher, on separate ends of the schoolyard of course. Jahrra, Gieaun and Scede found a large granite boulder resting against the side of the hill with a great sprawling oak wedged between. While the three new friends sat waiting for their instructor they quietly endured the unkind comments drifting across the meadow to their side of the schoolhouse.

As Jahrra listened, the tears that had been welling up in her eyes finally spilled over.

"A dragon!" the girl called Ellysian exclaimed, managing to sound amused and shocked at the same time. "And did you see her uniform? How horrible! I bet it is made of old potato sacks that her mother dyed blue!"

Gieaun hugged her new friend tightly when she saw the look of hurt and confusion on Jahrra's face. "Oh, don't listen to her! She screamed the first time she saw me and Scede. She was frightened by our dark hair!"

Jahrra looked at the two siblings, eyes wide with surprise. Gieaun closed her eyes and nodded somberly.

"She had no idea that anyone could have black hair, and when my mother walked by her and her mother I could hear her saying, 'Mama! What kind of people are those? They have hair like a crow!' Scede and I were upset at first but then our mother said to us, 'Just imagine how sad it is that she knows so little.' "

They then had a good laugh and Jahrra soon stopped crying. The three of them had been so caught up in the talk from across the yard that they almost didn't notice a man on horseback coming up the path. When they finally noticed, all three of them sat stark still and appraised the man who could only be their school teacher.

He looked younger than middle-aged and his clothes were not as fine as most of the other children's, a fact that somehow warmed Jahrra's heart. He wore brown pants and a faded dark green riding jacket, along with a pointed hat complete with an exotic bird's feather.

The man slid off of his tall chestnut horse and led it around to the back of the school building. Jahrra, Gieaun and Scede watched as he took the horse to the small stable out back, not once acknowledging the curious students glancing his way. After he was done caring for his horse he turned and walked over to the children. He immediately noticed that Jahrra, Gieaun and Scede were on one side of the schoolyard while the others were on the other.

"What's this?" he asked in a warm voice, his hands placed casually on his hips. "Did these three try to bite you?" He lifted one long arm and gestured towards Jahrra and her friends.

# Surviving the First Day of School

Ellysian and Eydeth blushed at the comment but kept their faces stern. Jahrra, on the other hand, saw the amusement in their new teacher's eyes. She smiled. She was glad to have another person with a light heart here; the other children were much too serious for her.

"I'm waiting," the man said, crossing his arms and tapping his foot in a falsely annoyed fashion.

It was the boy Eydeth who spoke up first. "That girl is Nesnan, and those two Resai want to be her friend."

Jahrra frowned. So what if she was Nesnan or Resai? Why did it matter if she had less elf blood in her veins than the rest of the class? It mattered to Eydeth and Ellysian, apparently.

The man raised one eyebrow and scrutinized Eydeth for a while. "What's wrong with that?" he finally asked.

Jahrra allowed herself a more abundant grin.

"She's lower in class than us! We can't learn with her, our parents won't have it!" Ellysian insisted, stamping her foot in a small fit.

The man curled one hand under his chin and gazed at the group in a pensive manner. By now, the oldest students had stopped what they were doing to gaze on in interest. Finally, after what seemed like several minutes, the man spoke, "My mother was Nesnan, and therefore I'm half. Will that be a problem as well?"

Ellysian simply stood where she was, mouth clamped shut, not knowing what to say.

"How about we forget about who is Nesnan and who is Resai and focus on our studies instead? Now, everyone into the classroom, we're wasting the day!"

The man walked briskly up the stairs and pulled open the door, smiling in Jahrra's direction. Jahrra, Gieaun and Scede quickly ran over to the building and went inside.

"Come on everyone!" The man called out to the quiet crowd. Slowly and reluctantly they all piled into the building, Eydeth and Ellysian coming in last.

Once inside, Jahrra narrowed her eyes and gazed around the spacious room. It was quite large with many windows that let in little light due to a thick layer of dust. At the front of the classroom was a huge black board for writing and in the right hand corner was an enormous stone fireplace. The room was lined with small wooden tables and chairs, and at the front there was a larger desk and chair for their teacher.

Maps covered the wall on either side of the chalkboard, and Jahrra stared at them in wonder. One map had the word *Ethöes* scrawled across it, the other *Oescienne*. Jahrra didn't yet know how to read all that well, but she knew those two words from looking at the maps Hroombra had shown her. She approached the front of the room to get a better look at them and was severely disappointed to see how devoid of details they were.

These maps merely showed brown land masses surrounded by black, squiggly lines with a few cities shown as red dots. They weren't colorful and stuffed with landmarks, lakes, rivers, trees and mountains the way maps should be. Jahrra was irked. She'd only ever seen a map of Oescienne at the Castle Guard Ruin and was eager to see one of Ethöes with all the details. For now she'd have to do with the boring, brown blob representing their world.

"Alright, everyone find a seat," their teacher said loudly over the murmuring students.

Jahrra and her two friends found desks near the front of the room and the other seats gradually filled in behind them. To Jahrra's profound relief, Eydeth and Ellysian sat as far away from them as possible.

Once everyone had chosen a desk and the murmuring finally dissipated, their teacher addressed them, "Today we'll just be introducing ourselves and making this classroom our own. As you can see it's rather dusty from lack of use. I also have many pieces of parchment for you to draw pictures of yourselves, your families and some of your favorite things. And yes," he paused and shot a stern look at the older students rolling their eyes, "I even want to know what *your* favorite color is, Brethen."

Jahrra risked a peek behind her where she could see a tall, floppy haired teenage boy being jabbed and prodded by his snickering friends. She smothered a grin, liking her new teacher more and more by the minute.

# The Legend of Oescienne – The Finding

The man clasped his hands together cheerfully and then continued on, "So, let's start with me. My name is Mr. Cohrbin. I'm two hundred and eighteen years old and I live here in Aldehren. I'm originally from Aenaith in the northern part of the province and I first came here to teach about fifty years ago. My favorite hobbies are hiking, gardening and reading. My favorite color is brown."

Jahrra smiled inwardly, feeling optimistic for the first time since arriving at the schoolhouse. The rest of the class soon followed suit, and everyone gave their names, where they lived and their favorite things to do. Jahrra explained that she lived in a small stone cottage on the Great Sloping Hill, that she lived with her parents and that they owned a small orchard. She told the class that she didn't have a favorite color, she liked them all, and that what she liked best was starry skies, climbing trees, catching bugs and exploring.

Eydeth and Ellysian sniggered as she spoke, but luckily Jahrra didn't hear them. Scede even opened up a little when he and Gieaun told the class that they lived with their parents on a large ranch just outside the tiny village of Nuun Esse, also on the Great Sloping Hill. They said that they loved riding horses and watching the sun set on the ocean, which they could see from the bluff's edge.

When it came to be Eydeth and Ellysian's turns the twins made no effort to be humble. They not only spoke of their mansion in the northern canyon of the affluent city of Kiniahn

Kroi but also of their vacation home in Hassett Town. They mentioned how their father was the richest Resai man in Oescienne and how he owned half of the Raenyan Valley.

The twins talked about how many outfits they had a piece, or how many music lessons Ellysian had taken or how many trophies Eydeth had won for fencing, or about how many different places they'd visited. The list went on and on. Jahrra sat listening to the two, almost entranced by how much they had but annoyed at how much they still wished they had.

After introductions the day went by rather smoothly. The students helped clean out the classroom (something Ellysian and Eydeth refused to do) and then they got to decorate their tables. Jahrra thought this was absolutely wonderful and soon everyone was busy drawing and gathering together what they would be keeping on their desks.

Around mid-afternoon the class let out and the students went outside to wait for their rides home. The carriages that had brought the twins and all the other students were waiting as they emerged. Ellysian and Eydeth climbed into the lead carriage with everyone else left to fill up the others.

Jahrra wondered why the rest of the class rode in these carriages and Gieaun quickly explained, "They're just showing off. Most of them live nearby. Eydeth and Ellysian are just trying to get them to be their friends by bringing them to school."

Jahrra stared after the retreating wagon train, glad that the mean children were finally gone. A few minutes later Mr. Cohrbin emerged from behind the stone building on his horse. "You three haven't been forgotten, have you?"

His voice was kind once again and Jahrra replied, "We're waiting for Master Hroombra, he should be here any minute."

Just as Jahrra finished explaining the great dragon came clambering up the narrow path, detaching himself from the shadows he matched so well. As soon as he saw their teacher, Hroombra gave a great, wide smile.

"Ahhh, Cohrbin! I was hoping you'd be the school master again this year. How did the first day go?"

Cohrbin nodded at the children and led his horse over to where Hroombra stood. "If it isn't Hroombramantu, out and about! I haven't seen you in ages."

He looked genuinely glad to see Hroombra and Jahrra grinned happily knowing that her teacher didn't have nasty things to say about him like her classmates had.

"I don't often get out, only on special occasions and a first day of school is a special occasion." Hroombra beamed at the children and they smiled right back.

Hroombra and Cohrbin chatted for a little while longer, discussing everything from news around Oescienne to the politics of the classroom. The three friends merely played around the little yard as the adults spoke, grateful that they were free to explore without the twins to make malicious comments.

Hroombra watched them out of the corner of his eye, glad to see Jahrra in higher spirits since the morning.

"So, tell me Hroombra," Cohrbin asked quietly as he leaned forward in the saddle of his edgy horse, "any news from outside the province?"

Hroombra turned his amber eyes back on his friend. He'd known Cohrbin for a long time and he knew he could be trusted.

"As far as we know, the Tyrant remains dormant. There has been little change in the east but there's a strangeness hanging in the air, a sensation I can't describe. Almost like the prickling feeling one senses before lightning strikes. I don't know if it bodes ill will or good."

"Perhaps the time is drawing near for the child of the prophecy to be born," Cohrbin whispered cautiously, his eyes bright with enthusiasm. "There has been much talk in the north about it you know. More than usual, so I've heard."

Hroombra stiffened but not so much for Cohrbin to notice. *Have the elves of Crie been careless?* he wondered with icy fear. His alarm only intensified when Cohrbin spoke again. The Resai man had settled back in the saddle and was now gazing casually at the children.

"Now I know the two dark haired children, their parents raise sheep and horses on the Sloping Hill. But the blonde girl I've never seen before."

A casual change of subject in Cohrbin's eyes perhaps, but not in Hroombra's. His friend's first mention of the prophecy and now this curiosity about Jahrra, as innocent as it may seem, made Hroombra even more uncomfortable. He trusted Cohrbin, but not nearly enough to convey to him the deep secret he kept.

The dragon took a deep breath, "She came to two friends of mine as an infant. Her parents died shortly after her birth but she's been a blessing to my friends Lynhi and Abdhe." Hroombra kept his answer short and simple.

"Well, I have my hands full with the usual privileged, troublesome children this year but those three are definitely a delight to have in the class."

Hroombra breathed a mental sigh of relief, grateful that Cohrbin's interest in Jahrra didn't linger. The two adults spoke for a little while longer until the children came skipping up, ready to be on their way home. The group said their goodbyes and soon they were once again atop Hroombra and heading south. Once outside of Aldehren the three children spilled everything about their first day at school.

"Our teacher is great!" Jahrra remarked. "He let us decorate our desks."

"Yeah, and we got to draw and learn about the history of Oescienne. Did you know that *humans* used to live here?" Scede said in wonderment, no longer the timid boy he had been earlier that day.

"Really?" Hroombra smiled, knowing all too well that they had. "You don't say."

"It was fun," Gieaun added, "except for the twins."

And then the three went into great detail about Ellysian and Eydeth and how they had turned the whole class against them.

"Don't worry, young ones. Most of them will grow out of it and learn that there's nothing wrong with being different from one another. Just have patience."

"Like when growing a beard!" Jahrra piped, remembering what the mailman had once said.

"What?" asked Hroombra in bewilderment.

Jahrra told him all about the beard and the conversation soon returned to more pleasant talk. By the time the dragon and the children arrived at the Castle Guard Ruin it was late afternoon and Dharedth was already waiting for them at the top of the hill.

"So, how did the first day go?" he asked with much eagerness.

"It was alright," Jahrra said simply.

"Alright? That's it?"

"The other children weren't very nice," Gieaun explained solemnly.

"Oh, I see," Dharedth said knowingly. "Don't you worry, they'll soon see what wonderful children you three are, just give it time."

Jahrra looked up, feeling a little better. Maybe Dharedth and Master Hroombra were right. Maybe their classmates just needed time to get used to school as well.

In no time the mail cart was clacking down the road carrying the new friends in the direction of home. Hroombra watched them slowly fade into the distance, looking rather grave in the rich light of the approaching sunset. He smiled as he recalled the first day Jahrra had been brought to him. She'd been all alone then, a human being in a world of Resai and Nesnan elves. He smiled once more as they turned to wave one more time before disappearing over the rise in the road, feeling truly grateful that Jahrra had made some real friends today. *They'll be a great help to her in the coming years,* he thought soberly.

The old dragon exhaled strongly, stirring the dust upon the road and mixing it with a plume of acrid smoke. He only wished that Jaax would visit soon. The younger dragon needed to see how big Jahrra had grown and he needed to update Hroombra on news of the outside world. The conversation with Cohrbin had shaken him at first but it was good to know that there was still uncertainty about Jahrra's existence.

The great reptile yawned and stalked into the one huge, remaining room in the Ruin. Winter was approaching and Jahrra would soon turn seven. The past six years had already gone by so quickly, Hroombra was afraid he would blink and Jahrra would be grown. He only hoped he was doing the right thing by withholding the truth from her until she was old enough to understand. As long as she was satisfied with school and her friends, however, he didn't have to worry, at least not for now.

# -Chapter Five-

# Tricks and Traps and Fighting Back

Jahrra's first day of school was definitely not what she'd expected it to be, but with the encouragement of her parents, the companionship of her two new friends, and mostly from the promise that Hroombra would teach her on her days off, she willingly faced the inhospitable Resai twins day in and day out.

To Jahrra's great relief, the school week only lasted four days, leaving the last day free for her lessons with Hroombra. The old dragon would help her refine her writing and reading skills and teach her about the history of Ethöes through stories of times long past. Jahrra always looked forward to these lessons; at the Castle Guard Ruin she didn't have to fear the laughter and taunting of her classmates.

On weekends, Jahrra would either help out at home or go over to Gieaun's and Scede's ranch where she would learn how to ride horses. Learning to ride quickly became Jahrra's favorite thing to do, especially since it meant spending time with her two best friends.

Wood's End Ranch was the largest piece of land on the western end of the Sloping Hill, easily a hundred acres if not more. It was called Wood's End Ranch because it backed into the Wreing Florenn on its southern side. Jahrra didn't hesitate to mention that her own orchard met the feared forest and asked her friends if they'd ever seen the terrible beast that was said to live there.

"Father has told us many stories about the monsters of Oescienne, but we've never actually seen them," Scede said matter-of-factly.

Jahrra looked at him with wide eyes, too distracted by the fact that there were many monsters living in Oescienne to be disappointed that he already knew about the one in the Wreing Florenn.

"Don't worry, if you ever get to go camping with us I'm sure father will tell you all about them," he continued after seeing Jahrra's reaction.

Jahrra crossed her arms and squished up her face, "I *would* like to hear about them," she claimed. "I need to know what exactly is in the Wreing Florenn. I'm going to go looking for the monster someday when I'm older and braver."

Gieaun looked simply terrified at this comment but Scede, surprisingly, looked as if he'd nurtured the same idea for a long time. After much pleading and teasing Gieaun said that she'd only go with them when they were much older and only during broad daylight. The children laughed at their bravado. If only they could be so bold at school. The schoolhouse was Jahrra's least favorite place to be since it had become a place of both emotional and physical conflict inside and outside the building.

Her first few months studying with the other children had proven a challenge, especially with the twins and their devotees. They always had something negative to say to her and the younger students dying to be part of the popular crowd would chuckle and snigger in support of a recent slight to prove they disliked Jahrra just as much as the twins did.

Eydeth and Ellysian often tried to corner her on her own, but luckily they often failed since Scede and Gieaun were always at her side. Jahrra was able to ignore them most of the time since she wasn't completely alone, but they always found a way to get to her. She was convinced that if Eydeth and Ellysian hadn't been part of the class her other classmates wouldn't be so eager to ostracize her.

"It's because they're afraid of Eydeth and Ellysian," Gieaun often told her. "Not because they don't like you."

Jahrra tried to take this to heart, but with or without supporters, the twins were always looking for ways to ruin her day. Very early on they noticed that Jahrra, Gieaun and Scede liked to sit in a far secluded corner of the schoolyard. Before the first week was over, the twins had made it their place to sit during recess.

When Jahrra and her friends moved to another location, they followed. At first Jahrra had been intimidated by this tactic, but soon she learned to avoid her classmates by lingering inside after class had been dismissed. Once she saw where Ellysian was going she'd head in the opposite direction with Gieaun and Scede.

"Thank goodness Ellysian is so snooty," Gieaun whispered as they headed for their favorite corner of the yard for the first time in weeks.

"I know. She's so busy talking about how wonderful she is that she didn't even notice us!" Jahrra said, unable to conceal a smile.

Scede merely nodded, trailing after the two girls quietly as they crept across the yard. He may have opened up at home but he barely ever said a word at school.

Jahrra knew that if she remained in the shadows and didn't draw attention to herself, she could usually make it through the day. But no matter how hard she tried she never could quite shake them off for good. If Ellysian ever came down from her imaginary castle or if her horrible brother had the notion to realize they hadn't tortured Jahrra and her friends in a while, the tables would turn.

Eydeth had taken up the sport of hunting the "Dragon Dung Dweebs" as Jahrra, Gieaun and Scede had come to be known. While his sister sat at the lunch tables crowing about her six white ponies, Eydeth would sneak off, leaving the main crowd of children in order creep up on Jahrra and her two best friends. He would sneak up behind the great granite rock they sat on and listen quietly to their conversation, waiting for them to say something he could tease them about.

One particularly awful incident occurred the day Jahrra told Gieaun and Scede about the nightmare she'd had over the weekend.

"It was terrible! Strange men came to the Castle Guard Ruin and started teasing and throwing things at Master Hroombra," she said, her eyes filling with tears. "I had Nida and Pada take me to the Ruin first thing the next morning to make sure he was alright."

Jahrra was sitting on top of the flat, cold granite, her arms wrapped tightly around herself as the chill of the stone combined with the chill she felt from the image of the dream. Suddenly, Eydeth jumped out from behind the stone, nearly causing the three of them to tumble to the ground from fright.

"Ha-ha!" the evil boy chirped, pointing a menacing finger in their direction. "The Dragon Dung Dweebs are over here crying about that stupid lizard!"

Before the stunned friends could comprehend what was happening, Ellysian had them surrounded by her band of followers. With tears streaming down her cheeks, Jahrra watched and listened helplessly as the entire class, except for maybe five or so students her own age, closed in and maliciously chanted, "The Three D's the Three D's, nothing more than babies!" over and over again.

Jahrra turned bright red and Gieaun and Scede moved in closer to her. This wasn't the first time that Eydeth had snuck up on them, but Jahrra decided right then and there it would be the last. After Mr. Cohrbin came out to break up the commotion, Jahrra and her two friends remained on the rock for a little while longer.

"I've had it!" she fumed. "How dare he? I only wanted you two to know about that dream!"

Jahrra allowed one last tear of anger to run down her face, burning her skin like acid. Gieaun and Scede put their arms around her to comfort her and Jahrra took a deep breath.

"I know what to do," she said stoically after calming a bit. "I'm going to trick Eydeth, just like he tricks us. I'm going to build a mud trap and see how he likes to get caught!"

Gieaun was surprised at Jahrra's sudden thirst for vengeance. "Oh, Jahrra, do you think that'll work? What if he tells on us and we get in trouble?"

"It has to work," Jahrra insisted. "And I don't care if we do get in trouble!"

During the next week they worked quietly on Jahrra's plan. They dug a hole behind their granite perch and slowly filled it with water from the school's well, making a muddy, boggy mess at the bottom of it. Gieaun and Scede even gathered some rotting vegetables from their garden to make the mud even nastier.

Finally they covered the gaping hole with branches and leaves and simply waited for Eydeth to taunt them again. They didn't have to wait long. Two days after they finished their trap they got their chance. Eydeth snuck up on them again and started teasing them, but this time the three friends were prepared.

"That's right," Jahrra said, shaking nervously, "we *are* the Dragon Dung Dweebs, and here's some dung to prove it!"

She scooped up a prepared blob of muck off the top of their granite slab and launched it at Eydeth, watching in delighted horror as it splacked against his white uniform shirt. Eydeth looked down at the black muck sticking to his chest in hollow shock. He turned his squinty eyes up at Jahrra, his alarm slowly turning to anger as his face flushed red.

"You'll pay for that Nesnan!" he breathed and rushed at the low stone.

"Quick, down the other side!" Jahrra hissed giving Scede and Gieaun a shove.

By now the whole class had noticed that something unusual was going on in Jahrra's corner of the yard. Eydeth wasn't chanting like he usually did after scaring the Dweebs. Instead, he was shouting and scrambling up the rock. Jahrra, Gieaun and Scede slid down the back of their boulder, side-stepping their mud trap and secretly hoping that Eydeth didn't notice.

As they clambered up the trunk of the nearest oak tree, Eydeth heaved himself on top of the rock and it wasn't long before he jumped down the side to follow them. He sprinted to catch up to his prey and as he made the last leap to snatch at Gieaun's ankle, his own feet went crashing through the thatching that hid the mud-lined hole.

The angry boy made a strangled screaming sound as he tripped face first into a trough of sticky, smelly mud. Jahrra watched breathlessly from a high branch in the tree as the boy started screaming and crying, his own sister reluctant to help him up out of the trap. Jahrra had to stifle a laugh as Eydeth dragged himself out of the filth, looking like an angry, muddy rat. The class sniggered and laughed at the fuming boy who was carrying on and on about how Jahrra and her friends had thrown mud at him.

"Honestly, Eydeth," Ellysian said, her arms crossed and her face twisted in disgust, "you fell *into* the mud, you didn't have it thrown at you!"

Ellysian and the rest of the children slowly moved away, hiding their giggles as the filthy boy gaped and bellowed at them.

Jahrra, Gieaun and Scede were beside themselves with glee.

"At least he should leave us alone for a while," Scede said between giggles.

"Or he'll be twice as mean," Gieaun added nervously.

"Either way," Jahrra laughed, "it was worth it!"

Though the attack on Eydeth hadn't completely ended the assaults from either of them, it had put a dent in their dominance over Jahrra and her friends. They seldom ever came around the boulder any longer and only harassed Jahrra if she wandered too close to their side of the schoolyard. Whenever their behavior was particularly nasty however, Jahrra simply recalled what it had felt like to throw the ball of mud at Eydeth. That pleasant memory was usually enough to get her through a tough day.

Jahrra gratefully welcomed the winter break when it finally came, thrilled to have a long vacation away from the tension at school. She was able to enjoy her very first birthday party with her two best friends, and Gieaun and Scede were even allowed to stay the night.

"I can't believe she is already seven years old," Lynhi commented to Hroombra as they watched the three companions chase each other around the orchard pretending to hunt the wild beasts of the forest. "It seems just yesterday she was a baby."

"It's amazing how quickly the time goes by," Hroombra agreed solemnly. He'd dropped by for the day to wish Jahrra a happy birthday and to tell her a special birthday tale, one about unicorns.

Like all good things, however, the much appreciated time away from school eventually came to an end. The first several days back at the schoolhouse went well but it wasn't long before the twins were back into the habit of tormenting Jahrra.

"Nesnan girl," Ellysian chirped the second week back, "we hear that you live in a house that's as small as a dwarf's basement."

They'd dropped the phrase "Dragon Dung Dweebs" and were singling Jahrra out by simply referring to her as the 'Nesnan', ignoring Gieaun and Scede completely. Jahrra couldn't possibly imagine why two seven year olds, who should be more concerned with playing tag and hide-and-go-seek, would put so much effort into tormenting someone else. Her mother and father and Hroombra had always said that all the peoples of Oescienne were equal, but for some reason the twins didn't think so.

When the name calling started to wear off they moved on to more cruel tactics. For instance, they still found it shocking that Jahrra was being tutored by a dragon and didn't hesitate to make their disapproval known, in less than kind terms of course.

One morning, Jahrra was telling Gieaun and Scede about her lesson with Hroombra the weekend before.

"Have you ever heard of semequins!" she breathed excitedly, thinking she was out of earshot of the evil twins. "Master Hroombra told me all about them. They're the most amazing creatures! He told me that they're horses that have a unicorn mother or father!"

"You mean you didn't know about semequins?"

To Jahrra's great annoyance, Eydeth had heard her. "How dumb can you be!" he laughed. "My father owns over a hundred of them, the best in the land!"

Gieaun and Scede gave Eydeth an annoyed look and swiftly made efforts to ignore him, but it was what he said next that captured their attention. He was irritated that his initial insult missed its target, so he tried a different tactic.

"Don't you dummies know that dragons are evil creatures that steal treasure and set whole towns on fire!"

Many of the other girls and boys who had at first ignored Eydeth's usual tirade gasped at this remark and stepped away from Jahrra as if she were sick with the plague. Jahrra tried to remain cool and tried desperately to think of a good retort, but all she could do was hang her head low and walk away with her two friends. She tried so hard to enjoy school but the silence one day and laughter the next truly disheartened her.

A few weeks later Ellysian made another nasty comment about Nesnans right in front of Jahrra, but this time she reacted. Just as Ellysian finished telling a group of girls how the Nesnan people never did anything worth praising, Jahrra shouted back without thinking, "I don't care what you say! Master Hroombra told me that we're all the same!"

*Oh yes, that showed them,* Jahrra thought to herself bitterly as the laughter around her strengthened. She flushed terribly as she once again became a spectacle.

# Tricks and Traps and Fighting Back

Eydeth had been right across the yard and quickly joined in the foray.

"All the same?" he squeaked with delight. "You? The same as us? That dragon isn't only horrible, he's stupid too!" The evil boy could barely hold back his laughter.

Jahrra just stood there, frozen in frustration and anger as the entire class laughed at her.

"Stop it!" Gieaun shouted, seething with rage. "Master Hroombra isn't horrible or stupid! You're all just too afraid of Eydeth's lies to believe anything else!"

The laughter, if at all possible, grew louder. Jahrra felt like vapor being spread thin throughout the air around her. Gieaun quailed in shame. Almost every last person in the class was now surrounding Jahrra and Gieaun, pointing and making faces.

"Dragon Dung Dweebs! Dragon Dung Dweebs!" they chanted again and again, resurrecting the old phrase once more. Eydeth and Ellysian stood back and watched with malevolent grins of satisfaction on their smug faces.

Then, without warning, Scede did something no one was expecting. He'd been sitting on the great granite boulder beneath the oak tree when all of this had started. He'd watched helplessly as Jahrra walked over to defend herself and remained seated in fear as his sister joined her. But as the cacophony unfolded before him, his fear slowly turned to rage and he just couldn't stand it any longer.

"Stop it! All of you stop it right now!" he screamed as he jumped off the stone slab, looking as dangerous as an angry wasp.

Scede's sudden outburst caught everyone off guard and the laughing ceased instantly.

"Master Hroombra is much smarter than any of you, and he's nicer too! We know you don't like us or him, and we don't care. So why don't you just leave us alone! And you had better watch out," he pointed a shaking finger at Ellysian, "or you'll end up getting a mud bath just like your brother!"

Scede was breathing hard and his teeth and fists were clenched. Even Gieaun and Jahrra backed away, slightly afraid he might explode. Ellysian had turned white and the smile on Eydeth's face became a hard frown as he recalled the memory of falling into the mud.

Scede darted his eyes around, trying hard to think of something else to say, but nothing came to mind. Every child in the schoolyard, oldest to youngest, stood still as if waiting for him to strike at them like a snake.

When he finally spoke again everyone cringed, but the only words he could muster were, "Why don't you all go wait for your stupid wagons over there!"

He pointed furiously towards the front of the schoolhouse and surprisingly, everyone obeyed.

"Yeah, we will, and you can go wait for your hay cart over there," Ellysian said, sounding like a deflated balloon as she and her brother turned and headed towards the front of the yard.

Gieaun, Scede and Jahrra slowly walked back to their oak tree, the two girls keeping their distance. Like the victims of a massive earthquake, they waited for Scede's aftershocks but they never came. They sat a long time, watching as all of their classmates quietly climbed into their respective carriages or rode off on their own horses they kept in the school stables.

Finally, after what seemed like ages, the mail cart came creaking up the path. Gieaun, Jahrra and Scede climbed up next to Mr. Dharedth as if under a spell, content with riding all the way home in complete silence. The two girls had no idea what to say to Scede, but finally Dharedth, sensing the strange tension surrounding the three friends, spoke up, "What seems to be the problem? Ever since I started taking you to and from school eight months ago, you always talked up a storm on the way back. Why are you all so silent?"

Scede was the one to answer, his voice strangely calm, "The other children were saying some mean things about Master Hroombra and Jahrra, so I yelled at them."

"Is that all? Well, 'tis about time those ruffians get told a thing or two. Don' worry," Dharedth said seeing the look of dread on the children's faces. "I won' tell anyone you did it."

He smiled, and the icy silence surrounding the three friends melted away.

"Did you see the look on Eydeth's and Ellysian's faces when you yelled at them? It looked like they'd seen a ghost!" Jahrra said, relieved Scede wasn't going to erupt again.

"I know. I was so afraid of you Scede! I've never seen you so mad, even after the time I kicked apart the sand castle you made at the beach," added Gieaun, stifling a giggle.

By the time they reached the crest of the Sloping Hill an hour later, they were their normal selves again. Dharedth pulled the cart to a groaning stop and the three of them jumped out, waving goodbye as they began walking towards the Castle Guard Ruin. The school week was over and Jahrra had invited Scede and Gieaun to stay over for the weekend. But before they went home for the night, Hroombra had asked Jahrra to stop by after school on her way home.

They trekked down the narrow dirt path leading from the main road to the Ruin, engrossed in a discussion about what had happened at school that day. Jahrra looked up and saw Hroombra standing beside the crumbled building and her heart leapt. She was hoping that the old dragon had a special story to tell them today, for why else would he ask them to stop by after school? She waved vigorously at her mentor's figure and got back to her friends' conversation. What Jahrra hadn't noticed, however, was the other dragon waiting patiently just inside the Ruin and out of view, his eyes fixed entirely on her.

# -Chapter Six-

# Phrym

Jaax wasn't surprised the children hadn't spotted him; he was standing behind the great wall, his head barely stretching through the large side entrance of the Ruin. His blue-green scales, like chips of aquamarine granite, blended seamlessly with the lichen plastered stone, his eyes standing out like pale emeralds set in a statue. The children were much too far away to notice that particular detail, however, but the young dragon's silvery-green gaze remained unfalteringly focused on the little girl walking between the two dark haired Resai children.

Jaax smiled, grateful for his keen eyesight. It gave him a chance to sum up Jahrra from afar, to get a sense of what she was made of before meeting her. He'd heard much praise from Hroombra already, but he had to make this judgment for himself.

More than seven years had passed since he'd left her in this land and he watched now in amused amazement as she approached. She still had the same golden hair that he remembered but she looked much different from the infant he'd left behind. She was tall for her age and from this distance he could see that she was going to be strong and sturdy, not petit and delicate like the races of elves. *Strong and sturdy, just like a human,* he thought. He narrowed his intense eyes, pulling the young girl's face closer into his vision. Her eyes were still blue, but now they were the blue of rainclouds retreating over the ocean after a storm, a blue that was only a shade or two away from gray.

Jaax took a breath and focused his attention on her face. It was a determined face, slightly rounded with high cheekbones. He noticed a few freckles and a dimple when she made a comical face at what her friends were saying. She pulled at her collar unconsciously and he couldn't blame her. The uniforms the children were wearing looked absolutely uncomfortable.

As the companions drew closer to the Ruin, Jahrra shot Hroombra a cheerful look, but beneath the look of happiness Jaax detected something more. Fear, sorrow, anticipation, all of these emotions fought behind her eyes like swarming fish in a clouded pool. He cast these aside as simple childhood whims: a stubbed toe, a lost game, a beloved pet gone missing. What captured most of the dragon's attention, however, was the fire and spirit he saw residing there.

When the children were about a hundred yards from the Ruin, Jaax decided to leave behind his safe hiding place and face the child he had come to see. He felt a little guilty, for he only planned to meet Jahrra and then be on his way. For the past several years he'd been trying to find time to check in on Jahrra and Hroombra, but something had always delayed or thwarted these plans. Hroombra had been ecstatic when he'd received word of Jaax's planned visit and the younger dragon now wondered if maybe he should've told Hroombra this stay would be an extremely short one.

Jaax took a deep breath, set his thoughts aside for later, and stepped out from behind the stone wall. He moved gracefully for such a large and powerful creature and was so silent that the children didn't hear him at first. To his great delight, however, Jahrra was the first to look up and see what had moved in the corner of her eye. She gasped, and stopped dead in her tracks.

Jaax merely gazed down at her with a look of interest. Her blue eyes changed in an instant, moving closer to that shade of gray he'd noticed earlier. Jahrra was frozen in place and the two other children walked right into her, knocking her slightly off balance. When they looked up to see why she'd stopped they also caught sight of the Tanaan dragon that had appeared out of nowhere.

"Whoa!!" yelped Scede, unable to stop himself. He quickly clasped his hands over his mouth and ogled up at the strange dragon towering above him. Gieaun stood rigid, mouth hanging open, looking very much like she did earlier in the schoolyard. The children were used to Hroombra's calm presence but they could all tell right away that this younger dragon was nothing like Hroombra.

Although slightly smaller than the Korli dragon, Jaax moved with the fluidity of a warrior, all well-controlled strength and raw power. It was clear that this dragon was a determined, dominant and clever creature with shrewd eyes that did not easily betray what he was thinking. Next to the placid and gentle soul that was Hroombra, Jaax was a lion poised for battle.

"Hello children," Hroombra's greeting rolled through the awkward silence like distant thunder. He turned and acknowledged behind him. "I'd like you all to meet Raejaaxorix. He was once a student of mine."

Jaax kept his gaze locked on Jahrra's face the entire time Hroombra spoke, making her feel uncomfortable. When she heard her mentor speak his name, however, she miraculously found her voice.

"Raejaaxorix?" she repeated almost indecipherably, gaping up at Hroombra. "Like the Raejaaxorix in the stories you told me?"

"Yes, the very same," Hroombra said cheerily with a wide smile to match.

Jahrra returned her gaze to the Tanaan dragon, but instead of remaining dark with veiled unease her eyes sparkled with enthusiasm as she beamed brightly. He was younger than she imagined him, since the stories Hroombra told her were from hundreds of years ago. Then she remembered how long dragons actually lived and regained some of her composure.

"Stories?" Jaax found his voice as well, taking his stony gaze off of Jahrra.

His eyes now landed on Hroombra and his mood went from interested observance to inquisitive suspicion.

Jahrra jumped slightly when she heard the dragon speak for the first time. He had a strong, authoritative voice. It wasn't as deep as Hroombra's but it was much more intimidating. Where Hroombra's voice earned trust and respect, this one demanded it.

"Yes Jaax, I've told Jahrra many tales of the past, those of when you were still a very young dragon. When so many followed you."

Hroombra's smile began to fade as his speech trailed off.

Jahrra could tell that Jaax had somehow upset him and a tiny feeling of dislike began in the pit of her stomach.

Jaax blew hot air from his nostrils, almost releasing out a snort as he did so. He turned his gaze to the distant Wreing Florenn before answering shortly, "I'm no hero Hroombra, you know that."

An awkward silence fell over the group, but not for long. "We'll discuss this later, but for now I'd like to introduce the young children to you."

Hroombra sounded disappointed and uncomfortable, but Jahrra pushed this aside as she waited nervously to be introduced to the famous Raejaaxorix.

"This is Gieaun, and her brother Scede. And this, of course, is Jahrra." Hroombra nodded to the children as he named them.

"I see you've grown up quite well, Jahrra," Jaax remarked placidly, returning his gaze to the young girl, seeming to forget his rebuke of Hroombra. "I haven't seen you since you were an infant."

Jahrra shot Hroombra a look of surprise.

"That's right," the old dragon smiled. "He brought you here to us from the north, to your foster parents."

"Really?" said Jahrra in bemusement.

She'd never really known how she'd come to be placed with her parents. Before now she always imagined coming to Oescienne with a large party of traveling merchants who had stopped to trade with her mother and father, only to discover that they would be the perfect people to raise the orphan child they'd found in the wilderness. Jahrra suddenly wondered if Jaax might know something about her original home and perhaps her real parents, but she felt too unsettled to ask any questions.

"Jaax has come to see how you've grown and he's also brought something for you. Follow me."

There was a twinkling in the old dragon's eyes as he spoke, and soon all three children were being led eagerly around the side of the Ruin and out into the field just south of the old building. *Raejaaxorix brought something for me?* Jahrra could hardly believe it. She was afraid to breathe, thinking that such a simple act might destroy this strange dream.

"Where're we going?" she queried as she jogged to keep up with Hroombra's slow but long stride.

Gieaun and Scede were right behind her with Jaax taking up the rear. His gait was much smoother than Hroombra's and when Jahrra quickly glanced back at his alert figure she came to the conclusion that he never let his guard down.

"We're going to the old stables that used to house the horses of the guards who, long ago, kept watch over the castle grounds from here," Hroombra finally answered, tearing into Jahrra's wandering thoughts.

The three children quickened their pace and started guessing at what the great Raejaaxorix might've brought for Jahrra. Gieaun guessed a robe woven by fairies, Scede a magical stone from the elves, but neither Jaax nor Hroombra would give in. After several failed guesses Jahrra and her friends gave up and focused on reaching their destination.

Jahrra scanned the edge of the field up ahead and discovered another ancient stone structure that must have been the stables Hroombra had mentioned. She'd never really thought about this other building before, imagining it was just the remains of an old storage shed.

The old stables were in much better shape than the Ruin itself, however. Most of the roof had rotted away and the wood gates that once stood in the openings had long ago disintegrated, leaving a gaping entrance framed in stone.

The group closed in on the stables and Jahrra immediately spotted something crumpled upon the ground. It looked like a discarded blanket lying within the stone walls. As she got closer, however, she realized that the blanket was in fact a tiny colt, grayish in color, huddled on a bed of fresh straw.

"Ohhhhhh!" she exclaimed in pure delight as she recognized the rather small creature. Gieaun and Scede also ran over, emitting sounds of excitement at the sight of the foal.

As the children sat adoring the tiny, sleeping horse, Hroombra turned to Jaax.

"Tell me where you found him again," he asked in a low voice. All the cheer he'd used with the children had vanished and now a look of deep concern settled upon his weathered face.

"Just north of Lidien, at the base of the Hrunahn Footmountains," Jaax answered grimly.

He then took a deep, troubled breath and continued on, "His mother was the unicorn Nihll, and his father was a semequin. The elves that found and cared for Nihll told me that a mercenary of Cierryon had wounded her. She was able to communicate to them that she was east of Lake Hronah in the Arghott Forest where her herd lived before the Tyrant's men found them and killed them all. She was shot as well but somehow she lost them in the hills. She traveled as far west as she could, gave birth to this young one and died of her wounds."

Jaax concluded his tale in a weary tone. He looked over at the children, who for now were well protected from such horrors.

"So it seems the Crimson King is no longer dormant in the east," Hroombra said in a serious tone, still not loud enough for the children to hear. He blinked at Jaax and whispered, "Then it has started?"

"Something must have stirred his interest, yet I can't say for sure how much time we have left. The Creecemind emperor has finally agreed to another meeting with me, but I'm afraid it will come to nothing, just like it did seven years ago. He remains stubbornly adamant about remaining neutral, at least until he sees the human child with his very own eyes."

Jaax paused to let Hroombra turn this information over in his head before he continued.

Quietly and severely, he went on, "From my inquiries and observations throughout the west it has become clear to me that entire villages and towns are growing restless. Their citizens act like wounded prey being stalked. They know the Crimson King is watching and they know he means to attack but they don't know when or how. It could happen in a month or ten years, I cannot tell you for sure. Some have even begun asking questions, more than before, questions I cannot afford to answer or to ignore. Yet we cannot take any risks; Jahrra must be kept safe from the outside world even if it means further distancing ourselves from our allies." The Tanaan dragon took a deep breath and released it wearily. "At least for now."

Hroombra simply nodded in response to this statement. *So,* he thought, remembering Cohrbin's comments, *it was an ill wind I detected after all.*

"Then you must go," the old dragon said somberly, looking away from Jaax. When he turned back around his eyes twinkled with emotion. "It seems to be a new habit of yours. Dropping off young orphans and then leaving the very next moment."

Jaax simply looked towards the dark forest once again, not knowing how to respond.

"Go now, and be safe. Do what you must so that she can still live here in peace, at least for a while," Hroombra said in a whisper.

Jaax turned to look at him, matching his morose demeanor.

"I shall," he breathed. "Take good care of the young foal. I would have left him with the elves but I thought that Jahrra would need a good, strong horse when her fate called her. This little one will be perfect when he is grown."

"Very well," Hroombra answered quietly. "You'd better be off then. I'll explain to the children why you've left."

"Thank you. I hope to return again soon, when I know more."

Jaax glanced down at Jahrra. She was too busy mooning over the young semequin to notice him turning to leave. *Yes,* he thought, *we must keep her safe, and secret.*

The young dragon walked back across the field and out to the road, rather stealthily for his size. He spread his great wings and just as silently, lifted off into the darkening spring sky. Hroombra watched him disappear like a dark cloud over the sun-gilded mountains, fearing for him the way he feared for Jahrra. He shook off his feelings of doubt and trepidation, despite an instinctual need for them, and turned to the three children.

"So what do you think?" he asked, donning a fresh smile.

"He's marvelous! What's his name?" Jahrra asked, not yet noticing Jaax was gone.

"I think Raejaaxorix wanted to leave that up to you."

Jahrra tore her eyes away from the sleeping colt, finally seeing that the other dragon was nowhere to be found.

"Where did he go?" she asked, sounding disappointed as her smile faded. She had so many questions to ask him about the outside world and about his many adventures, that is, when she had worked up the courage to address him personally. Now it seemed she would never get that chance.

"You'll learn, young Jahrra," the old dragon answered in a wearied tone, "that sometimes we adults have many obligations to fulfill that you can't understand. Jaax has many duties outside of Oescienne; he has many things he must take care of, things a young girl wouldn't understand. We're just lucky he was able to visit us at all."

Hroombra knew this was a lame excuse, and he saw how disappointed Jahrra was, but he could think of nothing else to tell her.

"Don't fret young one," he continued after a while, "he'll visit us again someday. But I don't want you wasting your time waiting for him, for it may be a long time before he comes this way again."

Jahrra nodded, her eyes trained on the ground. She knew she should take her mentor's advice, but she felt she couldn't wait until the next time Jaax paid them a visit.

"Well," said Jahrra finally, looking down at the sleeping foal, "I guess I'll call him 'Phrym'."

Hroombra smiled as the name sparked a memory. He'd once used the word in a lesson, a dragon's word, forgetting who he was teaching. Although he meant to teach Jahrra the language of the dragons some day, he knew that it was too soon. Jahrra liked the word, so he'd told her what it meant: '*Phrym*, it means *friend* in the dragons' tongue.'

He smiled down at Jahrra now, completely enchanted by the young semequin lying in front of her. "Yes, Jahrra, I do believe he'll make you a good friend."

❀ ❀ ❀

The warm spring months crept by and the flowers and trees slowly faded into the soft and warm hues of summer. As the days grew longer, Jahrra kept busy with the new responsibility of caring for the young semequin Jaax had left her. The foal was only a few weeks old when he arrived in Oescienne so he was placed with one of the mares at Wood's End Ranch.

During the early weeks with Phrym, nothing seemed to bring Jahrra down, not even the long days at school with Eydeth and Ellysian. Fortunately, Scede's tirade the day Jaax arrived kept the twins at a comfortable distance for a few weeks, but like always, that wore off with time. If they sniggered in her direction or whispered as she walked by, however, all she had to do was close her eyes and picture her young foal waiting for her to come home and play with him.

At first Phrym was a light silver color all over, looking exactly the way Hroombra had described unicorn foals, but as he grew the silver faded into a variety of grays that dappled his smooth coat. His mane and tail turned into a deep, storm cloud color and his long legs were spotted until they blended into a dark gray towards his hooves. His eyes, light blue at first, became a rich, smoky quartz.

As he grew older the timid colt became much more animated and learned to trust Jahrra unwaveringly. Sometimes, late into the afternoon on the weekends, she would play with him in the fields of her friends' ranch. She'd sneak up on the young colt and he would take off running, tossing his head and bucking in good humor. Jahrra would fall to the ground laughing and Phrym would trot over and add his own chorus of cheerful whinnies.

All of this time spent with Phrym distracted Jahrra from her other troubles and before she knew it, the school season was drawing to an end. Jahrra was beside herself with anticipation. There was so much to do over the summer: camping with her two best friends, extra lessons (and extra stories) with Master Hroombra, aiding her father with the orchard and assisting her mother with the garden. Gieaun and Scede promised to help Jahrra clean out the old stables by the Castle Guard Ruin so that she could someday keep Phrym there when they visited Hroombra. Even Abdhe and Hroombra volunteered to help the children when they found the time.

"Oh, Phrym," Jahrra would say with glee, "at the end of the summer, you'll be able to visit and stay with Master Hroombra if you'd like!"

Then she'd turn to the Korli dragon, whom would stand out by the old degraded stables and imagine it in pristine condition alongside her, and add, "And when I'm older, I can come and visit you anytime I want!"

Hroombra smiled down at the young girl with her eyes closed in happiness, envisioning the completed stable before her. The old dragon may have been disappointed by Jaax's short visit, but he couldn't help feeling pleased with how his gift was affecting Jahrra.

# Phrym

On the final day of school before their long-anticipated summer break, Jahrra, Gieaun and Scede patiently endured the presence of the twins and their gang, but even Eydeth and Ellysian seemed too distracted by the prospect of long days away from the schoolhouse to waste much time on them.

Jahrra was barely able to pay attention in class with all the images of the upcoming camping trip dancing around in her head. She was going to stay the night at Wood's End Ranch and the next morning she'd be leaving for Ossar Lake with her friends. Ossar Lake, according to Gieaun and Scede, was the most wondrous place in Ethöes.

"If there is any magic in Oescienne Jahrra, it's at Lake Ossar," Scede had told her dreamily.

Jahrra sighed heavily, wishing the hours would move by faster. The school day dragged on but finally, after what seemed like years, it was all over. Master Cohrbin wished them all goodbye as his impatient students fled through the doors to freedom, reminding them not to forget what they had learned over the summer.

Jahrra, Gieaun and Scede were the last to leave the schoolyard, darting to the mail cart when it finally rattled up the shaded drive.

"What's all this rushin' about?" Dharedth asked in a slightly aggravated tone. "You all may be in a hurry, but Rhuda sure isn't."

"Summer has started!" the children exclaimed in exasperation as if such a thing should be fairly obvious to the mail carrier.

"Ah, I see. Can' wait to make use of the free time, eh?"

And with that he clicked Rhuda into a steady gait. The long ride home, which was usually Jahrra's favorite time of the day, was almost unbearable. Each field they passed and each road they crossed was one more minute lost from her summer vacation, but finally the mail cart came to a jerking halt in front of Jahrra's long drive.

"Alright, little Jahrra, run and get your things. We'll wait," Dharedth called after her as she sprinted down the walk.

"Nida! Pada!" she yelled breathlessly as she burst through the front door.

"Oh!" Her mother jumped and dropped the dust rag she'd been holding. "My goodness child! Are you trying to kill me?" Lynhi breathed, clutching her heart.

"Sorry," Jahrra interjected, "but Gieaun and Scede are waiting with Mr. Dharedth!"

She jumped up and gave her mother a kiss on the cheek, still breathless from running up the drive. Lynhi smiled warmly. "Go say goodbye to your Pada. He's out tending the trees."

Jahrra darted into the small yard and through the wood pole fence, causing the family's small flock of chickens to go scattering in terror. She found her father atop a ladder wearing his wide brim straw hat, thinning out the young fruit on the trees so they would produce a healthier crop.

"Pada!" she shouted up at him.

He looked down, not at all surprised to hear his daughter shouting from below. "Yes Jahrra? How was your last day of school?"

"It was alright. But Gieaun and Scede are waiting out front," Jahrra said, trying not to sound overly enthusiastic. "Remember, I'm going to Lake Ossar?"

Abdhe climbed down the ladder and scooped his daughter into his arms. "Oh, that's right. I guess I'd better come in and say goodbye then."

He carried her back to the house and set her down in the kitchen, taking a seat on one of the old kitchen chairs.

"Have you packed?" he asked seriously, looking at Jahrra through his wispy hair.

Jahrra's eyes popped open and she turned and clambered up the stairs. Abdhe just chuckled, causing Lynhi to glance over at her husband with veiled eyes.

"What is it now?" he asked in a tone that declared he was used to this silent protesting from his wife.

"Are you sure it's safe to send her there for the weekend? I know we've already discussed this a hundred times, but what if something happens, even with Nuhra and Kaihmen watching over her?"

Abdhe took out his pipe and carefully lit it. After taking a few puffs he glanced back at his wife. "She can't be kept safe forever, and it's only for the weekend. Jahrra deserves to enjoy her childhood while it lasts."

"You're probably right," Lynhi sighed, getting back to her dusting. "But I can't help but worry."

Abdhe smiled. "It's a mother's job to worry."

Jahrra scampered back down the stairs, complete with a small sack stuffed with what her parents could only imagine were her clothes.

Her father smiled and kissed her on the cheek. "Be careful my dear, and have a good time."

Jahrra then turned to her mother, who gave her a hug. "Come home soon."

"I will," said Jahrra, and then added cheerfully, "I'll only be gone for a few days!"

Jahrra fled out the door and flew down the path, eagerly joining her friends before Dharedth coaxed his horse into an easy gait. A wiggling, barking pack of dogs greeted the children when they finally reached the end of the long road trailing through Wood's End Ranch. Jahrra smiled broadly as she gazed upon the ranch house she loved so much. It was built of clay brick and looked snug among the low rolling fields that made up most of the land surrounding it.

After greeting Nuhra and Kaihmen, her friends' parents, Jahrra, Gieaun and Scede strolled over to the stables where

# Phrym

Phrym was kept. The semequin heard Jahrra before he saw her, poking his curious head over the top of the stable door. Jahrra grinned lovingly; he was growing so fast and becoming so tall.

"Hi Phrym!" She ran the remaining distance to meet him. He was only five months old now, but Jahrra could hardly wait until he was old enough to ride.

During dinner, the three friends chatted about the highlights of their school year.

"I don't know if I like school very much," Jahrra answered when Nuhra asked her how her first year had gone. "The only good thing about it is Master Cohrbin and Gieaun and Scede."

After dinner, the three friends begged Kaihmen to tell them stories.

"Please father, tell us about the monsters that live in the Wreing Florenn!" Scede pleaded.

"Oh no, those tales are for tomorrow when we're out in the wilderness," Kaihmen answered with a grin.

The children tried in vain to get him to budge, but he refused. Instead, he pulled out a flute and played a few songs for them until they became drowsy. Once they were all tucked into bed, however, they found it extremely hard to sleep. Jahrra couldn't tell when she finally drifted off, but when she did, she had dreams of riding Phrym across her friends' ranch in pursuit of the strange beasts of the Wreing Florenn.

# The Legend of Oescienne – The Finding

Morning came quickly, and before the sun showed his face, Kaihmen and Nuhra had all of the camping gear gathered and tied to the horses. They both had their own mounts, a pair of Palominos, the ranch's trademark, while Gieaun, Jahrra and Scede shared a much older and gentler paint named Strohda. After a small breakfast of biscuits and bacon, the group set off heading west, following the road that ran through the town of Nuun Esse and past the Castle Guard Ruin.

The trip to the lake took most of the morning, but it was one filled with color and light and sound. Once at the base of the Sloping Hill, the trio of horses made their way easily through Willowsflorn, full of yellow, brushy willow blooms in the early summer. They crossed over a wide stone bridge that lay across a chattering stream and waved energetically when they met other travelers. Birdsong and the soft whispering of branches being jostled by the breeze filled the air and the fresh, sweet smell of the wilderness tickled Jahrra's nose. Finally, after what seemed like hours, they arrived at their destination.

Lake Ossar wasn't only the largest of the dune lakes, but it also had a boardwalk running straight across its width. Ossar was rimmed mainly by lazy, languid oaks with rows of willows, tangles of blackberry bushes, bunches of poison oak and forests of rushes and reeds fencing in its shore.

"We'll have to return later in the summer when the blackberries are ripe," Nuhra remarked to the children riding just behind her.

Gieaun, Scede and Jahrra all exchanged smiles of delight. Jahrra loved blackberries, especially those that were still warm from soaking in the sun. Nuhra and Kaihmen led the horses to a clearing surrounded by a few willow trees just out of reach of the boardwalk. As the adults set up camp, the three children climbed down from their horse and went running onto the wide bridge.

"Don't wander too far you three. Your parents will kill me if anything happens to you Jahrra!"

But they were too thrilled and distracted to hear Kaihmen's warning.

Once out on the boardwalk, Jahrra could finally see the full beauty of the lake before her. The boardwalk was wide, wide enough in some spots for people to sit on benches and fish. Two empty docks, bobbing and splashing in the weak current, protruded from either side of the wooden bridge like the fins of some great sea animal. Jahrra stepped up onto one of the benches on the turnout closest to her and rested her arms on the edge of the railing, staring out in wide-eyed wonder.

Ossar was more of a large pond than a lake, but it was breathtaking nonetheless. Scrubby woods dotted the landscape to the north and east and just a hint of creamy dunes peeked between the trees in the west. The sky was clear and the sun was shining brightly upon the small ripples of the water's surface. The Oorn River flowed into this lake and then out into the smaller, marshier Nuun Dein until it finally spilled into the ocean.

Jahrra's eyes trailed the current of the river, obviously cutting along the surface of the water. Waterfowl of many shapes, sizes and colors floated along in the river's undertow, prattling on in their bird language. Every now and then one would dive beneath the surface after something moving below, resurfacing many yards away with a tiny silver fish in its beak.

Jahrra spotted a heron foraging among the many bunches of reeds growing in the center of the lake and a duck with her ducklings hiding on the shore. Enormous mats of submerged grasses and plants darkened the water like bruises and when Jahrra focused her eyes on one particular spot, she noticed small minnows darting about just below the surface. If she listened carefully she could detect the sound of the ocean, just a whispering murmur in the distance sending a cool breeze that brushed past her cheek, pulling a tendril of her hair with it. It smelled of salt and the uniqueness of sea and felt refreshing on this warm day. Jahrra took a deep breath and closed her eyes. She lost herself in those several minutes of observation, knowing that this place would always be special to her.

Nuhra found the children soon after their escape from camp chores and told them that lunch was ready. When they finished eating they found the boardwalk once again, desperate for a swim. Kaihmen and Nuhra sat on one of the many benches against the railing as the three friends lowered themselves timidly into the water.

"Be wary of the lake monster!" Kaihmen teased when they were finally fully submerged.

"What?" spluttered Jahrra, taking in a mouthful of water as she sank. She resurfaced to tread water next to her friends. She shot them a nervous glance and the two rolled their eyes.

"He says that every year, and he *always* thinks he's going to trick us," Gieaun said matter-of-factly, her hair spreading out like ink in the water around her. "Don't worry, though. You've never been here before, so he figures he could try to scare you."

Jahrra relaxed when she saw that her friends weren't about to get out of the water anytime soon, but she still stayed rather close to the pilings of the low boardwalk. After several minutes of coaxing, Gieaun and Scede talked her into swimming out to a large matt of reeds towards the middle of the lake.

"Come on, Jahrra! Even if the lake monster does exist, it only comes out at night!" Scede yelled from the halfway point between the island and the boardwalk.

"Jahrra, you're the one who wants to go hunting for the monster that lives in the Wreing Florenn, remember!" Gieaun shouted, already standing upon the dark mud of the islet, dripping dry from her swim. "Don't be such a scaredy cat!"

Swallowing her fear and polishing her pride, Jahrra pushed away from the pier supports and swam vigorously towards her two friends, half frightened she would be eaten and half annoyed at herself for being such a coward. Once on the island the three of them laughed at their silliness and stretched out upon the damp soil, staring off into the deep blue sky. They watched clouds scudding by and listened for the soft crackling sound of dragonfly wings darting overhead, all the while becoming very sleepy.

Before they could drift off to sleep in the middle of the lake, however, Nuhra called to them from the dock, reminding them it would be dark in a few hours. Jahrra had completely forgotten about the lake monster, that is, until they got back into the water. Once again she swam as quickly as she could towards the shore.

The evening around the fire proved just as exciting as swimming in a potentially monster-infested lake. As the sky darkened and the firelight cast an orange glow upon everyone's faces, Kaihmen began telling the ghost stories and local legends he'd promised. Jahrra listened in rapt horror as he told them of the terrible witch that lives in the Black Swamp, only a few miles from her house. It was a terrifying tale of a missing girl and her brave brother who went searching for her deep in the Wreing Florenn.

"It happened a long time ago," Kaihmen began dramatically, the camp fire crackling with malice between them. "The young boy thought the Witch of the Wreing took his little sister, so he went into the forest to get her back. He wandered for many hours among the frightening trees, trying to ignore the sounds of the wildlings at night."

Kaihmen paused for effect, and Jahrra, huddled safely under her blanket, coaxed up enough gumption to ask in a timid voice, "W-wildlings?"

"Yes, any unnatural creature living in the wilderness of the world, we call them *wildlings*," Kaihmen explained.

Jahrra curled back up next to Gieaun and Scede, both equally as terrified as herself.

"Now, where was I?" Kaihmen said, rubbing his chin. "Ah! Yes!" he barked, causing all three children to yelp.

Nuhra rolled her eyes as she cleaned up the dinner dishes, thinking her husband was having far too much fun.

"The boy wandered far into the Black Swamp until he could go no farther. When dawn finally came, the boy's friends told their parents and the village elders what had happened and a search party was organized. Only the boldest of the village men went into the swamp looking for the poor lad. After a day of tedious searching, all they found were his tattered boots and his torn red coat.

"From that day on, no child has ever gone into that forest and come back out again. Sometimes, even to this day, someone or something dressed in red is seen in the woods. Some believe it is the lost soul of that poor boy. Others think it is the witch, reminding people to stay out of her swamp."

Kaihmen finished his story, giving the children a solemn look. Jahrra shivered from the thought of it and vowed she'd never again play in the orchard alone. She looked over at her two friends, eyes wide with terror, and said in a shaking voice, "I ch-changed my mind. I don't want to go looking for a-anything in that forest!"

The next morning arrived in splendor, and to Jahrra's great delight, they *hadn't* been eaten in the night. After a quick breakfast and packing, the group ventured west to see the coast. Jahrra soaked in all the sights and sounds around her; the rumbling ocean and the pungent scent of sage, salt water and wild herbs. They stopped every now and again to locate a singing bird or to allow Jahrra to sketch a wildflower in her journal.

As soon as the high piled sand flattened out and met the churning shore, the group stopped for a break to admire the view. Jahrra gazed north up the beach that expanded as far as the eye could see, and south until the sandbank crawled into the Thorbet Foothills. The spray of the surf misted her skin, sending goose-bumps up and down her arms. She laughed when Gieaun pointed out the sand pipers scurrying away from the ever encroaching water, always managing to stay a few inches ahead. Scede encouraged the girls to help him build a sand castle, and so the day passed cheerfully as they built towers and moats and walls.

That night the family camped near another lake, Nuun Dein, and once again Kaihmen wove frightening tales of monsters and goblins. This time, he told them about the lake monster he tried to fool Jahrra with the day before.

"But it really does exist!" he exclaimed when Gieaun and Scede tried to assure Jahrra it was all made up. "It only feeds at night and only during a full moon when it can see its victims. During the day, the monster sleeps on the bottom of the lake, in the middle where the water is deepest."

Jahrra quailed at the mere thought. Scede nudged her and whispered, "We're sure he's making it up, but if there really *is* a lake monster it doesn't come out during the day, so I think we're safe."

Scede did his best to look unabashed but Jahrra noticed that both he and Gieaun weren't ready to dismiss the legend completely.

The next day dawned as beautiful as ever, but Jahrra abhorred the fact that they'd be heading back home today. This trip had been so much fun and now it was all over. She sighed deeply as her friends stirred next to her.

"What's the matter?" Gieaun asked.

"Oh," Jahrra answered gloomily, "I just wish we could stay longer, that's all."

"Don't worry," Scede said, still lying down with the blanket pulled around him. "It's only the very beginning of summer and we've got lots of time to come back."

Later that day, after all had been packed and the climb up the Great Sloping Hill had passed, the horses and their riders reached the front of Jahrra's drive. Jahrra jumped down and grabbed her bag and blanket, turning to thank Nuhra and Kaihmen for such a wonderful weekend.

"You're welcome, Jahrra," Nuhra answered with a smile. "Now, you'd better get inside, I'm sure your parents will be eager to hear all about it."

Jahrra nodded sleepily and turned up the path, heading towards the tiny stone cabin she called home.

After that first weekend, the summer months passed by easily. Jahrra spent most of her days with her two friends and Phrym, but when she wasn't out riding horses and catching lizards, she was at home helping her parents with the everyday chores of a country home.

Sometimes, when Jahrra was helping Abdhe, Lynhi would pause in the kitchen and gaze out the window only to catch sight of her husband galloping around in the tall grass like a horse with Jahrra perched upon his shoulders, laughing in delight. When this happened Lynhi would smile warmly, her arms often resting in a tub of hot, soapy dishwater. Abdhe looked so ridiculous with his glasses askew and his hair messier than ever, but the joy on his wearied face erased all thoughts of how absurd the scene appeared.

Jahrra's expression would be just as heartwarming. She had come home so often during the school year with a cloud over her head that it brought her mother some peace of mind to see her now. Lynhi shook her head, clucking her tongue good-heartedly as she got back to scrubbing the greasy dishes. *Those two will never get any work done,* she mused.

When Jahrra wasn't kept busy around her little cottage or at the Castle Guard Ruin learning reading and writing with Hroombra, she was at Wood's End Ranch visiting Phrym and riding the other horses with Gieaun and Scede. Still relatively new at riding, the three friends chose calmer, older horses, and when they charged out across the fields Phrym would whinny impatiently after them.

"I'll be back soon!" Jahrra called, waving as her small colt watched her disappear into the distance.

Phrym was disappointed that he had to stay behind, but so long as Jahrra came back, he was happy. Sometimes when she was gone for a long time he'd make his way across the vast fields to the fence that ran along the edge of the forest. Once there, a kind stranger would sometimes come and feed him some bizarre but very tasty fruit. Somehow the young colt knew that it wasn't such a good idea to take food from someone he didn't know, but this creature didn't feel dangerous, and if a semequin could count on anything, it was his instincts.

The kind creature was there today, standing just on the edge of the woods. Phrym spotted it and picked up his pace, crying out happily as he trotted closer. This person reminded him of his best friend, Jahrra. It almost had the same shape, but it was hard to tell with all the cloth it wore.

Once he was pressed against the fence, blowing and sniffing for his treat, the creature reached out to stroke his neck or rub his forehead, but then thought better of it. *Not yet,* the stranger thought, *there'll be plenty of time in the future for that.*

Phrym munched contentedly on the snack offered to him, not noticing the glint of some strange emotion flickering in the being's eyes. *Such a fine animal . . .* it thought.

Suddenly, the stranger sensed the children returning from their ride and hastily withdrew back into the forest leaving the curious Phrym to stare after it as it disappeared into the woods.

"Patience," the stranger whispered to the shivering trees as it crept along, "patience . . ."

# -Chapter Seven-

# The Stranger and the Dragons' Court

Jahrra yawned and stretched against the fragrant grasses growing beneath the shady fruit trees of her orchard. All of the wonderful memories of the past summer had made her sleepy and she had to fight to stay awake. She'd been thinking about the trips to Lake Ossar, her days spent playing with Phrym at Wood's End Ranch and the half-finished tree house that sat perched like a decrepit shack in the old eucalyptus tree behind the barn. She and her friends, with the help of her father of course, had made good progress on the elevated hideaway, but it still needed much work. *Next summer,* she thought with rapture, *we'll have our very own tree house next summer.*

The lovely images left a warm glow behind, but her thoughts took a sharp turn as she realized that it was all over and the beginning of the school year was just around the corner. *One more week before I have to be around Eydeth and Ellysian again!* she thought ruefully. As awful as the prospect of facing the twins seemed, however, she couldn't help but smile when she remembered that Hroombra had promised to take her and her friends to the marshlands in the Longuinn Valley for one last summer camping trip.

Jahrra sat bolt upright, startling a covey of quail relaxing in the shade several feet away. They were leaving early tomorrow morning and she still had to pack for the trip. Jahrra lifted herself up out of her grassy nest and ran down the shady lane between the trees and into her tiny cabin.

By mid-morning the next day the three friends were atop Hroombra, clinging to one another as they looked fearfully into the depths of the Wreing Florenn.

"Come now children, this is the main road into Edyadth. It's perfectly safe," he said to encourage them. "Besides," he continued with a mischievous grin, "what monster or creature would be brave enough to attack a dragon?"

"You know about the monsters that live in the forest?!" Jahrra asked in a harsh whisper.

"I've heard stories, yes, but I've never seen them," he answered, leaving the frightened children to draw their own conclusions.

It was a long walk, for the Longuinn Valley was on the opposite end of the Great Sloping Hill and the Wreing Florenn was a rather large forest. When Hroombra finally emerged from its dark depths and descended onto the main road into Edyadth, Jahrra, Gieaun and Scede gave a great sigh of relief. Soon all thoughts of monsters, ghosts and witches left their minds as they crossed the rolling farmlands and the valley came into view. The town of Edyadth itself lay between the edge of the Wreing Florenn and a crop of hills in the east in the middle of the Longuinn Valley.

As they drew closer to the valley town, Jahrra peeked around Hroombra's great neck to get a better view. A sprawling group of tavern-like buildings were hunched together along the side of the road running through the center of the settlement. They looked like giant heads buried halfway in the ground, their windows like secretive eyes glancing warily at passersby, their roofs like giant mushroom-shaped hats concealing their devious intentions.

Most of the structures were made of wood, but here and there a stone house would stand out like a cheerful friend among glowering strangers. There were no trees nearby, apart from a few scattered oaks and those in the Wreing Florenn that loomed behind them like a dark cloud. The land surrounding Edyadth was strangely barren and it had the look of the dead of winter hanging about it, even on this warm summer day.

Jahrra glanced down at the street as Hroombra traipsed along past the silent and brooding buildings. They'd left the sandy road behind and were now sloshing through a shallow river of mud.

"Master Hroombra," Jahrra whispered above the sucking and smacking sound of the dragon's footsteps, "why are the streets so wet?"

"Do you see that creek to the east?" Hroombra answered, pointing his head towards the hills. "It flows out of the hills, and a natural spring keeps it fed all year long. Therefore, the streets are always soggy."

"Is that why there are so many sidewalks?" Gieaun asked.

"Yes, Gieaun. Everybody likes to avoid mud, well," he paused and smiled down at his own feet, "maybe not everybody."

Jahrra gazed at the scenery unfolding around her, watching the locals strolling on the sidewalks or riding their horses through the damp streets. There was something strange about them, something different. They walked around vigilantly, hunched over as if trying to sneak away from a crime they'd just committed. When Jahrra made eye contact with one or two of them, they quickly glanced away, covering their faces with their hats or jacket collars.

"Master Hroombra," Jahrra prodded silently, still watching the last man that had hidden his face from her, "why are these people acting so strangely?"

"They fear dragons, Jahrra, like those in Aldehren. It's one of the reasons I seldom leave the Ruin." He sighed wearily. "They'll act strangely with me walking around."

Jahrra nodded in compliance, not needing any further explanation. That first day of school had been so long ago that she'd almost forgotten the effect her reptilian mentor had had on its inhabitants. Hroombra hadn't gone into town with her since, well, not until today.

As the group approached the southern end of town a rather large field filled with a crowd of people fell into view. Hroombra slowed his pace to pass by the raucous mass, many of its members spilling from the swampy field onto the street. Jahrra leaned forward to get a better look. A few people glanced back grumpily to learn who had nudged them, only to move forward nervously when they noticed Hroombra walking past. A few began to whisper warnings to their comrades, and the outer circle of the crowd began pressing inward as more and more people turned to see the approaching Korli dragon.

"Who are all those people there in the middle of the crowd?" Scede asked aloud.

Jahrra glanced up then and immediately saw what her friend was talking about. In the center of the muddy field stood a line of ten or so people all with their heads bowed. They were dirty and thin, their hands and feet bound in chains and ropes and dressed in nothing more than rags. Jahrra gasped when Hroombra drew breath to answer Scede's question.

"Those people are slaves Scede, taken forcefully from their homeland and brought here to be sold," he said solemnly, ignoring the stares and jeers being thrown his way. "Usually slaves aren't brought as far west as Oescienne, but every so often a slave trader makes a point to try his luck here. It's a most horrendous and despicable thing to buy and sell another being. Unfortunately, not everyone feels this way."

Jahrra turned her head to look at the poor creatures once more. She frowned as the first person in line, a young man with dark, tangled hair, was pushed upon a pedestal to be bartered off like an animal.

"Master Hroombra, how can some people sell other people?" she asked, a spark of anger coloring her voice.

"Because no one is willing to put an end to it," he answered simply, masking his own fury and frustration. "At least, no one is brave enough to defy the Crimson King and his minions. It's up to those of us who know better to find a way to do away with it."

"How can we do that?" Gieaun asked.

"By growing up and teaching others that such things are wrong, young Gieaun. When enough people in the world know that owning another person is wrong then perhaps there will be enough people to change it."

Hroombra continued on past the mustering crowd as quickly as he could. As they walked on, Jahrra turned to look upon the dismal scene behind them. The shouts of the bidders broke free from the general murmur and soon the first man was replaced by another slave on the pedestal.

# The Stranger and the Dragons' Court

Jahrra furrowed her brow and glared at the stuffy men and women, imagining that the twins' parents were probably here somewhere. Those people bidding on the slaves wore robes of silk and fur and were attended by servants, or more likely, other slaves Jahrra realized. They resembled brightly plumed birds, fluffed up and shifting discontentedly in the filthy street.

The fancy women and spotless men were all quite impressive, but as Jahrra scanned the far edge of the crowd one man in particular caught her attention. This person's impeccable clothing and tall, finely dressed horse were quite a contrast to the muddy streets and plain clothes of many of the common town folk. Even the other well-dressed men and women looked grungy standing next to him. He was slightly taller than most of those around him, and although he didn't look at Jahrra, his gaze on the enslaved people was a hard, focused one. He wore what looked like green velvet, so dark it was almost black, but Jahrra suspected it was something more intriguing than just that; some rare fabric that had been woven with magic by elves. The reins he held belonged to his snow-white horse, or more likely, a semequin.

Suddenly, the man turned and looked directly at her, his bright, piercing green eyes locking with her own. Jahrra had never seen eyes like this, eyes that seemed to pierce her soul. Beneath a closely trimmed beard and mustache his features were fine and strong. He didn't look old, but he didn't look young either, and his face was grim and stony, as if he were trying to make a thousand difficult decisions at once.

The man eventually turned his attention back to look at the row of chained people with glum faces, releasing Jahrra from his overpowering gaze. As his head turned, Jahrra caught a glimpse of a sharply pointed ear resting against his dark hair. Her eyes grew wide as she let out a small gasp, quiet enough for no one else to hear. He *had* to be an elf; his ears were even more pointed than the twins', and those two were always claiming to be almost pure elf.

Jahrra was enthralled by the strange elfin man, but her stomach turned as soon as she realized that he was here to buy slaves like everyone else. She didn't know why, but she felt terribly disappointed in him for doing such an atrocious thing. Yes, she expected the evil twins and *their* family to do something as appalling as trade people like merchandise, but why was she so shocked to see this stranger doing it? Jahrra quickly turned her head and tucked her chin against her chest, trying to squeeze those bright green eyes out of her memory. They had been so cold, but so sad. It was almost as if the soul inside of the body had burned out long ago and there was just an emptiness left behind.

"Master Hroombra, how much farther are the marshlands from here?" Jahrra asked once Edyadth was behind them.

"Not long. I know it's been a dull journey, but believe me, what is at the end of it is worth the wait."

"Are the marshlands better than Lake Ossar?" Scede asked.

"I wouldn't say they are better, but I think you'll enjoy them just the same," Hroombra said with a smile.

The lazy minutes ticked away as the dragon and his riders moved farther southward. The wide dirt road they traveled passed through golden green fields sprinkled with fading wildflowers and fell and climbed with the rolling landscape. Much of this land was grazing land, so the three friends took turns pointing out cows, horses, sheep and goats wandering freely through the open fields. The Longuinn Creek twisted and turned below the road, complimenting them with its cheery babble as they traveled along.

It was late afternoon by the time the group reached the wetlands. At first glance the marsh was a refreshing splash of brilliant green nestled between the dull olive and ocher hills, but as they moved closer Jahrra took note of the differences from Lake Ossar. Instead of sand dunes and the salty scent of sea water, the marshland was guarded by the rising land and the sweet aroma of a thousand wildflowers.

White water lily blossoms shone like a thousand moons upon the water's dark surface, and rows of brilliant blue bog irises waved in the breeze like the standards of an army. Dragonflies and other insects darted and floated over the glimmering water paradise, their wings and legs clicking faintly in a summertime chorus. Birds and butterflies of all shapes and sizes painted bright spots against the blue sky as they visited flower after flower or searched for shallow places to bathe.

Jahrra closed her eyes and breathed deeply. She felt the sun's warm caress on her skin, a sensation akin to a great, golden blanket enveloping her in safety. She smiled inwardly, happy that this beautiful scene was slowly taking the place of the oppressive images she'd witnessed in town.

"Now, children," Hroombra said softly, breaking into Jahrra's dream world, "we need to make camp, and we still have a little farther to go before we can do so."

"But we're at the wetlands," Jahrra blurted, tightening her grip on one of Hroombra's spikes. "Isn't this where we're supposed to be?"

Hroombra smiled. "Yes dear Jahrra, but I wish to camp in the hills, there, where those towering rocks are."

He nodded to a group of large stones sitting atop a natural shelf on the hillside above the great marsh.

Jahrra, Gieaun and Scede tilted back their heads and gaped up at the cairn. Jahrra thought it resembled a crown of stone atop the head of a giant trapped in the earth.

Hroombra began his trek up the narrow path twining along the hillside, the children stretching their necks to capture the changing view from his back. The sun was low on the horizon now, but there was still plenty of daylight left before dusk. The marsh below was a glimmering mirror rimmed in emerald, reflecting the slanted light of sunset. In the distance, the town of Edyadth looked like a collection of ant hills cowering beneath the shadow of the Wreing Florenn.

Jahrra shivered, imagining monsters crawling out of the forest in order to terrorize the townspeople. She quickly turned her gaze back to the path ahead and wondered what could be up this hill among the stones that interested her mentor so much.

It didn't take them long to reach the rocky outcropping, but once they did, Jahrra, Gieaun and Scede glanced around in wonder.

"What *is* this place?" Scede asked, his mouth hanging open as he clung to his sister in front of him.

Hroombra stepped past the first few stone columns encircling a large patch of bare earth. Jahrra couldn't help but notice that most of these rocks stood taller than her mentor's head. Beyond the outer rim of stone pillars, the hillside dropped away, becoming lost in a scattering of oak and chaparral shrub.

"This," Hroombra said smiling, "is called the Dragons' Court. Long, long ago when dragons lived in Oescienne, this is where they met to discuss important matters. Sometimes even the king of Oescienne would be invited."

Jahrra blinked in wonderment, suddenly feeling the importance and significance of this sacred place. Her skin began to prickle and she thought she could hear whispering on the gentle wind sloughing past her cheek and fingering through her hair. She scrambled off of Hroombra's back when she felt a cool absence behind her, but her unease forced her to stay close to the dragon's side even as her friends began to explore. *Why does this place make me feel so anxious?* she wondered, raking her eyes over the brush beyond the edge of the wide stone ring as she pressed up against Hroombra's foreleg.

Jahrra was shocked from her veiled restlessness when Hroombra yanked on the great blanket folded across his back, almost burying her beneath it. With a great jerk of his head he spread it out upon the flat ground for the children to rest on. He then instructed them to gather some fallen branches and pile them together for a fire.

Jahrra reluctantly joined her friends, fearing to move beyond the ring of stones. Nevertheless, the thought of exploring this new place seemed too tempting to pass up, despite her earlier disquiet. Once the three of them had a good pile of kindling Hroombra breathed a stream of ruby flame upon it, causing the wood to leap with fire. The children huddled together on the blanket and Hroombra lay down as well, folding legs and wings as he settled in for the night.

The sun winked before disappearing below the horizon just as the cheery blaze replaced its light. The sky slowly turned from crimson to deep indigo, and the sounds of the night began creeping up all around them. Over the chorus of crickets, the whirring of summer beetles and the solitary mourning of an owl, Hroombra began telling the children the myths of the past.

# The Stranger and the Dragons' Court

"Now I wish to tell you an old story, a story almost as old as Ethöes herself," Hroombra said in a quiet, humming voice that blended with the hushed sounds of the night.

The children clustered together anxiously, preparing themselves for another good tale. The old dragon told them then the story of Traagien, the first warrior dragon that Ethöes ever created. He wove a legend of loyalty and bravery, of sacrifice and forgiveness, explaining to the children that it was because of Traagien that Ciarrohn first fell, and because of his compassion that the elves got a second chance at their immortality.

When Hroombra finished his story he sat in regal stillness, looking ancient painted in the orange firelight. Jahrra felt awed and slightly saddened by the tale. When she peered over at her friends, she saw that both were staring up at Hroombra with impressed expressions on their faces; she knew they felt the same way she did.

After a few moments of silence, the great dragon pointed his head towards the sky. The stars shone more brightly in this valley for some reason, and as Hroombra instructed the children to look up, he pointed Traagien out to them.

"There," he said, "in the northeastern sky. He watches over us all the year round, circling the constellation Aelhean and the north star, Noiramaebolis."

Jahrra looked up and traced the shape of a dragon over the eastern hills with her finger.

"What's that bright star called? The red one?" she asked, pointing to the center of the dragon shaped in starlight.

"That is Atrova, the Dragon's Heart," Hroombra answered knowingly.

Jahrra smiled, settling back between Gieaun and Scede. She knew that from now on she would always have something to draw courage from if she ever felt alone or afraid. In life, Traagien had protected the weak and helpless, and perhaps he could watch over her now from the heavens.

Hroombra told them a little more about the summer constellations as the three friends lay on their backs gazing up in wonder and a meteor shower began shortly after he finished his lesson in astronomy.

"Ah, this reminds me of the story of the Oak and the Pine," Hroombra said, smiling at the brilliant streaks of colorful light above. "When Ethöes created her very first trees, the Oak and the Pine, she drew them in the sky above and set the bright stars to outline them. The Pine kept its leaves all the year round, never shedding a single one while the Oak lost them completely in the winter."

The dragon glanced down at the three pairs of eyes watching him, glittering from the firelight.

"After some time, the Oak began to wonder why she had to lose her leaves while the Pine kept his. So the Oak went to Ethöes with her plight, *'Why must I lose my leaves for half of the year while the Pine is allowed to keep his always? Why can I not keep mine as well?'*

"Ethöes thought about this and told the Oak she had always imagined her this way, and so that is how she was created. The Oak was saddened and returned to her place in the sky, but the Pine had overheard what was said. *'Dear Goddess,'* he said to Ethöes, *'I too wonder why the Oak cannot keep her leaves all the year round. Is there not a way to make this so?'*

"Ethöes knew she couldn't grant the Oak her wish without disturbing the balance of nature, but eventually she thought of a way to please both the Oak and the Pine. She called the Oak back to her and spoke to both trees at once, *'Dear Oak and Pine, I have made you the way you are and there is no way I can change that. Unless the Pine is willing to sacrifice his leaves as well, then the Oak must remain as she is. If you are both willing to have leaves on your boughs all the year round, then you must constantly pay me with those leaves and re-grow them to show me the promise you have made.'*

"The Oak knew that this could never be, for how could the Pine make such a sacrifice? But he agreed to the solution, giving the Oak her one true wish. And so that is why we see the falling stars, for they aren't stars at all, but the pine needles and oak leaves that the Pine and Oak are giving back to Ethöes for the bargain they made. That is why we call those constellations the Wise Oak and the Noble Pine, for the Oak was wise to see that she lost her leaves, while the Pine was noble for aiding her in her plight. And this is why the oaks and pines today lose their leaves and re-grow them all throughout the year, for the pact they made with Ethöes."

Jahrra stared up in wonder, not wanting it to end. Blazing streaks of blue, green, red and white whizzed by as tiny highlights or brilliant fireballs. She imagined that the larger meteors were the Oak's leaves and the smaller ones the Pine's needles, falling to the earth from the heavens just as they fell from the branches of the trees in Oescienne. Jahrra tried hard to keep her eyes open for the entire show, but the long journey to the valley had proven exhausting, and she, Gieaun and Scede were soon fast asleep.

Hroombra looked down at the three young ones and smiled. He secretly hoped they would always remain as intuitive as they were now, and he hoped even more that Jahrra would always have her two friends with her. As he curled around the children like a wolf around its pups, he thought of Jaax and wondered where he was now. He often thought of the younger dragon, especially since Jahrra had arrived on this earth. How wonderful it would be, thought Hroombra, to have Jaax here now. How happy he would be if he didn't have the outside world to distract him, but then again, how wonderful it would be for all of them.

Hroombra kept his eyes pointed towards the stars as he tried to remember when the last time was he'd seen Jaax content. He shook his head in regret when he realized it had been far too long ago. He let out a slow sigh as he slowly drifted off to sleep.

## The Stranger and the Dragons' Court

The gap between the conscious and unconscious world slowly closed, and the old dragon found himself wondering if Jaax would ever truly be happy again. He hoped that somehow, someday, Jahrra could make them all happy again.

# -Chapter Eight-
# A Long, Cold Winter

Abdhe realized the second he let the apple drop that Jahrra wasn't staying on task.

"Jahrra, pay attention to what you're doing!" he called down to his oblivious daughter.

She was daydreaming again and the loose apple narrowly missed her head. Instead, it hit the leaf littered ground with a loud, hollow *thlunk*.

Summer had been over for weeks now and the autumn season was well under way. The first several weeks of school had been grueling, what with the twins' taunts and jibes, but Jahrra had expected that. Her school lessons were proving to be harder than last year's, but she really didn't mind as much as she claimed to. She enjoyed learning; it was her classmates she couldn't stand.

"Be sure to add that apple to the basket, Jahrra. It may be bruised, but it's still good," her father added as he reached carefully for another bright red fruit several feet in front of him.

# A Long, Cold Winter

"Why must we pick so many apples?" Jahrra asked wearily, struggling with the heavy whicker basket as she bent down to pick up the apple that had almost hit her.

"We don't want to be unprepared for winter. After the frost arrives, there's no going back."

Jahrra plopped the apple into the basket churlishly and looked up. All she'd been doing after school lately was harvesting and preserving fruits and vegetables. She heaved a great sigh and got back to picking the apples still within her reach.

"I know a seven year old has more interesting things to do than pickle beets and dry potatoes, but you'll be grateful when you have food for the winter," Abdhe commented matter-of-factly as he climbed down the creaking ladder.

"Seven-and-three-quarters," Jahrra corrected, taking a bite out of one of the crisp fruits.

"That's right," her father laughed, hopping onto the ground and ruffling her hair. "I'm always forgetting."

Jahrra made a face. How could her own father forget how old she was?

"Well, that's the last of the apples." Abdhe dusted off his hands and straightened his coat. "I'll go check on the smokehouse and see how the meat is coming along. Go in and see if your mother needs any help."

He lifted the great, bulging basket of fruit Jahrra had collected and headed toward the small wooden hut leaking smoke like a sleeping dragon. Jahrra scampered into the family's warm kitchen, eager to get out of the chill air while she anticipated the mashed potatoes and roast chicken her mother was preparing for dinner. Like her father said, winter was approaching and she had a feeling it would be a long one.

Autumn passed by rather slowly with everyone lying in anticipation of the harsh months ahead. Before long, Jahrra and her family were finished with all of the pre-winter chores. Now the only thing left for them to do was to sit and wait anxiously for the first frost. Sobledthe, the celebrated harvest day, came and went, and soon the winter Solsticetide was only a month and a half away.

The first frost came early, just as the farmers had predicted, and Jahrra's parents insisted on dressing her more warmly against the chill. Jahrra hated it, but she could always take the miles of clothes off at school. This, of course, elicited rude remarks from the twins.

"I didn't know your parents could afford so many clothes!" Eydeth exclaimed the first day they had been forced to dress against the icy weather. "They must be going around wearing nothing but rags!"

The laughter grated at Jahrra, but she was determined to ignore them this year. The three friends moved as far away from Eydeth as possible, and on their way to their secret corner of the schoolyard, they heard Ellysian preaching to a flock of girls scuttling after her, "You must always dress appropriately for each occasion, and you must always act like a lady so the boys will like you."

"Yick, how boring!" Jahrra said, making a face through the scarf that covered most of it.

"I bet she doesn't even know how to ride a horse!" Gieaun added in disgust.

Scede simply shook his head in distaste and the trio went about their own business, climbing their favorite oak and pretending to be the heroes in Hroombra's stories.

The Solstice break seemed like it would never come, but like all things it eventually did. Jahrra's eighth birthday arrived two days later and she received the archery set she'd wanted so badly. Her parents had scraped and saved for nearly a year to get her the best bow, quite large for such a young girl but guaranteeing she'd never outgrow it. Jahrra was moved to tears from the gift and she treasured it above everything else. Hroombra gave her a small book on the wildlife of Oescienne, written and illustrated by the elves of Felldreim (so he claimed), and Gieaun and Scede bought her a rather nice quiver for her arrows.

Jahrra rued the day that their vacation came to an end. She'd enjoyed her rest from the twins, her lessons with Hroombra and her free time with Gieaun and Scede and a constantly growing Phrym. The time off had renewed her outlook on everything around her, giving her a new appreciation of what she had.

# The Legend of Oescienne – The Finding

It would be hard going back to the schoolhouse in Aldehren, but by the end of the Solstice break, even the knowledge of facing Eydeth and Ellysian didn't get Jahrra down. Nothing, not even the twins, could take away the joy she felt for having such wonderful friends and family. Nothing, that is, except the one thing she couldn't possibly prevent or prepare for.

❀ ❀ ❀

The days passed and the winter proved to be much worse than predicted, and yet the land still had to endure a few more months of its deadly grasp. Every morning Jahrra woke to find the pastures and fields coated with ice. There'd even been snow on the lower hills, something that never happened in this part of Oescienne. Everyone was living on a short supply of food, for no one had prepared for a winter quite as long or harsh as this one. Sometimes people would even come by the cottage, begging for food. Luckily, Abdhe and Lynhi had stored up plenty.

"Now, aren't you glad we did all of that extra work this fall?" Abdhe whispered to his daughter as she peeked past him at the thin woman standing at their door.

She looked weary and cold and her five children clung to her as if she were the source of a great heat. Jahrra felt a pang of compassion towards the family and dashed off to get one of her toys, a wooden horse, to give to them. Abdhe had carved it for her, but she knew her father wouldn't mind. The woman thanked her and the children smiled weakly but appreciatively. Jahrra was grateful to have been able to do something, anything, for those suffering people, even if it was as insignificant as sharing a homemade trinket.

Although everyone was living off of a limited food supply, no one was expected to starve to death. Food was short, yes, the weather was cold and wet and windy, but there was wild game to hunt if provisions ran out. Unfortunately, the cold and hunger wasn't what threatened the people of the region. Something far deadlier than ice was creeping throughout the land. No one had prepared for the lethal epidemic that crept quietly over the mountains to settle into the heart of Oescienne.

There'd been some word about a dangerous fever outside the province, but since no one ever dared cross the Thorbet or the Elornn Ranges, and since shipping had slowed for the winter, the people living in the south of Oescienne had little to fear, or so they thought. Despite all the obstacles, however, the sickness managed to find its way into the Oorn Plain and Raenyan and Aldehr Valleys. Signs of the fever were soon being reported all over the land.

Entire families would come down with the sickness and perish within the week. Anyone seen coughing or even looking pale would be avoided like a rabid dog. A medicine to fight the disease had been obtained and shipped in, but only the wealthiest could afford it, leaving the poor and underfed to the whims of nature. Many of the Nesnan commoners were left to fight off the illness on their own. Some scraped through, but others, especially the young and the old, didn't survive.

A black hand of death squeezed the land in its grasp, seeming to drain every last drop of hope from its people. The loss and sorrow lingered like a cloud of evil in the icy air and more than ever, the people of Oescienne yearned for an end to the unrelenting winter.

❋ ❋ ❋

Jahrra returned home from a particularly odious day of school to find her little cabin to be quieter than usual. The air around the place seemed darker, even though the sun shone brightly through the frigid air. The chimney registered no smoke, despite the fact that it was quite cool and would be getting colder, and the curtains in the front window were drawn shut. Jahrra knew that her family hadn't run out of firewood because her father had just chopped a large amount four days before and her mother never closed the front drapes before dark.

Jahrra exhaled into the frosty air as she approached the front door cautiously, her boots crunching quietly upon the chilled earth. She feared something might be wrong, but she couldn't imagine what. She pushed open the front door, its hinges complaining grumpily, and was met with darkness and a strange, still staleness in the air.

"Nida, Pada?" she called timidly.

She walked into the small living room just opposite the kitchen and the stairs leading to the second story. The room was dark because the windows were covered, but not so dark that she couldn't see. She found her father asleep in his rocking chair, yet even in sleep he looked worried. She walked up to him.

"Pada? Are you alright, where's Nida?" she asked in a small, frightened voice, her mitten-clad hands hanging on the arm of the chair.

Abdhe fluttered awake at the sound of his daughter's voice, but his weariness showed more than ever. For the first time in her life, Jahrra saw his true age. The lines in his face seemed deeper, his hair greyer, but it was his eyes, glazed over with years of hardship, that gave away the truth he wished to hide.

"Oh, there's my girl, how was school?" he queried with a weak smile that failed to mask his sorrow.

"What's the matter Pada?" Jahrra asked more seriously now. She barely recognized the man before her; he was completely different from the happy, carefree man chopping wood only a few days ago.

"Nothing dear, your mother and I have a little winter cold. We just need our rest."

"Where's Nida?" Jahrra asked worriedly.

"Upstairs, the doctor is just attending to her."

He gave that anxious smile again, and at the very same moment the doctor came down from upstairs, looking just as grim as Jahrra's father. He looked to be about to deliver some bad news, but saw Jahrra and quickly changed his somber expression to a less bleak one.

"Ah, young Jahrra," he said with a weary breath. "My, how you've grown."

The doctor was round and balding and was wearing a clean white shirt that hung far over thick brown pants. He held his medical bag tightly and closely in his right hand, as if it held a dark secret within. In his other hand he clutched a battered felt hat that looked a lot like a scrap of tanned hide. A tired smile graced his face when he saw Jahrra, giving him the semblance of a withered plant.

"Jahrra dear, could you please go feed the chickens while I talk to the doctor?" Abdhe's voice broke the odd silence and his eyes drooped sleepily.

Jahrra stood up right away, not wanting to argue in front of another adult. She walked through the kitchen and out into the back yard, leaving the gloomy cabin behind her. The yard was the same small patch of earth it had been since Jahrra could remember, but it seemed strangely small and unfamiliar now. The rectangular section of the land that had been fenced off using odd shaped tree branches lay fallow in the cold winter world, and instead of a garland of wild roses growing along the fence there stood a tangled mass of thorny branches, looking dead and threatening against the bleak winter backdrop.

Jahrra sighed and stepped through the opening in the fence, walking towards the faint call of hungry chickens. To get her mind off of what might be happening inside, she begrudgingly recalled what had occurred in class earlier that day. Master Cohrbin had asked her a question and as she was about to answer it, Ellysian had butted in. Stealing questions from her in class had become the twins' newest form of attack.

"You wouldn't have known the answer anyway," Ellysian told her after class when Cohrbin wasn't listening.

Jahrra knew she should just shrug and walk away, but she was getting tired of it, and she was tired of everyone telling her to forget about their cruel treatment of her.

"Just ignore them!" Gieaun had said, coming off more exasperated than helpful. "They *want* you to get mad, that's why they do it!"

"It's easy for you to tell me to forget about them, they aren't bothering you nearly as much as they're bothering me!" Jahrra had snapped.

Gieaun was taken aback, shocked at Jahrra's outburst at her. "Well, most of the time you act like you want them to pick on you!" she retorted, more out of anger than truthfulness.

Jahrra had been hurt by her friend's words and she hadn't spoken to either Scede or his sister on the ride back home that day. She sighed again in the cool, crisp air, breathing out a cloud of steam like a dragon. She'd had her first fight with her best friend, and now there was something wrong with her Pada. Jahrra felt like crying, but she didn't want her father to see that she'd been upset when she came back inside.

It took her longer than usual to feed the chickens. Maybe it was because she secretly dreaded going back into the house, maybe it was because she was still thinking about her fight with Gieaun. Either way, by the time she stepped back through the kitchen door it was almost dark. She found that the fire had finally been lit and she gladly welcomed the wonderful smell of smoke and the warm heat baking her cold cheeks.

She stepped into the living room and found her father still in the same spot, staring at the folded, withered hands resting in his lap. She approached him cautiously. "Pada, is Nida alright?"

Jahrra was afraid to ask, but she had to know. Her father kept on staring glumly at his gently folded hands.

"Pa?" Jahrra urged, her voice shrinking.

"Oh, I'm sorry dear. I didn't hear you come back in." The gruff answer was forced.

"What's wrong with you and Nida?"

He didn't seem to hear her question; he just kept staring downward with the same faded expression on his face.

"Everything is going to be fine, don't you worry. Everything will turn out right," he whispered sadly, not seeming to address anyone but himself.

Jahrra was confused. Of course everything was going to be all right, she had only had a small fight with her friends at school, that would pass, and winter was almost over and soon the weather would be cheerful again. The flowers would come up and the apple trees would begin to blossom. They had enough food left for the rest of winter, at least that's what she thought, and they had plenty of firewood. All they had to do was wait a little bit longer, so why was her father so worried?

Abdhe looked down at Jahrra crouched beside the rocking chair like a timid puppy. *What am I to do?* he thought, brokenhearted and vulnerable. Lynhi had contracted the horrible fever, the one responsible for so many deaths. The doctor had told him she had at the most a week left to live, and that he was already showing signs of the fever as well. *What will happen to our Jahrra?* he thought mournfully, *who'll make sure she grows up safe?* Abdhe could no longer hold back his tears.

The sight of her father's pain caused Jahrra to crumble. "Oh, Pada!" she cried, "What's wrong?"

Abdhe looked at his young daughter through glistening eyes and saw the future of Ethöes in her face. He smiled quietly, the smile of one who'd been defeated but still had so much left to give. He and Lynhi had lived a good life, many years long. He didn't fear this fate, but he did fear for Jahrra.

*Oh little one, my daughter. What trials and tribulations you will someday face. If only I could be there with you. At least this disease can't hurt you. You don't know it, but you are immune; your pure human blood resists this plague* . . . he thought sadly as Jahrra cried freely against his shoulder. He wrapped his arms tightly around her, cherishing every second he could still hold her close.

Two days later, Lynhi died from the fever. She'd lost consciousness the day Jahrra had come home to find her father in his wife's rocking chair, her patchwork quilt wrapped around him. Abdhe himself lasted a little while longer, but Jahrra watched him deteriorate over the next week. Abdhe knew he was doomed the day the doctor arrived and told him of the fever, but he couldn't worry about that, he had to find Jahrra a new family to live with. The obvious choice was Kaihmen and Nuhra, but before they could be consulted, Hroombra stepped forward insisting that Jahrra become his ward.

The doctor, not surprisingly, didn't approve. "A dragon raising a little girl? It's unheard of!" he had puffed.

But he was in no place to challenge a full-grown dragon.

As soon as Hroombra had heard about Abdhe's and Lynhi's condition, he'd immediately sent word to Jaax informing him of the tragic events, begging the younger dragon to bring the anecdote. By the time Jaax received Hroombra's frantic message and found the medicine, it was too late.

Jahrra was never supposed to know of this, but sometimes adults are not as careful as they think. She'd taken to sleeping in the living room after her mother's death, but most of the time she spent the night awake, crying into her pillow. The doctor had turned the room into a makeshift hospital, and although he tried in vain to keep the girl away from his contagious patient, she refused to leave her father's side.

It was during one of these restless nights that Jahrra overheard a conversation between Hroombra and the doctor, informing him that Jaax was being summoned to bring the cure for the sickness. Jahrra pretended to be asleep and listened quietly to the two adults whispering to each other through the window.

"Raejaaxorix knows where the medicine can be found. If only this province hadn't run out of it!"

Hroombra sounded very angry and frustrated, a frightening combination in one usually so calm. Jahrra quietly wondered if Hroombra felt this way often, but only revealed it when she wasn't around.

"Will he get it here on time?" the doctor asked nervously.

"We can only hope," Hroombra replied solemnly.

Jahrra's hopes rose a little despite her sorrow, *Jaax will save my Pada!* she thought fervently. She was still rather numb from her mother's death, but losing her father as well would be unbearable. As she snuggled under her thick quilt she hoped beyond all hope that Jaax would come with the medicine in time.

When the remedy finally did arrive, Jaax himself did not bring it. Rather, it was delivered by a man whose face and name Jahrra never learned. He rode up in the dead of night, speaking to Hroombra in what sounded like a strange language. Jahrra slept more easily that night, believing that her father would be saved, saved by the dragon she'd always thought of as a hero. But it had been too late; the fever was too far gone.

On the day that Abdhe died, Jahrra was brought to sit next to him. "She must be allowed to be near him or she'll regret it for the rest of her life." Hroombra told the doctor who still feared the young girl might contract the disease.

Jahrra sat down beside her father's bed and set her face obstinately against the tears forming behind her eyes. *You'll be alright Pada, I know it. Jaax brought you the medicine. I heard them talking, you'll be alright,* she thought stubbornly.

The final hours were hard, with Abdhe falling in and out of consciousness and finally passing into some kind of delirium where he no longer recognized his daughter. Jahrra kept clinging to her small shred of hope, believing he would survive because Jaax couldn't have failed him, couldn't have failed her.

But Abdhe kept calling for his daughter and his wife, and Jahrra kept saying, "I'm here Pada, I'm here!" through angry and desperate tears.

When her father finally passed, Jahrra lost all faith in hoping, and she began to hate Jaax more than she hated anyone or anything in the world. It was a resentment he didn't deserve, but it was the only way for such a small girl to deal with her sorrow. Her grief and anger distorted her thinking and although she should have realized that her father's death was no more

Jaax's fault than it was her own, her young mind equated the two.

Jaax, the hero of all those stories, the one who'd brought her Phrym, had failed her when she needed him most. The great dragon she once admired now became a vessel to deliver all of her pain; all of the sorrow she felt for losing her parents, all of the anger she felt towards those who taunted her at school, and all of the fear she felt towards being suddenly alone in this world.

The weeks that followed became a black, empty space in Jahrra's mind. She walked around as if in a fog, unaware of the world and people around her. Kaihmen, Nuhra, Gieaun, Scede and Hroombra watched her carefully and often had to say her name several times before she heard them. Jahrra was drowning in her grief and even avoided Phrym while she stayed at Wood's End Ranch.

After her parents' funeral, Jahrra moved into the Castle Guard Ruin with Hroombra. She shuffled through the small entryway without even gawking at the high, vaulted ceiling. She walked past Hroombra's massive desk littered with scrolls, parchment and its usual variety of glass jars containing an odd assortment of objects, but this familiar scene held no magic for her today. She almost lost her footing when she stepped down into the enormous living area, her boots scuffing against the stone floor. The great, black yawning mouth of the fireplace on the northern wall matched her mood, but she hardly realized it was there. Even the floor-to-ceiling bookshelves on either side of the fireplace went unnoticed.

Hroombra came quietly in through the larger entrance at the north end of the building, making plenty of noise to disturb the eerie silence. Whenever Jahrra was here it was seldom silent, but he could understand why she hadn't said a word the entire time it took him to carry her from Wood's End Ranch. She was now staring into the small room he'd once used as a storage space, staring but not seeing. Kaihmen had helped him clean it out the day before and now Jahrra's bed and scant furniture occupied the room.

The dragon took a weary breath and let it out slowly. "That," he said tentatively, "will be your new room, Jahrra."

A single tear slid down the girl's cheek. She didn't say a word, she didn't even nod. She simply moved forward like a ghost and sat down heavily on her bed. Jahrra missed her apple trees and cottage terribly. She missed the pigs, chickens, and their dairy cow, always happy to see her with a bucket of feed. She was far too distracted now to be grateful they'd been taken to Wood's End Ranch instead of being sold away to strangers. She missed the crooked walls and the roses growing helter-skelter on the fence, and she especially missed the half finished tree house she and her father had started last summer.

Hroombra's heart broke as he watched the girl, once so full of life and vigor, sitting defeated and broken before him. He wished more than anything that he could comfort her somehow, but he knew the only true comfort was time, the slow and healing passage of time.

As Jahrra lay in bed that first night in her new room, she tried so hard not to cry while she thought about her lost parents and her abandoned home. *It's hard now,* a quiet voice inside of her said, *and it'll take a long time to heal, but you'll heal, and life will get better.* Jahrra's last image before she drifted off to sleep was one of her mother and father, smiling down at her, their heads surrounded by a garland of pink apple blossoms.

# -Chapter Nine-
# Moving On

In the end, it took Jahrra more than a year to get past her parents' deaths. She finished her schooling with Hroombra that spring, not once stepping foot in the classroom in Aldehren. The old dragon knew this was the best for Jahrra, believing that being away from the hateful Resai children would speed up her recovery. Gieaun and Scede, no longer on bad terms with their best friend, visited her every day, filling Jahrra in with what she was missing at school. At first, she found it hard to concentrate on her lessons, but by the time summer arrived she was as fluent in history, mathematics, science and grammar as her friends.

Jahrra appreciated the delicate kindness everyone bestowed upon her, but it was Phrym who was the biggest comfort of all. The young semequin offered something no one else could by simply being present to listen to her sorrows without casting her sympathetic glances.

# Moving On

"Soon, I'll be able to ride you across these fields Phrym, and maybe I won't feel so sad anymore," Jahrra would whisper quietly as she leaned her head against his warm shoulder.

He was nearly full grown and it wouldn't be long before he'd be old enough to ride, but even that pleasant thought did little to pull Jahrra out of her misery.

When summer arrived, Jahrra found herself looking forward to something for the first time in months. She spent much of her time at Wood's End Ranch, perfecting her horse riding skills with Gieaun and Scede as the three of them raced along the edge of the Great Sloping Hill. They'd start at the Castle Guard Ruin and sweep in a long curve, dodging around the great eucalyptus trees on the bluff's edge until they reached the border of the Wreing Florenn. They would leave their horses tied several yards away and then venture towards the dreaded forest. They would move as close as they dared until becoming so spooked they'd run screaming in the opposite direction, leaving anyone who might be watching staring in puzzlement.

"Someday I'll go in there! I mean it!" Jahrra breathed as they skidded to a halt in front of the startled horses.

"Yeah right!" Gieaun exclaimed. "You won't even swim in Ossar Lake without getting scared!"

That statement caused the corners of Jahrra's mouth to curve upward in an unfamiliar way. It'd been such a long time since she last smiled that it actually hurt to do so. The laughter continued all the way back to the ranch, all three of them clutching their sides. When Hroombra, Kaihmen or Nuhra saw them together like this their grief for Jahrra would melt away, if only for that moment.

The summer passed by rather quickly now that Jahrra had taken notice of time again. By the beginning of her third school year, she'd become much more knowledgeable in the many subjects Hroombra had taught her, and she actually felt ready to face her old classmates. The first day of school began on an oppressively hot fall day with Mr. Dharedth picking Jahrra up at the Castle Guard Ruin instead of in front of her little cabin.

The mailman seemed to treat her more delicately now, knowing that she'd faced tragedy. He spoke more gently and laughed less aggressively, softening everything about him. Jahrra appreciated his kindness, but she missed the jovial mailman of old. When they arrived at the schoolhouse, Jahrra's fragile confidence shattered. The second they set foot out of the mail cart they learned that their old schoolmaster, Mr. Cohrbin, had left to teach in another town.

Their new teacher was a middle-aged Resai man who had shrewd black eyes, a balding head and wore a sneer of disgust whenever Jahrra, Gieaun or Scede brushed by him on the way to the classroom. He had a narrow face and was shorter than most of the older students but walked around like he was the tallest person in the world. He wore mostly black except for a white, tight collared shirt that seemed to stretch his neck out, making him look like a sallow-faced crane.

The small amount of graying brown hair he did have left on his head was pulled tightly into a neat ponytail at the base of his skull. Jahrra was tempted on many occasions to pull it as hard as she could, but feared it might come right off. He was a despicable man that disliked non-Resai children and had extremely high standards, which included his insistence on the children calling him "Professor" Tarnik.

The worst part about their new teacher, Jahrra decided, was that he favored Eydeth and Ellysian above all the other students. He constantly complimented them, admiring the impeccable way they wore their uniforms or praising their shoddy class work. Jahrra often made a face at Gieaun and Scede when Tarnik extolled Ellysian's terrible art project or gave high marks to Eydeth's atrocious grammar.

"He only likes them because their parents are rich!" Gieaun said in distaste.

"Father and I saw him in Toria Town a few days ago bowing as Ellysian's father walked by. He almost fell down trying to impress him!" Scede said, trying hard not to snigger.

The three had a good laugh over it time and again and soon found comfort in mocking their horrible teacher in secret. Jahrra wouldn't have minded their awful teacher so much if Tarnik's fawning hadn't made the twins more conceited than ever. Their teasing had gone from occasional quiet comments under Mr. Cohrbin's careful watch, to daily public berating under Tarnik's blind eye. Eydeth and Ellysian insulted Jahrra right in front of their biased teacher and had even started calling her the "Nesnan Orphan."

"Oh, poor little Nesnan Orphan!" Eydeth exclaimed placing his hands on his cheeks dramatically. "No one wants her now that her parents are dead, not even her friends. She has to go live with that old lizard!"

Some children would laugh hysterically at these comments, but others became disgusted.

"What's wrong with you!" a small girl with auburn hair said one day. "How'd you like it if your mom and dad died and people made fun of you?"

Jahrra, who'd been blasted with a sickening wave of anger and hurt from Eydeth's comments, stood gaping at the girl. No one, besides Gieaun and Scede of course, had ever stood up for her before. As grateful as she was, she couldn't help feeling sorry for the girl. She and her brother were new students this year and they hadn't yet learned the pecking order at the schoolhouse yet.

Eydeth just sneered at the comment and said, "You'd better be careful what you say Rhudedth or you'll be joining the Nesnan and her two loser friends."

The girl simply crossed her arms and scowled, obviously not wanting to cause a scene but determined to show Eydeth she wasn't afraid of his threats.

# Moving On

The girl called Rhudedth walked away with her brother to the other side of the yard, and Eydeth, gratefully, forgot about Jahrra and her friends. The three of them climbed up into their oak tree and listened blandly to what Ellysian was saying across the yard. It turned out that she and Eydeth could trace their pure elf ancestry back just three generations, and she had no problem blaring it in her whiny voice for all to hear.

"My father," she piped obnoxiously, "is the grandson of a very important *pure* elfin noble who lives in the east."

She then began strutting about the yard like an overstuffed peacock, shouting out orders and demanding that every student do as she said. Eydeth was no better. He acted as one of her guards, making absolutely sure that the "queen" got her way.

"Bow before the Queen!" the young boy would snarl.

"Queen Ellysian's" tour of the yard continued with Eydeth keeping everyone in line. Jahrra, Gieaun and Scede laughed into their hands wildly, trying not to make a sound as the children following Ellysian scattered about the meadow, desperately looking for them as she screamed, "Find the evil Nesnan and her traitorous friends!"

Luckily, Ellysian and Eydeth grew tired of this after a few weeks as the other students became less inclined to do their bidding. Once again, to her great relief, Jahrra became invisible, an outcast both inside and outside of school. Anytime she saw one of her classmates in town or at Lake Ossar, they gave her a wary look and quickly moved away as if avoiding a rabid animal.

Jahrra knew that this was mostly because of the twins' influence, but she wondered if some of it had to do with her constant depression. She tried hard to be the person she was before her mother and father died, but most of the time she was withdrawn and morose, as if she had a raincloud following her around all the time.

The crimson and gold of fall faded into shades of grays and blues, and Jahrra found herself dreading the approaching winter. The Harvest Festival and Solsticetide crept by and Hroombra, Kaihmen, Nuhra, Gieaun and Scede were careful of what they said around her during this dark time of the year. Jahrra's ninth birthday passed pleasantly, but her improvement of spirit suddenly began slowing down and came to a standstill when the first anniversary of her parents' deaths arrived.

Jahrra spent that day alone, looking out over the edge of the Great Sloping Hill, allowing the sun's distant warmth to flood over her. She thought of her parents and wondered how she'd survived this first year without them, but she already knew why.

In the end it was because of a familiar figure, not in her daily life, but in her dreams. Jahrra used the day's quiet somber mood to recall the strange dreams that had haunted her for nearly a year, dreams that she kept fiercely to herself. During the months following that tragic week, Jahrra had woken regularly in the night, crying uncontrollably. Hroombra had stood outside her door, his great head looking dark and menacing as he did his best to calm her, wishing he could do more than just whisper comforting words.

Jahrra appreciated Hroombra's kindness, but she longed to work the dreams out on her own. What had they meant? She sighed deeply and shut her eyes, remembering how they started and how they'd progressed. At first, the dreams would wake her in a burst of terror and grief, but over the months following the tragedy, they began to change.

The dream would always begin the same; a pleasant scene of Abdhe and Lynhi walking down a beach with her, swinging her from her arms between them. At first the blue sky was decorated with a few puffy, pale gray clouds being pushed along by a warm breeze. But soon the sky turned dark and those clouds became black and churned like thick smoke. A fierce wind would pick up and the air would turn cold.

A great beast would emerge from the angry clouds, overwhelm them and pluck Lynhi and Abdhe from the beach. It was a horrible, demon-like monster larger than even Hroombra. It had great horns and a skull-like face and its horrible, bone-thin body was covered in what looked like rotten, burned leather stretched so tightly it appeared to be on the verge of tearing. It had great claws instead of hands and feet, and its massive tail wrapped around the cold, gray sand of the beach. When it moved, the pounding of its steps surpassed the sound of the whipping waves and the roiling sky, and its stench, akin to a week-old battlefield, was enough to make her collapse. It was the most horrible thing Jahrra had ever seen and it filled her with a dread that froze her blood and melted her nerves.

As time passed and the nightmare became more familiar, Jahrra came to know at what point to expect the monster. She tried desperately to warn her parents early in the dream, but it was no use. They always stayed by her side, walking along as if it were a sunny, cheery day. No matter how much Jahrra pulled on them, the monster always came and took them.

This carried on for several weeks, but one day her dream changed. Instead of waking up after her parents were taken, Jahrra would remain in the dark, crying. Just when she thought she would die of sorrow right there on the cold beach, a light would begin shining far off in the distance. At first, Jahrra woke up just as the light began to grow, but gradually the dream became longer and the light became brighter, transforming the stormy beach into a misty orchard.

It only took Jahrra a minute the first time this happened to realize that this was her recurring dream of the misty woods and the hooded green figure. At first, the hooded man would only arrive after Abdhe and Lynhi were taken, but as time went on the man became a witness to the horrifying scene that played over and over in Jahrra's dreams. It was as if her two dreams were growing closer to one another and overlapping.

# Moving On

The hardest nights were the nights when the cloaked being would stand by and watch her nightmare unfold. He stood with his great arms crossed, like some horrible master watching in wicked approval as the monster swooped down for Abdhe and Lynhi. Jahrra would cry out desperately for him to help her, but no matter how much she cried and begged, he did not move and he would not help her. He only stood solemnly in the distance, his head covered and his face hidden in shadow, watching noiselessly and motionlessly as the wind whipped his cloak around like an emerald banner.

After several recurring dreams of this horrible scene, Jahrra became angry with him. Why wouldn't he help her parents? Why did he just look on like nothing was happening?

As the weeks went on, this didn't change. Her parents were always torn from her and the hooded figure always watched like a statue. Jahrra thought this torture would never end, but gradually, as gradually as the earth itself changes, she found herself looking to the hooded figure, finding comfort in his mere presence. It was then that she realized he could do nothing, for this wasn't his dream, this wasn't his sorrow, but hers. He was doing all he could just by being there on the edge of her nightmare.

Soon, Jahrra no longer saw the monster as it took her parents away, and she no longer felt as mournful as she had before. This being, this person, whoever he was, had helped her get past the loss of her parents more than she could ever know.

She no longer hated him, but looked to him as a beacon of comfort when the dreams came, and soon, sooner than she would have thought, she was no longer waking up in tears.

The soft, mournful hooting of an owl reminded Jahrra that the day was over. She put her hands to her cheeks to wipe away her tears only to be surprised to find them warm and dry. She took a deep breath, shaking the remaining images of her dreams from her mind. It had done her some good to think about them, even if they had been terrifying at first. Her dreams had shown her the truth of her pain, of her sorrow, and that it was time for her to move on. Jahrra walked back to the Castle Guard Ruin in the twilight hoping that this coming year would pass with less pain and sadness. Somehow, she knew that it would.

❀ ❀ ❀

Spring was a whirlwind of activity with Jahrra much improved from last year, despite her winter-time gloominess. It was almost as if she had been a dormant tree, bursting into life once the weather warmed. She was much more animated, actually smiling and laughing at least once a day. She even lashed out at the twins' rude comments every now and again, something she hadn't done since numbly joining the class once again in the fall.

Summer took an eternity to arrive, as always, and all because Kaihmen and Nuhra promised to help Jahrra saddle-train Phrym at school's end. Her best friends were already riding their own horses, Bhun, a chocolate gelding for Scede and Aimhe, a palomino mare for Gieaun. Jahrra was in a constant pout about this until Kaihmen informed her that Phrym had finally grown big enough to start riding.

"You have to go easy on him. He's still very much a foal," Kaihmen told Jahrra the first time she got in the saddle with Phrym.

At first, he reacted as any horse would; uncomfortable and edgy with an extra weight on his back. Once he realized it was Jahrra, however, he calmed down and became quite agreeable. Kaihmen had been nervous about Jahrra being the first to ride Phrym; he was so strong and so *tall*. And if she fell off . . . But he really didn't need to worry at all.

"Well, would you look at that! It must be a new record," Nuhra said, as Jahrra went tearing across the fields atop Phrym after only a few minutes of sitting on his back.

The Resai woman had been thrown so many times by new horses that she was almost jealous of Jahrra's success, but in truth, she was beyond pleased for the young girl.

Now that Phrym was suitable for riding, Jahrra, Gieaun and Scede spent the better part of the summer fixing up the old stable on the grounds of the Castle Guard Ruin. Phrym wouldn't be visiting here, like she had once thought when she first got him, he would be living here. Jahrra quickly dashed the memory away, fearing it would bring on tears, tears that wouldn't bring back her past life. Instead, she distracted herself with work.

"Just think!" she said as she dragged the old rotting wood out of the stable bed with Gieaun and Scede, "We'll all be able to ride to school in the fall!"

On the summer weekends, Kaihmen and Nuhra took the children to the lakes to go fishing. They would swim on the warm afternoons and catch frogs and insects, build forts on the shores and just catch up on the things that had happened that week. Many of the local youngsters came to the lake as well, but they were all either much younger or much older than Jahrra, Gieaun and Scede, and more often than not, they were here to work, not play.

Jahrra watched in slight pity as the youngest would help their mothers gather reeds or freshwater shellfish along the muddy banks. The older boys helped their fathers and uncles haul bulging nets of slippery fish out of the water and the older girls would clean the catch the men brought in.

Once their work was through, the young children were permitted to play, kicking around a ball constructed of tightly wound strips of hide. Jahrra always smiled her best when she saw the looks of joy on the children's faces as they went careening down the boardwalk after the lopsided ball, laughing and shrieking in fun.

Sometimes she would join them with Gieaun and Scede, but today they were busy floating on rafts across the cool lake surface. Jahrra took a long, deep breath and let it out slowly. The raft she was floating on had drifted towards the middle of the lake, but she hadn't noticed.

"Jahrra!" Gieaun's voice invaded her calm mind. "The lake monster will get you!"

Jahrra closed her eyes and smiled, having half a mind to pretend to get pulled under by the mysterious beast. She rolled over onto her stomach and began paddling back towards the boardwalk where Gieaun and Scede were lying upon their own homemade rafts.

"Gieaun! Will you ever give it up? There is no lake monster!" Jahrra proclaimed once she'd reached them.

"Sure there isn't," Scede teased, his impish grin matching her own.

The three friends enjoyed the rest of the afternoon along the banks of the lake searching for frogs and turtles before finally making the journey home. The summer had flown by as usual, but Jahrra had enjoyed it more than any summer she could remember. School would be starting again soon and she cringed at the thought. *Oh well*, she sighed inwardly, *I'll just have to make the best of it.*

The twins weren't at school on the first day back, and Jahrra almost burst with happiness at the idea that they might not be coming back at all. The very next day, however, they showed up in one of their fancy carriages, going on and on about how they got delayed on a vacation to some castle in the north.

Jahrra was bitterly disappointed, but she wasn't going to let it get her down, not this year. The summer had revived her in a way and her renewed spirit inspired her to create a garden outside her bedroom window in that tiny enclosed space that was once another room. She'd spent so many lonely afternoons staring out her window that she felt she needed to do something to the sad, empty space.

"This is for Nida and Pada," she told Hroombra one early fall day when he finally abandoned his studies to see what the young girl was up to. "I want to grow things like they did."

The old dragon watched thoughtfully as Jahrra toted an armful of various plants and bulbs towards the western edge of the Ruin. He smiled broadly; Jahrra was back, the spirited little girl who loved life so much had returned. He didn't know what had brought her back, but he was grateful nonetheless.

Jahrra, Gieaun and Scede spent most of that fall gathering seeds to plant in the garden. Hroombra didn't mind that the Castle Guard Ruin was becoming a pile of earth and plant debris, he was just happy that Jahrra had found something to occupy her mind. *She's finally healing*, he reminded himself as he listened to the chatting children through the window of his study.

Of course, Jahrra had come to terms with her sorrow the winter before, through her dreams, despite the fact that they had begun as nightmares. The soothing passage of time had worked out the rest for her.

"It's not that I've stopped missing them," she said to Hroombra one fine winter day as she lay next to a blazing fire in the Castle Guard Ruin. "It's just that I've grown used to them not being here."

Hroombra looked up from his work and glanced at the girl who was drawing by the firelight. He smiled a sad smile, one that portrayed his understanding of the rushed wisdom of one so young. *That's it then,* he told himself, *she's no longer an innocent child. She's begun the slow passage into adulthood, and although her child's years will linger yet, she'll never be quite the same again.*

The winter season caught everyone unawares with an early, but mildly dangerous frost. During those early winter days the fields became dusted with a fine crystal-white powder that sparkled and held the land hostage in its icy breath.

Most mornings Jahrra would rise early to check on Phrym in his new stable. She would dress in many layers and cross the gently sloping field that stretched beyond the Castle Guard Ruin. The ground always crunched delightedly beneath her boots as she pulled her wool jacket tight around her, puffing clouds of steam as she made her way towards the stables. Phrym was always waiting for her, no matter how quietly she approached, and the two would go out riding, allowing the icy air to numb their senses.

# The Legend of Oescienne – The Finding

As the second anniversary of her parents' deaths approached, Jahrra, despite her resilience and recent happiness, found herself once again burdened by a heavy and dull sorrow. Hroombra kept an especially close eye on her and asked that Gieaun and Scede watch her at school. He knew that even the smallest remark from hostile spectators could lead to trouble, and he wanted to make sure that her road to recovery continued to be a smooth one.

The winter passed, agonizingly slow, but Jahrra got through it with much less trouble than Hroombra had anticipated. At school, the twins had been too preoccupied with Solsticetide and telling everyone about the extravagant presents they were hoping to get that they'd almost forgotten about their favorite victim. Only when Jahrra stood idly around the schoolyard did they bother to antagonize her, but that almost never happened.

Solsticetide and Jahrra's tenth birthday passed, but the celebrations were empty and cold without her parents. As spring approached, however, Jahrra became distracted by her new garden. The seeds and bulbs were coming to life, and the lazy flowers were awakening to the warm spring days. The garden out-shown the surrounding wildflowers of the field, and soon the small pond she and her friends had dug was teaming with frogs and dragonflies, birds and butterflies. She had even transplanted a small sapling that was now showing brilliant pink blossoms. It was like her own personal oasis and she tended to it every day after school with Gieaun and Scede.

Hroombra often listened to the children chattering away amongst the flowers as he sat at his great desk in the Castle Guard Ruin. He found himself listening to the young laughter that drifted through the window behind him like one would listen to an orchestra. Against his better judgment, the great dragon allowed his mind to float away with the fragrant breezes and happy conversation, bringing him to a place long lost in time.

He found himself in another age, when this Castle Guard Ruin was not a ruin at all, but a proud building that kept a lookout for the great castle on the edge of the Sloping Hill. He heard the ghostly echo of innocent laughter of the children from the past. His heart froze and his blood became ice water when he saw the young prince and the beautiful queen. His heart seemed to melt and seep through his veins as liquid sadness, a sadness that flooded his cheerful reverie . . .

"Gieaun! Scede! Come and look at this butterfly!!! I think these are the caterpillars that belong to it!"

The sudden rise in voices broke up Hroombra's dismal thoughts. He breathed a great sigh of relief, grateful to escape the world he had entered. It had been a place of darker times and he didn't want to think about such things, at least, not right now.

"Whoa!!"

Scede's reaction to Jahrra's find caused Hroombra to chuckle to himself. *I think I'll rest now while they're busy being distracted outdoors* . . . the old dragon thought to himself. He curled his neck and tail around his enormous desk and rested his head upon the worn stone floor. *I think it's time that Jahrra know a little more about the past, but it can wait until after my nap.* He soon dozed off, promising himself he'd save the painful memories for later.

# -Chapter Ten-
# The Castle Ruin

Hroombra had been awake from his nap for quite some time now, but his mind was still focused on the images of the past. He took a deep, weary breath and released it with a tinge of smoke. He needed to find Jahrra and the silence outside made him wonder if she had taken Phrym to Wood's End Ranch, but he rose from the stone floor anyway. Perhaps the children had just walked up to the stables. *It is time*, he reminded himself with a slight shiver as he stepped out into bright daylight. *It's time for her to begin to know . . .*

He checked the garden first, and to his delight he found the young girl there. She was lying on the stone flagging of her tiny paradise, watching dragonflies skitter across the surface of the pond. He smiled warmly then brushed aside the last dregs of his reticence, "Jahrra, come over here please."

Jahrra turned her head lazily and looked up at her guardian, his massive reptilian face gazing down at her over the garden wall. She smiled as she gazed up at him quizzically. Hroombra often left her alone when she was outside, so she wondered if anything was wrong. Her mentor's tone of voice had been casual, but it had a lingering note to it which held a hundred possible emotions.

"What is it?" she asked without moving.

"You shall see, but if you're thinking about staying right where you are, you'll be severely disappointed."

Now his voice held mischief, and Jahrra knew that he was up to something, something mysterious. She jumped up enthusiastically from where she lay and easily cleared the wall.

"Where have Gieaun and Scede gone so early?" Hroombra asked curiously, his great brow creased in scrutiny. "It's only a few hours past midday."

"They had to go home for riding lessons. I would've gone too, but I wanted to sit in my garden," Jahrra answered matter-of-factly, picking at a daisy growing as high as her garden wall. "I told them I might come over later."

"You little ones, I just can't seem to keep up with you these days." The great dragon shook his head in humor.

"So, where're we going? Should I get Phrym?" Jahrra asked, becoming curious in this sudden venture.

"Oh no, it's just a little over three miles. Let's make it a good walk, shall we?"

"Alright, which way?"

Jahrra had been lying still for so long that she gratefully welcomed a long walk.

"Head north, along the path leading through the woods," Hroombra said, and then called as she bolted off, "Not too fast! I don't move as quickly as you do!"

Jahrra stopped running and instead began dashing back and forth from one side of the path to the other, searching for more plants she might like to add to her garden. She'd been in these woods before, but no deeper than a few hundred yards. The Wreing Florenn began somewhere behind them and she didn't want to end up in there. After only a few minutes she became bored with her hunt and noticed that they were following what appeared to be a wide, overgrown path.

"Was this once a road Master Hroombra?" she asked between skips.

"Yes, once. A very long time ago this used to be an important road. It led to the great castle that used to stand where we are now going. Now all that is left are the ruined walls of what was once the pride of Oescienne."

Jahrra stopped dead and looked up at Hroombra, her eyes round with excitement. "Do you mean we're finally going to the Castle Ruin? The one that's guarded by those two old towers?"

Hroombra smiled down at Jahrra. She'd asked him every time they passed the towers if they could visit the castle, and each time Hroombra had an excuse not to. "Yes Jahrra, we are finally going to the Castle Ruin, but don't get too excited; little remains of the great fortress that once stood."

"Oh, tell me what it used to look like so I can imagine it when we get there!" Jahrra begged, setting her gait to match Hroombra's pace so as not to miss a single detail.

Hroombra glanced hesitantly down at Jahrra, knowing that recalling such memories would be a burden to him. But how could he deny such an eager request?

"I'll tell you Jahrra, but don't be too disappointed when you see what remains."

"I won't," she assured him, holding her hand over her heart as if to make a pledge.

"Very well."

Jahrra straightened up, becoming disinterested in the wayside flowers and the startled insects. The old dragon now had her full attention as they trekked along. He took a deep breath and reached into that part of his memory that held the tale he now told.

"The castle was once called Estraelh Castle, home to the king of Oescienne, the most beautiful palace in all the land," he began. "It was built on the highest end of the Great Sloping Hill, for the very first king of this province wished to see all of his land from its walls. With each passing generation, the royal family would add something new to the castle, building it slowly into the palace it became. The first king's son had the patio gardens constructed; one queen insisted a studio and art gallery be added to one of its many turrets. A later king designed a music room, while one royal family built an observatory in another tower.

"Finally, an extensive library was added to the southeastern wing. A sweeping driveway, several more gardens, and a small orchard of trees were included in their own time. Those trees became the wood that now surrounds the castle; the trees that encroach upon the Wreing Florenn. It was once a place of magic Jahrra, built with the palest green granite and marble containing small flecks of all the colors of the natural world."

Hroombra paused and huffed a small sigh. When he went on, a hard note peppered his voice, "It's hard to see all of that now, due to the years of decay. Now the mossy green stones have become dull and faded, looking more like mud-caked slate. The gardens have gone wild and the walls have crumbled."

Jahrra slowed her already unhurried walk to gaze up at her guardian with a furrowed brow. He seemed to be distracted, but he blinked, took a breath and continued on as if not a second had passed.

"The inside of the castle was even more glorious than the exterior. As I mentioned, it had an observatory, a library, an art gallery and a music room, but it also had an enormous dining hall and ball room for great feasts, parties and dances. Throughout the halls and rooms there hung or stood many works of art and sculptures of man and beast alike. The bedrooms were extravagant with great carved canopy beds and enormous fireplaces just like the one at the Castle Guard Ruin. The kitchen could serve just about any dish imaginable and employed the most gifted chefs, but the most magnificent part of the castle was the entrance hall."

Hroombra spoke more enthusiastically now and Jahrra gazed off dreamily into the trees, imagining all of the decorations and details of the castle, forgetting the miles as they walked.

"The hall was enormous, large enough to fit a large party of dragons," Hroombra continued. "In those days dragons were not feared as they are now. The ceiling was high and domed, and painted on the floor was the great symbol of the dragons, the three point star, with the qualities that we strive for written around it in the dragons' language. The kings and queens and all of the people of the land tried hard to meet the standard of the dragons, so they had our code etched upon their fortress. Ahhh," said Hroombra breaking off his lesson, "here we are at last."

Jahrra had been so wrapped up in her guardian's story that she hadn't noticed how far they'd walked. She gazed up the path in front of her and gasped; several yards before them stood the skeleton of a once great structure resting quietly behind a screen of trees. Jahrra blinked, fearing this wonderful new place might disappear, but it didn't. She swallowed her wonder and focused all of her energy on the scene before her.

# The Castle Ruin

In the center of the thick wall rising before them was a crumbled arch that had once been a great doorway. Beyond that stood the remains of a staircase, looking very much like an old, arthritic man hunched over from age. Many more broken arches receding farther into the structure suggested the intricate ceiling system Hroombra had talked about. Jahrra decided that the arches and buttresses looked like the rib cage of some great beast that had perished long ago.

Ferns and mosses, lichens and liverworts grew between cracks in the granite. Patches of sod, covered in forest violets and tiny star lilies covered the multitude of broken staircases, making this place seem like a fairy realm directly out of Felldreim. As Jahrra stepped through a gaping hole in the outer wall, she noticed that the layers of this castle continued on forever.

A strange feeling of magic and mystery tickled Jahrra's skin, a feeling similar to the one she'd experienced at the Dragon's Court above Edyadth a few years ago. The sudden memory caused her to trip over a solitary stone, tossing up a large chunk of black earth and debris in the process. She looked back, slightly heated from her clumsiness, and saw evidence of a stone floor hidden beneath. Jahrra scrunched her eyes in scrutiny.

Hroombra spoke, however, before she could query, "I'm afraid the floor beneath our feet has been completely covered."

"How exactly did it come to be like this, the castle I mean?" Jahrra asked forlornly, running her fingers over a moss covered stone.

"That, my child, is a very long story." replied Hroombra, not making any attempt to elaborate.

Jahrra nodded solemnly, deciding not to complain in this quiet, empty atmosphere.

"May I look around?" she asked Hroombra suddenly, hoping that by moving or talking she could shake free of the strange feeling that surrounded her.

Jahrra looked up at the dragon when he didn't answer and froze when she saw his eyes. He was gazing into the heart of the old castle with an emotion Jahrra had never seen before playing across his face, turning his golden eyes to amber stone. It frightened her a little, so she kept quiet, not repeating the question. After some time, however, Hroombra looked down at her, suddenly realizing that she'd asked him something.

"You may look around," he said automatically, his voice seeming to be stuck in some other time.

Jahrra took off running towards the building before Hroombra could say anything more. He chuckled to himself, crossing the shadow of what was once a great courtyard, slowly following the girl. When Hroombra reached the great arch that had been the entryway for the dragons, he found Jahrra there, standing with her face turned towards the dappled canopy above.

"What on Ethöes are you doing now, Jahrra?" he asked with a wrinkled brow.

"Oh!" The girl jumped with a start. "I was just thinking about the great ceiling and I was trying to imagine it here."

She smiled at Hroombra, and he couldn't help but smile back. "Do you know," he began, "that this used to be the great entry hall for the dragons?"

Jahrra shook her head, but kept her gaze on Hroombra.

"Oh yes, as I was telling you before, the races of dragons were welcome here. In fact, many of the king's relatives had been tutored in the way of the dragons, by dragons themselves."

Hroombra stepped forward and took a deep breath, expelling a great blast of air across the floor, causing black soil, moldy leaves and grime to go shooting in great chunks through the air. Jahrra closed her eyes and waited for the debris to settle. When she opened them again there was no longer the rotting carpet of the forest floor, but rather, patches of ancient worn and faded tiles below her feet, stained from the decay of many centuries' worth of leaves.

"Wow!" Jahrra exclaimed. "What's that!?"

The colored tile below was not random, but revealed an intertwined triangular symbol set in a mosaic pattern. The symbol, which was only partially revealed, looked as if it covered the entire center of the enormous floor.

"That, Jahrra, is the Great Crest of the Dragons, something we call the Baherhb in our language. Each point stands for one quality, and each quality has two more aspects."

Hroombra closed his eyes as if he were mentally flipping through an ancient book. He took a small breath and continued, "The three qualities are Knowledge, Strength and Loyalty. Knowledge isn't the capacity of knowing or not knowing, it is so much more. In order for Knowledge to exist, one must have Truth and Understanding. Only true Knowledge can be gained when one knows the truth and when one understands it.

"Strength is not just the power that one can enforce. True Strength requires both Patience and Endurance. Without patience and endurance, one can never be strong of heart, mind, body and spirit; they can only be strong of body.

"Loyalty is the third quality of the Baherhb, and it is composed of Love and Honor. One cannot be loyal to another if they do not love and honor them. It is our way, and it binds us all: Korli, Creecemind, Gilli, Lendras, Tiynterra, Aquandaas, and now Tanaan as well; all the kruels of dragons created by Ethöes."

Jahrra stood still as Hroombra recited the ancient code of his kind, soaking in every word. Although she didn't quite understand what all of this meant, she could tell from his tone that this symbol, this code of words, was important to him.

# The Castle Ruin

Silence followed Hroombra's lesson and soon the songs of the late afternoon birds drifted through the woods, echoing strangely against the eroded walls.

It was Hroombra who spoke first, several breaths later, "So young one, are you through with exploring? You can't have gone much farther than this spot."

Jahrra was snapped back to the present at the sound of the dragon's voice. "Oh no, I want to continue exploring, if that's alright."

Hroombra grinned and nodded as she padded off to another location on the vast grounds.

He waited a little while longer this time before following in her wake. This place had meant so much to him so long ago, and now that he had returned he realized it still did. The great, withered reptile closed his old, tired eyes and stood as Jahrra had, staring close-eyed at a ceiling that was no longer there. Yet the longer he stared, eyes tightly shut, the more he could see the great arching ceiling of times past.

He saw the beautiful paintings of the gods of Ethöes surrounding a great image of the Baherhb, complete with the three qualities written in his language. In his mind's eye he witnessed the light streaming in through the tall windows that once lined the walls. Great bundles of vine and brilliant scarlet flowers spilled through the upmost vents on this bright spring day long past, their sweet fragrance drifting in with them.

# The Legend of Oescienne – The Finding

Hroombra began rebuilding the walls of the castle in his mind, walls covered in artwork created by people from all over Ethöes. He noted the collection of marble statues in the hall and the tapestries that hung from ceiling to floor, following the arched line of staircases that led to the many wings of the great castle. He smiled as he heard the people of the past taking part in pleasant conversation. Humans, elves, Nesnans, Resai, dwarves, dragons; every beast imaginable that lived in Ethöes, all were welcome to this place.

His smile grew when he recognized the great king that last ruled this land. He passed by, hand-clasped with his beautiful queen, her blond-red hair falling behind her like an autumn field. He could feel their happiness flowing around him; it was impossible for them to hide it. The seven eldest princes stepped in behind them, all fair haired like their parents. They laughed jovially and intermingled easily with the visitors of the castle. No person or being was turned away, rich and poor walked side by side.

Then, out of the corner of his eye, Hroombra saw another child, the youngest son of the king, his final child. The boy was no more than seven or eight in this scene of the past that played across his memory, but Hroombra's heart ached with regret like it hadn't in a very long time.

The young prince had been the Korli dragon's favorite, and now he saw the boy as he had known him, happy and carefree, completely innocent and unknowing of the fate that would someday befall him. He looked like his father, tall for his age and strong featured with golden hair. His eyes were also like his father's, bright and clear and shrewd, but they held the intelligence and fervor for life that defined his mother the queen.

Hroombra began to grow morose, and this colorful, blissful image began to fade from his mind. *That's enough for now,* he thought to himself forlornly, *I mustn't dwell too long on that time. It has passed, and I cannot change it.*

Hroombra shook off the last vestiges of his fantasy and opened his own amber eyes. He'd expected to see darkness and blandness, but he was surprised at the scene before him. True, the beautiful castle had disappeared, but the sun still shone as brightly as it had those many centuries ago. The dragon sighed and began to head in the direction that Jahrra had run off. *May she have a better fate than those who came before her,* he thought.

In the time that Hroombra had been reminiscing on the previous life of this haunted place, Jahrra had been further exploring the grounds. She poked her head in and out of every emaciated room she could find, wandering into a few of them to see what she would discover there. She climbed a few disintegrated steps of an ancient staircase hugging a massive wall, only to find that it abruptly dropped off ten steps up. The walls that somehow survived the ages were veined with massive holes and cracks. It was like walking around in a maze, Jahrra thought, a maze that had no beginning and no end.

Jahrra tried with all her might to imagine what this pile of eroded stones might have been like so long ago, eventually forming a clear picture of a shining castle in her head. *Oh*, she thought delightfully, *how Gieaun and Scede would love this place!*

She relished this thought as she passed through a particularly large broken archway into what might once have been a grand hall. Jahrra pushed past the bushes that had grown up here and there, wondering if this had been one of the ball rooms Hroombra spoke of. She pictured smiling people dressed in flowing gowns gliding around the candlelit space, hardly noticing the towering dragons that would have been sitting in the corners of the great room.

A gentle breeze rustled the canopy above, creating a whispering rhythm the imagined dancers could sway to. Jahrra smiled at her illusion, letting it pass through her mind the way she passed through this enchanted space.

Jahrra released a relaxed sigh and turned her attention to the worn stones stacked before her, forgetting the obscurity of a time long past. After brushing her eyes along the injured walls for several minutes, she spotted something out of place in front of her. It wasn't anything spectacular, but just enough of a change in the stone's color and texture to catch her attention.

She squinted and tilted her head as she peered at the strange inconsistency that seemed to be calling out to her. She approached the wall and ducked behind the tall bush that was hiding most of what she'd seen. Reaching out a timid hand,

Jahrra began rubbing away the loose grit and thread-thin roots that stretched along the layer of soil caked against the vertical stone surface.

Hroombra found his ward there, pressed between a shrub and the ancient stone, following a design with her finger, her eyes narrowed in concentration.

"There you are!" he announced jovially, trying to mask the hollowness he imagined lingered in his voice.

"I've found something," she said simply, not moving or looking away one inch from the obscure image.

Hroombra pulled his entire length into the remains of the room, turned his head, and caught his breath in a strangled gasp too quiet for Jahrra to hear. He knew this room. A clear, bright picture of it coursed behind his eyes like a flash of lightning, and he realized then exactly what Jahrra had found.

He allowed her to study the wall a few minutes more, forcing his mind's activity to ebb; his startled heartbeat to relax. When she attempted to brush away some more of the dust and grime, Hroombra decided it was time to speak up. His voice sounded like a deep, dry cavern.

"Here, this might help things a bit."

He motioned Jahrra to stand back, and then took one mighty breath and let out a massive blast of air, just as he'd done in the entrance hall. The effect of this act was immediately visible, and what was now revealed was astounding.

"Wow!" Jahrra gasped, her mouth hanging open and her eyes wide. She no longer looked at a grimy old wall covered in stringy roots, but a faded painting that must have continued on under the layers of dirt all along the entire interior of the massive room.

"What *is* this?" Jahrra whispered, looking up at Hroombra.

"It's a mural, a story painted upon the wall. This was once the great dining hall of the castle, and this is where the history of Oescienne is recorded. It starts over here somewhere with the story of how Ethöes created this earth we live on," Hroombra nodded to the opposite side of the entrance, "and it continues all the way around the room to about where you are standing."

Jahrra was standing about twenty feet away from the entranceway, and decided she had been looking at part of the final installment of the great mural. She moved closer to the paintings on the wall and began soaking in the faded images.

"Here, let me clear some more for you."

Jahrra stood back as Hroombra let out several more blasts of air, clearing one whole wall and the small section on one side of the doorway.

"That should be enough for now," he said, nodding.

Jahrra began in the corner of the northwest wall and worked her way southward, following the painted scenes with her eyes and her fingers the entire time. She found dragons and elves, dwarves and a strange variety of other beasts and beings. The mural depicted battles and celebrations, births and funerals, peaceful times and periods of turmoil.

The colors were dull now, but Jahrra could tell that this painting once held immense detail and more pigments than she could name. She placed her hand on the wall and closed her eyes. She could almost hear the clash of weapons, the music and laughter at a wedding celebration, the intense silence of the night sky painted above much of the scene. A feeling of wonder crawled over her skin, and when she looked more closely at the wall in front of her, she realized that she'd finally reached the end.

Disappointed to be finished so soon, Jahrra concentrated on the small section in front of her, trying to make the tale last a bit longer. The story, at its end, began with a frightening looking figure surrounded by large, shadowy dragons. Jahrra gasped and a shock of fearful memory burned through her. The menacing figure, despite its worn and degraded state, looked exactly like the one from the nightmares she'd had after her parents' deaths.

Jahrra shivered and forced herself to keep looking at the scene. She pulled her eyes from the dark demon and instead focused on the dragons, creatures that didn't frighten her. When she saw the winged reptiles, however, her heart sank even further; these dragons looked nothing like Hroombra or Jaax, they looked ominous and evil, like the monster they surrounded.

Jahrra covered the frightening animals with her hand and tried to finish the end of this tale. Much of the painting had been eroded, and about halfway to where Hroombra stood, there was a large portion that was horribly damaged, as if time had taken it upon itself to chisel away at this particular scene. Fortunately, it didn't impede Jahrra's progress in following the story.

Near the final section of the mural she spotted a proud figure on a great horse, and soon her attention was drawn away from the sinister creatures. As she drew closer, she noticed that the elf on the horse seemed unafraid of the fearsome, dark dragons. His face was faded and chipped away and try as she might, Jahrra couldn't conjure up an image in her mind. *That's strange,* she thought, *I can usually imagine anything!*

The young girl frowned and focused on his other features. His clothes were ancient, like those worn by brave warriors in the fairytales she read. He held a great sword, broken in half from a missing piece of wall, and the color of his great cloak had faded over time, making it impossible to decide whether it had been blue, green or violet. She couldn't tell why, but as she gazed at this figure she felt a vague familiarity towards him. *Maybe I've seen him in one of Master Hroombra's books,* she pondered, not giving the subtle feeling of acquaintance any further thought.

Jahrra moved on to the final scene of the painting, a picture of more elves fleeing the black, menacing figure from before, now billowing overhead like a great, poisonous cloud that engulfed the sky. The elves were extremely frightened, and in the background their twisted shadows looked like black, screeching dragons.

"What does all this mean Master Hroombra?" Jahrra looked up at the great dragon, her brow creased in concern. "Who is that horrible creature, all black and red, and who're all these elves?"

Hroombra gazed down at her in cloaked consternation. Was he really ready to tell her this story? *Yes*, his conscience told him, *yes*.

Hroombra drew a long breath and said very slowly, "Jahrra, those people aren't elves. They're humans."

# -Chapter Eleven-

# The Legend of Oescienne

J ahrra gazed up at her mentor with a blank look on her
face. "Humans?" she said disbelievingly.

She thought humans were just a myth, a fairytale like
everything else. Had they really once existed, or was this mural
just another story? She waited patiently for Hroombra to go on.

"Yes, Jahrra, humans. The king and the queen of this
land were human beings."

The old dragon paused, as if to gather the thoughts that
churned in his mind like autumn leaves caught in a whirlwind.

"I have a story to tell you now," he continued after some
time, "a story that I believe you're finally old enough to hear."

Jahrra sat down upon a piece of crumbled wall and gazed
up at him, not believing her luck today. *I finally get to come to the
Castle Ruin and now new a story?!* she thought with delight, trying
not to look overly eager.

"Long ago, before even the land of Oescienne existed,
the god Ciarrohn was born. He was the youngest son of Ethöes

and Haelionn and as he grew he became twisted and evil. He turned the elves against the world, and because of that he was thrown to the earth from the heavens during the great battle with the dragon Traagien.

"Now, I've told you part of this story before, and you know that Ciarrohn's form became the Elornn and the Thorbet mountains, but what you don't know is the story of the people who were brave enough to cross those mountains and settle in the land beyond them, this land."

Hroombra snuck a peek at Jahrra and noticed she was sitting attentively, a gleam of anticipation in her eyes. He smiled slightly and continued on, "This is the story of the Tanaan Tribe, the human race that became the rulers of Oescienne. Their people came into this land when the world was in turmoil, many ages ago after the defeat of Ciarrohn but before Ethöes was able to restore peace. When the Goddess finally divided her world into the present day provinces, she gave this province for them to rule.

"For many years the Tanaan ruled their realm in peace and prosperity. They built this great castle and the people thrived under their fair reign. The Tanaan were happy and knew their world was safe, but as the years passed and one generation took the throne after another, talk of a great evil in the east reached their province.

"A young man in the cursed province of Ghorium had seized power over the land and in turn had gained the aid of the dreaded god Ciarrohn. This news struck a great chord of fear into the hearts of the people, for not only had Ciarrohn awoken from his deep slumber, but the evil god and his mortal accomplice had destroyed all the other races of humans in the world. All but the Tanaan."

Hroombra paused to draw breath, taking stock of Jahrra's enraptured state. He cleared his throat and continued, "The world was no longer safe, and the king of the Tanaan knew that he had to do something before more damage could be done. He sent messengers to the different kingdoms of the world and gathered together an army of allies to march upon the east and purge the land of the evil that had awoken. He took with him seven of his eight sons, leaving his queen and the youngest prince behind."

Hroombra paused, closed his eyes and took a breath, looking very much like he was trying to unravel a difficult riddle. When he opened his eyes again he looked down at Jahrra and felt a shiver when he saw the slight despair in her eyes.

Oh, how he knew that despair . . .

He shook his head slightly and cleared his throat, "It took the king and his allies nearly a year to reach the east, and when they did they were met with devastation. The evil king who'd taken over the land with Ciarrohn's help killed the Tanaan ruler and his sons, along with many of the other warriors who'd joined them. They were laid to waste on the Desolate Plain, and those who escaped fled west, towards home, hoping against all hope that the god Ciarrohn and his new pawn, the tyrant Cierryon, didn't follow them.

"Another two years passed before the remaining, defeated Tanaan came crawling over the mountain pass and through the ancient canyon their ancestors had used when they first settled in Oescienne. Soon word spread throughout the land of their return and the forlorn men were brought to the castle. The queen waited eagerly for any sign of her husband and sons, and when she learned of their demise, she fell into despair."

Hroombra took a deep, calming breath and shut his eyes. At first, Jahrra wasn't sure if he would continue, but after several agonizing minutes he trudged on, his voice sounding strange, his eyes still shut.

"A great Korli dragon, the royal family's mentor and tutor had gone to the fight with the king and was the one to break the news to the beautiful queen, now lost in anguish.

"The dragon had regretted the king's decision in the beginning, but he'd refused to let them go alone. Now it all seemed such a waste, such a horrible, impossible waste. So many had died and now the queen and her young son were left without a family. The dragon knew that the only thing he could do now was teach the young prince everything he knew so that he may learn to be a good king like his father.

"The Tanaan people eventually healed from this terrible blow, but one of them did not. The queen, who had become overcome with grief on the day the bedraggled soldiers returned, had remained bed-ridden since, slowly slipping away. Her heart couldn't take such a loss, and although her young son was there beside her his love couldn't keep her in this world. She died only a few months after learning of her husband's fate, perishing of a broken heart.

"The prince lost all hope after that, and no matter how hard the great dragon tried to aid his new student, the boy simply couldn't comprehend such a loss. His mother had been the last thing keeping him anchored to the world. After her death, a shadow fell over the boy, and he was never again to be the laughing, bright child he used to be.

"Ten years passed and the boy grew into a young man, his Korli tutor watching him like a hawk every waking hour. The prince learned everything the dragon taught him, but he never learned how to move on or how to forgive. He desired vengeance, a vengeance that inspired him to organize a group of men bent on revenge for what had happened to them. Secretly, the prince and his alliance planned a march against Cierryon, now known to all as the Crimson King, hoping to attack before the Tyrant gained more power.

"Another year passed before the prince found a chance to enact upon his revenge. His great mentor, who had no idea of the prince's plans, was absent from Oescienne. The prince saw his opportunity and gathered his men together to march on their common enemy. By the time the dragon returned, the prince had been gone nearly two months. Panicked and desperate, he called together as many dragons as he could and flew after the young man and his army, hoping that somehow they'd been delayed in their quest. The desperate dragons soared over mountains and plains, great ravines and deserts, the whole while calling upon the aid of old friends and former allies.

"Finally, they reached Ghorium, the dreaded land of the Crimson King. What they found there, however, was a nightmare. A chill that nearly extinguished the fire within his stomach crept through the great dragon, guardian of the prince. He didn't find his beloved Tanaan humans, but the evil Morli dragons he recognized from before, surrounding a race of dragons that he didn't recognize.

"With a cold heart, the prince's guardian realized that these new dragons were their very own Tanaan humans, the humans they were supposed to care for and nurture. The soldiers who had been bold enough to attack the Crimson King had been transformed into the creatures the evil god Ciarrohn despised the most. He had conjured up a dark curse, a curse sealed in hatred and blackness.

"Despite the odds against them, however, the Korli dragons and their allies managed to free the new Tanaan dragons and together they fled westward, as far away from the blighted east as they could. When they finally arrived in Oescienne, exhausted and dejected, they found that their families too had become dragons."

Hroombra sighed and shook his head ever so slightly. He hated telling this story, but Jahrra had to know. He adjusted his posture then continued on, "The royal mentor lost heart then and fell into despair. The Tanaan had been the last race of humans in the world of Ethöes, and the Crimson King and the evil god Ciarrohn had taken the first step in conquering the world. Not one human being was left to take the throne of Oescienne, so now it lay open for the evil king to rule as soon as he desired to take it.

"After the transformation of the Tanaan, the great castle which they'd built over several hundred years began to crumble. The same curse that made them dragons also began to destroy their castle. Not a single stone mason, no matter how hard he tried, could repair the eroding palace. It seemed as if the fortress itself was a living part of Oescienne and was weathering away in despair. That was five hundred years ago now, and since then the castle has remained in disrepair, forgotten, just as the story of the curse of the Tanaan has been forgotten in time."

Hroombra ended his somber tale suddenly, the final sentence hanging in the air like a resounding, mournful note. He took a few moments to let it pass before looking down at Jahrra once more. When he finally did, he couldn't help but give in to the smile that pulled at the corners of his mouth; she stared up at him as if he were changing colors before her very eyes.

"Now," he said, his tired voice sounding slightly strained, "I'm sure you have many questions, so I'll allow you to ask three."

Jahrra's eyes, if at all possible, became even rounder. *Questions?* she thought, *I never get to ask questions after a story!* She sat quite still for a while, not wanting to waste her three precious questions.

Finally, after what felt like hours, she asked, "If the humans were turned into Tanaan dragons, where did all the dragons go?"

Hroombra smiled knowingly. He'd been expecting this inquiry, and it would be an easy one to answer, easier than some at least.

"They still exist in the world, only not in Oescienne any longer. As a matter of fact, you've seen one before. Jaax is a Tanaan dragon; his ancestors are the very same people who were cursed by the Crimson King so long ago."

Jahrra started at the mention of Jaax's name but simply nodded, her lips sealed tight. Hroombra smiled secretly, however, when he realized that her mind was fighting against itself, the evidence of this portrayed in her facial expressions. He was sure she wanted to ask a million more questions about this answer but knew she only had two questions left. He suppressed an urge to laugh out loud and waited for her next query.

"Did the Crimson King ever take over the world?" she blurted.

Jahrra knew of his existence of course; she had learned so in class and from Hroombra, but she never knew if he really ruled the world or if he just ruled the province of Ghorium.

"No, Jahrra, he hasn't yet taken over this world. It is thought that the curse he set upon the Tanaan and their castle weakened him so severely he is still, centuries later, recovering. Many believe that he is building up an army that will be unconquerable, but no one is brave enough to venture into Ghorium to find out for sure. For now we sit and wait, hoping he'll never inflict war upon the lands. Now," Hroombra breathed deeply, "one last question."

This time it took Jahrra longer than before to come up with her question, but when she finally asked it, Hroombra knew she had picked a good one.

"Whatever happened to the Tanaan prince?" she said timidly, gulping slightly. "Did he die when he fought the Crimson King?"

Hroombra took a breath and spoke, "It is said that he survived the battle, but it's uncertain whether he escaped with the rest of his people. You see, once they became dragons, the Tanaan no longer recognized one another. It's hard to say if the prince was one of the many to escape or not. Some say the prince's mentor believed he survived the battle and took to searching the ends of the earth for him, only to perish in his hunt. I myself like to think the prince is still out there somewhere, waiting for his second chance at revenge."

Jahrra listened and when Hroombra was done, she nodded her head contentedly. She closed her eyes and mulled the story over in her head, making it into something beautiful the way an oyster makes a pearl. After several minutes she stood up and walked back to the mural, to the end where she had seen the figure on the horse facing off the dark, menacing form.

"So, this is the whole story of how the Tanaan became dragons, the story of why Oescienne has no king," Jahrra whispered with a heavy heart, her hand pressed against the brave, faceless figure challenging the Crimson King, her eyes locked with Hroombra's.

"That's right," he said, "before the castle began to crumble, someone painted the last part of the story upon this wall. But they left several feet of the wall at the end there. I like to think they held out hope that somehow, someday, the land and the castle would return to the way it was." Hroombra sighed. "Many believe that someday the Tyrant will be defeated and there will be nothing left to fear."

"Master Hroombra?" Jahrra asked, furrowing her brow. "What exactly is a "tyrant"? Master Tarnik has talked about the Crimson King, but he has never called him by that name."

Hroombra curled his lip grimly and answered, "A tyrant is someone who rules by fear and oppression, but I don't want you to worry about it now, Jahrra. The king is far away and can't hurt you, but it would be best not to talk about this at school."

Hroombra released his breath, suddenly realizing that he'd been holding it, as Jahrra nodded her head in agreement. He knew that this statement may be true now but it was only so long until the king would want to find Jahrra, to destroy her. *I'm sorry young one, I lied,* the old dragon thought in private agony. *The king can hurt you and I fear someday he will. But not now, I won't let him harm you now.* Hroombra shook these awful thoughts from his head and looked back down at Jahrra.

She was now peering more closely at the people running in terror, those casting the shadows of dragons. Hroombra imagined she was trying to impress the pictures into her mind so that they matched up with the story he had told her. Jahrra trailed her fingers over the images slowly, but halted her hand when she spotted something else. It was a strange writing that followed the tale along the bottom of the mural. She had ignored it before, figuring she didn't need to read it. Now she was dying to know what it said.

"What is this writing?" she asked shortly.

"That, young one, is Kruelt, the language of the dragons."

Jahrra looked up with innocent eyes. "What does it say?"

"Oh, more or less what I just told you, but those words tell much more of the story . . ." Hroombra said in amusement.

"How much more!?" Jahrra exclaimed, nearly falling over as her hand glanced off the wall. "Master Hroombra! You've got to read it to me!" she insisted.

"That, I won't do."

Jahrra looked simply crestfallen.

"Don't fret, you'll know it in time." He laughed, sounding cheerful for the first time this day. "In fact, it's about time you began to learn Kruelt. I have always meant for you to learn it since you live with a dragon, and now is a good time for you to start. Once you've mastered the ancient language you can come back here and read the entire story for yourself."

Hroombra smiled and Jahrra made a sour face.

"Learn a new language?" she said. "Just so I can read this story? Wouldn't it be easier for you to read it to me?"

The young girl gazed up at Hroombra with a look of slight annoyance on her face.

"No, you shall learn Kruelt," Hroombra pressed adamantly. "Someday you may be grateful you learned it. And when you do, you can come back here and see what these words say."

"I don't see how I could someday be grateful for extra lessons," Jahrra grumbled, pushing her hair behind her ears and crossing her arms.

Hroombra grinned and said, "You'll understand, Jahrra . . ."

"I know, I know," she cut in impatiently, rolling her eyes, "all in good time."

Hroombra chuckled, his eyes crinkling in good humor, "Very good, young one. Now, is there any other part of the Castle Ruin you would like to see? It is growing late, and the sun will be setting soon so we must be moving along soon."

"No, I think I've seen it all," Jahrra said, forgetting her annoyance.

"Very well. Meet me out front. I'll catch up to you."

Jahrra disappeared through the broken archway and ran off to get lost once again in the stony labyrinth. Hroombra exhaled with another one of his great sighs, allowing his suspended thoughts to return to the front of his mind.

"How could I have forgotten?" he whispered to the walls. "How could I have forgotten reciting that terrible story as it was being painted on these walls?"

Hroombra shook himself like a great, wet dog and stared at the doorway through which Jahrra had disappeared. He was enormously grateful that she hadn't asked the question he knew he couldn't answer. He'd feared she would ask him if he'd been there, if he'd played a part in that painful chapter in history. *You may be ready to know some of this, but you are not ready for the truth to that question yet,* he thought astringently, *and I'm not ready to tell you.*

He looked back at the mural and let himself remember, just as he'd done in the entrance hall. He let his eyes wander upon the faded yet beautiful portraits and landscapes. His eyes darted from figure to figure, until they fell upon one figure in particular. It was the man Jahrra had seen riding the horse, proud and unafraid, but the old dragon saw more than what Jahrra had.

He focused hard on the portrait and once again closed his eyes. He could see the man more clearly now, a young man, charging upon a foe with full passion and purpose. The man's eyes had been eroded away from the wall, but now Hroombra saw eyes blinded by suffering and hatred. The memory of what had become of him cut Hroombra like a knife. This young man was happy once, before the great tragedy had befallen him. Once upon a time his life meant more than just a vessel for revenge.

Hroombra exhaled a low, tired breath, like ancient air pouring from a cave. He knew that this place in time was long past, yet he couldn't help but wish there was something more he could've done for this unfortunate person.

The Korli dragon breathed deeply once more and reminded himself that the past was the past, and try as he might, he couldn't change it. He thought of Jahrra and suddenly realized how much like this young man she was turning out to be. She was proud and strong, and she'd lost her family too soon as well. *May I be able to save her when the time comes,* Hroombra thought, *may she not share his fate.*

The great dragon let his mind drift away from the hurt and sorrow, the heartache and abhorrence. He let it float back to the present, and before he left the great room he whispered to no one in particular, "Do not give up, there is still hope."

Jahrra was waiting for him in the front of the castle, climbing over fallen stones and examining their color and texture.

"Are you ready?" he asked when she glanced up. "The sun will be down in a little under an hour and it would be foolish of us to stay here after dark. I fear this small wood is no longer as small as it once was; it is more than likely that it has encroached too far upon the Wreing Florenn. We wouldn't want to be in the woods after dark. Come, you can ride on my back."

Jahrra leaped from the giant square boulder she was standing on and landed on the dragon's back. As they left the Castle Ruin behind, Jahrra peered back once more. It looked more daunting in the fading light, but it still intrigued her. She'd discovered a deep secret when she found the mural on the wall, she could tell. True, Hroombra had told her a story and had even let her ask him questions, but she knew there was much more to it than what he'd told her.

There had been something short of fear in Hroombra's voice. She'd heard it when he recited the story behind the mural, and she heard it now, when he told her they must leave. *What could possibly frighten Master Hroombra?* she thought to herself. *Maybe the stories of the creature in the forest are true after all.* Jahrra inhaled and exhaled nervously, clutching even tighter to Hroombra's neck as he ambled along.

"Do you really think there are terrifying monsters in the Wreing Florenn?" she asked, making her thoughts known as she worked hard to keep her balance atop the rocking gait of her carrier.

Her guardian took his time answering. "I've never seen one personally. Yet again, I've never wandered into the forest at night."

Hroombra didn't actually think that fearsome beasts lived in the deep forest, but he did know that many strangers and travelers used it to avoid the superstitious local folk. He also knew that these people could often be more dangerous than wild beasts and he would rather have Jahrra frightened of being eaten than to take the chance of her being taken or seen by the wrong person in the deep of the woods.

By the time Hroombra and Jahrra exited the small grove surrounding the castle, the sun had already set. Luckily, the Castle Guard Ruin was under a mile away from the edge of the trees, and Hroombra and Jahrra no longer had to fear the beasts and strange things of the woods. They were almost safely home.

What the dragon and the girl didn't know was that they hadn't altogether left the forest unseen. As twilight fell upon the wide field that spread between the woods and their home, a pair of eyes watched diligently from behind a clump of trees. The eyes were odd indeed, full of curiosity and wit and some other undetectable emotion, but for now they stayed completely focused on the dragon and the girl.

For quite some time now, perhaps even for years, the creature belonging to those eyes had felt a presence in Oescienne, a presence it couldn't explain. It had always known about the dragon, that fact was understandable. It was the dragon the creature had followed to this corner of Ethöes to begin with, but the glimmer of an emotion within the great reptile had sparked the creature's recognition of this young girl now traveling with him.

The old Korli dragon had hope in his heart, something the spying creature had felt for a very long time, but not so strongly until now. For some time, the hope in the old dragon had been growing, and with it, the suspicions of the creature that now spied on them. Now, after what had been witnessed tonight, it knew *exactly* what it was that nurtured the old reptile's hope.

*He has found the one, the one He searches for!* The spy thought with glee and bewilderment, chills shivering over its clothed skin. *The time has finally come.*

Suddenly, the dragon, which was many yards away in the distance, stopped and began sniffing the air. The pair of watching eyes shrank back behind the closest tree, and as the great reptile turned his head to look back, the eyes closed slowly, hiding their presence. Hroombra stared at the spot where the being had watched him for a long while, but after some time he gave up and turned back to the decrepit building he called home.

The eyes opened once more and continued watching the dragon and the girl, the *human* girl. *Yes*, thought the creature as something crackled in its eyes, *she has to be the one.* The strange being smiled, a smile no one would ever see, a smile that some might call wicked. *Protect her now Old One, but you can only hide her from me for so long. I'll have my say in this and somehow, some way, I'll get to her.*

With a cold, unnatural voice the creature whispered, "I will not make the same mistake twice."

The eyes closed for a second time, but this time they closed and withdrew behind the tree for good. The creature slid back into the woods, back into the heart of the Wreing Florenn to wait.

# -Chapter Twelve-

# Blue Flames and Draggish Words

The weeks following the visit to the Castle Ruin were both fulfilling and frustrating in Jahrra's opinion. First of all, it was thrilling to know the story of the Tanaan king and the missing prince, as tragic as it may be. It seemed like such a tantalizing tale, one that couldn't possibly have happened but one that Hroombra insisted was in fact, true.

Jahrra would spend the evenings by the great hearth in the Ruin's common room, gazing at the flames and running an endless stream of questions through her head. How did the evil king turn the Tanaan into dragons? Did he use magic? Could the curse be broken, and if so, would the Tanaan dragons turn back into humans? Were any of those who were once human still alive? Would the castle return to what it once was if the curse was broken? Jahrra was dying to ask Hroombra, but every time she attempted to bring it up, he simply shook his head and told her he didn't know.

This was beyond frustrating, for she couldn't tell if he was serious or just trying to dodge her questions. Over time, she found herself enduring her unbound curiosity in thoughtful silence, especially when the school year began winding down. Fortunately her preoccupation with the Tanaan legend kept her mind off of the daily torment she faced at school. Ignoring the twins was easier than ever when she had the mystery of the legend of Oescienne on her mind.

This helped during actual school lessons as well. Jahrra took her education seriously, but not her educator. Tarnik's method of teaching math was convoluted and confusing, his grammar lessons could bore a statue to tears, and when it came to Ethöen history and mythology, Jahrra often found herself tempted to launch her pen at him. He never got anything right, often obscuring facts or making heroes out to be twisted or idiotic. Jahrra usually went into daydream mode during his lectures, but one day his lesson was so outrageous she couldn't even lose herself in her own thoughts.

"I wish we didn't have such an awful teacher," Gieaun groaned as they streamed out of the stuffy classroom on their final day of school.

"I know! Claiming dragons are mere figments of our imaginations!" Jahrra was simply flabbergasted and she had actually laughed out loud in class, earning her thirty minutes detention after school.

"Maybe you should invite him over after school someday. I'm sure he'd love to meet Master Hroombra and discuss his theory."

Scede cast Jahrra an impish grin and she snorted. "Yeah, he'd think he was hallucinating!"

Jahrra pursed up her face and stood rigid, speaking in a harsh, pinched voice that sounded remarkably like Tarnik's, "I tell you, dragons are creatures invented by story tellers to add drama to their tales. You see, you see! I'm imagining one right now, do you see it?!"

Jahrra jabbed her finger as if pointing to an imaginary Hroombra, towering over them at the Castle Guard Ruin.

By the time they arrived at the stables to fetch their horses, Jahrra, Gieaun and Scede could barely walk from laughing so hard.

"Ugh!" Jahrra cried, wiping away a few tears and taking on a more serious tone, "Sometimes I just wish he and the twins would disappear!"

"Is that so, Nesnan?" asked a smug, cold voice from behind. "If anyone should disappear, it should be you."

The three of them turned quickly, fearing for a split second that Tarnik had actually been behind them.

"What do *you* want?" Jahrra said distastefully when she recognized who it was.

Eydeth just stood there and sneered silently. Three of his friends, all bigger, older boys, came walking over to stand just behind him, their arms crossed menacingly like a trio of body guards.

"If you dislike us so much, why do you go to such trouble to follow us around?" Gieaun asked coolly, crossing her arms to match the thugs.

"Nobody asked you!" Eydeth snapped ferociously, glaring both at Gieaun and Scede. "You should be ashamed of yourselves, both of you, for associating with this Nesnan!"

Eydeth was obviously out of insults to throw, and Jahrra wasn't in the mood to stand there and have him glare at them the rest of the afternoon. Summer vacation had started after all, and it wasn't going to start out on a bad foot, not if she could help it. She took a deep breath and gave Eydeth her most menacing glare.

"Look," she said rather boldly, "if you're just going to stand there and look stupid, then waste your time somewhere else. We've got a long ride home and the last thing we want to do is stick around here and look at your ugly face."

Gieaun and Scede had to turn away to hide their laughter, and even a few of the boys standing behind Eydeth found it hard to keep a straight face.

Eydeth, however, turned vermillion with anger. "What'd you say to me?!" he spat with rage.

"I said," Jahrra answered slowly, as if speaking to a very small child, "I'll be leaving now, so if you have anything else to say, then say it. But my guess is that your vocabulary isn't large enough."

Jahrra crossed her arms aggressively, flung her braided hair over her shoulder with a toss of her head, and stood up as tall as she could, a whole head taller than Eydeth.

The group of boys moved in closer, and Eydeth looked like a volcano about to erupt as he stood there contemplating what he should do next. Jahrra took advantage of the stalemate, turning and continuing the short walk up to the stables, a snickering Gieaun and Scede on her tail.

"Don't you turn your back on me!" Eydeth screamed as he began walking briskly after them.

Jahrra heard his approach, but she ignored it and kept on moving, her heart beginning to race. Just as Eydeth was closing in, she reached Phrym's stable door. With one swift motion of her arm, she lifted the rope loop that kept the door shut, and Phrym came bursting out, driving Eydeth back. The tall semequin began swinging his head and stomping his heavy hooves on the ground, knocking Eydeth completely off of his feet.

"AAAAGGGHHH!" he shouted as the young stallion pushed passed him, frightening off the other students.

Eydeth's friends scurried away from the agitated animal while Jahrra walked over to grab his halter. As soon as he sensed that Jahrra was no longer upset, Phrym began to calm down. She patted his cheek and whispered calming words to him, but Phrym never took his eyes off the boy who had been trying to hurt his friend. He snorted and drew his ears back in irritation.

Once Eydeth saw that the semequin was no longer running amuck, he scrambled to his feet and began limping off. In a last ditch effort to insult Jahrra, he whipped his head around and shouted in a voice that broke more than once, "You'd better learn to control that stupid horse! It's bound to get you into a lot of trouble some day!"

Jahrra simply smiled and retorted, "He's not a horse. He's a semequin, and he would never get me into trouble."

Eydeth smiled smugly at this statement, barely masking his grimace of pain. "Ha! Where would a poor Nesnan like you get a semequin?!"

He seemed amused by this and even straightened up a bit from his slumping posture. But as Eydeth began looking Phrym up and down, his maniacal grin crept away as he saw the truth in what Jahrra had said.

Jahrra tossed her head and chirped, waggling the fingers of her free hand, "I got him from an *imaginary* dragon."

Eydeth's smile disappeared completely. Whatever he might have wanted to say next, however, stayed unsaid. He turned and limped back towards the schoolhouse to wait with his sister for their carriage.

"Jahrra! You shouldn't have told him that!" Gieaun hissed.

"Oh, don't worry. If Eydeth believes the rubbish that Tarnik has been teaching us, and I'm sure he does, then he won't believe what I said," Jahrra answered briskly as she assessed Phrym, checking to make sure he hadn't hurt himself while breaking free of his stall.

"Jahrra, this is no joke! His father breeds semequins! He knows for sure that they're hard to find and really expensive. He'll make up some story of how you stole him!"

Gieaun seemed to be getting overly anxious, and Jahrra began to have second thoughts about antagonizing her enemy. Maybe she should've just let Eydeth have the last word and leave it at that.

"Hopefully he just thinks I'm crazy, like he always has. Come on, we need to get moving," Jahrra answered.

When she saw the look on her friend's face, however, she said, "Oh, Gieaun, don't worry so much!"

As they rode through the schoolyard, Scede nodded at the pair of twins glaring menacingly at them. "No doubt he's told his sister what happened," he commented.

"Yeah, and exaggerated it ten times worse than what actually *did* happen," Jahrra sniffed, sitting taller in the saddle.

By the time the three companions made it to the Castle Guard Ruin, the yellow glow of the daylight hours had faded into hues of washed-out indigo. Jahrra turned Phrym down the narrow path that led to the withered building and stopped, turning to her friends.

"I'll see you later, maybe tomorrow?" she asked.

"Mother and father might need us to help out in the fields with the horses, but I'm sure they wouldn't mind if you joined us," Scede offered.

"I'll see what Master Hroombra has planned. Goodbye!"

They said their farewells and Jahrra jogged Phrym across the field to his stable. As she took off his saddle and rubbed him down, she talked with him as if he were Gieaun or Scede. "One more school year gone. I can't believe it."

Phrym just whickered contentedly, nibbling at the oats in his trough. Jahrra looked off into the west and sighed. She wondered if next year would be any different. *If the twins are still in school, then probably not,* she thought ruefully.

Jahrra finished up with Phrym and took her time walking back to the Ruin, the chirping of crickets and alarm calls of frightened birds accompanying her the entire way. She stepped through the small door of her home to find Hroombra crouched in front of the massive fireplace in the equally massive common room. She looked past him, a little surprised not to find him at his desk, and saw a large pile of logs stacked in the center of the stone fireplace. Jahrra looked up at her mentor, her brow furrowed.

"Are you building a fire?" she asked, thinking of how ridiculous the idea was on this warm evening.

"Yes, I am," was Hroombra's simple reply.

Jahrra sighed, knowing out of experience that he wasn't about to explain. "And *why* are you building a fire? It's the beginning of summer."

Just as Jahrra was beginning to think that her guardian had lost it, he smiled brightly, eyes glittering. "This will be no ordinary fire," he said.

Jahrra was growing frustrated with Hroombra's lack of information, so she threw her hands up and exclaimed, "Alright, what do you have planned now?"

His grin deepened as he chanted, "This fire will be neither hot nor cool, and it will neither burn nor freeze."

Jahrra was flabbergasted. *What kind of a fire could freeze?* she thought with a befuddled look on her face.

Hroombra stood and walked over to the fireplace. He took a short breath and quickly exhaled, blowing a vibrant ball of red flame onto the pile of wood. The dry timber caught fire immediately, crackling and sparking aggressively, but the red flames soon turned to a blue-violet color, and they began rippling like water.

Jahrra was no longer confused, but intrigued. She slowly walked over to look at the strange flames, reaching out a hand to see if it felt hot, but there was no sensation of heat whatsoever.

"Go ahead and brush your fingers through it, it won't burn you."

Jahrra looked up at Hroombra and saw the truth of that statement in his honest eyes. He nodded his great head, so she quickly trailed her hand through one of the ripples. The effect was nothing more than that of a tiny puff of wind passing through smoke. Jahrra pulled her hand back and looked at it. No mark had been made, and she didn't feel a thing. It felt just as it would if she were waving goodbye to her friends.

"What *is* this?" she asked in wonder, still staring at her hand.

"It's ancient magic, long banished by the Tyrant King. The wood is ordinary, but the herb used to light the fire and the words I spoke over it earlier are magical. I have much of the plant stored away, but I only use it on special occasions since it is near impossible to come by these days."

Jahrra thought of the locked room in the back of the building and suddenly wondered what else might be hidden in there.

Hroombra reached his great foreleg out and passed his own hand over the flame, leaving it there for several seconds. His claws began to glow the same color as the fire, and Jahrra became worried. "Master Hroombra," she began anxiously.

"Don't fret, you'll see." he answered before she could continue.

He left his massive hand there for awhile longer, and then pulled it out slowly, his glowing claws leaving a trail of hazy blue smoke as they cut across the space between the fire and the floor. He then pulled his toes in and began to draw something on the ancient stone floor with the claw of his forefinger.

Jahrra watched carefully, the blue light of the fire and weak yellow flames of the few lit candles throughout the large room casting strange shadows on Hroombra's stern face. The old dragon looked to be writing something, and when he was finished, the marks glowed blue-violet upon the floor. Jahrra stared at the characters, which looked oddly familiar.

"What does that say, Master Hroombra?" she whispered as a log crashed behind her, sending indigo sparks flying through the enchanted air.

"It says *Kruledth, edth chormiehn epit edth Krueldhnen*, and in the common tongue, *Kruelt, the language of the Dragons.*"

Jahrra looked even more perplexed than before, blinking up at Hroombra like a dazed bird.

"It's time, young Jahrra, that you begin learning the language of the ancients, the language of the dragons."

Jahrra returned her gaze to the glowing letters. "Is this the language you spoke of when we went to see the castle a few months ago?" she asked.

"Yes, it is." Hroombra looked down at the child with serious eyes and took a breath. "I've found a few empty books for you to copy down the characters in, so tonight I'll write out the Kruelt alphabet for you, and you are to copy it down. During the summer you'll take out this alphabet and practice it each night. When you have learned the alphabet and can read it confidently, you'll begin to learn the words of the dragons."

Hroombra had been pacing back and forth as he said this, and when he stopped, he turned his head and looked down at Jahrra once more. She appeared to be slightly overwhelmed, but set her mouth in a determined manner just the same.

"Another thing you must know Jahrra, is that this language has been forbidden by the Crimson King of the east, and you must never tell anyone about it, not even Gieaun and Scede. You must promise me that."

The glance that Jahrra received from her mentor was a most serious one, and she nodded heartily. Hroombra didn't often ask her to keep secrets, so she knew that she must keep this one.

"Very well, let us begin. I'll first start with the capital letters, and tell you what each one corresponds with in the common alphabet. The characters will remain glowing upon the floor as long as the fire burns, so take your time in copying them properly."

Jahrra grabbed one of the empty books and a quill and inkwell and slowly began to copy down the strange letters that glowed before her eyes. For the next few hours, Hroombra reached into the fire and pulled its magic into his sharp claws. He carefully wrote each letter, telling Jahrra what it stood for.

He insisted that she write it down several times on one line and go back later to make a single list. By the time they reached the lowercase characters, Jahrra's fingers were stained black and her hand was cramping up.

Finally, after what seemed like ages, she had the entire alphabet, upper and lower case, copied down. Hroombra, who'd been watching her aptly, faced the fire and blew red flames upon the violet ones. The two colors melded in a beautiful dance, and soon the violet fire completely dissipated as a natural orange fire took over, taking the glowing characters with it. Jahrra was sad to see the strange fire go, but equally glad that her writing was over.

"Now," Hroombra said suddenly, allowing the wood to burn its natural way, "it's time for you to learn the story behind this language."

He invited Jahrra to make herself comfortable and then he began, "The language that you are about to learn is called Kruelt, or Draggish."

The old dragon had Jahrra repeat the words a few times both for pronunciation purposes as well as for memory purposes.

"The Kruelt language is the ancient language of the dragons. As you well know from what I've taught you, there are separate races of dragons, just as there are separate races of elves and other creatures of Ethöes. Dragons call their races "kruels".

# Blue Flames and Draggish Words

"Now each kruel of dragons that has the ability to speak has its own dialect, but they're not so different that one cannot understand another dragon from a different kruel than their own. A long, long time ago, only dragons spoke Kruelt. There were other races in existence, but they spoke their own languages. The elves spoke Elvish, the dwarves, Dwarvish, the Aandhoulis spoke Aandhoulin, the Nephaari, Nephaarye, and so on and so forth.

"But when Ethöes created her final race, the humans, she gave them no language and gave the dragons the responsibility to look after them, so naturally we taught them our way of speech. Each tribe of humans picked up the dialect of the group of dragons that taught them. You'll be learning the Tanaan dialect of Kruelt, because my kruel of dragons, the Korli, were responsible for the Tanaan race."

Hroombra paused to make sure Jahrra was following, continuing only when he saw that her eyes were wide with curiosity.

"The interesting thing about Kruelt, or Draggish as I have mentioned, is that true Kruelt can only be pronounced by a dragon. The humans however, created their own dialect using the same words and emphasizing the same syllables. The only difference was that their tongues couldn't handle certain accents, so they sounded slightly different from the dragons who taught them. If you keep to your lessons of this language, then eventually you'll be able to read the writing on the walls of the Castle Ruin."

Hroombra looked down at Jahrra and was glad to see she was still paying attention.

"Do you have any questions?" he asked delicately.

"I do have one question," she began hesitantly.

"Go on," Hroombra encouraged.

"I was just wondering, not that I don't want to learn Kruelt or anything, but why is it important that I learn it? I'm Nesnan, and everyone else speaks the common language here, so why learn a language that's forbidden?"

The old dragon smiled broadly. Jahrra wasn't trying to be insulting or insolent; she simply didn't see the importance of this. *And of course she doesn't,* Hroombra thought quietly. *But someday she will.*

He took a deep breath, exhaled and said, "That's a very good question Jahrra, and I have a very good answer. First of all, I'm a dragon, and I speak Kruelt, and I'd like to be able to communicate with you in my native language. It's been far too long since I've had that pleasure.

"Secondly, I'd like you to be able to read the many ancient documents and paintings in this old place. I know that as time goes by you'll have many questions about the history of Ethöes, and I'll be too busy to answer your questions. Fortunately, everything you need to know is written down in my scrolls and documents, only it's all in Draggish. So as you can see Jahrra, you're learning Kruelt because it will someday be convenient for me."

He smiled again, and Jahrra realized that he was teasing her.

"Oh, I don't mind learning Draggish, I was only wondering," she said nonchalantly, smiling back.

"I know you were young one, I know. But remember, you mustn't tell anyone about this. I cannot stress enough how important it is that this remain a secret."

Jahrra nodded soberly, promising once again to keep the secret between the two of them. If she was being completely honest with herself, the idea of learning a secret language no one else knew was both intriguing and quite appealing. Perhaps all those questions she had about the story of the Tanaan would be answered after all . . .

Hroombra yawned widely and stretched both his useless wings. "Well, I don't know about you, but I'm tired. We're done for the evening, but tomorrow night we'll start practicing writing common words in the Krueltish alphabet. You'll start by writing lines of letters."

Jahrra groaned as she flexed her ink-stained hand, surprised to feel that it no longer felt tired.

"I'm off to bed. Will you be staying up much longer?"

"Oh," Jahrra answered, forgetting about her hand, "only for a bit longer, I want to re-write the characters more neatly and next to the common alphabet in one column. I'll see you in the morning."

As Jahrra plopped down on her stomach by the fire with her feet dangling in the air, her full concentration on writing the characters down properly, Hroombra couldn't help but feel a sense of joy in his heart. She was so eager to learn, so happy to listen to him. *How long will it last?* he thought ruefully, *How long until she grows tired of my stories and no longer wants an old dragon around?*

Hroombra sighed and tried to shake off his morose thoughts. *Jahrra isn't like that. She would never shut me out*, he thought, sorrow clenching his heart. *But she's so much like, like him, like he was at that age. She's full of spirit and curiosity, just like he was. She's intelligent and strong, just like he was.* He looked at Jahrra one more time, humming softly and writing down her characters. *No*, he convinced himself, *she'll persevere; she'll not succumb to the horrors of this world.*

All Hroombra could count on was to do his best in guiding her towards her destiny and keeping her happy today. Beyond that he couldn't know, he could only hope.

He yawned once more and peered down at Jahrra's fresh writing, the still wet ink glistening in the light of the dimming fire. It did him good to see the old language written by a human again, even if it was only one. *As long as I'm here with her, she'll be alright. She'll be safe.* Hroombra rested his head beside the glowing fire, content in knowing that Jahrra was protected for now, and drifted off to sleep.

❊ ❊ ❊

The remainder of the summer consisted of the typical activities that any summer would be made up of. Jahrra, Gieaun and Scede occupied their time riding horses, helping on the ranch, going on camping trips to the lakes and on occasion, making a few trips into town.

The camping trips to Lake Ossar were definitely their favorite thing to do however, despite the ghost stories Kaihmen still tried to spook them with. The Resai man was sorely disappointed to discover that the children weren't as frightened of his stories as they used to be, often grumbling to his wife as the three friends giggled under their blankets.

"Kaihmen, they're getting older, they know your stories aren't true!" Nuhra would tell him.

"Oh, but they *are* true!" he'd insist as the children let loose a fresh round of laughter.

The trips into Aldehren or Toria Town were a welcome change from riding and camping. That is, they were until they spotted Eydeth and Ellysian stepping gingerly out of one of their ridiculous carriages, their puffed up mother just behind them. Jahrra stared in wrath as the crowd of commoners parted out of their way like abused dogs avoiding an angry master. It took Jahrra and her friends less than three minutes to collect their horses and head straight home.

"We see enough of them at school," Gieaun commented dourly.

"Besides, there are much more interesting things to do than wander around town," Scede said severely.

Gieaun simply huffed and slouched her shoulders, loosening her grip on Aimhe's reins. She wanted to go looking in all the trinket and clothing shops, but Scede thought this was the most boring thing he'd ever heard of. Jahrra thought that some of the stores were appealing, but she really would rather camp and ride Phrym all over the less populated parts of Oescienne than wander around through cramped, overly-perfumed shops. She didn't mention this to Gieaun, however, and tried not to look too elated that the evil twins had ruined this particular expedition.

While Jahrra spent most of her summer days seeking out adventure, her nights were spent by the fireside with Hroombra, learning the delicate intricacies of the language of the dragons. It proved much harder than she'd anticipated, and although Hroombra was supportive and patient, Jahrra was disappointed with her slow progress. The pronunciation was the hardest part for her, and by the end of the summer, she'd only learned a few dozen words.

"At least I know the alphabet by heart," she told Hroombra in a disappointed voice.

"Don't worry, Jahrra, you'll learn it. Languages take time," he encouraged.

# Blue Flames and Draggish Words

Summer came to an end with little fanfare, and the first half of the school year seemed to pass with ease, but Jahrra assumed it was only because of all the extra work she was now doing. Although her school work took precedence over her Draggish lessons, Jahrra found herself spending a good deal of time on the ancient and intriguing language. Instead of going to Gieaun's and Scede's for the Fall Festival this year, Jahrra stayed home and listened to a Sobledthe story from Hroombra. Jahrra was thrilled to be hearing a new tale from her mentor, that is, until Hroombra informed her it would be recited entirely in Kruelt.

Jahrra slumped and pouted the entire time, only to realize that by the end of it she had followed the story line pretty well.

"Wow!" she told Hroombra afterwards. "I didn't think I'd be able to understand!"

The great dragon smiled, his eyes twinkling. "Now you see, I told you that you'd get it after a while."

Hroombra didn't have the heart to tell her that he'd used only the easiest of words and the simplest of pronunciations for this particular story.

The fall gradually drifted into winter and Jahrra began counting down the days to Solsticetide. She was especially excited because Gieaun, Scede, Kaihmen and Nuhra would be joining them for Solstice dinner.

"I can't wait!" Jahrra told her two friends on their way to school the final day before the winter break. "It'll be so much fun with you all over for the holiday."

She smiled wistfully, not at all worried about what Eydeth and Ellysian might say to her this day. It was going to be the best Solsticetide ever and nothing, not even the twins, could ruin it. At least, that is what she told herself.

# -Chapter Thirteen-
# An Unwanted Invitation

"I'm *not* going!" Jahrra growled irritably, crossing her arms in distaste as Hroombra frowned down upon her.

*Curse Ellysian!* she thought angrily, trying to ignore her mentor's disapproving glare. *He can't seriously want me to go, to their house! On Solsticetide Eve!*

Jahrra felt herself turning red with fury as she recalled the day before. During the lunch break Ellysian, with all of her usual drama, had announced that her parents were hosting a Solsticetide party which the entire class was invited to attend.

"Classmates, I must make an important announcement on behalf of my mother and father," she'd crooned over the heads of the on-looking children.

Jahrra, Scede and Gieaun stopped what they were doing in their far corner of the yard to look up at the scene.

"My parents are having a grand party for the holiday, and you're all invited to join us."

Ellysian put on her most horribly sweet smile, and Jahrra made a gagging face at Gieaun and Scede who promptly giggled into their hands.

Ellysian looked over to their corner of the yard, narrowed her eyes, and said, "I'd like to remind you, that to mine and my brother's horror, my parents have insisted we invite the *whole* class, including you three."

The Resai girl spit out the last part of her sentence like it was a foul tasting medicine or some hot liquid that had burnt her mouth. Jahrra immediately stopped giggling and looked up at the vile girl. She glowered at them, purposely not making eye contact, and drew in her lips as if she had just sucked on a lemon. Gieaun and Scede simply stared up at her in surprise. Jahrra actually gaped in shock.

Ellysian pulled her glare away and continued haughtily, "The celebration will take place the day before the Solstice at our home in Kiniahn Kroi. Dress," Ellysian paused and smiled malevolently down at Jahrra, "is *formal*."

As Ellysian passed around the envelopes containing the information on where to meet and how long the party would last, Jahrra whispered harshly to Gieaun and Scede, "Let's just throw these out when we get them, no point in holding onto them!"

As if waiting for Jahrra to say this, Ellysian piped up once again, "Don't worry if you happen to lose your invitation, my mother has also sent copies by mail."

"Oh great," Jahrra seethed, "now Master Hroombra will know about this!"

"Oh, don't worry," Scede said. "I'm sure he won't make you go. I know mother and father won't make us go either."

"You know, you're probably right," Jahrra conceded. "Master Hroombra knows how much I hate them."

That had been yesterday, and now Jahrra stood in the great room of the Castle Guard Ruin, face to face with her mentor. He'd received the invitation from Dharedth the mailman that afternoon and thought going to such a party would be a good lesson for Jahrra.

"Of course you'll be going," he said casually. "It's a chance for you to witness a different side of Oescienne, not to mention a chance to see Kiniahn Kroi. Besides, Eydeth's and Ellysian's parents invited you, and it's rude to turn down an invitation of this merit."

A burning log crackled and popped in the giant fireplace, mimicking Jahrra's mood just then.

"Master Hroombra! You can't expect me to go!" she exclaimed, arms dropping to her sides in frustration. "They hate me! And I'm sure their parents hate me too! They won't even call me by my first name! Why can't I just stay here with you and Phrym and invite Gieaun and Scede to come over a day early?"

"I doubt they'd be able to make it," Hroombra said, eyes lowered on a pile of manuscripts strewn atop his massive desk, his voice holding not even a hint of amusement. "I've a feeling they'll be attending a party in Kiniahn Kroi."

"No, they won't," Jahrra insisted, the words grating against her throat. She crossed her arms quickly and continued, "We made a pact. None of us are going."

"Something tells me that their parents won't allow them to turn down the invitation either," Hroombra answered calmly, still poring over his work.

"Their parents won't want to torture them like you're trying to torture me! I'm sure they only invited me to make a spectacle out of me!"

"You'll be fine, Jahrra. Don't be so dramatic."

Jahrra clenched her fists at her sides and tried not to panic. Hroombra's calm attitude only made her more frustrated, but it didn't matter, she knew she'd already lost this battle.

The old dragon finally looked up at her. She stood there in a stubborn display of defiance, thinking he might actually yell at her, but after several seconds, he took a breath and spoke evenly once more, "You'll be going to this party, Jahrra, so there's no use in arguing with me any longer."

Hroombra's gaze was stern and unbending, and for once in her life Jahrra felt intimidated by him. She realized she wasn't getting out of this. Just as she was feeling completely defeated however, she remembered one little detail that shone like a light at the end of a tunnel.

"Well," she said, her mood lifting substantially, "there's one more thing."

She let the statement hang in the air for a while, waiting for Hroombra to look up at her.

When he continued his research without acknowledging her, she plowed on, "The dress code for this party is formal, and formal standards for Eydeth and Ellysian are far greater than what I've got to wear. So, I guess I won't be able to make it after all."

"Oh, is that all?" Hroombra said, trying hard not to smile. "I just happen to know a very good tailor in Aldehren who owes me a favor."

Jahrra gaped in outrage. She was so sure that not having the proper wardrobe would get her out of this mess.

"I still refuse to go!" she shouted, as she marched off to her room to fester in her temper.

Hroombra shook his head in amusement. He couldn't blame her, and if he were in her place he wouldn't want to go to this party either. But it was a chance for Jahrra to escape her protected little world and see a little more of Oescienne, even if it was only a city just on the other side of the Raenyan River, and even though it meant, for a time, she had to endure bad company.

The Solstice season began the next day and although Jahrra had only a day ago been looking forward to a great feast with her friends, she was in the worst mood ever. In just over a week's time she'd be in the dominion of her most bitter enemies. Hroombra was taking her to the tailor the next day, so Jahrra used her first day off to visit Gieaun and Scede and hear what their parents had to say about the matter.

"They won't make them go, will they Phrym?" Jahrra asked the semequin as she saddled him for the short journey.

He just nickered and looked over at her with his great smoky eyes. He'd grown to be such a tall and fine animal that Jahrra couldn't help but look upon him with pride. Phrym had been her guiding light and her anchor for the past few years, and he never grew angry with her the way Gieaun and Scede sometimes did. Nor did he make her go to stupid parties. She sighed, hoping something would come up and she wouldn't have to go after all.

As the colt and his rider loped across the barren fields, the cool breeze of winter whipping both hair and tail into streams of gold and dark silver, Jahrra thought more about the dreaded party. Why did she have to spend Solsticetide Eve amongst her enemies? Why was Hroombra doing this to her? *I should think he'd at least let me decide whether I wanted to go to a party or not!*

As Phrym puffed down the long drive leading to Wood's End Ranch, a pack of overly-excited dogs came bursting down the road to greet them.

"Calm down," Jahrra shouted over the din as she reined an edgy Phrym around the leaping animals, "it's just me!"

She finally managed to climb down from the semequin and was immediately knocked over by the happy creatures, all nine of them, tails wagging madly. When Jahrra eventually escaped her eager admirers, she led Phrym over to the fence to tie him up and then made her way up to the front of the house. She walked through the open gate and up the short stone path onto the wrap-around porch. The railing and edge of the roof were decorated in ivy and holly for the Solsticetide, and Jahrra even spotted some mistletoe tucked in with the evergreen garland.

As she made her way up the few steps and onto the porch, she noticed that the entire family was standing just inside the door frame waiting for her.

"Well, well, well, if it isn't Jahrra. What're you doing up at such an hour?"

It was Kaihmen who spoke down at her. At first Jahrra thought he might be angry with her so she froze. Then she noticed that everyone was attempting, very unsuccessfully, to hide smiles.

"I have to talk to Gieaun and Scede, it's urgent," she managed.

"You're just in time for breakfast. Have you eaten?" Nuhra asked cheerfully, looking more awake than Jahrra felt.

"No, I'm afraid I've forgotten," Jahrra answered truthfully. She'd been in such a hurry that she hadn't thought to eat.

"Gieaun, Scede, help Jahrra put Phrym in one of the corrals and then you three can come in and help get ready for breakfast."

As Nuhra began frying some bacon, the three friends skipped away to take care of Phrym. On the way to the stables, Jahrra learned that Hroombra had been right about the Solsticetide party. Gieaun and Scede told her that their parents insisted they honor the invitation as well, no questions asked.

"How can they make us go?!" Jahrra breathed in frustration as they hung on the fence and watched the other horses welcome Phrym.

"I don't know, but we don't really have a choice do we?" said Scede glumly.

"I wish Master Hroombra had given me a choice. He even has a tailor making me an outfit!" Jahrra made a face. "I was so sure that I would've gotten out of it since I don't have any nice clothes!"

"I think we shouldn't talk about it in front of mother and father," whispered Gieaun fretfully as they trekked back to the house. "They'll get angry at us again."

# An Unwanted Invitation

After breakfast, Jahrra spent the day riding and exploring with her two friends. They took the horses down to the Oorn Plain and raced along the bank of the river until they reached Lake Ossar. They spotted a few of the birds that frequented this part of Oescienne during the winter months and they even saw a small herd of deer drinking cautiously along the shore. Jahrra sketched all of the creatures they spotted in her journal.

"You've got to make a copy for me someday," Scede said admiringly, as he watched Jahrra sketch a cinnamon teal.

Jahrra just smiled at the compliment. She'd been making both her friends copies that she planned to give to them for Solsticetide.

A few hours before dark Jahrra bid her friends farewell, grumbling about getting up early to go to the tailor's in the morning. She rode home much more quickly than she'd come the first time, worried she might run into someone unpleasant as dusk settled in. She waved to townsfolk who were closing shop in Nuun Esse on her way through, and by the time she was coming up over the slope that led down to the Castle Guard Ruin, it was already twilight.

Jahrra led Phrym into his stable and patted him goodnight, then began her trek across the field, puffing and rubbing her sides to keep warm. She found Hroombra lying by the fire looking at some old maps. He turned his head in inquisition as Jahrra's dark figure became awash in firelight.

"Ah, there you are. Did you have a good day?" he asked casually.

"I guess so," she shrugged.

"So . . . ?" Hroombra said with smiling eyes. "Are we all going to the party then?"

"Yes," Jahrra mumbled in a defeated voice.

"It won't be all that bad," Hroombra replied, turning back to the old papers strangely illuminated by the crackling fire.

Noticing the unfamiliar documents and looking for anything to distract her from negative thoughts about the twins, Jahrra walked over to the hearth and stood beside Hroombra's shoulder.

"What maps are these?" she asked. "I've never seen these ones before."

"More maps of Ethöes," Hroombra answered. "See, here's the known world up until a few hundred years ago, before the threat of Cierryon discouraged the mapmakers from continuing their work."

Jahrra gazed down at where Hroombra pointed with his great forefinger. She recalled the map hanging in the classroom in Aldehren and remembered seeing a few smaller ones in Hroombra's study, but nothing of this detail or size.

The old worn map was large enough to be a quilt. The document showed the entire Norwester Arm, the part of the world that was known, at least to the peoples that inhabited it, and was enhanced with detailed topography and natural wonders.

The Great Hrunahn Mountains in the north, so tall that they pierced the clouds and almost touched the heavens, were drawn towering over the lower peaks below them. The Great Rhiimian Gorge, a huge canyon that cut long, deep and wide into the desert of the east, looked cavernous, an effect she was sure the mapmaker intended.

Jahrra noted the huge blue splashes representing the giant lakes of the west and the enormous Samenbi Desert, depicted as a blush painted across the land, in the center of the great continent. She let her eyes travel southeast and they fell upon the gold-tinged Dunes of Ehrann, and then to the lost mountain range that cut the Norwester Arm off from the south. The map faded away after this range, showing that these lands hadn't yet been explored by the people of the Norwest.

After admiring all of the shapes and colors, Jahrra took a closer look and found that the map was also labeled quite clearly. The names of these places were both in the common language and, just below, in Kruelt. Jahrra immediately loved this map, and she soon became entranced, grazing her eyes over it again and again. She read out some of the names in the dragons' language as best as she could pronounce them, looking to her mentor for help.

"Here," chuckled Hroombra, pushing over a much smaller map, only as big as the top of a small table, "you might want to start out with this one."

Jahrra looked dazedly at the new document and saw that it was just as detailed as the first one, only this map showed all of the province of Oescienne.

"The landmarks are printed in Kruelt, but you need the practice anyway. You can copy it and carry it with you so you won't get lost."

Hroombra then pushed over a blank scroll small enough for Jahrra to keep in Phrym's saddlebags, but large enough for her to copy the major features of the Oescienne map. He also pushed a box of drawing and coloring pencils in her direction and Jahrra soon began her work, completely forgetting about her anger at the old dragon and the dreaded party she had to attend.

"You may help yourself to the roast on the fire as well. I figured you might not have eaten." Hroombra nodded to the remains of a large wild pig roasting deliciously over the large fireplace.

Jahrra lay in front of the hearth for hours, working on her map and looking at the others, eating the roasted pork and enjoying the warmth of the fire on this cold night. Hroombra answered all of her questions about the many maps he pored over and even helped her with her own map.

When Jahrra finished all of the details, she scribbled in the names of the different places and checked to make sure everything was as accurate as she could make it. She gave the map the same colors as the old one in front of her, but the newer drawing glowed with the vibrancy that time had not yet stolen.

When the hour grew late, Jahrra yawned hugely, realizing just how tired she was. Her map was not yet finished, but she could work on it later. As she stretched her back and bid good night to Hroombra, he reminded her of her fitting at the tailor's tomorrow.

Jahrra groaned, suddenly remembering the past two days. She shuffled off to her room, feeling the warmth from the fire slowly seeping away. She climbed reluctantly into bed, dreading the arrival of morning, but managed to calm her anxious thoughts with painted scenes from her new map.

The next day Hroombra and Jahrra traveled to Aldehren in hopes of finding the perfect outfit for the Solsticetide party. The journey was slow going and although Jahrra loathed the idea of spending a day away from her friends, she couldn't help being curious about the many fabrics the tailor might have to offer.

The bustling town of Aldehren was busy with the clamor of the season and Jahrra suddenly remembered the last few times she'd walked through town with a huge dragon. Once it been her first day of school, and she frowned as she recalled the menacing scowls and guarded whispers from the early morning crowd that autumn day so long ago. The second time had been during a trip through Edyadth, when they had witnessed a slave auction. Jahrra shivered as she recalled the chained people and a pair of bright green, elvin eyes that had made her uneasy. And just like the first time in Aldehren, the people of Edyadth had regarded Hroombra with disdain, moving away and muttering as he'd passed. Jahrra now wondered if her guardian would get the same treatment today.

Either the people of Aldehren had finally gotten used to the fact that a mystical beast lived on the great hill above their town, or they were so caught up in their own business of the day that they hardly noticed his presence now. There were the few stares and pointing fingers of the enthralled children being dragged along by their mothers from one over-stuffed shop to the next, but nothing like what Jahrra remembered. Everyone, except for a few wagons drawn by two or four horses, stuck closely to the sidewalks, easily distracted by the glittering and bedecked storefronts. No one seemed to care about the dragon passing by.

Jahrra relaxed a little and looked around. She smiled at the people shuffling about, tripping over decorations and long ribbons or trying hard to balance gift boxes piled high in their arms. The air held the dancing scents of hot-baked cranberry cobbler, spicy cinnamon cider and roasting chestnuts. Jingling bells hanging from polished harnesses played throughout the city streets, and Jahrra felt a pleasant chill creep over her skin as the smells and sights of the Solstice season overwhelmed her.

Hroombra eventually stopped in front of an obscure little shop painted a dark, brilliant blue with a wooden sign hanging above the holly-draped door. The sign read *Gahlen's Fine Clothery*, and Jahrra realized with a tiny grimace that this must be the tailor's shop. She reluctantly slid off of Hroombra's back as he stood blocking the flow of traffic. It seemed people were taking notice of him now, giving puzzled looks and muttering irritably as they shoved past him.

"I'll wait right here for you Jahrra," he said in a low voice, eyeing the person-sized door in front of them.

"Alright," she gulped.

Jahrra turned the handle of the door and pushed, causing a cheerful jingle of bells to chatter above her head. She stepped cautiously into the small, cramped tailor's shop, the buzz of the crowd ceasing as the door swung shut. Jahrra blinked as her eyes became overwhelmed with an explosion of vibrant color.

Cotton, silk, satin, denim, lace, linen and wool, every type of fabric in every color imaginable populated the small space she stood in. Streams of cloth hung like banners on the walls and huge folded squares of it were piled as high as the ceiling. Jahrra had never seen anything so colorful in her life. It was like all of the rainbows of the world had been trapped in this tiny place and were trying desperately to escape.

The light that flooded in from the many tall windows facing the street glowed with the color of whatever pattern stood in their way. The aroma of cinnamon, shoe polish and something more stringent, perhaps the fumes from the dye used to create these brilliantly painted fabrics, tainted the room. It was a strange combination of scents, but Jahrra liked it, smiling despite her wariness.

A grunt from somewhere in the back of the room made her yelp. A very tall and thin older Resai man came dancing into view, loaded down with an armful of even more fabric. When he dumped the folds onto the already crowded cashier's counter, Jahrra noticed that he had no hair but a long grey beard he kept braided. His legs and arms were so long and gangly that if he had another set of each Jahrra would have been convinced he was an oversized daddy-long-legs spider. She giggled at the thought, but quickly stifled her laughter knowing that it would appear rude.

The tailor seemed preoccupied, so Jahrra politely cleared her throat. The man stopped his humming and whirled around to gaze quizzically down at her. He had bright, pale brown eyes and almost as many wrinkles as Hroombra.

"Why, I didn't hear you enter! How may I help you dearie?" he asked in a melodic voice, straightening up to an even taller height.

Jahrra quickly and awkwardly explained who she was and why she was there. After a swift glance through the window to find Hroombra smiling in encouragement, the tailor got straight to work. Although Jahrra had grown to be one of the tallest in her class so far, the kind man still had to bend down in order to pat her on the head, which he did quite frequently.

"What a lovely child!" he said enthusiastically. "Such good bone structure, and look at that hair! Like threads of gold."

Jahrra thought the man was exaggerating about her hair, but she liked him anyways. He cheered her up and actually looked happy, not annoyed, to see Hroombra loitering outside his door.

The fitting took longer than expected, but Jahrra was much amused by the tailor's chatter. He placed her up on a small stool and began draping acres of fabric over her as if he were trying to build a mountain. Then he would scurry around the small room muttering to himself while constantly measuring her with yellow tape.

"Tsk, tsk," he would say with chin in hand. "That color won't do, no sir-ee. AHHH!" he exclaimed, making Jahrra jump as he pulled off several layers of cloth, almost knocking her off her perch. "This'll do much better."

What he thought would do was a pretty blue and silver patterned fabric that looked like silk. Jahrra was wondering where it had been because she didn't remember being draped with that particular color. She liked it very much though, and wondered what he would make with it.

"What do you think?" he flapped the fabric boisterously in front of Hroombra, who was now peering in through the door so he could hear everything.

"Very nice. It'll do well, very well indeed," was the dragon's approving reply.

"Yes, it goes well with her eye color," said the tailor, once again distracted with the aesthetics of his job.

He then found a solid blue material that matched the blue highlights in the first fabric.

"Good, good, good." he twittered, trailing blue and silver sheets of fabric over to his crowded desk. "I'll work on this for a few days. Then I'll need you to come back, young lady, for a fitting."

The tailor smiled and patted Jahrra's head once again before releasing her to Hroombra. They left for home with Jahrra feeling a little more than dazed by the strange experience.

"What exactly is he making?" she asked once they left the noisy town behind.

"I would think he's making a skirt and a blouse," Hroombra said knowledgeably.

"A skirt!" Jahrra blurted. "Are you crazy, I can't wear a skirt!"

"Oh, yes you can. It's formal dress, remember?" Hroombra answered firmly.

Jahrra groaned aloud. She hated the idea of wearing anything girly. She hated girly things, plus, they were uncomfortable. All she knew was that Ellysian was always girly, and the last thing she wanted was to be anything like Ellysian. Jahrra crossed her arms with a disgruntled huff. *A skirt! Why a skirt?* she thought miserably. *Well,* she sighed inwardly, knowing there was nothing she could do about it now, *at least it's blue.*

The next week passed quickly, with Jahrra and Hroombra traveling to town twice more to try on her outfit, buy shoes and jewelry to match, and to finally take the whole lot home to prepare for the party.

Finally, after two weeks of uncomfortable anticipation, the day of the dreaded event arrived. Jahrra rode Phrym to her friends' ranch early in the morning on Solstice Eve. Kaihmen and Nuhra had offered to drive the children into town, and Hroombra thought it best if Jahrra got ready at Wood's End Ranch.

"Be sure your skirt and blouse are tucked well into the saddlebag so they won't get dirty!" Hroombra shouted after Jahrra as Phrym tore across the frost coated fields.

Jahrra had half a mind to get them dirty on purpose. *That'll show the twins, showing up in stained clothes to their fancy party!* she thought slyly. Then she remembered the trouble Hroombra had gone to in order to get the outfit made for her. She quickly forgot about how she could sabotage the twins' evening and turned her focus on how to survive it.

Once she reached the ranch and Phrym was put away safely into the stables, Jahrra went inside to greet her friends.

"What're you going to wear?" Gieaun asked gleefully dragging her friend upstairs. Apparently, the notion of dressing up had suddenly overshadowed the reality of where they were going, at least in Gieaun's eyes.

"A skirt and blouse."

Jahrra's response was barely audible, but Gieaun heard her anyway and let out a squeal of delight.

Jahrra turned crimson as Gieaun pulled her into her room. Scede snickered after them, but just before Gieaun closed the door to the rest of the house, Jahrra turned and gave him a deadly glare. Scede stopped laughing immediately. The last thing he wanted was to suffer the wrath of his ill-tempered friend. Once in the other room, Gieaun helped Jahrra into her long skirt and blouse.

The Resai girl simply adored her friend's outfit. "Oh, Jahrra! The skirt is so lovely, and the blouse too!"

The clothes had turned out quite nicely, Jahrra had to admit. The tailor must have sensed her distaste for too-feminine clothing from their few meetings, so he'd kept it simple. The long-sleeved blouse was a pale blue with a beautiful dark blue and silver embroidered pattern of oak branches and wild roses trailing around the collar, sleeve ends and hem.

The sleeves, although long, flared out at the ends so that her wrists wouldn't feel constrained. The skirt, the same color as the dark blue thread in the embroidered pattern, was long and flowing with delicate plaiting. The hem ended in a flurry of small tassels that had silver beads sewn on them.

Hroombra also had the tailor fit her for a jacket of supple blue suede, stitched with a large leather thread and lined with soft wool. This jacket complemented her clothes quite well and matched her dress boots perfectly.

Of the entire outfit, Jahrra loved her boots the most. They were made of the same blue suede of her long coat and lined with the same wool for the winter cold, and although they had small heels on them, they were quite comfortable.

The jewelry that Jahrra picked out was a plain necklace made of blue glass and silver with matching earrings and a bracelet. Hroombra had pointed out some nicer pieces, but Jahrra insisted on the simpler ones, feeling that he'd already given her plenty for this accursed party.

Jahrra sighed as Gieaun pulled her over to the mirror so she could see what she looked like. Jahrra gawked when she saw the unfamiliar figure standing in front of her, a figure that looked so much like all of the rude girls in class.

Gieaun simply beamed at her. "Oh! You look so nice Jahrra! You should dress up more often!"

Jahrra blushed with embarrassment. She never dressed up and didn't know how to take all of her friend's compliments.

"Oh, let me do your hair too, will you?" Gieaun pleaded.

Gieaun pulled Jahrra's hair up into a fancy half twist, braiding part of it into a tight rope that held up the rest. Gieaun was next to get into her dress, a lovely shimmery green material with a forest green, capped-sleeve velvet vest to match her eyes. She opted to pull half of her dark hair back in a ponytail, leaving the rest down. For shoes, Gieaun wore embroidered slippers that had green glass beads sewn onto them.

An hour later, the two girls came out of Gieaun's room to meet Scede and their parents. Everyone was impressed by the girls' appearance, especially by Jahrra's.

"Why Jahrra, look at you!" Nuhra said cheerily.

Jahrra, unable to be rid of her blush, gave a weak smile and dropped her eyes to focus on her boots. A few minutes later Scede entered the common room where everybody stood. Jahrra raised her head just enough to see that her other friend had on a nice pair of pants, also green, but much darker than Gieaun's vest. The tunic he wore was a light moss color, embroidered in emerald and gold and covered in emerald, copper and gold glass beads. He had his longish hair slicked back for the occasion. Jahrra resisted the urge to poke fun at him, knowing he would return the favor.

"Are you three ready?" Kaihmen asked enthusiastically.

"Yes," they said simply and morosely, once again remembering exactly where they were going.

The instructions had been to meet at the schoolhouse one hour before midday. It was now three and a half hours to midday, so the three children and two adults piled into the family carriage and made their way towards Aldehren. On their way they stopped briefly at the Castle Guard Ruin to greet Hroombra.

"You all look so grown up, especially you, Jahrra. Remember your manners and try not to let the other children get to you." Hroombra smiled at them as they headed down the drive to the main road.

The ride to Aldehren was much more pleasant in a carriage than on horseback, and along the way the children chatted about what their classmates might be wearing.

"I bet Eydeth'll be wearing royal robes, and Ellysian'll be wearing furs and a big frilly dress," Scede commented boorishly, tucking his loose hair behind his slightly pointed ears.

The three friends laughed heartily at the thought of the "Royal" twins glaring down at everyone from their high perches.

As the carriage clattered into Aldehren, Jahrra, Gieaun and Scede stopped talking about their classmates and began imagining what the city of Kiniahn Kroi might look like.

"I hear they have houses made of silver and gold there!" Gieaun said.

"Yes, and they keep unicorns for pets!" Scede added in wide-eyed wonder.

Jahrra hoped very much that they did keep unicorns for pets; she'd never seen one before.

# The Legend of Oescienne – The Finding

Aldehren was busy with all of the ongoing Solsticetide festivities, and it took Kaihmen longer than anticipated to maneuver the horses towards the schoolhouse. Finally, they reached the small grove of redwood trees and turned up the narrow road into the hidden gully. Jahrra breathed in the crisp air, shivering a little as she stuffed her hands into her jacket pockets. The schoolhouse and its surrounding yard were deserted, and Jahrra imagined the dull red building was a great wild creature, hiding from everything that was happening in Aldehren.

Jahrra released a great sigh into the cool air, hoping that they were too late and had missed their ride to the party. Ten minutes later, however, their classmates started trickling up the path in a variety of carriages. Jahrra swallowed her disappointment and she, Gieaun and Scede all gazed curiously at the other children stepping out of the coaches to gather on the school steps.

Jahrra stared in awe at the variety of costumes. The girls all wore dresses, much more sophisticated than her own skirt and blouse, in intricate patterns and designs. Glittering necklaces and earrings, most definitely not glass, hung from their ears, necks and gloved wrists and a few were wearing jackets lined with rare furs. It appeared as though everyone had their hair done up by a professional barber as well, and Jahrra felt a little self conscious with the simple style Gieaun had done for her. The boys looked just as impressive, their pants and shirts a little fancier than Scede's.

Finally the twins arrived leading a wagon train that was made up of eight pristine white carriages, each pulled by a pair of matching snowy horses. Jahrra's jaw dropped. She remembered the twins arriving in yellow carriages the first day of school and was impressed, but they had *white* ones as well? These new carriages were more embellished than the canary-hued coaches from before, and they all had garlands of holly branches and evergreen boughs hanging from them.

Jahrra blinked dazedly and turned her attention to the horses instead. They were the same horses from before and now that she was taking the time to get a good look at them, she realized they weren't horses but semequins. Jahrra gulped. Four semequins for each carriage. She was flabbergasted. How rich *were* the twins' parents?

She shook her head and tried to forget about Eydeth and Ellysian, returning her attention to the semequins. Their harnesses were red and had large silver bells sewn onto them, jingling cheerfully as the animals approached. Stiff men in ivory colored suits pulled heartily on bell-laden reins, bringing the carriage train to an elegant halt.

Jahrra was overwhelmed by the whole display. She suddenly felt as though she were wearing rags and as she shrank down in her seat, the door of the first carriage opened and out stepped the twins. They were both attired in shades of yellow, not far off from the description Scede had imagined.

Ellysian wore a full-skirted dress the color of butter. The sleeves were short and she donned white satin gloves that ended just below the puffed sleeves adorning her shoulders. The tiara perched in her ridiculously styled hair sparkled blindingly and her earrings and necklace glittered like crystal fire. A white fur shawl completed the ensemble and she stood, not surprisingly, with the air of a smug queen.

Her brother looked just as bad. Eydeth's mustard colored pants, polished boots and embroidered dandelion silk jacket actually hurt Jahrra's eyes. He looked like a giant banana slug. *Looks like a banana slug?* Jahrra thought with a smirk, *he is a banana slug.* The costumes would've been better in another color, but for some reason gold was obviously important to the two.

"Why do they always wear yellow?" Gieaun asked harshly, voicing Jahrra's thoughts.

"Probably has to do with a stupid family crest or something," Scede added bitterly.

"Hello everyone, I hope you're all doing well this morning," Ellysian said, even more pompously than when she'd invited them all to this ridiculous celebration. "You can get into the carriages now."

And with that, Ellysian swept her gown up as gracefully as she could and her brother, who had followed her, helped her into the first carriage. Stuffed her, more like. Jahrra had to suppress a laugh as Eydeth abashedly jammed his sister's billowing skirts through the carriage door.

Gieaun rolled her eyes and gave Jahrra and Scede a disgusted look.

"Well, I guess we'll see you tomorrow morning then," Kaihmen said to them.

Jahrra was sure she heard a hint of laughter in his voice, but she couldn't say for sure.

Reluctantly, the three exited their wagon and swiftly made their way to the last carriage in the line, hoping that no one saw them. To their delight, everyone was crowded around the head of the wagon train trying to sit with Ellysian and Eydeth, but only the privileged few were granted the honor of sitting in the lead carriage. Gieaun, Scede and Jahrra breathed a sigh of relief when no one climbed into their cart.

"At least we'll have some peace for now," Scede commented.

Jahrra nodded her head in agreement, but still dreaded what would happen once they arrived in Kiniahn Kroi. She took a deep breath and felt her stomach lurch as their carriage jolted forward.

# -Chapter Fourteen-

# A Party, a Prank, and a Near Death Experience

The caravan traveled at a steady pace, clattering down the smooth dirt road that wound through the wide, green Raenyan Valley. From an eagle's point of view, Jahrra imagined the small train of carriages would look very much like eight glittering pearls strung out on a necklace. Unfortunately Jahrra, Gieaun and Scede couldn't appreciate such a sight; they were stuck in one of the giant gem-like coaches rocking gently towards what they were sure was going to be an unpleasant experience.

In order to blot out the horrible images of dancing around a crowded ballroom with their malicious classmates, Jahrra, Gieaun and Scede focused on the landscape as it passed by. Deep green hills and wild, rolling fields stood on either side of them.

Jahrra pushed open the window nearest to her side of the carriage and poked her nose out like a curious mouse. The outside air stung her face, but it smelled wonderfully of thawing frost and distant fire smoke. The clattering of wheels, the chucking of hooves and the puffing and snorting of the horses made any other natural sounds obsolete. Great clumps of deep green oak groves dotted the fallow fields like huge, hulking beasts curled up against the cold.

Jahrra shivered at the sight and frowned when she noticed the stark white trunks of birches and sycamores lining the great Raenyan River. They looked, she thought, like the skeletal remains of giants, standing on either side of the waterway in an endless faceoff. Jahrra sighed and closed her eyes, imagining the noise that such a great battle might create.

The three companions kept a tally of all the animals they saw along the way, ranging from cattle and horses to deer, foxes, and the birds visiting Oescienne for the winter. As the carriages veered north, Jahrra peered out of the window once again and noticed in the far distance a large stream diverging northwest from the Raenyan River. Half an hour later the carriages turned off along a road that followed the tributary.

"Oh! This must be Itah Creek!" Gieaun exclaimed, now leaning gingerly out of the open window. "Father told us it flows out of the north canyon of Kiniahn Kroi, and South Itah Creek flows out of the south canyon into Itah Creek. We must be close!"

Both Jahrra and Scede plastered themselves against the inside wall to get a better look. A few minutes later their coach abruptly headed west and soon they came upon yet another waterway. Jahrra looked out the window once more and her jaw dropped in awe. Ahead of them lay a great stone bridge constructed from smooth, light blue-grey cubes of granite.

The structure was the most beautiful thing she'd ever seen, broad and strong and ornamented with carved stone pillars. Evergreen wreaths and brilliant red ribbons hung in garlands along the railing and two enormous wreaths crafted of the same evergreens bedecked the two tallest pillars at the bridge's entrance. It looked like a frozen fortress guarding the enchanted land of winter.

"This is the south fork of Itah Creek," Gieaun said knowledgeably.

As they crossed the creek, Jahrra's eyes widened even further. Ahead there lay something even more wonderful than the granite bridge spanning the stream. A great, beautiful city made entirely of polished stone in every color imaginable towered into view.

The carriage train moved smoothly down the main street of Kiniahn Kroi and immediately became surrounded by an assortment of sights, sounds and smells. Manicured yards and tall gleaming houses of stone flashed by, their small gardens kept tidy and contained by strong iron fences. Every shrub and plant was kept in top shape and every door was ornately carved and painted in rich ocean blues, brick reds, and blazing whites.

# A Party, a Prank, and a Near Death Experience

All of the houses were at least two or three stories high with a neat stone path leading to the front door; in every entryway hung beautiful oil lamps made of pale green glass. The streets were lined with ancient sycamores, lamps similar to those in the doorways hanging from their bare branches or perched upon lampposts on every street corner.

Everywhere the children looked, they saw the signs of the season. Bows and ribbons of silver and gold, bright red berries, rich green holly and branches of evergreen garnished the elaborate fences and lampposts of the massive labyrinthine town.

Along the way, the carriages passed many public gardens, large and small, their lily ponds now black and empty of life during these cold months. Everything looked very clean and Jahrra imagined that gnomes and fairies flitted and dashed around after dark to keep the streets and sidewalks immaculate.

If Jahrra hadn't known any better, she would've thought the entire city was enchanted. She closed her eyes and tried to imagine what those strange lamps would look like when lit at twilight. A smile crossed her lips as she pictured a thousand lanterns, emitting a soft green glow as noble couples strolled through the parks during a warm summer evening.

Jahrra inhaled deeply, the cold air reminding her summer was still far away, and realized this city wasn't filled with the unpleasant smells she usually recognized in the other towns of Oescienne. The air here was pungent with frost and the faint, clean odor of berries and apples, all infused with the deep, cool aroma of damp, mossy granite. In the distance she heard an orchestra playing a familiar Solstice song enhanced by the constant light jingle of bells.

Kiniahn Kroi was quieter than Aldehren, if a bustling city could be quiet. There was definitely something different about the noises here. People didn't shout across the street at one another and those driving horses didn't whistle, but seemed almost to lead the animals with their minds. Jahrra thought it was all very strange, but sat back and enjoyed the passing scenery anyway.

They passed fancy restaurants stuffed with well-dressed patrons, a clothing store selling nothing but silks and lace, and even a building with a sign that read *Hot Springs*. *Wow, wouldn't that be nice!* Jahrra thought, imagining hot water coming out of the ground and collecting into a deep, steaming pool. What she and her friends didn't see however, were livery stables, butchers' shops or smithies. Jahrra decided that such noisy and smelly places would not be acceptable within Kiniahn Kroi's boundaries.

The people here were different, too. Finely dressed men and women ambled down the wide sidewalks, rode fine semequins, passed by in expensive buggies or shopped for gifts while enjoying the crisp air. One woman, weighed down by yards of rich ruby skirts and topped with a ridiculous feathered hat, had a small covey of servants trailing after her, each one trying hard not to drop the mountain of packages they carried as she barked out orders. Jahrra imagined each of these decorated people had at least one relative who lived in a palace somewhere and wondered if any of them might be related to Eydeth and Ellysian.

Once through the main part of town, the caravan headed farther north along a wide cobblestone road that began to turn west. Jahrra stuck her head through the window and noticed, behind the screen of bald sycamores and birches, another arm of tall hills looming up ahead.

"Those hills split the two canyons," Gieaun explained. "And I think we're headed for the north canyon. It's where the *richer* people live," she continued with a slightly sour face.

Jahrra couldn't begin to imagine what the richer part of town might look like.

"Kiniahn Kroi is built right up against the tip of that range, placed directly between the two canyons," Scede added, seeing Jahrra's somewhat puzzled look.

The cobbled road followed Itah Creek around the hills and continued westward. Jahrra gaped at the huge mansions nestled against the wooded hillside, and as the white carriage train moved farther up the canyon, the houses gradually became larger and more ornate. Many of them were built right up into the side of the hills, making Jahrra wonder if there might be an entire second set of rooms reaching deep inside the heart of the earth.

# The Legend of Oescienne – The Finding

About thirty minutes after the wagons entered the canyon, the beautiful houses suddenly ceased and the caravan passed through a massive gate. Jahrra leaned out of the window once again and glanced at the buggies ahead of their own.

They were now traveling up a long cobbled road lined with evenly manicured holly bushes, all of which were adorned with bright red berries and glossy white and green leaves. The western-most tip of the canyon was draped in shade by the tall hills and the winter air here stayed hidden from the sun, remaining cold and unmoving. The world seemed frozen and secluded here and Jahrra sunk back into her seat, feeling like she was intruding in a land where she wasn't welcome.

The wagon train clattered along steadily for what seemed like hours until finally Jahrra, Gieaun and Scede felt their comfortable carriage slow to a halt.

The three friends stood up and peered shyly through the window on one side of their coach. At the end of the long drive there stood the most beautiful house Jahrra had ever seen. The drive circled around a great fountain and two massive, arching staircases led up to the second story.

The mansion itself was four stories tall and was built close to the eastern curve of the canyon's end. Jahrra blinked as she registered the color of the great stone house. It was a deep butter color, with a dark goldenrod tile roof speckled with moss and lichen. She'd always loved yellow, but now she wondered if she would ever consider it a happy color again.

# A Party, a Prank, and a Near Death Experience

The eight carriages all came to a crunching stop over the gravel drive and several men and women dressed in clean but simple uniforms came rushing out to help the children into the main house. Jahrra suddenly felt very nervous and glanced warily at her two friends, both donning a bewildered look. They purposely waited for all of their other classmates to line up behind the twins and proceed, entranced as they were, up the side staircase and into the main entrance hall. The awkward trio joined in at the back of the group, keeping their distance and hoping that the other children would be too hypnotized by their surroundings to notice the Nesnan and her traitorous friends.

As soon as they entered the huge, heavy double oak doors (opened by servants of course), the children were engulfed in a wave of color, sound and movement. Elegant and beautiful women were gathered in circles or sitting on overstuffed couches chattering away like hens. Some dashed across the room several times, whispering secrets to their friends only to burst into red-faced giggling when listening to the reply.

The men, smoking pipes and dressed in the most ornate clothing Jahrra had ever seen, didn't even notice the children come in. She found it peculiar that the men stood around talking openly to one another in the middle of the room while the women took a much more secretive approach to their style of conversation.

"I wonder if they're supposed to do that," Gieaun whispered once Jahrra pointed the strange scene out to her.

Nevertheless, the fancy patrons seemed to be enjoying themselves, eating refreshments and drinking what Jahrra could only guess was sparkling wine. The aromatic buzz of conversation was only interrupted by the light, cheery music floating in from another room.

Jahrra pulled her attention away from the busy environment and looked more closely at her surroundings. It was a large space, complete with a vaulted ceiling and a half-moon staircase leading to the upper levels of the house. The interior of the mansion was tiled with white marble, and many fine paintings and tapestries hung in the great hall, their rich blues, greens, reds, oranges and blacks contrasting with the pale lemon walls. The windows were beautiful as well; thousands of small diamond shaped panes, glittering like rough sheets of ice in the afternoon light, filled the space above the stairs from ceiling to floor.

The ceiling itself was exquisite, complete with an enormous crystal chandelier hanging from its center. Jahrra wondered quietly if the castle on the Sloping Hill had once looked like this so many centuries ago. She craned her neck to see the entirety of the amazing, high-domed ceiling. A mural told a story with the characters boldly painted, but before she could discern what the tale was about she felt a tug at her arm. It was Gieaun and she was pointing over to where the left wing of the crescent staircase began.

# A Party, a Prank, and a Near Death Experience

Ellysian stood there with all of their classmates gathered around her. Jahrra grimaced as the girl shouted over the din.

"Now, you all must come see mine and Eydeth's rooms. We have the finest bedding and furniture father could find."

She said something more, but Jahrra made no effort to listen. The last thing she wanted to do was see the twins' rooms. Gieaun and Scede agreed with her, and they decided to head in the opposite direction towards a glass door next to the other side of the staircase that opened out onto a nice shaded terrace. The three friends wove their way through the boisterous crowd, not worried about alarming the adults who were too intent on their noisy gossip to notice three wayward children.

They stepped out onto the stone terrace and saw that it was really a raised patio with the creek flowing below it. The patio cut into the side of the rocky wall of the canyon, creating a small, protected grotto. Several chairs and a heavy stone table stood within the small alcove, and feathery ferns and other shade-loving plants added an extra soft, delicate touch.

A carved marble railing enclosed the patio, and marble benches and statues stood in perfect harmony with the many curves and turns of the terrace. Jahrra, Gieaun and Scede took a seat on one of the benches facing into the canyon. Once settled, Jahrra breathed in the fresh air and plucked lightly at her skirt, grateful to be away from the stuffy drove of people inside.

"Well," Scede breathed, tugging on the sleeves of his tunic to mimic Jahrra, "if we stay out of the way, we may just survive tonight."

Gieaun and Jahrra nodded in agreement. Jahrra sighed deeply then glanced towards the western edge of the courtyard, only to notice a simple staircase leading down to a path running above the creek. It was a narrow path and it trailed away behind a curve in the canyon's wall. She immediately got up and headed towards it.

"Where are you going?" asked Gieaun with a perplexed look on her face.

"There's a path down there. Come on, let's follow it. We'll definitely be out of everyone's way if we do."

Gieaun and Scede gladly followed Jahrra, hoping the adults really hadn't noticed them before.

The pre-occupied Resai men and women may not have noticed the Nesnan girl and her two Resai friends, but Eydeth had. As they made their way up the narrow path, Eydeth watched them from the tall window at the top of the stairs.

He'd lingered behind as his sister led their classmates to her room. He'd been on his way up behind his classmates, but something had flittered in the corner of his eye, and when he turned to see what it had been, he caught sight of Jahrra, Gieaun and Scede wandering off onto the terrace. A cold smile crossed his lips and as he watched them disappear farther into the canyon, he thought of a way to humiliate Jahrra once again.

# A Party, a Prank, and a Near Death Experience

❀ ❀ ❀

The path crawled snake-like along the edge of the rocky tributary that fed Itah Creek. Every few yards or so, the stone path would widen, creating a nice little overlook with benches for sitting. The trail itself rose and fell along the way, and in some places it was only a few feet above the creek where in others it was much steeper. The hillside on the opposite side of the creek was shaded by low oaks, and the ground below them was carpeted with the crimson leaves of the now naked poison ivy branches clinging to the tree trunks.

Jahrra grinned as she and her friends traipsed down the tidy gravel trail, the crunching of their boots overwhelming the quieter sounds of the canyon. The cool taste of frosty air and the subtle voice of the bubbling stream below followed the trio as they gradually moved farther and farther away from the house, now standing like a beacon in the golden light of the late afternoon sun. Every now and then they would pause to gaze into the deep pools beside the creek, dropping small pebbles in each one and counting the tiny fish as they scattered for cover.

A half hour after they left the great house they came around a final bend in the path to find themselves at the canyon's end, or rather, the canyon's beginning. A narrow ribbon of black water, fenced in by a path of green ferns and moss on either side of it, trickled down the steep hillside and collected in a large pool below.

Jahrra, followed by Gieaun then Scede, walked down to the edge of the pond where the path spilled onto a stone patio surrounding the pool. More stone benches and statues adorned the dark corner of the gully, and when Jahrra looked up to locate the top of the waterfall, she frowned. Thick, green oak branches completely blocked the view.

"I bet this pond is deeper after a good rainstorm," Scede commented as he tapped the shallow water with the bottom of his boot.

"I bet it makes a great swimming pool in the summer, too," Gieaun added, plopping down on a nearby bench.

Jahrra squatted down next to Scede and reached out to touch the surface of the water. It seemed so smooth, so perfect; she wondered if touching it would be like touching the surface of a mirror.

"Don't even think about moving any closer," said a cold voice from above.

Jahrra yanked her hand back in surprise while Scede turned quickly to see who had spoken. It was Eydeth, of course, with what appeared to be the entire class crowded behind him. Jahrra was stunned, and although her heart echoed loudly in her ears, it didn't block out the voice she heard next.

"Eydeth, why on Ethöes did you leave the party to walk out here . . ?" Ellysian said irritably as she pushed her way through the throng to confront her brother. When she saw

Jahrra, Gieaun and Scede, however, her gaze of annoyance turned to a one of distaste.

"What are *you* three doing down here?" she demanded, thrusting her hands on her hips.

"We just wanted to get some fresh air," Gieaun said timidly. "We'll be heading back now . . ."

She moved to stand up from the bench she'd been sitting on, but Eydeth's movement in her direction forced her back down.

"Oh no," he said in a chillingly silent voice, a dry smile creeping across his face, "you've seen our secret swimming pond. The only way you can leave now is to fulfill a challenge."

Gieaun turned white as a ghost, looking slightly blue in the waning light, and Jahrra felt Scede tense up beside her. It was one thing to defy the twins at school but it was quite another to do so here. This was their territory; they were in control and Jahrra had no idea how to get out of this mess.

She stood and glared at Eydeth, despising him more than ever. "What 'secret swimming pond'? We saw no sign warning us off. We did nothing wrong."

She crossed her arms and waited for him to say something.

Eydeth turned slightly pink, and as their classmates started to fill in around him, he continued on.

"Do you think you can just walk past all of us then?" he demanded, waving nonchalantly at the small crowd surrounding him. "You must compete against me in a contest. You have to beat me to the top of the waterfall if you want to leave here unharmed. If you fail, you and your friends will spend the night out here."

Jahrra was horrified. She was certain that Eydeth could enforce such a threat at his own home. She glanced at Scede, and then Gieaun. Scede looked like he might have lost his ability to speak and Gieaun looked like she was about to faint.

Jahrra turned her eyes back on the malicious boy standing in front of her.

"Alright, I'll do it," she said, starting to feel angry and frightened at the same time.

The crowd began sniggering and whispering amongst themselves, the twins looked wickedly pleased, and Gieaun and Scede looked like they were melting from the inside out.

"Jahrra!" Gieaun hissed. "You can't do this, you'll fall for sure! And your clothes! What are you thinking!?"

Jahrra was afraid Gieaun would go into hysterics, but she refused to back down. She shrugged off her jacket and handed it to a rather stunned Scede, then pushed up her loose sleeves and stared up the face of the water-slick cliff with stony determination.

It didn't look *too* daunting. The tops of the oak trees grew right up against the wall about twenty feet up, and the top of the falls couldn't be much higher than that. Jahrra raked her eyes over the damp wall in front of her and saw a system of gnarled roots protruding from stone and soil. She smiled weakly, knowing that these would make the climb easier.

The two competitors moved towards the base of the narrow fall, Jahrra doing her best to step on the large stones protruding from the pool so that she wouldn't get her boots wet. She risked a glance at her friends. Gieaun had managed to snatch her suede jacket out of Scede's hands and was now clutching it in a very distressful way, her brother beside her looking just as anxious.

Jahrra glared over at Eydeth. He looked her up and down as if she were something unsightly, then turned his eyes towards the canopy above. Everyone crowded in closer to the scene and Ellysian stepped up onto the closest bench, raising one white-gloved arm.

"On my signal," she piped, sounding quite pleased. "Ready, set, CLIMB!" she roared and the two children grasped the closest root and began pulling themselves up.

Everyone began cheering excitedly, and Jahrra had to take a deep breath to clear her mind. Many of the children were cheering for Eydeth but most of them were just making noise.

"Come on, Jahrra!" Scede managed as his sister cringed.

The climbing proved slightly harder than she had thought and she lost her footing many times on the slippery rocks. Despite her slow progress, however, she was able to keep up with Eydeth, who seemed to be struggling just as much as she was.

By the time the two were within five feet of the highest oak branches, Jahrra was ahead. She pushed her way through the leaves and discovered that the top of the canyon was only another ten feet or so away. *Alright,* she thought to herself, gritting her teeth, *you can do this, you can beat him.*

She heard the crowd gasp slightly as she pushed her way through the leaves before Eydeth, smiling a little as she picked up her pace. A few moments later Eydeth rustled through the canopy behind her and the cheering increased. Jahrra risked a look back and saw that he was within three feet of her boots. She also noticed that they had been shielded from view by a thick screen of leaves.

The sun had already gone down over the western wall of the valley, and Jahrra shivered from the cooling temperature seeping into her bones. The icy water trickling down the wall had successfully soaked through her blouse and skirt, coating her skin with goose bumps and causing her to shiver. She quickly regained her focus and continued to pull herself upward, despite her numb fingers. She was almost there, a few more feet and she would be the winner.

Jahrra smiled triumphantly as she reached for the final hand hold that would aid her past the top of the cliff. Just as her fingers grazed the rough tree root, however, something tugged on her foot and she slipped, losing her grip and falling off balance. She glanced over her shoulder and saw that Eydeth was just beneath her, his right hand wrapped tightly around her ankle.

"Hey!" she shouted in frustration as Eydeth tugged again.

He was tightly wedged against the cliff with one arm hooked around a sturdy root, the other free to pull on Jahrra. He yanked again, even harder this time, forcing Jahrra to grab onto a clump of weeds, gratefully anchored securely to the soil. She hung from the side of the cliff like a fish on a hook, her now free feet kicking and scraping against the rock wall.

"What're you doing!?" she screeched, starting to feel herself panic.

"Do you really think this was about a competition?" Eydeth breathed. "Please, I wish you weren't even here, so now you're going to pay."

With a glint of malice in his eyes, Eydeth reached out, grabbed hold of Jahrra's ankle once more, and jerked down one last time.

With a stifled scream her grip failed, her icy fingers unable to hold on any longer. Jahrra grasped desperately for anything that might stop her from falling down the canyon wall, but it was no use. All she could get her hands on were the slicks of muddy earth that had been dampened by the fall and a few larger roots that snapped as she caught them.

She slid down the cliff face at an alarming rate, becoming muddied and scratched as she did so. She crashed into the canopy and broke through, screaming in fear. Just as she prepared herself for impact, something caught her leg and jerked her to a stop, throwing her violently backward to hang upside down fifteen feet above the ground. She glanced up and noticed her entire leg, from the knee down, was entangled in a net of branches. Jahrra swallowed past her tight throat as she tried to fight back the coming tears and overwhelming nausea.

"JAHRRA!!!"

The combined voices pronouncing her name sounded familiar but so far away.

Gieaun and Scede sprinted toward the cold, hard paving just below their best friend. The sight of Jahrra falling suddenly through the tree tops and then becoming caught in the trees' bows was enough to give them each a heart attack.

Jahrra simply hung where she was, too stunned to register what was being said to her.

"Jahrra! Jahrra! Oh no, are you alright!?" Gieaun was screeching in panic, still clinging to the jacket as if this would offer her some comfort.

Jahrra groaned and tried to piece together what had just happened. She looked around and saw that she was hanging in mid-air; she hadn't hit the ground. A wave of relief rushed over her, but she soon realized she was stuck, and when the shock of the ordeal gradually passed, she felt the pain slowly crawling up her leg. *Oh no, I've broken something!* she thought despairingly.

# A Party, a Prank, and a Near Death Experience

*Master Hroombra is going to kill me!* But she knew she couldn't stay there, hanging and dripping muddy water in misery forever.

"I n-need help-p-p ge-eh-etting d-down-n-n!" she chattered through clenched teeth and tears of pain, her frustration and embarrassment growing by the minute.

She was becoming light headed from her upside-down position and her shin felt like it was on fire. She blinked at the strange distorted world below her and wondered if it looked strange because of how she was hanging or because of the sensation of blood filling up her head. She did notice the entire class gathered around beneath her, looking glum and slightly worried.

"Quick! Someone go get help at the house!" Scede yelled to those surrounding them.

Two ginger-haired children, a brother and sister Jahrra recognized from coming to her aid before, hurried off to fetch help. Fifteen agonizing minutes later they returned with a servant from the house.

"Sorry it took so long, but he was the only one who would listen to us! Everyone else was too busy dancing and talking!" the boy yelled up at Jahrra.

She could barely see the people standing below her through her blurred vision, but she spotted the two children who'd run off to fetch help and a taller, dark-haired young man standing next to them. It was funny how friendly and concerned everyone became when she was in actual danger, Jahrra thought bitterly.

The young man promptly told Jahrra to hold on just a bit longer and began to climb the tree as fast as he could. Jahrra was comforted that help was finally here, but she was growing cold and tired, and her leg was throbbing, her head pounding.

What bothered her most, however, was the thought of what Hroombra would say when he saw her. She'd ruined the nice new clothes he'd gone to so much trouble to get for her and she'd let her anger and stubbornness get the better of her. She felt hot, fresh tears forming in her eyes again and knew that they were not meant for the pain and humiliation she felt at losing to Eydeth. They were for the shame she felt for letting Hroombra down.

The young man reached Jahrra in no time and managed to gently untangle her, carrying her back down the tree like an over-sized rag doll. Once on solid ground, he set her down to see if she could stand on her leg, and surprisingly she could, but not without a little help.

Everyone was gathered around to gawk at her as if she had narrowly escaped death, and Jahrra was starting to think that she had. She shivered and lowered her head, feeling suffocated by all of the staring faces. Her hair had come loose from Gieaun's earlier efforts and it was now tangled with twigs and dead leaves. Her palms and arms were covered in cuts and abrasions beneath the dirt and grime, and there was a raw scrape running down her shin.

Gieaun pushed her way through the crowd and flung her arms around Jahrra, her face shining with tears. The force of it knocked her off balance and both girls fell to the ground, adding a few more bruises to Jahrra's already bedraggled state.

Jahrra barely noticed. The entire unfolding of events had her dazed and all she wanted to do was get to somewhere warm, even if it meant being in a stuffy mansion full of disapproving, haughty party guests.

Scede came over and pulled them both up, looking very relieved that his friend was finally safe from immediate harm. Jahrra murmured a weak thanks as the young servant draped a blanket around her shoulders. Once she was able to walk without collapsing, the entire group began the journey back, Jahrra in the middle with the young man on one side and Scede and Gieaun on the other to help. Everyone clamored timidly around Jahrra like guilty marauders waiting to catch a wobbly vase before it crashed to the ground.

As they began their slow progress back towards the house, it was clear that Jahrra had become the center of attention. It was no surprise, then, that nobody noticed Eydeth's form climbing carefully down the canyon wall except for his sister. Once both his feet were on level ground Ellysian stalked up to him in that obscene dress of hers and demanded, "What on Ethöes just happened?! Did you push her or did she fall?"

Eydeth brushed off his mud-stained pants and tunic and turned to his sister with a sneer.

"I pulled her down, of course."

Ellysian was taken aback and donned a patronizing look.

"What?" demanded Eydeth, annoyed at his sister's condescending glare.

"Oh, I'm not disappointed that she fell, that was a nice little trick you just came up with," she answered haughtily, crossing her arms smoothly.

"Well, what's the problem then?" Eydeth growled.

"If mother and father find out what really happened . . ." began Ellysian angrily.

"They won't!" Eydeth cut her off. "And if someone tells them, I'll just say it isn't true. Who're they going to believe, those three Nesnan-lovers or their own children?"

Eydeth looked like a prize rooster who'd just lost the first fight of his life and Ellysian would have laughed at him, but it wasn't worth the effort.

After thinking about the situation for a while, Ellysian saw that her brother was right. She wasn't about to concede however, without adding her own thoughts. She screwed up her mouth in an unpleasant smirk and said, "Too bad your plan completely backfired."

"How do you mean?" Eydeth asked, pausing in his attempt to scrape off the layers of moss and icy mud. Jahrra may not have been hurt, but she had been ridiculed.

# A Party, a Prank, and a Near Death Experience

"Now everyone is sympathizing with *her*, and she'll most definitely tell them the whole story. Mother and father we may be able to fool, but everyone else knows how much we despise the Nesnan and her friends."

Eydeth stood up straight, dark, muddy water dripping from his hands, and narrowed his eyes. Slowly he began to see the truth in what his sister said and his expression turned from disappointment to anger.

"Don't worry," Ellysian added as they walked back to their house in the growing darkness, "we'll find a way to get back at her, somehow."

# -Chapter Fifteen-

# Friends in Unexpected Places

The sight of Jahrra being half carried, half dragged back to the house by her friends and one of the servants must have been quite a sight for the lord and lady of the great house to behold. Fortunately, they were too busy indulging their adult guests to notice not only the large party now approaching, but also the fact that they had been short twenty or so children for quite some time now.

The knowledge that she might've been missed didn't bother Jahrra one bit. In fact, she was greatly pleased by it. The last thing she wanted to do was draw more attention to herself by causing a scene among so many disapproving people. The large, strangely-silent mob stopped at the bottom of the staircase leading up to the back patio, eyes still wide with shock from what had happened in the canyon.

The young man who had come to the rescue turned, left Jahrra to lean against Scede, and addressed the other children, "Now, I'm going to take this young lady into the kitchens so she can clean up. I suggest the rest of you return to the party and enjoy the rest of your night."

The Nesnan man, who didn't look much older than Jahrra's oldest schoolmates, had a kindly tone of voice and seemed genuinely concerned about Jahrra's recovery. He also seemed quite aware of how this scene would be received by the host and hostess. Jahrra had a feeling that he knew the master and mistress of the house would be more horrified at the idea of a girl covered in mud than at the fact she'd nearly been killed.

The young servant looked over the children once again, his eyes dark and his mouth set sternly. He clasped his hands casually in front of him, as if patiently waiting for an unruly party guest to finish a long-winded complaint. It seemed to work because gradually the school children began shuffling their way up the stairs, leaving only Scede and Gieaun remaining.

"Now, how about it?" he asked, jerking his head toward the stairs after the other children.

"She's our best friend," Gieaun said, tears swimming in her eyes as she hugged Jahrra's overly-abused jacket. "Can't we go with her?"

She looked up at the young man with pleading eyes, and he sighed, dropping all pretenses. "Of course, of course. I just hope you three don't mind spending the rest of the evening in the kitchen with us lowly servants." He smiled warmly and Jahrra cheered up a bit.

The young man went on to explain to them that the two children who came and got him told him all about what had happened.

"It just isn't right, treating people so. I know how you feel."

He patted Jahrra on the shoulder and instead of heading up the stairs they took a narrow stone path leading under the raised terrace and across a narrow footbridge over the creek.

"Where exactly are we going?" asked Scede cautiously.

"To the lowest level of the house, where the kitchens and servants' quarters are," he replied. "Don't worry. The partygoers won't venture down here. You'll have a chance to clean up and get something to eat. And if you wish to stay, you're welcome to partake in our own humble celebration of the Solsticetide."

He smiled down at the younger boy and Scede returned the gesture weakly.

Jahrra thought her rescuer had a charming smile and although his face showed that he was tired, his dark brown eyes laughed when he grinned. At the other end of the footbridge there was another stone deck, one that was attached to the north wall of the house. The young man led the children up to a wooden door and knocked at it strongly. A few seconds later a short, rather round woman jerked the door open in alarm.

"Lahnehn! Where ya' been? We been lookin' all over for ya'!" she exclaimed.

# Friends in Unexpected Places

She seemed quite perturbed and relieved at the same time. Her face was pink and shining with sweat as if she'd been slaving over a stove all day. Her light brown hair was streaked evenly with gray and was tied back tightly in a bun, all except for a crown of lose tendrils that floated around her tired face. Her brow was furrowed and her small russet eyes were narrowed.

"Many sorrys Mrs. Addie, but you see I was called away for an emergency of sorts," the young man explained guiltily as he gestured towards Jahrra. "This young lady was enticed up the falls at the end of the canyon by our young master, and she fell only to be caught by a patch of oak branches."

"Oh, my!" the older lady retorted.

Her stern demeanor softened for a heartbeat but hardened once again as she placed her hands on her hips.

"That youngin' is too brash I tell ya', far too brash gettin' others into trouble. Come in dearie, we'll fix ya' up. I'll call in some of the younger 'uns to get ya' cleaned up and then we'll fetch ya' somethin' to eat. Thank goo'ness for the oak tho'. Ethöes herself musta been watchin' out for ya'."

The woman shoved her sleeves farther up her plump arms and fluttered off in a flurry of skirts while the young man led the children into what could only be the kitchen. The warmth of the room was welcoming to Jahrra, who was dripping and freezing from the cold mud that coated the entire front of her body.

As she stood waiting to thaw out, she scanned the large room now surrounding her. There were three long, heavy wooden tables stretched across the floor, all of which were covered in food awaiting preparation. Four great stone ovens were set deep in the wall at the far end of the hall with a doorway and staircase, presumably leading to the upper levels of the house, placed on either side of them. On the right hand side of the kitchen was a great basin for washing and preparing food, and on both sides of this basin was a door leading to another room.

The kitchen was buzzing quietly with the sounds of boiling water and simmering soups, but it wasn't yet clattering and roaring with the clamor caused by busy chefs trying to get dinner ready on time. Jahrra sighed sleepily, detecting the subtle flavors of fresh herbs and spices hanging in the warm air.

A few minutes later Mrs. Addie returned with two younger women, one skinny and sickly looking, the other tall and plump with smallish eyes. Both women looked worn down, but they had kind faces and managed to cheerfully lead Jahrra through one of the two doors near the gargantuan wash basin.

Jahrra stepped easily into the other room, realizing instantly that it was the living quarters for the house servants. She counted a dozen or so rows of beds with only curtains to give privacy, and just one large window on the far end of the room. Under the window there was an area with a tub for bathing and washing up. Jahrra stood grazing her eyes over the walls, floor and ceiling while the women hauled in hot water, soap, towels and spare clothes. Once the tub was filled, they left Jahrra to soak in the steaming, fragrant water.

"But my clothes, what'll I do with them?" she asked sullenly before the servants left.

"Don't worry lass, we'll put 'em to soak. Maybe they'll be all well after all," said the thin woman, smiling warmly.

After she was dry and bandaged, Jahrra returned to the kitchen to find Gieaun and Scede sitting below the great window next to the staircase leading up to the second floor. The window was recessed into the wall with a wide ledge, perfect for cooling an army of pies or providing a nice place to sit and take a break from kitchen work.

The window looked out over the creek and although it wasn't constructed of the beautiful tiny, diamond-paned glass of the upper level of the house, it was still majestic in its simple design. The walls on either side of it were draped in garlands of holly, ivy, pine branches and mistletoe and trimmed with delicate gold ribbon. Jahrra smiled at the sight, grateful to be in this wonderful place and not upstairs.

Gieaun and Scede were sitting on cushions that someone had acquired for them and were now watching the creek run by. Once they caught sight of Jahrra, however, they immediately jumped up from their relaxed position and nearly crushed her lungs with their hugs.

Once settled, Jahrra informed them of what really happened at the top of the waterfall. Gieaun had to help her hold Scede back when he tried to march up the stairs in search of Eydeth.

"I'll kill him!" he breathed.

Shortly after Jahrra assured her friends she would be fine, the young servant who'd helped her earlier came out of one of the rooms beside the basin carrying a bundle of blankets.

"I know they aren't much, but with the fire from the ovens they should keep you warm."

He grinned and dropped the bundle on top of them, causing them to laugh for the first time that day.

"Now," he continued with a sly grin, "I've got to go check on the guests right now, but later I hope to see you three drinking cocoa and cream and listening to the tales and music of these fine people down here."

He winked and left them just as the kitchen grew busy with life. There were many servants, young and old, men and women, of all shapes and sizes, but all Nesnan from the looks of it. There were five chefs and bakers, two men and three women, who prepared and cooked the food. The meat that had already been roasting when the three friends first arrived was now being removed from the spits and cut and placed on ornate dishes. Soups and stews were ladled out, fresh baked bread sliced and buttered, fruits and vegetables roasted and sugared. Puddings, pies and cakes were put into the ovens or arranged beautifully on plates.

The clanking and scuffling of utensils and feet upon the worn stone floor filled the air and blended with the hum of voices and the minute crackle of the oven fires. Jahrra's mouth began watering as the aroma of roasting meat and vegetables, creamy soups and baking pastries spread throughout the room. She leaned into her soft pillow with a contented sigh and wrapped the thick quilt more tightly around her. Her leg was feeling much better now that she had soaked it in the hot water, and the steaming tea that one of the kitchen workers handed her was easing the pain in her head. The only discomfort the three friends felt was their growing hunger, made worse by the tantalizing aromas of the feast.

After several minutes, Jahrra's rescuer returned from upstairs quite flustered, almost overlooking the three children he'd left on the windowsill.

"Oh, forgive me," he said once he finally noticed them. "Some of those high society types can be quite frustrating. Sing and dance for them indeed!"

The children giggled into their blankets and the young man soon forgot the rude guests.

"I'm terribly sorry, I never introduced myself," he said lightly once the children recovered from their amusement. "I'm called Lahnehn, and you three are?"

Jahrra, Gieaun and Scede introduced themselves in turn, shaking hands and smiling.

"Pleased to meet you all," Lahnehn remarked. "Now, I can only assume that you're growing quite hungry?"

They all nodded vigorously and Lahnehn invited them to join him in making a plate from the food on the tables. Along the way, he introduced them to the many servants and cooks, all of whom were delighted to have such young visitors in the kitchens. Once the four had their food they returned to the windowsill to watch the twilight sky turn inky blue. Jahrra, Gieaun and Scede sat back onto their cushions and Lahnehn pulled up a stool.

"So, where do you three come from?" he asked as they began to eat their meal of roast turkey, herbed potatoes, wild berry casserole and spiced apple cider.

"We come from the Great Sloping Hill to the south, but we go to school in Aldehren," Scede replied around a mouthful of stuffing.

"Ah, and this is how you became classmates of my young masters then?" Lahnehn commented with arched eyebrows, "How do you like school?"

"It's horrible," replied Jahrra truthfully. "I'd much rather learn all my lessons from Master Hroombra."

"Master Hroombra? I've never heard of a teacher by that name." Lahnehn stabbed at a few chunks of golden potatoes with his fork, and then turned his head back to Jahrra, waiting for her answer.

"He's my guardian," Jahrra replied, then added confidently, "he's a great dragon who knows everything there is to know."

Lahnehn looked up quickly, choking somewhat on his food. "A dragon? Here in the southern part of Oescienne? I've never seen such a thing!"

The look on his face was a mixture of delight and surprise.

"Do you travel south of the Raenyan Valley often?" Jahrra queried rather casually.

"Nay, once or twice a year I'll travel into Aldehren or to the coast, but that's as far as I go. I mainly stay here or visit Kiniahn Kroi."

"Well," interjected Jahrra rather pertly, "Master Hroombra rarely travels also. He can no longer fly and walks slowly, so he mainly stays at the Castle Guard Ruin where I live."

Jahrra lost her gumption when she suddenly remembered why she was in the kitchen in the first place and not up in the main part of the house. She'd let Hroombra down, and her dread and guilt suddenly returned at the memory.

Lahnehn sensed a change in her demeanor and tried to continue the conversation casually. "You live with a dragon? That must be quite interesting. What's he like?"

"He's kind, and is patient with me when I make mistakes. He'll not be happy with what I did today," Jahrra answered sadly, suddenly uninterested in her dinner.

Lahnehn realized he'd brought up a sore subject and tried to redeem himself. "Don't worry, he'll understand. He may seem angry at first, but it's only because he cares for your safety. Come now, let's talk about something else."

And so Gieaun and Scede took their turn at conversing and briefly told Lahnehn about their lives while Lahnehn told about his, how he was from the city of Glordienn to the east and how he'd once been a slave.

"I worked on a farm there with my family, and the man who owned my family had a bad crop and was forced to sell me. I knew as a slave I had no rights, but my master always treated my family well, so I tried not to be angry with him.

"I feared that my new master would be terrible, and when I was taken to the auction in Glordienn, I was bought by a rich stranger I'd never seen before. He wore a hooded cloak, and as soon as he bought me he told me that I was free, all the while not showing his face. He said he was a wealthy merchant who inherited most of his money and spent it freeing what enslaved people of Ethöes he could. He gave me a job on one of his merchant ships and I spent a few years at sea, saving what money I earned to set my family free.

"After those few years, I returned to Oescienne to find safer work here. My benefactor wished me luck and told me there was a city to the west of Glordienn called Kiniahn Kroi where I could find work as a house servant and make a decent wage. So here I am, no longer a slave and eternally grateful to the man who gave me the means to free my family."

Jahrra felt her spirit suddenly lifted by Lahnehn's story. She always despised the slave traders and the slave market, but she was glad to hear this story of hope. She also felt strangely disturbed by the story. As soon as Lahnehn had spoken of a hooded figure that had liberated him from slavery, she immediately thought of the stranger that had so often entered her dreams. Could this be the same man? Was she somehow connected to a freedom defender?

The eager questions of her two friends pushed Jahrra's secret thoughts to the back of her mind.

"Was the man who rescued you another Nesnan, or Resai? Ooooh, maybe he's a rich elfin king from the east!" Gieaun clapped her hands excitedly, her green eyes bright with delight.

"I don't know for sure," Lahnehn answered, mussing his black hair with his free hand. "He never told me his name, and I never saw him without his hood on. Now that you mention it though, he did act as an elf would."

"How does an elf act exactly?" asked Scede seriously, setting his empty plate down on the windowsill, its dull clink against stone having no effect on the kitchen's simmering bustle.

"Well," Lahnehn mused, mimicking Scede's action with his own dish, "this man stood in a rather dignified manner without coming off as smug. He never spoke unnecessarily and he had an aura of class that can only be natural, not learned."

Scede nodded his head, apparently accepting this answer as satisfactory.

After some more discussion of whom the mysterious liberator was ("Maybe a Nephaarene!" Gieaun squealed excitedly. "Why else would he hide his head in a foreign land?"), a bell was rung signaling the end of the banquet. Lahnehn and the three children had been so absorbed in conversation that they'd missed the hectic run of dinner to the upper levels and were now invited to take some dessert. Lahnehn rose and picked up one of the small pies and carried it over to the windowsill. He then grabbed four plates and some spare forks and the new friends happily delved into the fruit filled pastry.

As they ate, the cooks and servants began cleaning up the kitchen, recruiting the help of Jahrra, Gieaun, Scede and Lahnehn when the pie was gone. They splashed happily in the hot, soapy water as they were handed plates, bowls and utensils to wash and rinse. The cleaning only took about a half hour and as they were finishing up, the music suddenly grew louder upstairs signaling to the party goers it was time for dancing.

"That's the signal for our party to begin, too," said Lahnehn, winking once again as he disappeared through one of the doors beside the sink.

# Friends in Unexpected Places

He returned a few minutes later with a banjo. Another male servant left and returned with a fiddle. One of the women pulled a harmonica from her apron and another pulled out a flute. The group of musicians grabbed wooden stools and climbed atop a section of raised stone floor that was situated against the back wall. Everyone gathered together and lifted and carried the large tables to the sides of the room, clapping cheerfully once the instruments began peeling out a festive tune.

Jahrra, Gieaun and Scede climbed up onto one of the tables and began dancing with many of the maids and cooks. Even the reserved-looking butler replaced his serious scowl with a genuine grin as he leapt and jumped to the tune. The dying firelight from the ovens and the low glow of the candle-lined walls gave off just enough brightness to see everyone's cheery faces. Soon the whole room was dancing and clapping, thoroughly enjoying the rhythm of the banjo, fiddle, flute and harmonica.

Once everybody had worn themselves out from the merriment, the adults took turns telling stories. Gieaun, Scede and Jahrra returned to their windowsill lookout and, quite exhausted, lay down to rest as the tales were shared. Lahnehn put down his fiddle and fetched mugs of cocoa and cream for the children, pulling his stool up against the wall to listen to the folktales with them.

Gradually, the oven fires turned to smoldering coals and the atmosphere became much more inviting for the legends of lore. The maids and servants repeated accounts of faeries and magic from years past, while others told simple tales of good deeds and rewards. Some of the servants spoke of witches and goblins that roamed about during the winter time, often turning children stone cold as they slept in their warm beds.

Jahrra especially liked the tales about the pleasant spirits. These good spirits, or sephyres, showed themselves on Solsticetide Eve only if there was a full moon that night. They slept in the depths of the earth and were awoken when a portal, created by the light of the full moon casting a shadow behind a stone, opened to them. They brought good tidings and luck, and if anyone were fortunate enough to capture one or find one that was unable to make it back to their portal before moonset, they could keep it as a pet until the next full moon on Solstice Eve.

Jahrra listened in wonder as the storyteller described how a lost sephyre would take the guise of a white cat with rusty colored ears, paws and tail, and with eyes the color of deep amethyst. The sephyre would keep its finder free of misfortune for as long as the creature stayed in the mortal world.

Gieaun closed her eyes and donned a mystical smile, giving Jahrra a sudden, sneaking suspicion of what her friend wanted for Solsticetide. Jahrra herself imagined what it would be like to have a sephyre and wondered how it would help her evade Eydeth and Ellysian at school. She smiled once more and yawned, suddenly realizing just how tired she'd become since the festivities began. She grinned ironically as she recalled the unlikely day, the warm, comfortable room forcing her eyelids to droop.

She would've done anything to skip this ill-fated party, and up until the point that Lahnehn brought her into the kitchen, dripping and freezing miserably from Eydeth's attack, she'd held firmly to this opinion. Now she wished the night would never end. She smiled to herself as she finally gave in to the waves of drowsiness, imagining the faeries of the frost and the shadowy forms of sephyres dancing around her head.

It only seemed a second later when Jahrra was suddenly woken by a distantly familiar voice, "Jahrra, Gieaun, Scede, it's time for you to go now. The party's over upstairs and your classmates are returning home."

Jahrra tried to blink the sleep from her eyes as she looked up at Lahnehn. He was smiling but he looked tired from the celebration the night before. Jahrra sat up, feeling stiff and sore and suddenly remembered the ordeal from the day before. A wave of guilty dread flooded over her, but she shook it off as Gieaun and Scede slowly rose from their window perch. The early morning sun streamed through the windows, painting the empty kitchen with golden bars of light. Jahrra peeked out through the warped glass. The day looked very cold and the ground was coated with a layer of fresh, white frost.

"Uhhgh, did we sleep in?" Scede moaned, rubbing the back of his neck and fighting to keep his eyes open.

"Oh no, I made sure that you were up on time," Lahnehn responded. "We servants must be up early to tend to the masters and their guests." Lahnehn made a small face that forced Jahrra to stifle a giggle.

Mrs. Addie came bursting in through the door leading from the women's quarters. Jahrra, Gieaun, Scede and Lahnehn all jumped around, thoroughly surprised by the sudden spout of energy.

"Ohh!" she yelped. "Wha' are you children still doin' en here? The carriages are all lined up! Here young'n, quickly, get into your dress things, they're dry an' good as new."

Mrs. Addie quickly led Jahrra through the doors to the women's quarters and she was back in five minutes time, dressed in her clothes from the night before. They didn't look as bad as she'd imagined, but it was still obvious she'd been climbing up muddy walls in them. She looked warily to Gieaun and Scede, who'd climbed down from the windowsill in their own wrinkled clothing, but they just shrugged. *Oh great, I can't wait to get back home. I think I'd rather stay here under the wrath of the twins then have to tell Master Hroombra what happened,* Jahrra thought miserably as Mrs. Addie and Lahnehn hurried them up the stairs.

The two servants led them into the main entrance hall and wove them between couches draped with snoozing patrons from the night before. They managed to get through the front doors without too much trouble, but Jahrra suppressed a shiver of unease once there. The entire class was lined up outside, small groups climbing into each white carriage as they pulled up. No one seemed to notice the three friends and the young man and older woman who accompanied them, that is, everyone except Eydeth and Ellysian.

The twins stood at the top of the arched staircase, right beside the door they had just stepped through. As the three friends approached, the twins turned and looked at Jahrra. No, glared. Eydeth's stare was almost frightening and Ellysian's was poisonous.

Jahrra didn't let it get to her, however, and as she walked past the two children she turned and said, with an amount of bravado that surprised even her, "Thank you so much for a lovely evening. I don't think I've ever had such a great time before."

She smiled, gave a rough curtsey and even stifled a laugh when she saw the look of shock on both the twins' faces. She could feel Gieaun and Scede tense up next to her, but when she looked back, Mrs. Addie appeared rather smug and Lahnehn looked as if he'd just heard a particularly intriguing bit of gossip.

Jahrra and her friends were lucky once again to get the last carriage all to themselves. They waved goodbye to Lahnehn and Mrs. Addie, and told them, if by any stroke of luck they were invited back, they would be sure to come. As the caravan passed down the great drive and through the gates of the estate, the sun was just peering past the northern ridge of the canyon.

The morning was freezing, but the three companions were still glowing with the excitement from the night before. It had been wonderful, after all, and it was finally Solsticetide. Later on they would be enjoying the company of their families while exchanging the gifts of the season.

Jahrra used the long ride back to dream about the festivities to come. She'd made a bracelet out of shells for Gieaun and had finished an illustrated book of local birds for Scede, leaving many blank pages for him to add more. She'd crafted a cover out of dried fall leaves for the book and had spent months collecting the shells for Gieaun's bracelet.

For her friends' parents, she'd collected winterberries and made them into pies, a difficult thing to do when all she had to cook them in was the great fireplace in the Castle Guard Ruin. For Hroombra, she'd saved up old pieces of cloth all year to fashion a massive cushion for him to rest his forelegs on as he studied his documents and maps at the great desk in his study or by the fireplace. Gieaun and Scede had helped her with this, and it had taken her all year to finish.

Jahrra felt gloomy once again as she thought about Hroombra. She decided it would be better if she didn't tell him what really happened. She didn't want him to worry about how bad Eydeth and Ellysian had become; she felt that she could handle it on her own. She sighed and allowed herself to be distracted by the beautiful spectacle of Kiniahn Kroi on Solsticetide.

# Friends in Unexpected Places

"I never thought I'd be saying this," she said aloud after some time, "but I wish we could've stayed longer."

Gieaun and Scede nodded in agreement and soon started talking enthusiastically about all that had happened as the glistening city of Kiniahn Kroi disappeared into the distance.

The rest of the day passed as pleasantly as if the accident in the canyon hadn't happened at all. Hroombra, Nuhra and Kaihmen all accepted Jahrra's invented story of a slip into the creek while chasing after a frog. It helped that Gieaun and Scede backed her up.

After getting everyone settled into the Castle Guard Ruin, the girls got to work helping Nuhra prepare honeyed bread, potato cheese soup, herbed pork and winterberry salad. Scede and Kaihmen, with a little help from Hroombra, got the fire started and dragged blankets, pillows and old chairs into the main room. Later, Kaihmen pulled out his flute and played a few holiday songs.

As the food roasted, baked and simmered, the gifts were passed around. Hroombra loved his patchwork cushion, Gieaun adored her shell bracelet and Scede his book, and Kaihmen and Nuhra insisted on adding their pies to the upcoming feast. Jahrra was thrilled with the bulbs and seeds her friends gave her and cherished the small, brass telescope from Hroombra. After exchanging gifts the feast was ready, and once the children, adults and dragon were fed and lazing on the many layers of thick blankets, Hroombra began his traditional Solstice tale.

# The Legend of Oescienne – The Finding

Jahrra, Gieaun and Scede snuggled deeply into their quilt mattress as Hroombra took his place next to the giant fireplace. The logs had burned down to giant coals and the flames were no longer a crackling yellow but a whispering deep orange. Nuhra passed fragrant hot cider to the children and then carried away two cups for herself and Kaihmen, joining him on a chair against the western wall. The shadows cast by the fire made Hroombra look like a statue, and as he drew breath to start his tale, Jahrra could've sworn the flames of the fire danced higher for just a wink of time.

This year's tale was about the creation of the Great Rhiimian Gorge, a huge canyon that cut through the middle of the Norwester continent. Hroombra explained to his listeners that the Samenbi Desert once stretched from the western edge of the Aandhoul Plain to the eastern reaches of Terre Moeserre, before the gorge came to be.

Jahrra listened, eyes wide with wonder, as the Korli dragon described the stubborn dwarves of Doribas who risked everything to keep their treasure out of the hands of an evil king, hiding their gold and jewels in the great lake below their mines. She gasped when the king discovered their trick and broke the dam holding back the lake.

Scede clapped his hands over his gaping mouth when Hroombra described how the water spilled southward, taking the sunken treasure with it across the great desert as it cut a gash into the earth. Gieaun even whimpered slightly when they learned that the treasure eventually became the cursed gold dust dunes of Ehrann.

At the end of the tale the three children lay silent and still, allowing the tragic story to soak in. The king never got his hands on the coveted treasure, but the elves had lost everything in the process. The story made Jahrra think of what had happened with Eydeth. If she hadn't been so stubborn, if she'd only realized that Eydeth was baiting her, she would've left Kiniahn Kroi unscathed. *Oh well*, she thought with a mental sigh, *I won't let it happen again.*

Hroombra eventually broke the silence by offering to show everyone a map of Ethöes. Gieaun, Jahrra and Scede jumped at the idea and eagerly pored over the parchment the dragon unrolled in front of them. It was in the common language, Jahrra noticed; not a single letter of Kruelt in sight. She immediately pointed out the gorge to her friends.

Hroombra gazed down upon the three young children, all looking enchanted in the soft glow of the firelight. The great dragon smiled and breathed out a small laugh, enjoying their innocence for a moment, if only for a moment. These young ones knew nothing of the world that surrounded them, nothing at all, but he was almost glad of it.

Solsticetide evening carried on this way for a few more hours, with the children making up their own adventures across the map of Ethöes and the adults sitting back and reading or simply enjoying the peace. Jahrra brought out the maps she was working on and Gieaun and Scede happily started their own, Scede copying them down in the book Jahrra had given him.

*In two days she'll be eleven.* Hroombra sighed inwardly as he rested like a great guard dog by the fire. It seemed just yesterday Jahrra was a squirming little creature enveloped in cloth, and now, now she was only a few years away from becoming the distinguished young woman she was destined to be.

Hroombra shivered, grimacing at the thought of Jahrra growing up. The older she got, the sooner he would have to let her go. *No, I won't think of it that way. She'll not be lost,* the old dragon sternly told himself.

Outside the Ruin in the nearby wood an owl hooted across the clear, frozen, endless night. The stars stood witness to this scene, where a dragon once again taught the children of men and elves, and where Hroombra secretly hoped that Ethöes herself was watching as well.

# -Chapter Sixteen-
# Chasing Unicorns

The day looked very promising. The sun was out, the air was warm and it was the first day of the weekend. Jahrra lay in bed wondering what she would do this fine spring day. She yawned one last time and stretched herself out of bed, smiling gleefully at the thought of having the entire day free to do whatever she pleased. A chorus of birds camped out in her garden only added delightful charm to the mood of the morning.

Jahrra stood and moved to the window of her small room, looking out across the field to the stables. *Huh,* she thought with a grin, *I swear he can read my mind.*

Phrym had stuck his head out of his stable and was looking across the grounds right back at her, his face a tiny gray splash of color no bigger than her fingernail. He tossed his head a few times and let out a good natured whinny, weakened by the distance between them, but enthusiastic all the same. *You're right Phrym,* Jahrra thought dreamily, *a ride sounds just fine.*

# The Legend of Oescienne – The Finding

Things hadn't changed much since winter. The days had gradually grown warmer and longer, and school had started up again, but life still went along as it always did. The landscape had gradually turned from brown and grey to green and gold, and although it was still a few months off, Jahrra was already counting down the days to summer.

The schoolyard, not surprisingly, was still the last place she wanted to be. Eydeth and Ellysian were just as horrible as usual, but Eydeth seemed to have taken more of a role in terrorizing Jahrra. Before the mishap in Kiniahn Kroi, he usually just stood back and let his sister do all of the talking and sneering. But ever since the Solstice, Eydeth had been more willing to be the frontrunner in Jahrra's torment.

The increasing support from some of her classmates made it easier, but this only aggravated the twins more than ever. Granted, Jahrra's classmates weren't exactly walking over and befriending her, but they seemed to react less to the twins' remarks and often shot them small looks of disgust.

In fact, the siblings who'd run for help at the party in Kiniahn Kroi were the only ones who'd purposely approached Jahrra, Gieaun and Scede with offers of friendship. They introduced themselves as Pahrdh and Rhudedth one day after school and from that point on, they became good friends. Perhaps things were looking up after all.

Jahrra sighed and returned her thoughts to the present. *I won't think about school, I'm going to do something fun today,* she told herself.

She quickly dressed and headed toward the main room of the Castle Guard Ruin. Hroombra was already there, studying his books and manuscripts as usual. He peeked up over his reading glasses and smiled tiredly.

"Where are you off to this morning Jahrra?" he asked casually.

"Oh, just for a ride," she answered in all truthfulness. "Then maybe I'll go over to see what Gieaun and Scede are up to."

She often had something more mischievous in mind than a simple ride, but today she could explore with a clear conscience.

"Whatever you have planned, do be careful," Hroombra replied, looking back down at his work.

"Of course, I always am."

Jahrra quickly grabbed a few chunks of bread and cheese and packed a small lunch for later. As she crossed the uneven field that stood between the Ruin and the stables, she gratefully breathed in the fresh air. It was full of moisture and flavor and smelled and tasted of the rain that had fallen only a few days ago. Its scent was of warm, moist earth combined with the unique smell of new growth; the comforting aroma of spring.

She closed her eyes as she walked and happily imagined the field covered in blossoms, nodding and brushing softly against her skin; the bright yellow sun daisies, the blue and indigo lupines, the red paintbrush, the creams, butters, lavenders and violets of the wild pea plants, the deep yellow ochre of the fiddle necks, and the brilliant orange of the poppies. Jahrra began to skip as she got closer to the stable, and Phrym, sensing her gusto, joined in with a dancing of his head.

"Alright Phrym, I'm here," she laughed. "Ready for a ride?"

Phrym greeted her with a rough nuzzle, nearly knocking her over. She sighed in admiration, remembering when his shoulder came up to her own. Now it was above her head.

Jahrra saddled Phrym in record time and soon they were cantering across the lush fields, kicking up condensation and startled doves. Jahrra decided to take Phrym along the western edge of the Wreing Florenn and then on towards Wood's End Ranch. Gieaun and Scede were helping their parents with the sheep this weekend, and Jahrra figured they would be in one of the back pastures. Every spring, Nuhra and Kaihmen counted their stock and helped the ewes with the new lambs. Scede and Gieaun were now old enough to work alongside their parents and Jahrra wanted to lend a hand as well.

Jahrra kept Phrym a good hundred yards away from the looming forest as they traveled; she was still a bit leery of its deep shadows and strange quiet. When they were halfway to the ranch, Jahrra pulled back on the reins for a short rest. She and Phrym caught their breath and took in the wonderful scenery of the vast rolling fields spreading out all around them.

It was then that Jahrra had a sudden urge, almost as if someone were whispering into her mind, to glance over at the edge of the Wreing Florenn, only a stone's throw away. The tall trees looked suddenly peaceful, not menacing, in the bright, warm sunlight. Her whole life, Jahrra had been warned away from these woods. Kaihmen's tales and her own father's warnings from her earlier years had frightened her away from the Wreing Florenn. But now, seeing the silvery blue and green of the eucalyptus leaves and the cool, inviting depths of the wood, she had trouble curbing her sudden curiosity.

"I did tell Gieaun and Scede that I'd go in there someday, when I was braver," Jahrra whispered to Phrym while keeping her gaze glued to the forest's edge. With an unexpected spurt of gumption that seemed to come from nowhere she added, "Well, I feel brave now. How about you Phrym?"

Phrym let out a nicker of apprehension as Jahrra slowly led him towards the forest's edge, her eyes snared within its depths as if she were under a trance.

"It's alright Phrym, we won't go in too far," she encouraged, patting his neck gently.

They slowly approached the edge of the trees and Jahrra let out a quiet gasp when she noticed that their branches were covered in thousands of butterflies. Many were dancing around in the air all around them, their burning orange and golden-beige wings flashing vigorously like falling leaves.

"You see! Anything that attracts so many butterflies can't be that bad!"

Phrym, who was now stepping nervously and eyeing the shadows suspiciously, didn't seem as sure as his rider. Nevertheless, with a gentle nudge from Jahrra's knees, he crossed the barrier between field and forest and they immediately became engulfed in a sudden, profound silence.

Jahrra gazed up in wonder at the trunks and canopies of the massive trees. They were the tallest she'd ever seen in Oescienne, and they were absolutely beautiful. Beneath Phrym's unsure feet was a game trail littered with blackened leaves, stiff sheets of bark and fallen branches looking like the skeletons of tiny houses. Shoots of thin wild grass, imitating bright green needles, poked through the layers of leaves and bark. A soothing scent of eucalyptus oil, wild mushrooms and a strange smell Jahrra didn't recognize drenched the air, and her skin prickled warmly as if a magical breeze flowed over it. The silent forest seemed almost unnatural, particularly since Phrym's footfalls barely made a sound. *Wait until I tell Scede and Gieaun I was in the Wreing Florenn!* she thought smugly, *They'll never believe me!*

Just as Jahrra was imagining Gieaun's frightful reaction to going into the forest alone, something moved in the corner of her eye. She quickly turned her head and caught another flash of movement, the strange magical feel of her surroundings bending for a mere second. Something was retreating into the forest. It was too big to be a boar or a fox, too small to be another horse, yet it couldn't have been a deer.

Jahrra gazed into the depths of the forest, trying hard to catch just one more glimpse of the strange animal. Phrym drew closer to where Jahrra had seen the creature, and she saw movement again, this time deeper in the forest. She thought the blaze of color was gold, but she knew that nothing living in southern Oescienne could be that particular shimmering metallic color.

Making up her mind in a hurry, Jahrra clicked at Phrym, who had suddenly dropped his fearful anxiety and now seemed just as curious as she was. *If Phrym isn't afraid anymore it can't be too dangerous,* she mused.

The semequin stepped forward, snapping a large twig as he moved onward. It was the first sound he made after stepping past the tree line, and whatever it was that Jahrra had seen took off running into the heart of the woods.

"Yaah!" Jahrra kicked into Phrym, causing him to bolt abruptly into a quick sprint.

The beast, whatever it was, moved quickly and smoothly, almost as if it had been born to slide like liquid past the tree trunks and branches that hindered Jahrra and Phrym's way. It dashed and darted and zigzagged like living smoke, making it difficult to follow.

*Come on Phrym! Keep up!* Jahrra encouraged in her mind as they crashed awkwardly through the underbrush. After about ten minutes of pursuit Jahrra pulled Phrym back. He was exhausted from the constant ducking and dodging and both of them shared a good number of scratches and bruises from the trees.

"What was that thing?" Jahrra wondered aloud, out of breath from the excitement.

She was a bit discouraged they hadn't caught up with the animal, but the realization that they'd run deeper into the Wreing Florenn greatly out-weighed her disappointment. They stayed for a little while in the shade of the trees in order to recover from their pursuit and discover where they'd ended up. Jahrra grimaced when she realized they'd lost the trail they'd been following. A sudden chill prickled her skin as she wondered, not for the first time, if all the rumors about monsters and robbers were true.

The film of magic that had surrounded them at the foot of the forest had dissipated, and now Jahrra felt nervous and edgy. After a few minutes passed, she turned Phrym around to try and make out which way they'd come when suddenly the semequin turned his head and gazed back towards the center of the forest. His nostrils flared and his ears perked forward.

"No Phrym, we have to find our way out of here before we get even more lost," Jahrra hissed, pulling on the reins firmly.

But Phrym kept on looking in the same direction and snorted with a small nicker.

"No Phrym, no!" Jahrra pleaded, trying to keep the panic down in her voice.

Phrym began walking farther toward the heart of the forest and Jahrra kept whispering threats to him as she tried desperately to get him turned back around. He had never disobeyed her like this before and she again wondered, with cold dread, what it was they had chased. After another fifteen minutes of walking, trotting, and unsuccessful attempts at getting Phrym turned around, Jahrra and her semequin came upon a tall row of thick brambles.

Jahrra stopped fighting Phrym and looked up at the wall of thorns.

"Where are we now?" she asked as they followed a small path leading to an opening in the thick wall that stood over her head.

Phrym walked right up to a small slit in the bramble hedge and peered through, his smoky eyes wide with interest. Jahrra leaned forward in the saddle to see what was so fascinating to him and almost fell off his back in surprise.

There, in a large clearing in the woods, stood a small herd of unicorns. Jahrra had never seen unicorns in her life and had only been told by Hroombra what they looked like. He'd once told her that they'd inhabited Oescienne hundreds of years ago, but had since vanished from the province. Yet here she was now, gazing upon some of the most magical creatures in existence.

Jahrra rubbed her eyes and took a few breaths, thinking she was hallucinating, but when she glanced back through the gap in the wall they were still all there. The small, horse-like creatures looked like the many illustrations she'd seen in Hroombra's books and manuscripts: they had slender, petit bodies and were a little larger than a deer, a little smaller than a standard horse. Their necks and feet were feathered with generous amounts of corn silk hair and their tails, almost like that of a lion's, were smooth, ending with a generous amount of that same satiny hair at their tips.

The most interesting characteristic about the unicorns, Jahrra thought, were their horns. Not straight and twisted the way many people believed, but smooth and curved back slightly over their foreheads like a bow. Jahrra remembered Hroombra telling her that this was because it made it easier for branches to pass over the horns as the unicorns made their way through the thick forests they inhabited.

As Jahrra gawked at the magical creatures before her, Phrym moved ever so slightly and Jahrra's attention was shifted to a single animal. He had a mane and coat of gold and was slightly bigger than all of the others, and his horn was almost twice as long. *This must be the stallion*, Jahrra decided, *he must've been the one we saw at the edge of the forest.*

# Chasing Unicorns

The stallion stood proud and tall, the filtered light of the forest glancing off him like a great bronze statue. His color was breathtaking; like the sun reflecting off rippling water in the late afternoon, like the dew drops on a spider web caught between the morning light and the fading darkness. Jahrra had never seen such a color on any living creature before, and she was captivated by it.

Jahrra twitched convulsively when, suddenly, the gilded animal before her slowly, yet attentively, turned his head to look directly at her and Phrym. The stallion's gaze was cool and calculating, and Jahrra was sure he was debating whether or not the curious semequin and his rider were a threat to his mares. The stallion stared at the pair a bit longer and then turned his eyes back onto his herd. Jahrra realized, with a satisfied thrill, that they weren't considered a threat and the herd kept on grazing in peace while she and Phrym watched in wonder.

Over the next half hour or so Jahrra carefully counted seventeen mares, the one stallion and about six foals. She especially liked the foals. They looked very much like Phrym had when he had been young. The youngest ones didn't have horns yet and their feet were free of the fine, silky hair of the adults. The older foals had anything ranging from small nubs suggesting future horns, to several inches of new growth.

The colors of their coats were just as amazing as the creatures themselves. There was, of course, the golden stallion, but the mares and foals ranged anywhere from bright pearly white to dark silver, gold-red and copper. All of the unicorns had a metallic sheen to them and some of them had slightly darker manes than their bodies. Their hooves matched their coats, but appeared more metallic, as if made of pure gold or silver or bronze, and their horns were the same. The mares had horns that ranged between one and two feet and the stallion's horn looked almost three and a half feet long.

Jahrra took it all in, every last detail, because she knew that she may never see this sight again. Suddenly she had an idea. She quietly took out the journal she kept in Phrym's worn saddle bags and quickly began sketching the animals.

As she drew, Jahrra started looking around at all of the other details of this enchanted scene. The meadow the unicorns grazed in consisted of thick patches of dark green, mottled clover that was bursting with pink blossoms. Creamy yellow buttercups and periwinkle bluebells dotted the terrain and a faint burbling sound pulled her eyes towards the far end of the meadow where she spotted a shallow pool.

For the first time since arriving to this magical meadow, Jahrra noticed that the towering trees were not of the typical eucalyptus found in most of the Wreing Florenn. Aspen, elder and birch had taken their place, and instead of the thin, scraggly grass on the forest floor there grew the delicate clover, soft mosses and feathery ferns found near damper soil.

Butterflies, dragonflies and what Jahrra couldn't help but imagine were fairies, fluttered around the meadow lazily in the filtered, mid-morning sun. The entire scene was exactly what Jahrra would imagine finding in Felldreim or Rhiim, but not here in Oescienne.

A soft breeze soughed through the golden-green leaves above and jerked Jahrra's attention back to the stallion and his herd. He was looking back at Jahrra and Phrym again, bowing his noble head ever so slightly. The unusual gesture caught Jahrra off guard and she had to grab onto Phrym's mane to keep from falling. Had the stallion really greeted them?

While Jahrra sat wondering about the unicorn's acknowledgment, he reared up and emitted a melodic, chime-like whinny. The sound sent more shivers across Jahrra's skin and she smiled, tears welling up in her eyes against her will. She had no idea the sound of unicorns could make someone feel so happy and carefree. It was such a beautiful resonance, and it held a joy that reached straight into the soul.

His mares answered back in various chime-like tones, and Jahrra felt every scrap of sadness lingering in her heart shatter like a thin sheet of ice upon a stone floor. The stallion then turned and slowly led his herd out of the meadow and deeper into the Wreing Florenn while Jahrra and Phrym watched them leave. Once the very last one disappeared into the beckoning trees, the magic that had buzzed in the meadow seemed to seep away with the breeze. The brilliant colors of the scene faded away into the dull, ordinary tints of the world. The rich emerald turned to olive, the bright bluebells faded to cobalt and the rosy pink clover blossoms blanched nearly white.

Phrym had no objections to Jahrra turning him around now; he seemed mesmerized by what had just occurred and was easily led. When Jahrra had Phrym faced the way they came, she was surprised to see a tiny trail leading through the underbrush and back around the tall eucalyptus trees. Jahrra smiled, knowing that the trail was probably there the entire time; she'd just been too distracted to notice it.

Several minutes after leaving the meadow they came out of the forest exactly where they had entered it and soon Phrym was running across the field, heading south towards Gieaun's and Scede's ranch. They approached the familiar fence surrounding the back pasture, and Jahrra was pleased to see the family was nearby with a group of ewes and their newly-born lambs.

Jahrra pulled Phrym right up to the fence and called out to her friends enthusiastically, "Gieaun! Scede! Wait until you hear what I saw!!"

The two siblings looked up and then glanced at their parents. Jahrra saw Kaihmen and Nuhra nod and Gieaun and Scede came trotting over on Bhun and Aimhe.

"Mother and father said we could be done for the day. So what did you see?" Scede said, not sounding too excited.

"Come on, I'll tell you on the way," Jahrra replied, smiling impishly.

"On the way to where?" Gieaun asked suspiciously, opening the gate from Aimhe's back.

"You'll see!" Jahrra replied in exasperation.

The three walked their horses down the dusty road for about a mile before Jahrra finally stopped Phrym.

"Alright, you have to promise you'll believe me and promise you won't tell anyone!" Jahrra hissed in all seriousness.

Gieaun and Scede both adopted a worried look on their faces that said, *"Great, Jahrra has gone and done something foolish again"*.

"Alright," Gieaun finally said aloud.

"We promise," Scede added, holding his hand to his heart.

Jahrra pulled out her journal and opened up to the page where she'd drawn the unicorns. "Look," she said, holding up the book and smiling from ear to ear.

"Are those, *unicorns*!?" Scede gaped in disbelief, grasping Bhun's saddle horn to keep from falling off.

"Jahrra! Where on Ethöes did you see unicorns!? Are you sure they're unicorns?" Gieaun added, unable to contain her excitement.

"This is why you have to promise not to tell anybody!" Jahrra said sternly. "Phrym and I were riding in the fields and I happened to glance over to the edge of the Wreing Florenn. I know I promised not to go in there alone, but I thought that just going in a few yards wouldn't hurt."

"Oh, Jahrra! Are you crazy!?" Gieaun moaned in vexation. Aimhe shifted restlessly beneath her.

Jahrra just gave her a guilty look and continued on with her story, "Well, anyway, we only went in about ten feet, I swear. But then I saw something, something strange. I couldn't resist going after it."

"Jahrra!" Gieaun hissed again, her eyes wide with horror, "It could've been anything! It could've been a boarlaque!"

Jahrra ignored Gieaun's dramatic claims and continued on, "We chased after it for fifteen minutes or so, and then stopped. It was then I realized we had gone too far into the forest."

"You think so?" Scede inquired sarcastically, crossing his arms across his chest and giving Bhun free rein to pluck lazily at the field grasses.

Jahrra made a face at him and kept talking. "I wanted to turn back but Phrym started walking forward, farther into the forest."

"Oh, sure, blame it on Phrym," Gieaun huffed, placing her hands on her hips and giving Aimhe the same freedom as her brother's horse.

Jahrra pushed on, undeterred. "After awhile we came upon a small meadow surrounded by thick bramble bushes. Phrym stepped up to a gap in the wall of thorns and looked in. I stood up in the saddle and looked in as well, and there, before my very eyes, was an entire herd of unicorns!"

Jahrra sat back in the saddle with her hands resting on the pommel. She gazed, unsmiling but attentive, at her two friends. Gieaun looked flabbergasted and Scede had a smile of surprise on his face.

"Do you think they're still there?" he asked energetically, forgetting his officious posture.

"No," Jahrra said in a disheartened manner, "they left the meadow and that's when I left the forest."

"Maybe some of their hair got caught on a branch or something," he mused, shrugging slightly.

Jahrra sat up quickly in the saddle and stared, wide-eyed at her friend. Phrym nickered in slight irritation.

"I didn't think of looking!" she blurted.

"Are you thinking what I'm thinking?" Scede asked, unable to hide his grin.

"NO!" gasped Gieaun, horrified, knowing *exactly* what they were planning on doing. "We're NOT going into that forest. Are you nuts?!"

But Scede and Jahrra had already urged Phrym and Bhun into a steady trot down the gentle slope and Gieaun had no choice but to follow after them.

"You two are going to get us killed!" she yelled after them as she tried to catch up.

By the time the three friends reached the edge of the forest it was just before midday. They sat upon their horses several feet away from the woods, gazing into the trees.

"You go first," Scede suggested timidly to Jahrra.

"Are you afraid, Scede?" she teased.

"No! I, uh . . . you just know the way already, that's all," he recovered rather clumsily, fidgeting with Bhun's reins.

Jahrra shook her head with a smile and walked Phrym down the trail that led to the meadow. This time she paid attention to where she was going.

"Come on you two!" she called when she saw they weren't moving. "There's nothing to be afraid of!"

She could hear the two siblings arguing and finally, Gieaun stepped in followed by Scede. Jahrra could barely hear the other girl grumbling about "death" and "monsters", but she only grinned and focused on the path ahead of her. After half an hour the group found themselves in the place where Phrym and Jahrra had first stopped.

"Where are we?" asked Gieaun nervously, looking up at the trees as if their branches might reach down and strangle her.

"It's only a little while longer. This is where we stopped the first time."

Jahrra turned Phrym slightly to the right and up the tiny trail she hadn't seen before and in no time they reached the solid wall of brambles.

"We're here!" she exclaimed, causing her two friends to flinch.

Jahrra led Phrym into a quick walk and they came around the corner and up to the break in the wall. Phrym and the other two horses could easily step through, but Jahrra wondered if the unicorns wouldn't come back if they did. They tied up their horses and slowly stepped into the meadow.

"Wow!" Gieaun exclaimed. "This looks like a scene right out of one of Master Hroombra's fairytales!"

After soaking up the peace of the meadow for a while, Jahrra led her friends to where she'd last seen the unicorns before they disappeared into the forest.

"The stallion bowed his head at me. Then he led his herd this way."

"He *bowed* his head at you?" Gieaun asked in disbelief.

Jahrra nodded and Gieaun looked over at Scede. He simply shrugged his shoulders and continued after his friend. The way the unicorns had left was quite obvious; there was a large break in the brambles straight ahead and a well worn path leading out.

As the three approached the opening, Jahrra kept her fingers crossed that the unicorns had left some of their corn silk mane behind. She was the first to reach the brambles, and as her eyes raked the edge of the opening, her heart skipped a beat. Not only was there a chunk of unicorn hair, but there were several in a variety of colors.

"Wow!" Scede breathed, sounding more excited than Jahrra could ever remember.

"Real unicorn hair!" Gieaun put in, running the small distance to the opening in the hedge.

The three happily began to gather as much as they could shove in their pockets and carry back to their saddlebags.

"Too bad we can't show mother and father," Scede said, sounding slightly disappointed. "They'd kill us if they knew we went into the Wreing Florenn!"

Once they'd gathered enough hair to make their own unicorn if they wanted to, the three friends returned to their horses and began the journey out of the forest. They decided to spend the rest of the day helping Jahrra in her garden and then perhaps try talking Hroombra into telling them a story or showing them another map of Ethöes.

The ride back through the trees passed quickly but not uneventfully. By the time they reached the field, Jahrra, Gieaun and Scede were overcome by a fit of laughter. Gieaun had been trailing behind when she thought she saw someone in a red cloak following them. She instinctually tensed, spooking Aimhe and frightening the other horses into a run. When Scede and Jahrra looked back behind them, all they could see were several shrubs in full scarlet bloom. They laughed at Gieaun and told her she was paranoid, but something behind them made a crackling noise and all three screamed, urging their horses past the last row of trees.

"There very well could've been someone following us!" Gieaun said, trying to catch her breath.

"Yeah, the terrifying shrub monster!" Scede wheezed, barely able to stay in Bhun's saddle.

Gieaun just crossed her arms and tried to look annoyed. "Nothing is blooming right now, Scede. It's too early!" she insisted, but gave up when she couldn't hold on to her composure any longer.

"Come on. Let's race back to the Castle Guard Ruin," Jahrra said, wiping a tear from her eye.

"Oh, you always win! You have Phrym!" Scede complained.

They raced anyways. Phrym, Bhun and Aimhe tore across the rolling fields heading north. After several minutes they met up with the Danu Creek and turned to follow it westward. Jahrra and Phrym streaked far ahead of everybody else, frightening birds and other creatures that were bathing, drinking or foraging for food in the creek bed below.

Within ten minutes Jahrra came into view of the crumbled structure she called home. She gradually slowed Phrym to a walk and then turned him around to see where her friends were. A few minutes passed before Jahrra finally heard the horses thundering up the trail. She turned Phrym back toward the Ruin and kicked him into full speed once again, hoping Gieaun and Scede got the impression she wasn't too far ahead.

Jahrra smiled as Phrym trotted up to her home, her two friends and their horses trailing far behind. She turned and waited for them, grinning as they pulled up.

"You two almost beat us!" she laughed, knowing it wasn't true.

"Yeah, right!" said Gieaun. "You were so far ahead we never would've caught you!"

Jahrra smiled. "Sure you would've!"

Jahrra was so intent on convincing her friends she hadn't left them in the dust that she didn't notice the shadow of the Castle Guard Ruin suddenly growing larger behind her. Nor did she see the look of sudden disquiet crossing both her friends' faces or the sudden unease of Bhun and Aimhe.

"No, they wouldn't have," said an overbearing, stony voice above her shoulder. "You were much too far ahead."

Jahrra's smile instantly faded and her blood turned to ice water. She knew that voice, that cool, calculating, dominating voice. It had been a long time since she'd last heard it, but it wasn't a voice she could easily forget.

She turned her head, hoping that it wasn't who she thought it was, that her hearing had been affected by the magic in the meadow. She slowly looked up at the dominating figure standing just behind her and almost melted when she saw the large, unyielding Tanaan dragon smirking down at her. She closed her eyes and slowly realized that her perfect day had just come to an end.

# -Chapter Seventeen-
# Dueling with Dragons

It took a few minutes for Jahrra to realize why the sight of Jaax made her uneasy, and how long it had been since she'd seen him. Four years ago, she thought, when he brought her Phrym. Then it struck her; why she received a stabbing pang of distaste when she'd heard the dragon's voice. For three years now she'd subconsciously been blaming him for the death of her parents. She'd forgotten her anger in time, just as she'd learned to deal with her sorrow, but seeing the dragon now had the same effect as throwing stones at a hornet's nest.

Jahrra took a deep breath and forced herself to look Jaax in the eye. *Cold, granite eyes,* she thought with a shiver. "What are *you* doing here?" she finally said, her throat feeling constricted and her mouth feeling dry.

"I'm here on business," the dragon said simply, his voice holding a hint of amusement.

Jahrra still found Jaax imposing, despite the fact she was sitting high atop Phrym, and she wondered how she hadn't spotted him when they first approached. *He must have been waiting for me inside the Ruin, spying,* she decided with distaste.

She released a short breath and asked as pleasantly as she could, "Where's Master Hroombra?"

"He'll be out shortly. I couldn't help but overhear you shouting so loudly at your friends, so I came out to greet you all." He paused and then cocked his head to the side, eyeing her like a bug he was considering squashing. "Do you always take pleasure in deceiving your friends, Jahrra?"

The question took Jahrra by surprise, like a punch in the stomach. She glared up at Jaax, but he just kept looking at her as if she were insignificant. Jahrra turned her eyes away and suddenly felt the way she did when Eydeth or Ellysian looked at her. *Who is he to judge me?* she thought furiously, *I don't deceive my friends!*

Gieaun and Scede shifted on their horses somewhere behind her. She moved slowly to look at them, reluctant to turn her back on her enemy. They'd noticed Jaax before she did and had wisely stayed put where they were. Now they were giving her a fragile look as she sought them out with desperate eyes.

"Hello," Jaax said cheerily over Jahrra's head. "You are Gieaun and Scede if I'm not mistaken? I remember you two from last time I was here. You've grown quite a bit."

He smiled freely at them and they seemed to relax a little, both grinning sheepishly.

*What?!* Jahrra thought with her mouth hanging open, *how can he be so nice to them and treat me like dirt?!*

"Can you breathe fire like Master Hroombra?" Scede blurted, interrupting Jahrra's thoughts and taking everyone by surprise.

The boy blushed slightly at his own outburst; clearly he hadn't meant to be so forward. Jaax looked down at Scede and grinned, then took a deep breath and let out a huge burst of flame, blue in the center and green around the edges. Aimhe, Bhun and Phrym all backed up and pulled at their bits nervously, but Gieaun and Scede were ecstatic with joy.

"Whoa! How can you do that?" Gieaun remarked, not noticing the look of irritation on Jahrra's face.

"I'm not quite sure Gieaun, but all dragons have the ability to breathe fire, steam or ice," Jaax answered, as if discussing the weather. "I happen to be a fire-breather."

He then began to blow smoke rings, which only encouraged Gieaun and Scede to jump from their horses in delight. The next minute they were laughing and coughing as they tried to leap through the giant loops of misty smoke.

Jahrra remained seated on Phrym, infuriated that the dragon should put on such a show for her friends while treating her with such disdain. It was almost as if Jaax had *charmed* them with magic. *Why is he so rude to me but nice to them?* she wondered miserably. Then she remembered that she hated him, so it really didn't matter in the end.

"Gieaun, Scede, do you want to put the horses away now?" Jahrra said quite rudely as she finally climbed down from Phrym's back.

"Oh, yeah, in just a minute," Scede said shortly without stopping his game of dodging the smoke rings. "You go ahead, we'll catch up to you."

Jahrra shot one more angry look at Jaax before leading Phrym away.

"Is she always so bad-tempered?" he asked the siblings once Jahrra had turned away.

"What are you talking about?" Gieaun asked, allowing a stray smoke ring to pass through her.

"Never mind, it's not important," Jaax sniffed.

The Tanaan dragon narrowed his emerald eyes as he watched Jahrra march away across the pasture. *So,* he thought with a scowl, *that's how it's going to be, is it?* He'd been testing the girl, searching for weakness, knowing now she wasn't going to accept him back so easily after his long absence. What had happened to the young girl he met four years ago? She'd been impressed and eager to make friends then, now she seemed guarded and distant, a slow anger burning inside of her.

*What's causing this anger?* Jaax wondered, absentmindedly blowing another dozen smoke rings in Gieaun and Scede's direction as he watched Jahrra lead Phrym away. He wondered if it might still be the effect of Abdhe's and Lynhi's deaths. *After all, it really wasn't that long ago . . .* His brow furrowed and his mood darkened for a moment. *That could be it, but not all of it. She was cheerful until she saw me.*

He sighed and realized that he would have to figure this out in due time, but for now he was going to make good use of this opportunity to check in on Jahrra's progress. The business of the outside world had kept him away from this task for far too long, and though his time here would once again be short, he was going to make good use of it.

Jaax smiled wryly as he continued to watch the fuming girl kick irritably at stones and swat at the swaying grasses as she moved closer to the stables. *Yes, this will be interesting indeed . . .* he mused.

"Ugh!" Jahrra puffed angrily as she pulled Phrym up the sloping field alone. "He thinks he's so clever! They only like him because he can breathe fire!"

Phrym whinnied softly, as if voicing his agreement.

"I'm glad you're on my side Phrym," Jahrra said dejectedly, reaching over and pulling his head into an appreciative hug. Phrym just nickered cheerfully and shoved Jahrra softly forward with his nose.

Once they reached the stable, Jahrra let out a tense sigh. She was grateful to be away from that stupid dragon and her credulous friends. She looked over at the small yard attached to the enclosure and smiled as Phrym trotted around, trying to con Jahrra into playing with him.

"Not today, boy, maybe another time. I'm not in the mood."

Jahrra grabbed her pack from the saddle bags and turned to walk back to her traitorous friends and their unpleasant visitor. Phrym watched as Jahrra trudged back towards the Ruin, then shook his head and occupied himself with eating his oats.

As she moved closer to the crumbled building, Jahrra saw that Hroombra had finally joined the crowd. *Master Hroombra won't let Jaax be so rude!* she thought hopefully with a tiny smile. Once she was within a few yards of them however, she noticed that both the dragons were watching her intently and her two friends had their eyes to the ground. They all seemed like statues, standing stark still and rigid. Something that felt like an icicle slid down Jahrra's throat and settled in her stomach. *Why is everyone so quiet? What has happened?* she thought with a twinge of uneasiness.

"What's wrong?" she asked warily.

"Scede here was just telling us about your day," Jaax answered, his face for once without expression.

Jahrra glanced over at Scede, who looked as guilty as a fox in a henhouse. She then looked to Gieaun, who happened to be giving her brother a nasty look.

"What did he say?" Jahrra asked carefully.

"He said that you'd seen the most amazing thing today, and just as he was going to tell us he suddenly stopped talking, refusing to go on."

It was Hroombra this time, but his tone sounded more curious than accusing.

Jahrra looked daggers at Scede, and he cowered even more. *Great! Now what am I going to say!* she thought furiously. *I can't tell them I chased after a unicorn into the Wreing Florenn! Master Hroombra will kill me, and for Jaax to know too! He already thinks I'm a trouble-maker!* Jahrra fished around for an excuse in her head, and decided that the best method was to tell the truth, at least part of the truth.

"Well," she began delicately, "we were riding in the fields between here and Nuun Esse on our way back from Wood's End Ranch, and I saw something out of the corner of my eye. I looked towards the forest and saw what I thought was a herd of deer. But they weren't deer; they were unicorns Master Hroombra, real unicorns!"

Jahrra barely heard the gasps of relief, and disbelief, coming from her two friends. Jaax looked taken aback and Hroombra just gazed at her, as if trying to comprehend what she'd just said.

Jahrra continued after a while, "When they saw us, they went running into the trees, so Gieaun, Scede and I decided to see if any of their hair got caught in the brush they were grazing near. And it did, look!"

Jahrra reached into her bag and pulled out a wad of the hair the three children had collected in the meadow, hoping this proof would distract the dragons from questioning her honesty.

She knew she shouldn't have lied, but at least this way she'd told them some of the truth, and she wouldn't have to tell them she'd been in the Wreing Florenn. Hroombra was the first to step forward, with Jaax looking over his shoulder. Both dragons stared down at the unicorn hair as if in a trance, even Jaax, who always seemed to keep his true feelings hidden.

"Jahrra, did you happen to sketch them in your journal?" Hroombra asked, sounding like he could barely hang on to his excitement.

"Yes." Jahrra smiled and pulled out her journal. She opened it up to the pages where she'd drawn the stallion and some of the foals.

"Incredible!" Hroombra proclaimed, his multitude of wrinkles bunching around a huge smile.

Jaax, however, wasn't as enthused. He sat back on his haunches after looking at both the silky hair and the sketching. He glared at Jahrra as if she were someone untrustworthy, his usual cool gaze back once again.

"Jaax! Do you see this?" Hroombra asked, his voice still filled with awe.

The other dragon looked at Hroombra and said simply, "Has she seen drawings of unicorns before?"

Hroombra's expression went from complete joy to slight confusion. "Why, yes," he answered, his brow furrowed. "I've shown her many sketches and drawings of the creatures of Ethöes. Why?"

Jaax took a deep breath and said, "Isn't it possible she is making this all up? She could've drawn these from memory or copied them from your manuscripts."

Hroombra looked rather befuddled, and Jahrra gaped blankly at Jaax.

"What?!" she breathed, her blue eyes turning storm-cloud gray. "I didn't copy these from any other drawings, I saw the unicorns just today, I swear it! Here, I even have their hair to prove it!" Jahrra thrust out her hand, clutching the unicorn hair. "What more proof do you want?"

Jaax looked down at the hair wadded in Jahrra's hand. Then he moved his cool green eyes up to Jahrra's angry ones, saying quietly and calmly, "Some horses have fine hair. Your friends told me that their parents breed palomino horses. You could've taken the hair from them."

Jahrra couldn't believe that Jaax was accusing her of lying. She was severely tempted to kick him as hard as she could, but knew it would hurt her more than it would hurt him, not to mention give him one more thing to smile about. *Alright,* Jahrra thought miserably, *I did lie about where I saw them, but I saw them! And how can he tell I'm not being truthful anyways?* She knew it shouldn't bother her that Jaax didn't believe her. She hated him, so why did it matter? But for some reason it did.

"I'm telling the truth!" she demanded. "They were gold and copper and silver, they had one long horn that curved back over their forehead, and when they whinnied, it sounded like chimes!"

Then she added weakly as her shoulders drooped, "It made me feel very happy."

Hroombra, who'd remained quiet and pensive for the last few minutes, shot his head up immediately, his yellow eyes blazing.

"You heard them Jahrra? I never told you what they sounded like." His smile returned once again. "Jaax! There's no question about it, she did see them! She might've known what they looked like, but she didn't know what they sounded like!"

Hroombra was as giddy as the children had been the second they found the unicorn hair.

Jaax looked unnecessarily unhappy with this information and Hroombra's reaction to it, but for some strange reason, Jahrra didn't think it had anything to do with her.

"Jaax! Unicorns!" Hroombra said once again, wondering why the younger dragon was staying so calm.

Jaax turned his gaze to Hroombra and said simply, sternly, "Unicorns have not been in Oescienne for . . ."

"Nearly five hundred years."

Hroombra finished the statement with both a tone of wonder and revelation. Jahrra just stared back, not knowing what to say, not understanding the relevance of this fact.

The young dragon looked back to Jahrra, trying hard to read her expression. There was a glimmer of truth in the young girl's eyes; he couldn't deny that. But there couldn't be unicorns in Oescienne, it just wasn't possible . . .

"Hroombra, you and I know that what she claims is impossible!" Jaax snapped, growing irritated with his own thoughts.

He was no longer concerned with whether or not Jahrra was telling the truth. He was just concerned with what it meant if she *was* telling the truth.

"Jahrra, you may go and play with your friends now, we've detained you three long enough," Hroombra said, sounding serious all of a sudden.

Jahrra turned to Gieaun and Scede, grateful to be free of her small ordeal but wondering what had turned Jaax's mood so quickly. She shook her head in annoyance. The last thing she wanted to do right now was to untangle the inner workings of the mind of the great Raejaaxorix. Instead she began walking with Gieaun and Scede as they led the other horses up to the stables. When they were far away from the dragons however, Jahrra began chastising Scede for mentioning the incident with the unicorns.

"I'm sorry! I completely forgot. Those smoke rings were distracting!" he said between tight teeth.

"I'm sure they were," Jahrra answered sarcastically.

"Oh, it's alright!" she continued after seeing the crestfallen look on Scede's face. "We didn't have to tell them *exactly* where we went, so there was no harm done, after all."

They trudged along uphill in the warm afternoon sun, too busy chatting to pay any heed to the two dragons watching them carefully.

As soon as they were out of earshot Jaax immediately cut into Hroombra, "What could you possibly be thinking?" he snipped.

"Jaax, *unicorns*," Hroombra breathed dreamily, unaffected by the Tanaan dragon's shortness. "You can't ignore this. The return of unicorns to Oescienne was foreseen in the prophecy."

"You mean an amendment to the prophecy. Don't forget who it was that claimed to have foreseen unicorns returning," the young dragon growled. "The girl has a great imagination, you've told me so a number of times. She most likely saw a deer and let her thoughts run away with her. And that nonsense about hearing them, that was a coincidence. She could've heard about a unicorn's voice anywhere. She might've stumbled upon the description in one of your books."

Jaax forced out this last remark with a finality that stated the conversation was over. He turned aggressively and started walking more briskly toward the Ruin in what appeared to be a fouler mood than was necessary.

"Besides," he shot over his shoulder, "we can't follow the prophecy word for word. It's still possible that it's only a way to give us poor creatures hope in a time of hopelessness."

"There's always hope, Jaax," Hroombra retorted, "and I believe more than anything in this foretelling, I must. I've waited too many years and have seen too much suffering."

Jaax answered Hroombra without turning around this time.

He merely spoke louder so that the older dragon could hear him, "I'm through with this conversation Hroombra. The prophecy is and always has been simply a code to give false hope. I've spent hundreds of years trying to decipher its meaning and message to no avail. There's nothing absolute about it. Every claim and every statement within it can have a hundred different meanings. I've spent too many years getting my hopes up when I saw the signs, only to have them dashed away. I wouldn't rely on it if I were you."

"If that's the truth," Hroombra said with renewed determination, "then why did you bring Jahrra here to begin with? Why did you spend so many years looking for her? Admit it Jaax, we all cling onto hope, even if we have to wait centuries for our hopes and wishes to come true."

Jaax couldn't see Hroombra smiling, but he could hear it in the old dragon's voice, "I don't know what has happened since I last heard from you to bring you to say such things, but I know it's only a passing phase. You'll trust in the prophecy again, I know it."

The younger dragon eased a bit and nodded stiffly before he stalked off to go and rest in the main room of the

Ruin. His journey had been long, and he'd been traveling farther and more frequently than usual. He'd flown to Oescienne almost non-stop from Nimbronia, the great city in the Hrunahn Mountains to the north. The king of the Creecemind dragons was still refusing to choose sides in the festering turmoil that could boil over any day now, and Jaax was beyond frustrated with him and his people. Did they not realize the magnitude of the threat in the east?

It was this frustration that had put him in such a dire mood just now, and he regretted it. He now took the anger and disbelief he'd aimed at Jahrra and focused it on those who refused to help with the resistance of the Crimson King, especially the dragon king of the north. Jaax had been told to return only when he had the chosen one with him. He couldn't see how presenting an eleven year old girl to the Creecemind dragons would sway their allegiance to his side, and there was no way he could take Jahrra on such a long journey without telling her the truth. All Jaax could do was forget the north for now and hope the Tyrant remained inactive until Jahrra was older.

Jaax sighed as he suddenly remembered the main reason he'd made this journey to Oescienne in the first place. Jahrra may be too young to know the truth, but she was old enough to prepare for her future, even if she had no idea what that future was. His purpose in coming back to Oescienne now was to make sure she was learning what she needed to learn, and one of the things she was lacking in was self defense and basic fighting skills. Someday she would be taking on many foes, both elf and beast alike, and she needed to be prepared to defend herself.

Jaax laughed softly at this thought. She was only a child, what level of fighting skills could she possibly possess? That didn't matter, however, for no matter how ill-prepared she might be, she could become better with the proper training.

Jaax had expected this; he knew that Hroombra would not have thought of defense lessons. What he hadn't expected was this nonsense about a herd of unicorns in the fields just beyond the Ruin. And her reaction to seeing him . . . He'd expected the girl to be a little distant, but he hadn't expected the cold dislike that practically oozed from her. Now Jaax allowed himself to give this a little thought. Had Hroombra somehow left out some form of discipline on Jahrra's part? Had he softened because of her great loss and been easier on the girl than he normally would have?

Jaax had already seen signs of a lack of discipline in the young girl. Had she not been disrespectful the very moment she saw him? That was all he needed, an out of control little brat and her wild stories about magical creatures to make this visit less than unpleasant.

Jaax shook his head to clear his mind. If Jahrra was turning out to be an impossible child, then he would just have to find a way to work around it, or repair it. He already knew she would be averse to the trip they would be taking the next day, so Jaax decided to go to bed early and enlighten her in the morning.

*I'll need all the rest I can get if I'm to spend the day with her tomorrow,* he thought to himself as he stepped through the dragons' entrance of the Castle Guard Ruin. He walked into the great room and curled up in the corner away from the fireplace and slowly drifted off to sleep, trying not to think too much about the prophecy or of unicorns.

❀ ❀ ❀

Jahrra had been enjoying a particularly wonderful dream of racing unicorns through the forest with Phrym when a sharp, authoritative voice shattered the enchanted scene:

"JAHRRA!"

Jahrra woke with a snort, not quite sure what had awoken her. The flash of gold and silver and the musical notes of unicorns crying out still echoed in her mind.

"Wake up!" the rude voice came again. "Let's get this over with while the day is still young."

Jahrra turned one tired eye up to her window and saw the silhouette of Jaax's massive head glaring through, black dragon-shape against the near black of pre-dawn.

"What?" Jahrra said, closing her eyes again.

It was far too early to think, to do anything but sleep, and she had no idea what Jaax was talking about.

The dragon took a deep breath, let it out in a huff and said rather plainly, "I've come to Oescienne for one purpose: to see how good you are at fighting and defending yourself and I don't have all day to do it."

Jaax seemed a little irritated, Jahrra thought. Perhaps he was still angry about yesterday, or maybe he hadn't slept well. She didn't really care. All she cared about was being woken up so early. *Fighting and defending myself? What on Ethöes is he talking about? I must still be dreaming.* Jahrra pondered sleepily as the cool air enticed her to stay right where she was.

"I'll not ask you again!" demanded Jaax's grumpy voice, shattering all hopes of this all being a dream. Not a dream, a nightmare.

Jahrra tempted herself with the idea of staying in bed just to spite him, but she didn't want to see what would happen if she did. He was bad enough in his normal, non-agitated mood. She got up and dressed quickly, not wanting to anger him further.

"Good morning, Jahrra," Hroombra greeted as she shuffled into the main room of the Ruin. "Are you excited about your new lessons?"

Hroombra sounded a little guilty, and Jahrra gazed at him through half closed eyes and said, "New lessons? Huh? What's going on?"

She was too tired to be annoyed that she hadn't been told about this sooner, but it was too late to do anything about it now.

"We discussed it last night and decided that it would be best if you took part in some extra-curricular activities. I know you think going on adventures with Gieaun and Scede is enough, but I think this will be better for you. We've even found you two trainers who are excellent in teaching swordsmanship, archery and advanced riding skills. I'm sorry, I did mean to warn you in advance, but Jaax insisted you start right away."

*Of course he did,* Jahrra thought heatedly as she dug the heels of her hands into her eyes, attempting to drive away the sleep, *only Jaax would think up ways to make me miserable.*

She grabbed something for breakfast and made her way to the door, braiding up her hair while she held a biscuit in her mouth. She was still confused by this sudden change in her daily life, but she was curious nonetheless. She found Jaax standing in the great field, looking towards the north, towards the path that led to the old castle.

Jahrra tied off her long braid and took the biscuit out of her mouth.

"Should I go and get Phrym?" she asked, not caring if she sounded dumb.

Jaax just turned his head to the side and nodded once, slowly returning his gaze to where it had been before.

*I'll never understand that dragon,* Jahrra thought as she traipsed through the cold, wet grass. *Waking before sunrise and signing me up for some defense lessons without telling me.*

Jahrra's pants were soaked up to her knees by the time she reached Phrym's stable, but she didn't care, they would dry when the sun came up. *Hours from now,* she thought sarcastically. Phrym poked his head out over the gate, wondering what could be making so much racket this early in the morning. When he saw that it was Jahrra, he gave a happy whinny. Jahrra couldn't help but smile back at Phrym's cheerfulness. If only she had the same positive attitude about this whole strange morning.

"I brought you an apple as a peace offering for getting you up so early," she said as she fed him the fruit.

Phrym didn't seem to mind at all that Jahrra had awoken him early; he was just glad to get the apple. Jahrra quickly saddled him and cantered over to where Jaax stood. She pulled Phrym to a stop just behind the dragon's shoulder and waited. He still stared off into the woods, but Jahrra waited for him to speak first.

"Are we ready to go?" he asked sardonically, returning his gaze to her face.

Jahrra responded with the same tone, "Phrym and I are ready. I don't know about you."

Jaax gave her an annoyed look and then started off, Jahrra and Phrym keeping their distance behind him.

"So, where exactly are we going then?" she asked through a yawn once they reached the main road.

"Somewhere where I can test what skills you have, or lack thereof."

Jahrra ignored Jaax's last comment and wondered why they couldn't just stay where they were, but she wasn't about to question him further while he was in his foul mood. They walked down the well-worn road for several more minutes.

Jahrra thought the trip would've been more pleasant if there had been conversation, but she couldn't imagine a pleasant conversation with Jaax.

Instead of starting a discussion that would more than likely end in an argument, Jahrra passed the time by listening to the sounds around her and taking in the early morning grandeur. The birds were starting to sing and the owls were heading off to bed, and the smaller animals were searching noisily in their morning breakfast hunt. The sky was no longer solid ink but the washed-out blue and grey of the approaching dawn. Jahrra breathed in the cold air as the warmth of the sun's first golden rays touched her face.

Finally, after what seemed like ages, Jaax stopped walking and turned his head to talk to Jahrra.

"We'll stop here. This looks like a nice, flat open space."

The great dragon stepped off of the road, merely a small path to him, and started heading west through the new grass that was still quite short. Jahrra sighed and led Phrym after him. *I can't wait until this is over,* she thought to herself. A ring of tall eucalyptus trees decorated the furthest edge of the field, and Jahrra could see beyond the rim of the bluff just beyond. A sliver of the distant blue ocean and taupe-hued dunes, glowing brilliantly in the morning's golden sunlight, were visible between the trees.

Jaax's voice finally interrupted Jahrra's thoughts, "Shall we continue?"

"What?" Jahrra said, not realizing she'd stopped to ponder the scene before her.

"I want to be done with this as much as you do, so it would help if you paid attention."

Jahrra turned pink. Stupid dragon! He shouldn't be allowed to be so rude all the time. She clicked Phrym forward to catch up with the dragon, now walking towards the middle of the large field. Jaax stopped and began to gaze lazily at his surroundings, surveying the open space the way a deer might contemplate an unknown meadow. Jahrra just sat atop Phrym, who began to paw at the ground, and waited for her next order. She let out an obvious sigh, hoping that it would coax Jaax into speaking, and shifted in the saddle, causing the leather to squeak in protest. *For someone who's in such a hurry, he sure is taking his time,* she thought as she crossed her arms in vexation.

It seemed a full five minutes before Jaax finally spoke.

"Alright, I guess the first logical thing to do would be to see how you handle yourself on a horse, since you're already prepared for it," he said, looking Jahrra and Phrym up and down in a bored fashion.

"What would you like us to do?" Jahrra asked composedly.

She had no idea what Jaax wanted her to do with Phrym, but she figured it couldn't be too difficult. She'd become quite a good rider since she began her lessons with Gieaun and Scede, and Phrym trusted her completely.

"Take him to the edge of that small grove of trees and back." Jaax nodded to a few young eucalyptus saplings growing away from the main wood. "If you know any maneuvers or other "tricks", go ahead and show them to me."

Jahrra rolled her eyes and clicked at Phrym, bringing him into a sudden canter. The semequin easily covered the distance in a short time and soon Jahrra was weaving him in and out of the trees as she ducked and swerved adeptly from stray branches and limbs. She quickly turned Phrym, keeping her balance as he jumped over three fallen logs on their way back to Jaax. Jahrra was tempted to keep riding back to the Ruin, but instead she pulled her tall semequin to a sudden stop, causing foraging birds to scatter raucously and forcing a large cloud of dust to rise up around them.

"That was adequate," Jaax sniffed.

This was a surprise to Jahrra. She thought she'd done rather well. She just sat straighter in the saddle, trying to look unaffected by the dragon's judgment.

"Is that all you can do?" he continued.

"Wh-what do you mean?" Jahrra stammered, feeling somewhat flabbergasted.

"You ride well and move with Phrym well, but can you do anything else besides weave through trees and jump logs?"

Jaax was beginning to sound like Master Tarnik and Jahrra was starting to wonder what could be bothering him to make him so aggravated.

"Can you ride fast and shoot with a bow?" he continued fluently. "Could you cover rough ground and fight off five full-grown men while staying on Phrym's back? Could you make a higher or wider jump if you had to without falling from the saddle? These are things that you'll need to learn, so therefore, your overall horsemanship is merely adequate."

Jahrra was stunned. *Why on Ethöes would I need to fight off full-grown men!?* she wondered in exasperation. She didn't bring these questions up to Jaax, however. She thought that he was just being overly dramatic and assumed further questioning would only anger him more. Jahrra slumped in the saddle, waiting to receive her next set of marching orders.

"I guess we'll test your archery skills next," Jaax said shortly, and then added mordantly. "You did bring your bow?"

Jahrra slid from Phrym's back and untied her bow and quiver from the back of her saddle. She allowed Phrym to wander off to graze and then turned back towards Jaax. "Do I have a target, or am I to just shoot at whatever moves next?"

"I'll tell you what to aim for, and you'll try to hit it. That is generally how it works," the dragon answered to match Jahrra's cynicism. "Not all of your targets in real life are going to have bull's-eyes on them you know."

Jahrra burned with annoyance, but she pulled her gloves on quietly and readied an arrow.

"Alright, what am I to kill?" she said as pleasantly as possible.

"I'll go easy on you on your first attempt. Do you see that tree over there?"

Jaax nodded to a small apple tree, about fifty yards away that was covered in new leaves and unopened buds. Jahrra noticed the large knothole on its trunk and was happy to agree with Jaax on this next task being easy, that is, until he spoke again.

"I just want you to hit any of the blossoms growing on that tree for now."

He couldn't be serious. Most of the buds were smaller than her thumbnail.

"You must be joking!" Jahrra blurted out, making her thoughts known.

"No, deadly serious," the dragon whispered dangerously. "You can't always risk missing an exact target, you must be precise, or it could mean your life."

Jahrra stepped back nervously. She couldn't believe she was hearing this. *It could mean my life? Who could possibly be that threatening to me?* Then she thought with a slight panic, *Maybe someone told him and Master Hroombra about what happened in Kiniahn Kroi! Could Ellysian and Eydeth really be trying to kill me?*

Jahrra swallowed hard and pulled back on her bowstring, aiming at the largest blossom she could find. *It'll be a miracle if I hit any part of the tree*, she thought apprehensively. She released the arrow with a thick twang, but it sailed right past the tree, not even nicking a leaf. Jahrra stood there, turning bright red. Jaax didn't say a word, and Jahrra was sure he was savoring the moment.

Finally, the dragon spoke, his voice calm, "I am very glad I decided to start your training early. Now, the last thing I want to see is how you defend yourself when provoked. I'm going to attack you and I want you to fight back. In a sense, I want you to try sparring with a dragon. A dragon is probably the deadliest thing you'll ever have to face, so this is a good learning experience for you."

Jaax walked away from the numb and embarrassed girl and, using his teeth, broke off a dead limb from a nearby tree.

"Here," he said, spitting it out at her feet, "pretend that is a sword. You have a good imagination, something you proved with the story of the unicorns yesterday."

Jahrra's eyes were stinging with humiliation and rage, but she wouldn't allow herself to cry, not in front of him. She picked up the branch and broke off the end to a suitable length. She was somewhat afraid to attack Jaax. After all, he was a huge dragon and she was just a girl, but her pride ruled her more than she wished. She took a deep breath that was meant to steady her mind and stepped forward, holding the branch as best she could from what she'd gathered about sword fighting.

Jaax rose up on his hind legs and let out a mighty roar mixed with fire and smoke. Jahrra stopped dead. She'd never heard him roar like this before, and she became even more apprehensive. Now she understood why people feared dragons.

"Come on, attack me! Don't be afraid!" Jaax boomed down at her.

He was twice as tall as usual as he balanced on his hind legs and tail, his great wings stirring the air as they held up his great weight.

Jahrra lifted the stick she held and swallowed hard, bowing her head against the beat of his wings. She took a deep breath and let out a yell of her own, charging at full speed with her eyes shut tight and her heart racing. She felt a crashing as she sprinted forward, and before she knew it, she had been slammed to the ground, gasping for breath. She felt the earth shake slightly as Jaax returned his forelegs to the solid ground.

Jahrra opened her eyes and looked around dazedly. She was lying on her back and her lungs ached. Groaning, she rolled her head to the side and saw her imaginary sword lying on the ground a few yards away. Phrym was whinnying in distress but seemed too timid to approach. Jaax was standing above her, his great tail wrapped around the perimeter of the battlefield.

The dragon leaned his enormous head down right next to Jahrra's and said in a whisper, his breath moving the sand beside her head, "Never approach an enemy in anger, and never, *ever* close your eyes."

He lifted his head and walked off to the other end of the field and sat down, his back turned to the stunned girl. Jahrra sat up, furious with herself and extremely angry that Jaax had actually knocked her down. She shook the dirt and dead leaves from her hair and glared at him, hurtling as much hatred through her eyes as she could.

Since his back was turned, she decided to take the opportunity to surprise him by creeping up on his blind side. She kept her eyes wide open this time, and as she drew nearer, she lifted her wooden sword in preparation for an attack. Jahrra thought she was doing well. She'd gotten within a few feet of the dragon, but it was no use, his hearing was too good. He swiftly turned around, and as Jahrra swung at him, he grabbed the branch with his scaled hand and lifted both the girl and her weapon high above the ground.

Jahrra clung to her stick and hung helplessly in the air, kicking and flailing as Jaax held her up to his face.

"Not good enough, Jahrra. Come now, you should be able to hit me at least once!" he taunted, smiling in amusement.

He dropped her from five feet up, but this time when Jahrra hit the ground she got up much quicker than before, taking Jaax by surprise. The dragon began to lift up once again on his hind legs, but before he could get his front legs into the air, Jahrra swung her branch with all her strength. The hard wood cracked against one of his left knuckles, and to Jahrra's surprise and horror, a scale went flying off.

"Oh no! Jaax, I'm sorry!"

She dropped the branch and backed away, worried that he'd be furious. But the dragon merely shook his front foot as if to stop the stinging.

"Ha, don't worry. That scale has been loose for weeks."

The dragon's scowling mood was suddenly gone, and in its place Jahrra could almost detect a hint of approval. "You did well. You caught me by surprise and actually made contact. Unfortunately, if I were truly an unfriendly dragon, you'd be dead by now, but we'll worry about that later."

He smiled and Jahrra felt her strained muscles ease a little.

"Jahrra, go pick up that scale you knocked off and bring it over here."

The scale wasn't hard to find. It glinted with the blue, green and gold that made up the hue of all of Jaax's scales. Jahrra picked it up out of the grass and looked at it. It was heavier than she'd anticipated and fit nicely in the small center of her palm. If she didn't know any better she would've said it was a glittering stone she happened upon in the field. After admiring it for awhile, Jahrra brought it back over to the waiting dragon.

"What will you do with it?" she asked as she dropped the small scale into Jaax's opened paw.

"I'll find a use for it," he said. "Maybe the elves of the north can reattach it for me. Now, we'd better head to Aldehren, there is someone waiting to meet you."

Jahrra was glad to see that Jaax was no longer as disagreeable as he'd been earlier that morning, and she was even starting to feel more relaxed and optimistic. Maybe the loose scale had been bothering him and she'd actually helped him by removing it. Whether that was the reason for his sudden easy mood or not, she didn't care. She was just glad of the change.

Jaax watched as Jahrra went and collected Phrym from the edge of the clearing, his hard eyes dark with thought. She reminded him of someone he once knew, long ago, someone just as stubborn and just as unrelenting. It would be a long while yet, however, before the Tanaan dragon realized just how similar the two were.

For now, he needed to focus on her improvement. She had so much to learn. She had to become stronger, that was a must, and more flexible. Her reflexes needed improvement and her archery needed to be fine-tuned. She had to learn how to wield a sword, and although she rode quite well, she needed to become even better in the saddle. Perhaps she was too young to begin these brutal and trying lessons, but Jaax knew that it couldn't be helped; the sooner she learned how to survive the unthinkable, the better.

Jaax shook himself like a horse shaking off a shiver of unease. This whole process of delaying his busy schedule to check in on Jahrra had been a thorn in his side, and his patience had been worn thin by it. It had also saddened him in a way. He had always meant to have a greater part in Jahrra's life, that is, until other matters came up; matters outside of Oescienne that were so much more urgent than helping Hroombra raise a child. This in turn had angered him, for some of these issues could've been dealt with by someone else, and some of them, well, some of them Jaax hadn't anticipated on happening so soon.

Oescienne may be resting peacefully on the other side of the great Elornn and Thorbet Mountains, but outside of the province it was a different story. Although the signs were not obvious, it was apparent that the world was growing restless. For several years now, the wandering tribes of Rhiim and eastern Felldreim had been joining together, creating bands of warring criminals, raiding and attacking isolated villages. What was more disturbing, Jaax thought ruefully, was fresh news of the Tyrant's soldiers and mercenaries being spotted as far west as the Aandhoul Plain. Several years ago he'd heard of scouts and spies being spotted here and there, but now he was seeing troops of men on the move with his own eyes. *Has Cierryon somehow found out about Jahrra? Could he know where she is?*

The dragon squeezed his eyes shut, as if doing this would push the worries from his mind. He forced a blistering breath from his nostrils and opened them again with weariness. *I must focus on Jahrra while I have the time to do so. I can think about everything else later.* Including the dreams he had been having lately . . . *Later,* he reminded himself with determined vigor.

He looked over at the girl, now sitting patiently atop Phrym. He smiled and finally let his qualms melt away for now. He'd been impressed with the way she caught him off guard on her third attempt to attack him. *Perhaps she isn't hopeless after all.*

He grinned more purposefully as he thought about her reaction to his crude derision the day before. Most children would fear him or, in the case of her friends, be in awe of him, but not Jahrra. He had written it off as a bad attitude, a lack of discipline on Hroombra's part, but now that he gave it some genuine thought, he was starting to see that her will and her pride were much stronger than he'd previously believed. *At least now I have one less thing to worry about,* he mused, his anxiety dissolving a little. *But now she has to learn how to use those assets against her foes, even though she won't face them for some time . . .* At least, he hoped she wouldn't have to face them for some time.

The young dragon directed Jahrra to the road and on towards Aldehren. Jahrra led Phrym ahead of him without argument, and Jaax paused only long enough to watch them in the glow of early morning.

"Someday," he whispered to his surroundings as the semequin and the girl moved out of earshot. "Someday, you can know the truth of what you are, Jahrra, but not now, not yet."

# -Chapter Eighteen-
# The Elves of Dhonoara

The normally short trip down the Sloping Hill took longer than expected, what with Jahrra and Jaax stopping every now and then along the way to greet familiar faces. Jahrra couldn't resist saying hello to the mailman, Mr. Dharedth, whom she hadn't seen since she started riding Phrym to school.

"Jahrra! My how you've grown! You look a full foot taller than the last time I saw you." His kind eyes crinkled in amusement. "How old are you now?"

"Eleven," Jahrra answered proudly.

"You don't say . . ." the mailman mused. "She's gonna be a tall one, that girl," he added to Jaax. "Say . . ." Dharedth said, looking at the dragon more closely, "you don't look like Master Hroombra. Jahrra, who's your friend here?"

"Oh," Jahrra said in surprise, forgetting that Jaax only ever visited her and Hroombra. "This is Jaax. He doesn't visit often."

"Huh, well it's a pleasure to meet you. Jaax is it? I go by Dharedth. How do you do?" Dharedth didn't seem intimidated by Jaax one bit, and Jahrra was glad of this. The mailman was used to seeing Hroombra, so the sight of a dragon wasn't as shocking as it would've been to anybody else, she decided.

"I'm glad to meet you, and I'm well." Jaax cast a firm glance at Jahrra before continuing in a rather diplomatic manner, "I wish we could stay and chat, but we have an important meeting in town."

"Oh, I best be off now too. You two may have the day off, but we delivery folk don't. Have a nice day." He waved cheerily as he clicked his old horse on down the road.

"You too!" Jahrra called after the clattering mail cart. She stopped smiling when she turned and saw the look on Jaax's face.

He spoke before she could give his serious gaze any more thought.

"Jahrra, the lessons you'll be receiving and those who'll be training you must be kept a secret. You cannot tell anyone about them. And in case you're thinking of telling the whole world just to upset me, remember that this request comes from Hroombra as well. Luckily your mailman friend wasn't overly curious, but in case we see anyone else they'll receive the same explanation I gave him."

Jahrra risked another look at him, but when she saw more than just sternness and no trace of smugness in his gaze, she quickly focused her attention on the road straight ahead and nodded in subtle obedience. Had that been fear she saw behind Jaax's stony green eyes? Fear or not, Jahrra could see that this issue was very important to the dragon. As much as she disliked him, however, she felt that on this matter it would be best to do as she was told, no questions asked.

Jahrra cleared her throat as they came to the bottom of the hill and said, more to disrupt the awkward silence than anything else, "So these lessons are going to be like my Kruelt lessons? Top secret?"

Jaax didn't answer for a while so Jahrra shot him a sideways glance. He was smiling, though his eyes were trained keenly on the path ahead.

"So," he drawled, "Hroombra has finally started teaching you the language of the dragons."

Jahrra nodded. "Do you speak it?"

"Tehna."

Jahrra's heart skidded to a halt. She knew *tehna* meant *yes*, but she was suddenly terrified Jaax was about to start speaking to her in Draggish.

As if reading her thoughts, the dragon said "Shall we continue the conversation in Kruelt?"

"No," Jahrra said too quickly.

She immediately flushed. Now she was going to have to tell Jaax just how much of a challenge the language was for her. *One more point against me,* she thought miserably.

She was surprised when he answered, "Very well, another day perhaps."

Jahrra had been so absorbed in their conversation that she was surprised to look up and see a crossroads ahead marked by a crude sign. The arrow that pointed eastward read *Aldehr Lake & Edyadth* and the one that pointed northward read *Raenyan Wilders & Glordienn*. She remembered taking the eastern road when she and her friends went to Aldehr Lake once, but Jaax motioned her to lead Phrym down the northern road this time.

"I thought we were going into Aldehren," she commented, her voice overtaking the soft plodding of dragon's feet and horse's hooves and the delicate swish of Phrym's tail.

Jaax waited a long while before answering, "We're not going into the city but to the home of two elves, Viornen and his wife, Yaraa. They're old friends of mine and just happen to be excellent trainers in the arts of combat. They can teach you basic defense and attack maneuvers, fine tune your horsemanship and perfect your archery."

Then his grim mouth tweaked into a tiny grin. "Not to mention, they're the only people in this province that I can trust with this task."

Jahrra blinked at him and secretly wondered if Jaax truly trusted anyone. *But elves!* she thought with a thrill.

The path they now followed ran snuggly along the base of a range of steep hillocks. Jahrra looked around warily and frowned, despite the bright sunshine warming her skin. The trees along the dreary road appeared to be sick with a cold and the empty wood and its depressed surroundings would surely turn away any traveler that happened by; except for one girl and the dragon following her of course.

*Well, this path sure goes well with Jaax's personality. My new trainer is probably just as bad as he is.* Jahrra thought with a sigh, forgetting the wondrous images of magical elves she had envisioned earlier. She tried with all her might to make light of the situation, but she simply couldn't find anything pleasant to look at, even the occasional lizard or bird was dull and comatose.

They continued down the trail for another half hour or so and gradually the intermittent oaks became so crowded that any light making its way through the thick canopy was stopped before it could reach the ground. These trees, Jahrra noticed, looked less depressed than the others, but she was convinced it was only her imagination. A few more turns around the dusty lane proved her wrong, however, when they came upon a bright cottage tucked back into a secluded gully.

Jahrra gaped in surprise, astounded at the contrast the cheery white house made against its boring surroundings. It was a single storied place, constructed of stone and topped with a red wood pole roof. There was smoke of a peculiar purplish color rising out of the tall chimney, and the front door, a rich blue in color, was open to a stone path that led out onto the road.

Window boxes, painted to match the door, overflowed with flowers, and a trail of herbs, vegetables and wildflowers complimented the white fence surrounding the entire place. Glittering sunlight, looking like beams of golden magic, spilled through a great gap in the leaves of the tall oaks, giving Jahrra the impression of a fairy cottage she'd once seen illustrated in one of Hroombra's books.

"I'll approach first," Jaax spoke, jolting Jahrra from her quiet survey. "Yaraa and Viornen know me, and they're wary about strangers." He turned to gaze down at her. "That's why they live so far away from town."

Jahrra nodded numbly and watched as Jaax casually approached the beautiful little cabin. She finally felt at ease when a man and woman came out of the charming setting and approached the dragon peacefully. They were too far away for Jahrra to get a good look, so she busied herself with soaking up the enchanted scene while she waited. She raked her eyes over their small but impressive garden, picking out the plants she knew. She detected the fragrance of jasmine floating on the air, brushed aside every now and again by the smell of something wonderful cooking inside: a savory blend of roasting poultry and sweet, fresh bread. Her mouth watered against her will and she longed to climb down from Phrym and stretch out her legs, but she feared if she moved it would cause this wonderful place to disappear back into the dreary wood.

Several fat, mottled chickens wandered around in the yard clucking contently and looking for grubs. They were guarded by a watchful, grey-speckled rooster that gave her an accusing glare. A ruddy colored sow and her piglets ran by making quite a racket and kicking up dust off of the dry road. The family of pigs was trailed by a scraggly gray deer hound that seemed to find endless joy in harassing them. Jahrra smiled as the noisy bunch hustled by, completely ignoring the marble-gray semequin and his rider.

Jaax turned his head then to look back in Jahrra's direction. She saw him and quickly straightened in the saddle. She tried to look attentive, but the dreamy atmosphere made it hard to do so. It was almost as if this small house and its surroundings had been enveloped in some sort of magical bubble. It glowed with enchantment while the trees, hill and road nearby seemed to be sleeping under a cloak of dust and grime.

Jahrra kept her eyes on Jaax, hoping he would signal what she should do next. After several minutes of gazing directly at her without so much as blinking, he gave a single nod, letting her know it was safe to approach. She led Phrym slowly towards the edge of the path where the dragon and the two elves stood. She felt a strange tingling over her skin as she moved closer to the cabin, and she thought she could hear faint singing in the corners of her mind. She shook her head and focused on reaching Jaax, wondering if Phrym was being affected in the same way she was.

Once Jahrra moved closer to the couple, she could see that there was no mistaking them as elves. The man was slight and shorter than most adults she knew, and the woman was just the same. They both had dark green-brown eyes and long, rich brown hair that shone like gold. The man had his hair pulled back neatly into a ponytail and the woman's was fashioned into a long braid. They both stood attentive with their hands clasped behind their backs, the sharp features of their faces looking rather statuesque. If Jahrra had to guess their ages, she wouldn't know what to presume. The couple looked younger than middle-aged, but being elves they could be hundreds or even thousands of years old.

"Jahrra, this is Viornen and Yaraa, and you'll refer to them as Master Viornen and Mastress Yaraa. They'll be your trainers for your new defense lessons." Jaax nodded to each of them in turn.

Jahrra slid off of Phrym, not wanting to be disrespectful, and approached the two elves timidly.

"Nice to meet you. I hope to learn a lot from you."

The pair smiled brightly, and Jahrra relaxed a little.

"We're pleased to meet you, Jahrra," Yaraa said in a melodious voice. "We've heard so much about you."

She gave a welcoming gesture with her arm, the white sleeve of her simple cotton shirt fluttering with the movement.

Jahrra smiled again and gave a slight curtsey, something she felt odd doing in leather pants and an old stained, tattered tunic.

"We're eager to train you in the old ways Jahrra. We haven't had this opportunity in many years." Viornen spoke this time, his kind voice just as musical as his wife's.

Jahrra took a minute to wonder if this was an effect of the magic surrounding this place, but grew attentive when Jaax spoke again, using his most commanding voice, "As I have told you, Viornen and Yaraa are true elves, something that is not too common in these parts. You may also have noticed that they have inherited the gift of magic. It is used to help keep their home hidden. If the wrong people found out about them there could be trouble, so I want to stress the importance of keeping these lessons secret, even from your closest friends. They may mean no harm, but like I said, if the wrong people were to find out. . ."

Jaax let the end of his sentence hang in the enchanted air. He gave Jahrra another one of his steady, intrusive glares and Jahrra knew that he was serious. The grave faces of the two elves only supported the dragon's words and not for the first time Jahrra wondered about these secret lessons. She also wondered why these elves were hiding out in the first place. Surely they wouldn't be shunned in town? She took a deep breath and nodded to the dragon and her new trainers, signaling to them that she understood.

Suddenly, the intense mood was interrupted by an explosion of noise. Three young children, the spitting images of the two adults, came bursting through the front door of the cabin. Jahrra watched as two girls and one boy went tearing around the corner of the yard after the lazy chickens, which instantly became alive with terror. The dog that Jahrra had seen earlier trailed after them, barking and chasing the chickens in a playful ruckus.

"Oh, don't mind them," laughed Yaraa. "They have just all gotten over a spit of sickness and they've been cooped up for weeks." Then she added with a sly grin, "Looks like they've recovered from their shyness as well."

The children finished their lap around the house, breathless from their exertions, and stopped dead when they saw Jaax.

"Whoa!!!" said the young boy, eyes wide as saucers. "A dragon!"

The two girls skidded to a halt behind their brother, gaping in awe. Jahrra forced away a smirk as she reminded herself that these children wouldn't be so impressed if they knew what Jaax could really be like.

"Samibi, Strohm, Srithe," Viornen said, his arms crossed tightly across his chest, "don't stare, it's rude."

"Sorry Pa, but isn't it magnificent!" the little boy piped.

"It's alright, Viornen, I don't mind," Jaax laughed softly.

Jahrra looked up at him in surprise. *When has Jaax ever laughed before?* she wondered, unable to ever remember the dragon looking so much at ease.

"Hey, who are *you?*" asked the oldest girl when she spotted Jahrra.

Jahrra, who'd been standing back and watching in mild amusement, flinched when the attention was suddenly directed at her. It took her a moment to register what the girl had said.

"I'm, I'm Jahrra."

She blushed in embarrassment. She wasn't used to anyone taking such positive interest in her. Usually it was the opposite.

"I'm Samibi," the girl replied, not at all noticing Jahrra's awkward discomfort, "and this is my brother Strohm, and my sister Srithe."

Jahrra smiled and felt her muscles relax. She was so used to the laughter and sneers from the younger children in the schoolyard that it was a treat being so easily accepted here.

Samibi, Strohm and Srithe soon lost interest in their two guests and started a game of tug-of-war with their dog. While the children tried their best to wrestle the rope away from the hound, Jahrra tried to guess their ages. They looked to be four, six and eight in Nesnan years, but like their parents, they could've been much older considering the endless life span of elves.

# The Elves of Dhonoara

"Samibi, why don't you go show Jahrra your tree house and your garden?" Yaraa suggested kindly, tucking a loose strand of hair behind a sharply pointed ear.

"Oh! C'mon, it's grand!" the eldest girl chirped, her face radiating happiness.

The children grabbed Jahrra's hands and dragged her off behind the cabin to see their world.

Jaax turned to the two elves as soon as the four children were out of sight, and just out of ear shot. "So, what do you think? Will we be able to pull this off?"

"She definitely looks human, but are you absolutely sure Jaax?" Viornen asked quietly, donning a more serious face now that the children were gone.

"Yes, absolutely. I arrived in Crie as soon as I could," the dragon insisted, "and she was only a week old when I arrived. She had blue eyes as an infant. That could only mean she's human."

"After all these years . . ." Viornen said in a quiet voice, his face paling slightly.

"Oh, Jaax," Yaraa cried, hardly able to hold back her excitement, "finally, *finally* she's come to us! Jahrra will be the start of a new era, I'm sure of it!"

"Now, let's not get ahead of ourselves. She's still quite young and has much to learn," Jaax answered. With a more serious and warning tone he continued, "You must understand, she's been raised believing she is Nesnan. She mustn't know who she really is until she is ready."

"You're right to do so," Viornen said after a thoughtful pause. "I don't think she'd be able to comprehend the truth now. We'll prepare her for that day the best way we can."

"Very well." Jaax nodded agreement. "For now, we focus on getting her strong and capable to protect herself. I'm counting on you two, for you are the best ones for this job."

Yaraa flashed the dragon a look of slight confusion.

"Jaax, we're flattered by this honor," she began, her usually smooth brow furrowed, "but surely there must be someone more suited, what about . . ."

"No," Jaax interrupted, his voice like a whip.

There was a silent pause as the tension in the air nearly solidified. Finally, Yaraa went on delicately, "She deserves another chance you know, and she's skilled in more ways than we are . . ." but Yaraa stopped when she saw the threatening look on the dragon's face. Whatever memory or notion she'd been trying to evoke fell short and stayed buried in her mind.

"I know who you're thinking of, and that is absolutely not an option."

Jaax finished this sentence rather harshly with fire building in his nostrils.

Yaraa backed down timidly, something she didn't often do.

"Besides, the energy it would take to find . . ." Jaax began again, but stopped himself and shook his head to clear it. "No, like I said, it's not an option."

Viornen broke the awkward silence that followed with a light-hearted chuckle, "You'll just have to make do with us then. We'll start with the basics after tea. Did you test her already Jaax?"

Jaax didn't answer at first. He was staring at the ground, his thoughts clearly somewhere else. He squeezed his eyes shut and took a sharp breath, releasing a miniscule stream of smoke as he exhaled, "Yes, and I would start at the beginning. She has some skill, but it wouldn't hurt to start her from the bottom and work your way up."

"Will you join us for tea, then?" Viornen queried.

"Oh no, I can't. I have business outside of Oescienne that I've neglected for too long as it is. It's taken precious time stopping in Oescienne at all, but it had been so long since I checked in on the girl," Jaax said coldly, without emotion.

Yaraa, unable to be fooled by Jaax's iron facade, smiled lightly. She donned a maternal look and placed a gentle hand on the dragon's scaly foreleg, "Someday I hope to see you back to your old self Jaax, before . . . well, everything. Until then, promise me that you'll stop every now and then to relax a little and enjoy this life, however dismal it may seem."

Jaax gazed back with those silver green eyes of his and said shortly, "Life can't truly be enjoyed until the Tyrant is purged from his throne. Goodbye Yaraa, Viornen. I'll see you again, but at what time I don't know."

The two elves nodded somberly, as if honoring some ancient code that had been long since forgotten. Jaax returned the gesture just as quietly and just as slowly before turning to leave. As he started back down the lane he spotted Jahrra in the yard behind the cabin, bent over with her hands on her knees, examining the deep blue flowers the elfin children were pointing out to her. He must have lingered too long, because Jahrra turned her head and saw him. She stood up straight, said something to the children, and walked over to the dragon.

"Where are you going?"

Jahrra's question sounded sincere, catching Jaax a little off guard.

"I have to leave, but you are to stay here and begin your training. I take it you remember how to get home?"

Jahrra's earnestness vanished the instant Jaax's sarcasm registered, taking her feelings of disappointment with it.

Her cobalt eyes darkened as she crossed her arms ferociously and took on an unyielding pose, "Oh, so you're just going to leave me out in the middle of nowhere with perfect strangers while you go off to tend to your "business"?"

Jaax felt the beginning of a dry smile as he turned his gaze down the lane. He took his time to answer, something that chafed at Jahrra's patience.

"They're not complete strangers," he finally said with an amused sigh. "I know them quite well and am not at all worried about leaving you here with them. I just hope they can make something out of you."

Jahrra had grown too irate to answer, her face turning red like a boiled thermometer.

When she didn't reply to his rude statement, Jaax continued, "I'll see you in a few years, if I get a chance to visit this part of Ethöes again. If not, good luck with your training."

Jaax snapped open his giant wings and lifted effortlessly into the blue sky, leaving a flustered Jahrra to kick at the earth in irritation. She was angry that she had actually felt disappointed he was leaving; angry that she didn't have a snide reply for him. Now she wished she hadn't apologized earlier for hitting him so hard with that branch.

Jahrra tilted her head so that she was looking at the canopy of the giant oaks, closed her eyes, and exhaled slowly. She was overwhelmingly tempted to gather up Phrym and leave this bright little cottage for good. *Alright,* she thought to herself as the light from the sun filtered through the green leaves and onto her face, *I hate doing anything that Jaax says I have to do, but on the other hand these so called 'lessons' could be very useful against the twins.*

She smiled as she imagined dropkicking Ellysian and sparring with Eydeth in front of the whole school, only to leave him sprawled in the dust. *Oh yes, that would* definitely *be worth giving into Jaax's wishes. And besides, it's not like he'll be around to spy on me and make his rude comments.*

Feeling that Strohm, Samibi and Srithe were quite fine on their own, Jahrra headed back down the shaded lane to where Viornen and Yaraa patiently waited, watching her like a pair of attentive hawks. She felt guilty that they'd been kept waiting as it was, but she didn't want to approach them when she was still in a temper over Jaax.

Of course, the elves knew this already and used the time it took her to walk up the road to discuss their own private thoughts.

"That dragon sure has gotten into the habit of quick fixes," Yaraa whispered amusedly to her husband.

"He does seem to be in such a hurry these days," Viornen answered, just as quietly. "I wonder sometimes if he even thinks his decisions through."

Yaraa hugged her elbows in thought. "The girl is quite young, that's for sure, but she has spirit and although I admire her own unique wisdom, there is much she needs to learn."

"She'll be alright, I think," Viornen murmured as Jahrra closed the gap between them, leaving all other speculation for another time.

"Sorry," Jahrra said bashfully, "your children were so excited about showing me their garden, and then we found the toad . . ."

"Don't worry about it," Yaraa cut in kindly. "They do have a way of kidnapping newcomers; we don't get many visitors out here. Besides, it's only natural you'd want to talk to Jaax before he left."

Jahrra flushed at this statement. She hadn't realized they'd been watching her for so long.

"Oh, well, I wasn't . . ." she stammered, not wanting to admit she'd wanted to say goodbye to the dragon and feeling a bit ashamed they'd read her secret thoughts so easily.

"He shouldn't have left you so suddenly like that. You have every right to be angry." Viornen's kind smile seemed to relax their surroundings.

"How did you know I was angry?" Jahrra asked humbly, knowing that she'd done her best to let that emotion pass before approaching the couple.

"Well," Viornen said with an impish grin, "other than the fact that you attacked the road with your foot when Jaax flew off, I was born with the ability to sense the slightest change in moods."

Jahrra stared blankly. "You can be born with that ability?"

Viornen released a good-natured laugh, and Yaraa smiled along with him.

"I'm sorry!" Jahrra said apologetically, flushing once again. "That was extremely rude of me!"

She was completely mortified by now. These elves could read her emotions like words on a page and she didn't even know them.

"It's quite alright, I assure you," Viornen chuckled. "It's not as simple as that, so I'll explain. People, of all races and species, have a chance of being born with magical properties. Some have stronger ties to magic than others and some have none at all. It's not detectable at first, but once it is, depending on one's level of magic, they are trained to use it and recognize it.

"Now, elves are more inclined to be magical and so are dragons and dwarves, but that doesn't exclude all the other races. I myself happened to be born with a slight level of foresight. I can't read the future; in fact, a mere fortuneteller would put me to shame. What I can do is sense emotions in other people better than most, and I can bring out the good emotions in other living things as well. That's why our plants and trees seem so happy."

Viornen waved his hand around gracefully to point out what he was describing. Jahrra eased a little more, eager to learn all she could about these elves.

"But my abilities are nothing compared to Yaraa's. She can speak to animals." Viornen gazed at his wife in open admiration.

"You can, really?" Jahrra said excitedly, forgetting all about proper etiquette among new adult acquaintances.

"Now Viornen, I can't exactly *speak* to them, but I can touch their minds. Bring me your horse and don't tell me his name," Yaraa said calmly, shifting to a more relaxed posture.

Jahrra quickly scurried over to the other side of the road and grabbed Phrym by the reins, leading him grumpily away from the patch of clover he had been devouring.

"Now, this is what I can do."

Yaraa gently lifted her arm and stretched her hand out flat, placing her palm upon Phrym's forehead.

Phrym, who was usually twitchy around strangers touching him, acted as if nothing was happening. Then suddenly he became alert and looked Yaraa directly in the eye.

After some time, the elfin woman spoke, "He tells me that you gave him the name Phrym. He also tells me that he's not a horse, but a semequin, and is glad to have you as a friend."

Yaraa pulled her hand away from Phrym's forehead and Jahrra almost cried with happiness. She hugged Phrym's neck and he nickered lightly as if laughing at Jahrra for ever questioning his fondness.

"You can take him back now. He also told me those are the best clovers he's ever eaten."

Yaraa smiled as Jahrra led Phrym back to his snack. Jahrra took her time ambling back to where the two elves stood and gazed longingly at both of them, eager to learn more. Yaraa and Viornen may have thought their own abilities were insubstantial, but she thought they were fantastic.

# The Legend of Oescienne – The Finding

"You don't need to be so anxious Jahrra. We're going to help you grow into someone far greater than you know." Viornen tried not to sound so serious, and donned a fresh smile as he continued, "But for today, I think we'll just get to know one another a little better, that way you won't feel so overwhelmed when the real training begins."

The elves invited her into their home to have tea and Jahrra gladly accepted. When she stepped through the front door, she was immediately overwhelmed by the size of the place. The room they stood in was rather large and spacious. Two fat couches and a few comfortable looking chairs dominated the living space with a wide stone table set between them. The walls were covered in bookshelves from ceiling to floor, generously stuffed with books of every size and color. On the opposite end of the room was a pair of blue and green stained glass doors that led out into the backyard.

Jahrra gulped and peeked into the kitchen, just off of the main room. Great ropes of faded, dried flowers and vegetables hung in the rafters. A faint scent of cinnamon, vanilla and ginger spiced the warm, soft air pouring from the oven, and the age-polished stone floor that stretched beneath Jahrra's feet felt smooth and cool even through her leather boots.

Viornen motioned Jahrra to one of the overly stuffed chairs as he took a seat on the couch. Yaraa glided into the kitchen and poured some tea into three cups, setting them on a tray. She offered the cups to Viornen and Jahrra, and then took the tray back into the kitchen, disappearing from sight for a while.

"Now, we'll definitely start you with the basics, whether or not you've had formal training before. Have you?" Viornen stated, lifting his cup of tea from the unusual table.

It looked like a foggy multi-colored crystal that had been cut and polished to just the right size and shape. Jahrra had never seen anything like it, and didn't hear Viornen's question at first: she was too busy studying the stone's intricate beauty.

Viornen smiled as Jahrra continued to be lost in the beauty of the coffee table.

"It comes from our home land, the great valley of Dhonoara in the east."

"Huh?" Jahrra turned her goggle-eyed gaze to the elf.

"The stone slab that is the top of our table." He gestured towards the table top, not at all slighted by her bemusement. "It was extremely difficult to get it this far, but Yaraa and I had to have a piece of the walls of Dhonoara to remind us . . ."

The elfin man paused, cleared his throat and set his cup down, clacking rather noisily against the smooth surface of the table. Jahrra gazed at the polished stone with renewed vigor, absolutely flabbergasted at this new bit of information. *Dhonoara! That's miles upon miles away!* she thought, remembering that she'd seen the name once on one of Hroombra's maps of Ethöes.

She hadn't noticed the dark shadow crossing Viornen's face, however, but by the time she glanced back up at him, the shadow was gone.

"I thought it'd be a good idea to get to know each other a little better before we start training. How about we start by telling our life stories so far?"

Viornen smiled once again, shaking off his moment of dark reverie. "Yaraa, would you like to do the honors?" he prompted.

"Oh, most certainly," Yaraa answered cheerfully, sitting down on the great couch next to her husband. Jahrra jumped slightly, surprised that she had rejoined them so quietly.

Jahrra listened intently as Yaraa spun the tale of their past. Both the elves had been born in Dhonoara in a time of trouble and hardship. It was right around the time the Crimson King took power, when their unique abilities could be easily exploited by the Tyrant. Shortly after they married, they'd fled their homeland, seeking refuge in the west. Yaraa explained that it was extremely hard to leave Dhonoara Valley, so they'd brought a piece of the valley with them. She rapped her knuckles against the coffee table and grinned.

After settling in Oescienne, they started a family. They raised their first children, now grown and living in other parts of the west. As the years passed, they longed for more children and so came Srithe, Strohm and Samibi to fill their home and keep them busy.

Yaraa recited several centuries of history as if it had only been a decade, leaving Jahrra to sit and gape. *They've lived through all of that? Through the creation of the Tanaan Dragons?* Jahrra was astounded and desperately wanted to ask a thousand questions, but she knew she'd be treading on fragile ground. Instead, she sat there with her head buzzing, wondering how her own story could compare to such a broad history.

"I hope that wasn't too long for you Jahrra. I kept it as short as I possibly could."

Yaraa was smiling warmly once again, and Jahrra grinned reservedly.

"Now for your life story," Viornen encouraged, picking up his neglected tea once again and looking at Jahrra in anticipation as he took a cautious sip.

"There's not much to say," she said, rather modestly with a weak grin.

"Oh, I'm sure that's not true," Yaraa persuaded as she cuddled her own mug in her delicate hands. "Go on, it'll help us to understand your true character."

So Jahrra took a deep breath and dove into her own story, secretly thinking of how to make it more interesting so that it might be worthy of these elves. She told them about how she was found abandoned in Crie and how she was adopted by Lynhi and Abdhe. She described her own little cottage and apple orchard, home until her parents died and Hroombra became her guardian.

Jahrra paused when she got to this part of her story. She hadn't realized that talking about the death of her parents as a passing bit of information in a tale could have such an effect on her, and she had to take a few short breaths before continuing. She talked about Gieaun and Scede and how she acquired Phrym, but ended her tale explaining her feelings towards school.

"I don't enjoy school so much; some of my classmates are simply dreadful. There are two Resai children who absolutely despise me, but Gieaun, Scede and I find ways to avoid them."

Jahrra took a quick sip of her tepid tea and eyed the two elves nervously.

"Are you finished?" Yaraa asked kindly when she saw that the girl was not going to continue.

Jahrra nodded, breathing a sigh of relief.

"I know you may not believe it, but your story will help us in formulating your lessons," Viornen said, draining his cup and placing it down upon the polished stone table with a hollow *thlunk*. "We don't focus on just the physical nature of training, but also on the mental aspects of surviving in a challenging world as well."

For the remainder of Jahrra's visit, the two elves described some of the exercises she would come to learn. She listened in wonder as they depicted a few of the different skills she would gain as she progressed in the program. Viornen spoke of the many ways to break away from an enemy or wriggle free from a tightly bound rope. Yaraa explained the dexterity it took to sneak up on someone in the middle of a forest full of dry leaves without making a sound. Viornen then listed off the exercises needed for the various forms of fighting: using a sword, using a bow and using one's bare hands if the need to defend oneself or another arose. Once Viornen, Yaraa and Jahrra finished the last of the tea, the two elves stood to bid farewell to their new student.

"We've learned much about you today Jahrra," Viornen said after some time, "but it's getting late. We'll meet again tomorrow to discuss your training schedule and maybe show you a few maneuvers."

Jahrra looked up expectantly, but Viornen continued with a raised hand before she could form any words.

"Don't worry, these lessons won't interfere with your schooling. Your training will be taking place strictly during the summer months. As you grow older, however, we will expand your practice to also include the days you don't have school."

"This doesn't mean, however," Yaraa added firmly, "that you don't have to practice during the rest of the year. We expect you to keep up with exercises, flexibility stretches and meditation."

Jahrra nodded resolutely, her head still buzzing with this new endeavor, and went to gather Phrym from his clover patch.

Though she had a thousand questions on her mind, she thought it best to ask them later.

"One more thing," Yaraa added as Jahrra climbed into the saddle. "We wish for you to keep these lessons secret. We live far away from town for a reason. You may tell your closest friends, but don't tell them our names or where you take your lessons."

Jahrra promised them both that she'd keep their secret, just as she'd promised Jaax. She grinned secretly, however, when she imagined how satisfying it would have been to rub it in Eydeth's and Ellysian's faces. She was certain they would turn an awful shade of green if they knew she was receiving such privileged lessons from true elves.

Viornen and Yaraa waved one last time and then watched her in silence as she and Phrym walked slowly down the lane.

"She already shows an appreciation for Ethöes and all the life that she gives," Yaraa murmured once the girl and her semequin were far enough away. "The way she observes the life around her is astounding, especially for one so young."

"She's content with the wilds of the world, I can see that," Viornen added silently. "Yet, her mood is not happiness, and I wouldn't want it to be. Happiness about one thing or another can so easily turn. Contentment is the best, at least for now. With contentment one can never grow bored or disgusted.

She fits with the life of this world, and she always will. I can feel a strong spirit within her."

Yaraa smiled up at him, glad to hear her husband's wisdom.

"Yes, she's had to deal with much sorrow in her life, too much for someone so young. I feel she's lost her childhood in a way, but she's still far too young to be an adult. One thing is for certain, however," she sighed, her voice taking on a much brighter tone as her mouth curved in a sly grin, "she's definitely going to give Jaax a run for his money."

Viornen chuckled at his wife's comment, squeezing her tightly against him. They both stood gazing down the lane until the first star could be seen peeking through the black veil of the sky before going in for the night. They knew that this new responsibility would be a challenge, but they also knew the importance of what they did. They had the ability to mold the future of Ethöes, and they felt that finally, after all the years of waiting and hiding, their gifts could be used to help save their world.

# -Chapter Nineteen-
# Invasion of the Twins

The spring months slowly drifted away and the lazy rainclouds swept gently across the sky, draining their life-giving waters and pulling the soft air of summertime behind them. The last frosty clutches of winter had crawled away from the sleeping earth months ago, and outside the Castle Guard Ruin the little garden by the window was overflowing with fragrant flowers. Summer was in full swing in Oescienne, and another school year was finally over. Jahrra didn't mind this passage of time, however. Not only would she be free of her classmates during the warm months, but she would be starting her new lessons with Yaraa and Viornen.

The only bad thing about these lessons, Jahrra reminded herself, was that they took time away from Gieaun and Scede. They also meant following through with Jaax's wishes.

It was times like these that Jahrra would wonder about the enigma that was Raejaaxorix and how much he irritated her. She tried to convince herself she was glad the Tanaan dragon had arrived and left so abruptly, but if she wanted to be truly honest with herself, deep in her heart she was disappointed. When her curiosity finally overruled her stubbornness, she asked Hroombra about the other dragon's strange habit of visiting the Castle Guard Ruin then disappearing just as suddenly.

"He has obligations outside of this province Jahrra, and many of these obligations require extensive traveling."

"He always has excuses, he can't be that busy!" she complained, forgetting she didn't care either way. "And why does he get to tell me what to do anyways? He's never here!"

During the final weeks of school before summer, Jahrra told Gieaun and Scede about her new schedule. She kept her promise by not telling them about her mysterious elfin instructors, but she hadn't been able to hide her irritation with Jaax.

"I'm sure he isn't trying to be mean Jahrra," Gieaun encouraged. "It's probably his way of being supportive."

"Supportive!?" Jahrra snapped, and then she added with thick sarcasm, "That's right, you're not around when he insults my intelligence or accuses me of lying."

Gieaun flinched and didn't say another word. She knew how frustrated Jahrra got when discussing the Tanaan dragon, so Gieaun thought it best not to say anything else unless asked directly.

The weeks passed and Jahrra thought more about this sudden change in her life. She found herself wondering, not for the first time, exactly *why* Hroombra and Jaax insisted on the swordsmanship and archery lessons with the elves. She longed to ask her guardian, but she knew exactly what he'd say: 'You'll understand one day,' or 'It's for the best that you don't know', or 'These lessons will strengthen your character.' Why couldn't he just give her a straight answer for once?

As much as Jahrra hated not knowing the exact reason for these lessons, however, she showed up at the little cabin the first day of summer, more eager than when she had first begun riding lessons with her friends.

In those first few weeks of summer, Jahrra got to know the elves a little better. Both Viornen and Yaraa had a way of informing her of her mistakes without making her feel ridiculous, and for once in her life Jahrra didn't feel like she needed to prove something right away. Her typical week composed of rising early and spending anywhere from four to six hours a day working on archery, horsemanship, and fencing. Yaraa taught her meditation to help focus her mind and calm her nerves and Viornen taught her how to escape from several enemies without a weapon.

"Maybe they're training you to become an assassin!" Scede offered energetically one day as they stretched out in the field beside the Ruin, watching clouds sail by.

"Oh, don't be silly!" Gieaun scoffed. "I'm sure Master Hroombra has a good reason, but I can't think of any right now.

That is, unless he thinks Eydeth and Ellysian are truly dangerous."

"Too bad you can't come with me," Jahrra sighed, brushing a ladybug off her arm.

"I wish we could too, but mother and father need us to help out on the ranch during the summer," Scede complained.

Jahrra was grateful she didn't have to make up excuses as to why they couldn't come with her. Yaraa and Viornen did, however, encourage Jahrra to pass on what she learned to her friends. When Jahrra mentioned this to Gieaun and Scede, however, she got mixed reactions.

Scede, of course, was ecstatic with the idea.

"You're going to teach us fencing and self defense! Really?"

Gieaun, on the other hand, had no interest in participating.

"Learn to fight? I don't know, I think I'd rather just watch you two beat each other up."

She smiled wryly at her friend and brother and all three laughed as they imagined Jahrra and Scede sword fighting with branches and reeds.

When Jahrra was with her friends she almost forgot about all those questions she'd been asking herself lately, but a few important ones still refused to escape her mind. The most important concern being why Hroombra, and sometimes Jaax, two *dragons*, would be the ones responsible for raising her. Now that she was getting a little older, she found herself wondering why Hroombra had never placed her with another Nesnan family after her parents died. Before, when she was a child, she took everything for granted, but not anymore.

As her fierce anger for Jaax dulled, just as it always did after his brief visits, Jahrra began to wonder with a clearer mind what his role was in all of this. She knew that he'd brought her to Oescienne, but why? Why not leave her where she was? Why not find a family in the place where she was born? Why not let another Nesnan bring her here if it was so important that she be in Oescienne?

Hroombra would be the best one to put an answer to these questions of course, but she never worked up the gumption to ask. She would just write them down in her journal to save for a later time, whenever that time might be. Luckily, Jahrra had plenty to distract her restless mind with now that summer had begun.

The first month of practice was torture. The elves had her running long distances every day to get into shape, and then after that, myriad drills and exercises to help strengthen her arms and legs. By the end of her first week, Jahrra was so exhausted that she fell asleep atop Phrym several times on the ride home. When this happened, she would grumble to herself in embarrassment, praying that no one had seen her slumped in the saddle as she made her way up the Great Sloping Hill.

# Invasion of the Twins

As tough as those first weeks were, Jahrra's hard work was soon paying off. By the end of the third week, she was able to run to the waterfall below Lake Aldehr and back to the elves' cabin without even feeling fatigued. Her speed and balance were improving as well, and her reflexes were much quicker and more accurate than they had ever been. Jahrra was so pleased with her progress and her trainers' praise that she completely forgot about her lingering irritation at Jaax.

The summer progressed in this fashion and as her days of freedom ticked by, Jahrra felt a familiar dread growing in the pit of her stomach. The end of summer meant the beginning of school, and that meant another year of enduring the twins' wrath once again. Viornen and Yaraa gave Jahrra the last week of summer off, and she gratefully took advantage of her time by spending every day of it with Gieaun and Scede, going to Lake Ossar or visiting the ocean shore.

The three of them would race their horses down the beach and then lay out on one of the great sand dunes and listen to the waves and shifting shore grasses as they soaked up the blazing sun. They would breathe in the cool, salty breeze and think up new ways to avoid Eydeth and Ellysian this year at school.

"It'd be nice if they just stood there like dead fish," Jahrra said as she dug her toes into the warm, soft sand.

Her boots were off and she'd rolled up her pants to her knees, after shoving her short sleeves up over her shoulders.

Her long golden hair, usually kept bound in a loose braid, was gathered together with a leather band and now resembled a horse's tail. It was a hot day, hotter than usual. Jahrra shot an envious look at Gieaun, who was sprawled out beside her with a wide-brim hat shading her face. She'd had enough sense to wear a short-sleeved sun dress and sandals. Scede had on short pants and a short-sleeved tunic and sandals as well.

"But you know they'll have something to say back, and they *always* have friends with them," Scede said knowledgeably as he pushed aside a clump of needle-sharp dune grass so he could sit down.

"I just wish I could say something brave to them, without a nasty retort from Ellysian," Gieaun sighed, sliding down the sandy slope and causing an avalanche of powdery sand.

Jahrra and Scede went sliding down after her, laughing and squealing as they tumbled down the steep incline. Phrym, Bhun and Aimhe, who were nibbling on some willow leaves at the base of the dune, looked down at the pile of children below them, their ears perked forward in curiosity.

"I don't know about you, but I could sure use a swim to Reed Island," Scede said, standing up and brushing off the sand that stuck to his skin like sugar.

"Me too!" Gieaun breathed. "Let's enjoy a few more days of freedom from the twins while it lasts!"

The three friends climbed atop their horses and pointed them eastward. As they approached Lake Ossar, they heard the cheerful voices of other adults and children enjoying the warm summer day. Jahrra smiled as Phrym's hooves thudded against the boardwalk spanning the glittering lake. She smiled because she knew that not one of those voices belonged to any of her unfriendly classmates. They walked the length of the boardwalk and tied their horses up under the grove of willows just off shore.

"C'mon you two!" Scede called hurriedly as the girls dawdled behind him. "Let's see if our boat is still where we hid it last!"

He began digging around in a particularly large clump of reeds and let out a bark of triumph once he found the tiny vessel still intact. Once all three of them were inside the crude water craft, they began paddling out to the middle of the lake where their island of reeds sat waiting.

"We haven't been here in months!" Gieaun breathed. "I hope no one has taken over our island."

Jahrra agreed, but as they approached, they found their island just as they had left it: a small patch of dark, damp earth covered in moss and surrounded by a thicket of tall, shady reeds. Scede pushed the boat through a tiny gap in the rushes on the far side of the little islet and Jahrra jumped out into the knee-deep water to pull the boat closer. Scede and Gieaun helped her, quickly pulling it up over the reeds. The girls laid out some of the blankets they'd brought with them as Scede spied on all of the other people that were enjoying the lake. He saw families walking along the boardwalk, but no one he recognized. Many people were fishing, swimming or simply relaxing.

"Anything to report from the outside world?" Jahrra asked as she and Gieaun sat down on one of the blankets.

"No, just the usual," Scede replied, giving up his post and joining the girls.

After relaxing for a while, Scede and Jahrra decided to have a race from their little island to the boardwalk and back. The rules were that they would swim to one of the pier supports, swim clear around it, and then swim back. Gieaun was to be the referee, since she refused to swim so far out into the lake.

"Don't you two remember the lake monster father always talked about on our camping trips?" she queried teasingly.

"Oh, Gieaun, there's no such thing!" her brother groaned.

Jahrra laughed and glanced back at Gieaun, who looked a little vexed.

"Don't worry, Gieaun!" Jahrra snickered. "If it does eat us, think of it this way: at least you'll finally know for sure it exists. And besides, you'll be safe if you stay on Reed Island!"

"Very funny!" Gieaun chirped. "I remember you used to be afraid to put even a toe in the lake Jahrra!"

"Oh, that was ages ago!"

"Ugh, are you going to race or not?" Gieaun asked, sounding a little exasperated.

When Jahrra and Scede gave her a tense look she took a deep breath and said, "Ready . . . set . . . *GO!*"

They dove into the water and began swimming frantically towards the boardwalk. Gieaun watched them carefully, squealing dramatically every time something other than Scede or Jahrra broke the surface of the water.

"Look out! It's the lake monster!" she shouted after them.

When the two friends reached their post and started making their way back, they were neck and neck. By the time they were only ten yards from the small island, however, it was clear that Scede was trailing quite a bit. Jahrra reached the small island first and was panting over the muddy bank a full thirty seconds before Scede reached the shore.

Both were out of breath, but Scede managed to say between gasps of air, "Looks . . . like . . . those lessons . . . Jaax . . . is making . . . you take . . . are paying off."

Jahrra hadn't realized it, but swimming to the boardwalk and back hadn't been as hard as it used to be. It also got her thinking that maybe she should be working on swimming lessons as well as everything else. She made a mental note to herself to bring it up with Viornen and Yaraa the next time she saw them.

For the rest of the afternoon, the three of them stretched out on their blankets and watched the clouds roll by overhead. Jahrra spotted a variety of objects, everything from a mouse evading a cat to a kruel of dragons gathered in assembly. Behind them trailed a group of prancing horses and a watchful owl. Scede said he saw a centaur in one cloud, and Gieaun swore that the cloud she was looking at resembled Ellysian.

"It looks just like her!" she insisted. "You know, when she is marching around the schoolyard, telling everyone what to do."

The children had a good laugh and were soon on the subject of the evil twins once again.

"Ugh, I can't believe school is starting up in a week and we'll have to see them again!" Jahrra complained as she continued to stare skyward, her hands behind her head. "I wonder where they went on vacation *this* year!"

The twins always came back to school with tales of how they'd visited such places as the strange and tropical shores of Torinn or the mysterious and magical lands of Felldreim.

"No one can visit Felldreim!" cried Gieaun, watching the strutting cloud that was Ellysian break up and form into another shape, a mythical mihrcor. "I'm sure they were making that one up! Father says the entire province is surrounded by magic and only those who belong there can enter!"

Jahrra wondered if this was true as she watched what looked like a herd of gelbu taking form above them. Hroombra had taught her a little about the Northern Province, but he never went into much detail, even when she begged. She'd heard many stories from the children at school about Felldreim, but everything she'd heard seemed impossible. As much as Jahrra thought what her classmates said was total nonsense, she hoped in her heart that such a place really did exist. After all, she *had* seen unicorns in the Wreing Florenn once.

Jahrra rested her head deeper in the soft clump of moss she was using as a pillow and allowed the unpleasant thoughts of the twins to sink to the back of her mind. Before her eyes closed she caught one more glimpse of the streaming clouds above, appropriately shaped like a herd of dancing unicorns.

❀ ❀ ❀

Jahrra hadn't been asleep long, but already she was having a terrible dream. Gieaun and Scede were with her, setting out a picnic on Reed Island. She was breathing in the warm summer air and chasing after dragonflies when an unpleasant voice shattered the peaceful atmosphere, "Hey Nesnan! What're you doing, building your dream house? I guess reeds and mud are a step up from that dragon-infested pile of rubble you live in!"

The sound of Eydeth and his friends laughing hysterically from the boardwalk jerked her awake. She sat up, breathing harder than usual, and looked around. She was still on the island in the middle of the lake and Gieaun and Scede had fallen asleep next to her.

Jahrra closed her eyes and pulled in a deep breath. *Phew!* she thought, *what a nightmare!* But just as she was starting to relax, she heard something that made her stomach turn:

"Would you look at this place? It might be half-way decent if it wasn't crawling with Nesnans!"

"No!" Jahrra breathed silently, rising up into a low crouch.

She quietly scurried over to the edge of the island and peered out of a small gap in the reed screen. What she saw made her heart almost stop. It was Eydeth and Ellysian, accompanied by at least five of their classmates. They were in the middle of the boardwalk, looking out over the lake. Farther down the shore a pair of horses was strapped to a fancy paddleboat.

"No!!!" Jahrra repeated a little more hoarsely, her teeth gritting together in utter frustration.

Gieaun stirred awake, along with Scede.

"We must've fallen asleep," Scede said through a yawn as he sat up a little.

"Jahrra, what're you doing?" asked Gieaun sleepily.

When Jahrra didn't answer, they crawled up next to their friend and peeked out toward the boardwalk.

"Eydeth!!! What's *he* doing here?" Scede breathed scathingly.

"And Ellysian, too!" Gieaun growled. "Oh, look at that boat! I wonder who *that* belongs to! Honestly, is everything they own so, so *horribly* expensive-looking?"

Gieaun crossed her arms and sat down rather forcefully. Jahrra was still so upset she just continued to glare angrily.

"Well," said Scede, slumping down next to his sister, "I just hope they don't come out here."

Unfortunately, it seemed that's exactly what they planned to do. The group of children walked down the boardwalk towards the boat and climbed in, Eydeth and Ellysian giving the others orders to row. As she watched, Jahrra grew sick; they were paddling right towards her small island.

Scede saw them too and scrambled to his feet, almost knocking Jahrra into the lake.

"They can't possibly think of coming over here!" he hissed.

They quickly scuttled back to join Gieaun hampered down on the quilt, listening quietly for their classmates' voices. Several minutes passed before they could make out Eydeth's grating voice.

"Can you believe some of these Nesnans actually make a living fishing out here? There can't be anything worth catching! No wonder they're so poor!"

Jahrra held her breath, and her temper, wishing she was still dreaming.

Ellysian answered him after a while, "Speaking of Nesnans, I wonder if Jahrra and her Nesnan-lover friends are out here."

Jahrra froze. That was the first time she had *ever* heard Ellysian say her name, and it sounded like it actually physically hurt her to say it.

"Oh, they are," Eydeth said casually. "That was her horse in the clearing, I recognized it. If we can't find them, we could always torment that stupid animal. She acts like it's her best friend. How pathetic is that?"

Everyone in the boat snickered, and Jahrra shook with both rage and fear. Would he really do something to Phrym? If it wasn't for Gieaun and Scede holding her down, she would've jumped right into their approaching boat, practicing some of the skills she'd learned from Yaraa and Viornen on them. Instead, she was forced to secretly curse the twins and their gang of bullies from afar. She only hoped that Phrym would break away if they went after him.

"Should we dock at the other shore and continue on to the sea?" Ellysian asked in her mock-royal voice.

"No, I want to see what that clump of reeds is all about. Maybe we can find some bird nests or something," Eydeth said boorishly.

Jahrra quickly looked at Gieaun and then Scede with large eyes, the blood draining from her face.

"Find some bird nests!" Gieaun growled. "All he'd do with some bird nests is wreck them and break the eggs!"

The three friends hunkered down in the center of their blanket and tried to think of a way to distract the group.

"We could swim to shore!" Scede breathed quietly.

"No," Jahrra said solemnly, feeling herself turn green. "They'd chase us down in that boat and drown us before we got ten feet from here. Let's face it, we're trapped."

Fortunately, the problem was solved before any drastic measures were needed.

"No way!" Ellysian whined. "That clump of weeds is probably sitting in a pile of muck and we would end up covered in mud! A queen and her royal entourage never set foot in mud!"

They continued rowing past the island, but they were close enough for Jahrra to hear Eydeth's mumbled complaint and soon even the sound of the oars slapping the water disappeared.

"That was close!" Scede breathed, slumping onto his back.

Gieaun joined her brother in a huff, sounding as if she'd been holding her breath for the last several minutes. Jahrra, on the other hand, continued to glare after the boat now disappearing in the distance.

"What on Ethöes are they doing here?" she said so quietly it sounded like a hiss.

Gieaun and Scede both looked up at her, their relief quickly turning to apprehension.

"Maybe they ran out of people to bother in Kiniahn Kroi," Scede offered sarcastically.

Gieaun shot her brother a sour look and tried to break Jahrra's stern composure softly. "You know, they may just be exploring the area. I mean, it's not like Lake Ossar is a secret."

"They came here to torment us, I'm absolutely sure of it!" Jahrra shouted as she spun around.

Gieaun flinched and Scede quailed at his friend's anger.

"Look, Jahrra," Gieaun began gently, "they didn't see us, they only saw the horses. They probably think we're out in the dunes somewhere and I doubt they want to waste their entire day looking for us. Once they find out this place is too big to chase us down, they'll leave."

Jahrra was still fuming, but she saw the truth in what her friend said. Sighing, she dropped her clenched fists to her sides and took a deep breath.

"You're probably right, Gieaun. But I think we should head home, that way they won't run into us and have a reason to stay."

The three companions packed up their blankets and piled them into their homemade, rickety boat. Once back on shore, they quickly hid the boat among the shore plants and approached the horses. Jahrra breathed a grateful sigh of relief when she saw that nothing had happened to Phrym. While she rubbed his mane out of his eyes and touched his forehead with her own, she risked a glance at the horses the twins had used to haul their obnoxious water craft. The poor things were shifting uneasily and puffing in slight fear, pulling at the ropes wound snuggly around a thick tree branch. *I know how you feel,* she thought, *I would be afraid of them too.* Just then, an idea sparked in her mind like flint striking stone in the dark.

"Hey Gieaun, Scede . . ." she said quietly.

They looked up from their task of getting the blankets secured to Bhun and Aimhe.

"Yeah?" Scede asked.

"How about we give Eydeth and Ellysian a little reminder not to come out here again."

"What do you mean?" Gieaun queried, her voice hard and her green eyes narrowed.

Jahrra simply grinned and untied the lead ropes keeping the two horses in place, causing the animals to twitch and stomp their feet.

"Well, what if their horses accidentally pulled free and decided to go wandering off on their own?"

"Jahrra! No!" Gieaun gasped.

Scede, on the other hand, looked like he was quite fond of the idea.

Gieaun flashed him a threatening glare, but he brushed her gaze aside and said, "Oh come on Gieaun! How many times have the twins tormented us? Let's give them a taste of their own medicine."

Gieaun groaned as Jahrra dropped the ropes and Scede frightened the horses farther down the road.

"I hope you two are satisfied!" Gieaun complained on their ride back home.

"Oh, we are. Especially when I picture the twins chasing down their loose horses."

Jahrra let loose a peel of laughter and even Gieaun, who had been so well composed earlier, gave up and joined the fun.

"I still can't believe they came all the way out here," Jahrra mused after some time.

Gieaun gave her friend a meaningful look and Jahrra quickly added, "I'm just wondering how they knew about Lake Ossar at all, it's not like we talk about it at school."

They took the path that led through Willowsflorn and wrapped around the base of the Sloping Hill. By the time they made it to the Castle Guard Ruin the western sky was painted with the red-gold hues of sunset. Jahrra watched her friends ride away over the southern hill and shivered as the heat of the day gave way to the cool of the evening. She shut her eyes and breathed in the crisp flavor of the distant fog suspended out over the ocean, allowing it to fill her entire body.

Jahrra tried to relax in the beauty that surrounded her, but no matter how hard she tried, the thoughts of the past summer were alive in her mind. School would be starting up again in one week's time, and that meant no more daily lessons with Viornen and Yaraa. It would be hard for her to train on her own during the school year without their constant encouragement, but she was determined not to let them down.

"Even if you just practice your meditation and a few of your basic exercises, that'll help you greatly," Viornen had told her.

Jahrra jumped when Phrym nickered quietly from inside his stable. She'd nearly forgotten she was still standing out in the field so far from the Castle Guard Ruin. She smiled and reached out to scratch Phrym on the cheek.

"I'm not ready to go back to school yet, are you?"

Jahrra smiled tiredly and Phrym leaned his warm muzzle into her shoulder. She imagined that she could fall asleep standing right there next to him, for no one comforted her more than Phrym. After some time she reluctantly left him and walked down to the Ruin. She went to bed early, waving sluggishly to Hroombra and muttering some words of goodnight.

During the last few days of summer Jahrra didn't do much except tend to her garden and ride across the fields with Phrym. The weather was pleasant, but she could sense the wonderful, brisk approach of autumn. The air was warm but the breeze was crisp and cold and it held a hint of distant rain and the scent of the coming harvest. Soon the leaves would turn scarlet and crimson and the fields would turn gold and orange with ripening hay, corn and gourds. Jahrra closed her eyes and relished the idea of the coming season, hoping that her time at school would be just as pleasant.

On their final day of vacation, Jahrra, Gieaun and Scede decided to visit Lake Ossar one last time. They arrived cheerful and ready for a day of relaxation only to find the twins and their friends had beaten them there.

"Not possible!" Jahrra hissed between gritted teeth from behind a screen of trees.

Both Eydeth and Ellysian were walking along the boardwalk, trailed by an even larger crowd than the last time.

"Oh, how could they?" Gieaun said miserably. "I was so sure they wouldn't come back after last time."

"This was our only retreat from them!" Scede groaned. "Now what're we going to do?"

The three friends turned their horses in the direction of Lake Aldalis and fumed the whole way there. They enjoyed what they could of the day at the other lake, but Aldalis didn't have their Reed Island and it didn't have their boat or their boardwalk.

"If it's the last thing I do," Jahrra said angrily as they left Lake Aldalis behind later that afternoon, "I'll find a way to keep them away from Lake Ossar."

If being forced from her favorite retreat wasn't bad enough, dealing with the twins' recharged indignation at the schoolhouse was worse. Jahrra could only guess that this was

Eydeth's way of paying her back for his failed prank those few years ago in Kiniahn Kroi, and she was tempted to tell him that chasing them away from Lake Ossar was enough.

Gieaun, as usual, talked some sense into her however.

"The last thing you want to do is let him know just how much it bothers us."

So Jahrra was left to grit her teeth and bear the twins' daily assaults in silence, which in turn forced her and her friends dangerously close to the breaking point; the three friends barely made it through the fall months without resorting to violence.

The Solstice break offered them a chance to rise to the surface and take a breath, but it also somehow recharged Eydeth's and Ellysian's malice, if that was even possible. The second half of the school year was better, and in some ways worse, for Jahrra. One positive turn was the addition of Rhudedth and Pahrdh to their small group. Their presence helped increase the numbers against the twins and their fan club: it was harder to gang up on five instead of three, especially when the ginger-haired brother and sister constantly reminded the class of Eydeth's attempt to kill Jahrra in Kiniahn Kroi.

Jahrra was unfathomably grateful to her two new friends, but despite their added support, Eydeth and his sister refused to back down, especially when it came to her favorite retreat. The twins had made it a weekly habit to visit Lake Ossar, a routine that was worse than all of their horrible deeds combined. Jahrra had to be restrained on several occasions by her friends, for she had quite a few of Yaraa's techniques she wanted to use on Eydeth.

"No, Jahrra, it'll only get you in trouble!" Gieaun breathed desperately as she and Scede struggled to hold her back.

"I'm going to kill him, and his sister! I could flatten both of them in less than a minute!" Jahrra was livid, for Eydeth had done a very rude impersonation of her falling from the canyon wall in Kiniahn Kroi.

"Don't, Jahrra, it's not worth it!" Rhudedth squeaked as she and her brother ran over to help diffuse the situation.

As much as she wanted to pummel Eydeth to a pulp, Jahrra knew her friends were right. She gritted her teeth and took her anger out on a clump of grass in the corner of the schoolyard, kicking it until it ripped away from the earth. *I'm going to get those two one of these days, but Gieaun and Rhudedth are right. I can't just attack them, that'd be too easy.*

Jahrra sighed deeply, kicking the pulverized lump of grass one more time before climbing atop the granite boulder and slumping on her stomach. The great stone was hard and cold and Jahrra gladly welcomed its chill against her hot skin. As her anger ebbed, she watched as Eydeth and his sister moved to the other side of the yard, finally losing the audience that had grown tired of listening to their teasing. *Someday,* Jahrra thought once more, her irritation slowly becoming replaced with rancorous determination, *someday you'll pay for all of this.*

# -Chapter Twenty-
# The Dare

"Hey *Nesnan* . . ."

The snide remark came from Eydeth, as usual.

Jahrra sighed and rolled her eyes. It'd been a month since the end of winter break, two weeks since she'd almost attacked him after being mocked about the mishap in Kiniahn Kroi. Luckily, after that incident she'd remembered a way to deal with it. The meditation exercises she'd learned from Yaraa and Viornen had done wonders in the field of ignoring Eydeth and Ellysian, but today they'd been more resilient than usual, actually speaking *to* her and not *about* her. In fact, she'd grown rather bored with the twins' redundant insults of late. Really, couldn't they do any better?

Jahrra was sitting in the corner of the schoolyard with Gieaun, Scede, Pahrdh and Rhudedth, trading stories about their various adventures over the break. That is, until Eydeth's grating voice interrupted a rather intriguing anecdote Pahrdh was telling about an unfortunate run-in with a skunk. Pahrdh stopped speaking immediately and waited tensely for Eydeth to continue, wondering what insulting thing he would say next.

As the horrible boy slowly strolled over to her side of the yard, looking like a dog ready to start a fight, Jahrra was determined to stay put on the lichen-covered boulder with her friends.

"Rumor has it you live in the Wreing Florenn," Eydeth continued once he was within ten feet of them. "That's worse than swimming around in a mud-puddle with the Dune People!"

A wave of laughter ensued and soon the rest of the class was drawn to what appeared to be another show put on to torture Jahrra. Jahrra tried to remain cool, desperately grasping in her mind for something smart to say. She hadn't even bothered with her meditation exercises this time, and she could easily detect the frustration and anger in Eydeth's voice. He'd been trying hard to break her for days, and today he seemed full of renewed determination. Well, Jahrra felt determined too. She decided to respond to him this time; she was tired of taking his verbal abuse.

Gieaun and Rhudedth tensed up beside her as she drew breath to speak.

"Actually, I *lived* on the edge of the forest, not in it. Past tense, Eydeth."

Jahrra slid off of her perch and stood in front of the glowering boy, smugly reminding herself that she still had to look down at him.

"On the edge of the forest? How could you bear to live there? Mother says that only heathens and robbers live near the Wreing Florenn!" Ellysian said with delightful disgust as she joined her brother's side, obviously paying no attention to what Jahrra had just said.

Eydeth and Ellysian were enjoying this far too much, and just as Jahrra was about to comment on how dim-witted they were, Scede slid down to stand next to her.

"I'd like to see you go within five miles of that forest, Eydeth. Jahrra lived there for eight years without being afraid, but I've seen the scared look on your face when Professor Tarnik describes what lurks in there."

He stretched himself as tall as he could and laced his arms across his chest, glaring at Eydeth as he continued, "You have some nerve standing there making fun of Jahrra for living near that forest, but let's see you go within a hundred yards of it!"

The whole class quieted down at Scede's sudden outburst. He didn't often speak so boldly in front of his classmates, but when he did it was to make a point.

Jahrra smiled broadly in his direction and noticed that he looked even more irritated than she felt. He glared at Eydeth and Ellysian, looking like he was about to bite if they so much as blinked.

"You couldn't go near the Wreing Florenn if someone tied you up and dragged you there. That's how afraid I think you are."

Suddenly the laughter of their classmates turned from Jahrra to Eydeth, whose eyes had darkened dangerously. Gieaun, Rhudedth and Pahrdh joined their two companions, all three donning a look of determination as if Scede's insult had recharged them.

Discomfited as he was, Eydeth wasn't about to back down.

"Fine, so you don't live there anymore, but the only reason you did was because your dead parents couldn't afford to live anywhere else. Besides, it's not like you *actually* went into the forest. Only someone *brave* would go in there, not a lame little Nesnan like you."

Jahrra was suddenly livid, so she missed the tiny spark that flickered and vanished in Eydeth's eyes; the hint of triumph that glimmered behind the hatred. She forced herself to calm down and drew upon her measly arsenal: Eydeth didn't know about her little escapade with Gieaun and Scede after the unicorns. She knew she should let the evil boy's accusation hang, but she couldn't resist making him look like a fool in front of the entire class.

"Oh, but you're wrong," she crooned, examining her fingernails in a bored manner. "I *have* been in the Wreing

Florenn. It isn't so bad, unless you're afraid of trees, birds and butterflies."

A murmuring began bubbling around the crowd of children.

"You!? Going into the Wreing Florenn? A lie for sure," Eydeth spat venomously, his look of triumph vanishing as quickly as a dry leaf thrown into a fire. "You probably only went into Willowsflorn and thought it was the Wreing Florenn. The trees in Willowsflorn barely come over my head, what could be so frightening about that?"

"Trust me, Eydeth," Jahrra said with a sigh, her hands now placed squarely on her hips, "I would've noticed if I was taller than the trees."

Everyone suddenly burst out laughing, earning a poisonous glare from a red-faced Eydeth.

Scede took advantage of the opportunity of the horrible boy's moment of defeat.

"I've been in the Wreing Florenn too, and so has Gieaun!" he insisted. "We've all been in the forest, and Jahrra is right. You'd have to be a mouse to be afraid!"

The entire class continued sniggering at Eydeth while nodding their heads in apparent respect for the three courageous friends who had braved the Wreing Florenn.

Eydeth immediately overcame his embarrassment and snarled, "They're obviously lying! Remember how she lied about me pulling her down when we had the climbing contest at our Solstice party!"

It was right then that Jahrra realized what he was doing. *He's trying to coax me into going back into the forest. Fine, I'm not afraid, let him challenge me then.* Jahrra was partly eager to show the class that she wasn't afraid of the twins, and she partly wanted to let out all of her pent up frustration about everything he and his sister had done to her and her friends over the years.

Instead of just walking away like she should have, Jahrra glanced around and noted that the majority of the class seemed to believe her story and not Eydeth's. An overwhelming feeling of self-satisfaction overcame her, drowning out the tiny voice of caution in the back of her mind. For once she had Eydeth cornered, and she was going to milk it for all it was worth. Her enemy was vulnerable, and now was her chance to make *him* look like the buffoon for once.

"You just can't handle the fact that I, the Nesnan, am braver than you. That's why you keep telling everyone I'm lying. You're afraid and jealous, and I can prove it." Jahrra plowed on with a sudden burst of self-confidence, "Dare me to go into the forest, Eydeth. Go on. I'm absolutely sure there isn't one single animal or plant in there that could be even remotely dangerous. In front of the whole class I'll prove that you aren't as brave as a Nesnan."

Eydeth stood there speechless for awhile, everyone's eyes darting nervously between the Nesnan girl and Resai boy.

# The Dare

Jahrra could feel her friends tense up next to her, but she ignored them. They would say she had been too bold, that she'd not thought this through. But what was the big deal? They'd been in the Wreing Florenn before, and it was perfectly peaceful.

After a while, Eydeth opened his mouth and said, disbelievingly, "Anywhere in the Wreing Florenn?"

Jahrra nodded. "I'll even travel to Edyadth, taking the *scary* road that passes through the center of it."

She wiggled her fingers spookily and exaggerated her voice, receiving a few more chuckles from the crowd. She smiled broadly, enjoying this far too much.

Then she saw the gleam of spiteful victory in Eydeth's eyes and the evil grin of satisfaction on Ellysian's face. Jahrra changed the expression on her own face immediately. She'd almost forgotten about Ellysian, who'd remained oddly silent during this whole confrontation. *Why do they look so triumphant?* she wondered apprehensively, *I'm the one who's going to prove them wrong!*

After awhile, Eydeth spoke up, his voice quavering with anticipation, "Very well, I choose for you to travel into the Black Swamp. It's within the borders of the Wreing Florenn, and you said anywhere. You can refuse if you want, but that just proves you were lying all along."

Gieaun grabbed Jahrra's arm tightly as if trying to prevent her from stepping off a cliff. Scede made a strange choking sound in the back of his throat, and Rhudedth and Pahrdh, along with the entire class, gasped in shock.

Eydeth was grinning like a jackal and Jahrra could feel her face fading to white. *Oh no!* she thought furiously, remembering how haughty she'd been, *Oh no, oh no, oh no!!! You should've thought before speaking, you should've known they had something more devious planned! The Wreing Florenn is one thing, but the Black Swamp is quite another!* she told herself, panic welling up in her stomach like a thick, oily bubble.

She now understood why Eydeth had looked so victorious earlier. It wasn't because he was sure she hadn't been in the Wreing Florenn, it was because he knew that if he kept at it long enough he could con her into traveling into the deepest, darkest, most fearful part of the dangerous wood. The entire time he'd been acting scared he'd really been baiting her. He wasn't as dumb as she had so complacently convinced herself. She gave herself a mental kick, *How could I have been so* stupid*?!*

Jahrra's internal battle was interrupted by a cold voice.

"The Black Swamp." The words rolled off of Eydeth's tongue like ice water. "I've heard that there are monsters living in there, and we all know the stories about the witch. The bravest of men won't go within a mile of it, and I heard from the most reliable of sources that even dragons are afraid of it. Who would've thought, a dragon being afraid of a witch? But you aren't afraid, Nesnan, oh no, you're *brave*."

# The Dare

Everyone started murmuring again, but it was a low, secretive murmur that suggested they were exchanging their own personal fears and terror tales of the swamp. Jahrra burned with humiliation and horror, coming close to tears.

*No, I won't cry in front of them!* she thought, her fury suddenly engulfing her mortification. She tried hard to focus on anything else but the children sniggering and whispering about her, but all she could hear were Eydeth's words repeating themselves in her head: *I've heard that there are monsters living in there, and we all know the stories about the witch. The bravest of men won't go within a mile of it, and I heard from the most reliable of sources that even dragons are afraid of it. Who would have thought, a dragon being afraid of a witch? But you aren't afraid, Nesnan, oh no, you're brave . . .*

For some reason or another, one line in particular rung louder than the others: *Even dragons are afraid of it . . . Are dragons really afraid to enter the borders of the Black Swamp?* Jahrra wondered, grateful for something, anything that would distract her from the fear, aggravation and shame she felt for snaring herself in Eydeth's trap. Her common sense told her that this was a lie invented by the twins, yet she couldn't help but remember the time she and Hroombra had visited the Castle Ruin and his fear of lingering in the woods after dark.

Jahrra suddenly pictured Jaax being afraid of going into the dreaded swamp, but as hard as she tried, she couldn't get a clear image of that particular dragon being afraid of anything. *Has he ever gone into the Black Swamp of Oescienne?* she wondered.

*No,* she told herself with a slight tinge of bitterness left over from her last encounter with the dragon, *he's never around long enough to stretch his wings let alone explore the haunted corners of the province. But this is something he would definitely disapprove of.*

Eydeth continued to stare Jahrra down, waiting for her to back out, but she was feeling braver by the minute. *How bad could it be?* she wondered, *I've been taking defense lessons and I'm much more prepared than I normally would be to face anything that might be in there.* Jahrra shivered when she remembered the stories about the witch, though. Those frightening tales had caused her more nightmares than any of the others combined. *But they are just stories,* she reminded herself firmly.

Whether her face showed it or not, she couldn't tell, but Jahrra decided right then and there that she would accept the twins' challenge. If there was a monster or hag in the swamp she would just have to face it; there was no way she could back down after her overdrawn display of conceit.

She looked over at Gieaun and Scede and she could almost feel their eyes begging her not to accept. They'd be angry with her for her decision, but they didn't understand. She had to do this, she had to defeat Eydeth and Ellysian this time. As unfair as their dare might've been, she had to prove to herself she could be just as brave as she claimed.

"Well, Nesnan?"

The sudden question snapped her out of her train of thought. Eydeth gazed in her direction with a cold emptiness in his eyes. *I can't let him win,* she thought miserably, *I've got to see this through.*

"Do you think you're brave enough to go into the swamp?" he asked coolly. "Or are you just like all the other Nesnans around here, content with slaving away all day and giving into their superstitions? Do you think you're braver than a dragon?"

Jahrra shot Eydeth a fiery look, despising the way that he belittled everyone who was even remotely different or less fortunate than himself. She looked again at Gieaun and Scede, and Rhudedth and Pahrdh. She could see that even though their gazes begged her not to accept, there was a glint of knowledge in their eyes; they knew exactly what she was going to do.

Jahrra returned her stormy eyes to Eydeth and tried as hard as she could to look through him as he did her, and answered, "Name the time and the place."

The Resai twins bared their vile grins.

"Tomorrow morning," Eydeth said sadistically, "an hour after sunup, at the forest's edge on the bank of the Danu Creek. Don't be late."

❀ ❀ ❀

Jahrra found it hard to sleep that night for a number of reasons. First, she was still bristling about how easily she'd fallen into the twins' trap. Secondly, she was nervous and terrified about what she was about to do the next morning, no matter how many times she tried to convince herself the witch didn't exist. And finally, she was feeling overwhelmingly guilty about the lie she had told Hroombra.

The old dragon had warned her so many times not to go into the Wreing Florenn, and not only had she disobeyed him once, but she was about to do it again. Worse yet, she was going to wander into the deepest part of the forest. It was a long time before she finally drifted into a restless sleep full of strange and dark dreams.

Jahrra rose early despite her grogginess, dressing in her usual leather pants and loose tunic, adding a vest to help fight off the chill of the morning. She paused only long enough to pull her long hair into a messy braid before grabbing her thick riding cloak on the way out of her room. She hastily packed a lunch, sneaking around the Ruin so as not to disturb the great sleeping reptilian mountain that was Hroombra.

She saddled Phrym just as quickly, looking mournfully towards the Danu Creek flowing peacefully out of the Wreing Florenn. The creek was fed by a natural spring, deep within the heart of the forest. This spring also filled up the basin between the two rows of hillocks in the center of the great wood. This soggy basin was the infamous Black Swamp.

Jahrra shivered and wondered if Eydeth and Ellysian were already waiting for her on the edge of the forest. *Them and the entire school*, she thought, a feeling of dread slowly filling her hollow stomach. She'd been too nervous to eat breakfast.

Jahrra and Phrym walked gravely across the field, still gray in the early morning light. They met up with the creek and headed east towards the forest.

As they trudged along, Jahrra thought about her friends' offer to go along with her. Despite the fact that Gieaun was terrified out of her wits and still angry that Jahrra had actually accepted the challenge, she wouldn't let her friend go on such a dangerous endeavor alone.

Jahrra cringed when she recalled her friend's wrath from the day before.

"Have you gone quite mad?" the Resai girl had wheezed. "Jahrra, what's the matter with you? You can't go into that swamp! Don't you know what's in there? It's not just any witch but an evil witch of Ciarrohn that lives in the hollow of the hills, you remember the story. Jahrra! You'll most definitely be killed, and then Eydeth and Ellysian will have won for sure!"

Jahrra pushed Gieaun's voice and Scede's dark eyes to the back of her mind. In the end they had agreed to go with her, refusing to let their best friend go into dangerous territory alone. Jahrra had almost cried; she wanted to be brave, but she couldn't imagine doing this without them.

Phrym's rumbling whicker pulled Jahrra from her reverie. Up ahead, the towering trees of the Wreing Florenn were beginning to swallow the Danu Creek. Jahrra felt her heart drop into the pit of her stomach. She hadn't realized how far they had traveled. They came around one more bend of the shadowed stream and saw the entire school standing on the edge of the forest like a funeral procession. Jahrra thought she was going to faint. She spotted Gieaun and Scede off to the side on their own horses and she timidly led Phrym over to them.

"Am I late?" she whispered harshly, her mouth strangely dry. "I thought I left early enough."

"No, you're early, but they all got here even earlier," Scede said tensely, looking how Jahrra felt.

Jahrra gritted her teeth and fought the sudden waves of nausea. "I guess we'd better get this over with then."

She took a deep breath and led Phrym over to where Eydeth and Ellysian stood. Gieaun and Scede looked on in horror, their nerves slowly melting into pools of fear.

Jahrra addressed the twins, "Alright, what are the conditions, how far do I have to go in?"

She was no longer whispering, and she could hear her own voice trembling.

Eydeth reveled in her dread awhile before answering with a twisted smile, "You'll have to go all the way to the Belloughs, at the very end of the swamp, where the witch lives. Bring back some evidence that you've made it that far or else we won't believe you."

There was an audible gasp at the mention of the word *Belloughs*, but Jahrra forced herself to ignore it. The Belloughs was the worst part of the swamp. Going all the way to the Belloughs would be like diving into the middle of Lake Ossar where the lake monster supposedly slept as opposed to simply wading on the shore. Jahrra pushed the daunting comparison out of her mind and instead focused her attention on Eydeth's continued ridiculous suggestions.

"How could I possibly prove that!" she snipped, forgetting her fear for the time being.

"Oh, I don't know, bring back something that belongs to the witch."

Ellysian and a few of their friends snickered and Jahrra flushed with sudden anger. *That boy is so evil! He knows I can't bring back any proof!*

"Very well," she finally answered, straight-faced and unsmiling, "but if I do, I want something in return."

If she had to prove she made it to the Belloughs, then she wasn't going to do it for free. Something that looked like surprise flashed across Eydeth's face, and Jahrra felt her spirits lift just a little. He hadn't expected her to counter with her own demands.

"If I come back with evidence," Jahrra continued coolly, "then I want you, your sister, and all of your friends to stay away from Lake Ossar. *Forever.*"

Jahrra sat up rigidly in the saddle and held her head up as high as she could. A mixture of annoyance, anger and defeat churned behind Eydeth's cruel eyes. He was obviously fighting the desire to deny Jahrra what she wanted, but he was also deciding whether he should sacrifice one small advantage for her in order to ensure she would still go through with his dare.

Finally, after what seemed like hours, he spoke, "That mud hole? No problem! If you come back with believable evidence of the hag, then you and your Nesnan-loving friends can have that puddle all to yourselves."

Eydeth crossed his arms and smirked, trying to hide the fact that he was annoyed his enemy might be getting something out of this. Jahrra smiled widely and glanced over at Gieaun and Scede, both looking somewhat cheerful for the first time that morning.

"You've got a deal." Jahrra nodded to the twins and trailed her eyes over the rest of the crowd, reassuring herself that they had heard the bargain. She pulled Phrym's reins around and guided him towards the tiny path that eventually led into the heart of the Black Swamp. Gieaun and Scede followed suit on Bhun and Aimhe, Scede looking three shades of grey and Gieaun looking like a wilted flower.

"Hold on, what's this?" Eydeth said suddenly in feigned amusement. "An entourage?"

Jahrra turned around on Phrym, bracing herself for what she knew she was going to hear.

"You go alone, Nesnan. No buddies to help you out, or our deal about the pond is off."

Eydeth and his sister crossed their arms firmly, glaring even more contemptibly than before.

# The Dare

A dramatic muttering swept the crowd as Jahrra looked nervously around, not quite sure what to do. *I should've known he wouldn't want them coming with me!* she thought miserably. She looked at Scede, dread building in her eyes, but he just stared back, a look of helplessness on his own face. Gieaun appeared to be paler than a ghost and seemed to be beyond speech.

"Jahrra!" she finally managed to whisper hoarsely. "You can still tell them no!"

Jahrra turned away and took a deep breath. She knew that if she wanted to win this battle, to win back her favorite place in the whole world, she would have to do this alone.

She released the air in her lungs and with eyes still closed she said, "I'll go alone."

The crowd gasped, obviously shocked at her decision. Eydeth and Ellysian had expected her to back out, but she wasn't going to give them the satisfaction. She opened her eyes and looked at her friends one last time. Scede looked frightened, but encouraging at the same time and his sister was cowering next to him, on the verge of tears.

"Don't worry, I'll be fine. But don't you dare go and get Hroombra until the afternoon if I don't come back, alright?"

Gieaun and Scede reluctantly swore they'd give their friend plenty of time to complete her task. Jahrra hugged them both from Phrym's back and then turned and led him in the direction of the swamp once more.

"If any of you are expecting me to die today, you're wasting your time. I'll go to the Belloughs, but I don't plan on staying," she boldly shot behind her, guiding Phrym into a canter just before disappearing over the small rise in land that eventually dropped into the swamp.

After she crested the low hill, Jahrra let out a long sigh and slouched in the saddle. Her bones felt like rubber and her skin like jelly. *No point in looking brave now, no one is around to see,* she thought as her mouth became parched again.

Phrym walked tediously along the narrow trail stretching in front of them, his hooves making a sucking sound in the black, sticky mud. A sense of dread filled the air and the surrounding woods were oddly silent, the only noise, other than Phrym's feet of course, were his puffs of discomfiture. The air smelled woody, metallic and stale and it reminded Jahrra of the scent of blood. She shivered and tried hard not to imagine stumbling upon a massacre wrought by some horrific beast.

Despite her fear, however, Jahrra encouraged Phrym deeper into the darkening wood. Soon the tall, bright eucalyptus trees were replaced by black, crouching oaks and the first signs of the dark bog crept into view. The scent of putrid water filled the air, and Jahrra's restless mind unwillingly dredged up everything she had ever heard about the Black Swamp. At that moment her memory was recalling an excerpt from one of Hroombra's books:

# The Dare

*The Black Swamp, as it is so called by the many elfin tribes that inhabit Oescienne, is a stretch of wetlands nestled between the two small rows of hillocks within the Wreing Florenn.*

*The swamp gets its name from the blackish mud that makes up its belly, not to mention the dreary and dank atmosphere it exudes from the knotty, sick looking ancient black oaks that guard its boundaries.*

*Not many a soul ventures into the Black Swamp and only a few brave its borders to collect the coveted mushrooms and rare herbs that grow within its dark interior. It is also said that the best mistletoe grows in the canopies of the black oaks there, but even fewer people venture in deep enough to collect it.*

*The dreary environment and unpleasant surroundings are not the only reason people avoid the swamp. According to local legend, many fearsome and mysterious creatures are said to live there, and in the past many children have gone missing.*

Something splashed into the dank water only a few feet from the trail, stirring the cool, heavy mist that engulfed the landscape. Jahrra yelped and instinctively pulled on Phrym's reins, the disturbing thoughts resonating in her head quickly drowned out by the sound of her pounding heart. Phrym quickened his pace and made a few discontented noises of nervousness, but as Jahrra shakily coaxed him back to a slower pace, she noticed that the sound had been caused by a turtle taking cover under the water.

She closed her eyes and took a deep breath, laughing nervously as she released it. She reached down and patted Phrym.

"It's alright boy. It was only a turtle."

Phrym nickered and snorted, seeming satisfied with Jahrra's explanation. She encouraged him onward, and soon they were moving at a steady pace once again.

As they journeyed deeper into the swamp, Jahrra tried hard to be positive and not think about what might be watching her from the thick brush beyond the trail. She especially tried not to think about the legendary witch that may or may not live in the Belloughs, but the chilly woods conjured up memories of campfire ghost stories that kept the fear fresh.

She squeezed her eyes shut and tried desperately to repeat the words of meditation that Viornen had taught her, but all she could hear was Kaihmen's voice echoing in her head, *"The witch came from the far east, fleeing from the Crimson King. It is said that she double-crossed the evil king and is now hiding out in fear of him . . ."*

Jahrra shuddered. The idea of someone double-crossing the Crimson King terrified her; he sounded bad enough as it was without being angry. *I'm just being paranoid,* she told herself, *there's no one in this swamp except maybe some frogs and leeches.* But no matter how hard she tried, Jahrra couldn't get her mind off of the terror that had settled inside of her like heavy silt settling in a riverbed. Her hands were clammy and she could feel sweat trickling down her back, despite the cold.

# The Dare

Phrym nickered lightly, and Jahrra pulled him to a stop, hoping to recover her bearings and calm her mind. They'd been walking for about a half hour, and so far Jahrra hadn't seen anything to make her feel so nervous. She blinked and looked around at the surrounding scenery to distract herself. The swamp was tangled with a variety of plants ranging from tiny, almost luminescent toadstools of multiple colors, to the giant, dominating oaks that choked out everything else but the dark poison ivy that wrapped tightly around their trunks. The moss that hung from the twisting branches looked like thick, matted hair and was a dark, dry olive color.

Jahrra pulled her eyes from the thick canopy and glanced down at the path she and Phrym were following. The black tendril of soil stretched thinly above the bank of the wetlands before disappearing into the obscure, thick fog in the immediate distance. After several minutes, Jahrra took a deep breath and decided it was time to move on.

Regardless of the quiet atmosphere and the fact that nothing horrible had happened after an hour of walking, Jahrra still couldn't settle down. Phrym jerked back his head at the screech of a bird followed by a vigorous flapping of wings, and Jahrra had to take a few breaths to calm her racing heart. This was the first thing she'd heard since entering the swamp besides Phrym's horsey comments and the retreating turtle.

Phrym came to a stop once again and Jahrra took a few more deep breaths, the taste of the cool, mossy air calming her nerves a bit. The fog was thicker now; a result, Jahrra thought, of some dark, evil magic brewing in the hidden corners of the Belloughs. They had to be close now, she could *feel* it.

Jahrra shuddered and swallowed thickly. The Belloughs of the Black Swamp. Her stomach took another plunge at the very thought of the name.

"Phrym, you have to make sure I stay focused," she whispered nervously down to her strangely calm semequin.

Phrym merely turned his ears back towards her and kept on walking carefully past the brown ferns and oily green liverworts. A few minutes later the trail began to decline into the chill air of the belly of the swamp. The atmosphere not only grew colder and mistier, but darker as well, as if a premature twilight had begun to set in. *It's only because of the cover of the oaks; they're growing closer together here.* Jahrra told herself, trying really hard not to let the heavy atmosphere smother her.

A loud, sudden CRACK cut through the silence when Phrym stepped on a dead branch.

"Whoa!" Jahrra shouted, her entire body tensing out of instinct.

Phrym tossed his head and started to canter.

"Stop Phrym, slow down!" Jahrra pleaded as she pulled back on the reins which were easily slipping through her sweaty palms. She was trying hard not to panic and give in to her raw nerves as the cool air caressed her hot face. Phrym slowed after a few dozen yards and Jahrra slumped limply up against his strong neck.

"It's alright, Phrym, you only spooked yourself!" she breathed nervously, a little more loudly than she ought to.

She scratched his neck once more and his nervous snorting gradually calmed. But Phrym wasn't paying attention to her. He was standing stark still; his ears cocked forward, his stance tense. Jahrra froze. She was afraid to look up, but she forced herself to. She hadn't noticed the tall hills closing in on either side of them. She suddenly felt like a panicked insect rushing into a funnel spider's trap.

Jahrra blinked through Phrym's tangled mane, her blood freezing as she recognized the scene before her. The parallel rows of hills met up not too far ahead, forming the unmistakable crook of the Belloughs. She had made it, and she was still alive and in one piece.

*Well, here goes.*

Jahrra drew on every ounce of courage she possessed as she gently led Phrym down into the Belloughs of the Black Swamp.

# -Chapter Twenty-One-
# The Witch of the Wreing

Phrym released a small snort, his breath steaming in the chill air, letting Jahrra know in his own way that he was beginning to have second thoughts about this venture. Jahrra ignored him and surveyed the surrounding scenery, her senses on high alert. She squinted through the dense, gray mist, her heart thudding erratically when she realized the dark blotches against the base of the hills were caves.

Jahrra tightened her fingers around Phrym's reins, her knuckles growing white from the pressure, and tried to stop her mind from imagining what might live in those dark caverns. The cavern entrances themselves made her think of gaping, black mouths crying out in pain, and the ropes of moss clinging and streaming from their edges like the bedraggled beards of men long dead. The very thought sent chills down her spine, and she knew if a witch did live in this dank swamp, she would most definitely reside here.

# The Witch of the Wreing

Jahrra took a deep breath, inhaling the unpleasant scents of sulfur, stale dampness and old ashes. It was eerily quiet here, even more so than the stretch of swamp they had already passed. Nevertheless, Jahrra thought that if she strained her ears enough she might hear the strange whispering of a magical language or the black words of a terrible spell.

After surveying nervously for several minutes, Jahrra looked down at Phrym, trying to gauge his judgment. The semequin must have found the place safe enough after all, for he continued to look straight ahead, almost in curiosity. *Strange,* she thought, *how can he be so calm while I'm ready to turn and bolt?*

Terrified but unwilling to give up after coming this far, Jahrra grudgingly eased Phrym forward, her heart rate steadily rising until it pounded in her ears. The pair delicately wove their way around gnarled tree roots and through tangles of vegetation, coming to a stop when they reached the point where the land flattened out and became dry.

From this new vantage point Jahrra was able to see the Belloughs a little more clearly. There was life here, and not just the grim, depressed life she'd come to expect in a place without regular sunlight or fertile soil, but life that had been coaxed and pampered into existence.

Jahrra stopped Phrym and gazed around in wonder at the sight before her. There were strange plants that she'd never seen before, not even in Hroombra's books on botany: leafy plants with crinkled, bruise-purple foliage and woody plants with alien-like flowers. Jahrra was dumbfounded at this discovery. Of all the things she expected to find here, she had not expected to find a garden.

Jahrra continued to brush her eyes over the well-tended rows of plants, gasping when her eyes fell upon a huge colony of mushrooms. These were even more intriguing than the rest of the plants growing hodgepodge around the caves, and Jahrra soon forgot her overwhelming trepidation.

Fungi of all shapes and sizes, colors and patterns dotted the dark section of earth like the diverse buildings of a tiny city. There were mushrooms that appeared to be as tall as Phrym, some so tiny that hundreds of them together looked like a small blotch of blue or red or yellow paint spilled upon the ground. Jahrra noted red mushrooms with white spots and brown mushrooms with yellow stalks. There were even mushrooms that were covered in what appeared to be tiny taste buds, and others that looked like umbrellas turned inside out. She even spotted some of the incandescent toadstools she'd seen at the swamp's entrance.

Jahrra climbed down from Phrym and led him over to the edge of the strange garden. She stalked, wide-eyed, towards the mushroom patch, blocking out all other sights, sounds, smells and sensations. She dropped Phrym's reins as if in a daze and squatted down to get a closer look at the glowing toadstools. She reached out her hand to touch one of the more peculiar large mushrooms, a pale, creamy green thing that had short, nubby branches and tiny hair-like appendages all over it, when the silence was abruptly broken.

"Beautiful, aren't they?"

Jahrra screamed and fell awkwardly to the ground at the sound of the unfamiliar, crackling voice. Phrym panicked and backed up nervously, snorting and whinnying aggressively. He would've bolted, but Jahrra was on the ground in a vulnerable position and he wouldn't leave her. Jahrra quickly righted herself, putting her hands behind her to prop herself up. While still sitting in the soft, damp soil, she stared up at a much disheveled, very old woman.

*Oh no!* she thought with impending dread, *the Witch of the Wreing! I'm done for!* She tried to stand up, but her legs and arms were useless and her entire body felt like it had been drained of blood, leaving a sick, acidic feeling in her muscles. The woman rocked forward, and Jahrra desperately began crawling backwards, smearing black muck all over herself.

"Don't worry, I'm no witch, and I'm no hag," the haggard woman rasped. "Unless you think me a goblin or a troll, you have nothing to fear."

Jahrra would have sworn the woman was smiling, but she couldn't bring herself to look at her face. It was hard enough looking at any part of her at all. Jahrra decided to focus on her feet, which were actually hidden by a patched and worn skirt.

"Beautiful, aren't they?" the woman asked again, gesturing stiffly towards the mushrooms.

The pounding in Jahrra's ears had subsided enough to allow her to take notice of her voice. It wasn't gruff, but was worn and friendly, not at all threatening.

"It's quite alright, I won't harm you," the woman insisted.

Jahrra didn't know whether to be frightened or friendly. She breathed deeply and slowly like Viornen and Yaraa had taught her to do when faced with a potential enemy.

She then swallowed her fear and took a good, long look at the strange person in front of her. Jahrra blinked; the old woman wasn't overly impressive or frightening after all. In fact, she looked like she had risen right out of the swamp itself and Jahrra, after traveling through this strange landscape, wouldn't have been surprised if she had. She wasn't tall, maybe just a few inches over five feet at the most, and had flaming red hair unlike any color Jahrra had ever seen before.

Reluctantly, Jahrra forced herself to look at the woman's face, relief flooding through her when she didn't find the expected sallow features with hollow eyes and rotten skin. The woman did look quite old, however, and very haggard, with crooked teeth and wrinkled skin, and her heavy clothes were filthy and patched. Jahrra wondered again if this was the witch everyone feared, and understood why they would think that. If anyone had seen her from a distance wandering these misty woods, they would've run away in fear. But up close, she didn't seem frightening at all, and her voice, although scratchy and tired, was actually warm and welcoming.

Jahrra continued to stare as the woman took a few more steps forward, moving gracefully for someone who looked so fragile and weathered. As she drew closer, the woman's face became more visible in the dim light of the swamp. It was an old and bent face, and the lines were deeper than Jahrra had noticed at first, easily putting Hroombra and his wrinkles to shame. The old woman smiled once again, revealing missing teeth, but her topaz eyes overflowed with strength, fire, and a deep wisdom.

"You're a quiet one, not what I expected. Not what I expected at all."

She cackled softly, looking not at all deterred by Jahrra's rude staring.

Jahrra hadn't realized just how frightened she still was until a wave of calm washed over her, pushing away the feeling of faintness. Miraculously, she heard her own voice, although the words she tried to speak got caught in her throat, "Wh-who, wha-what . . .?"

The old woman's face cracked into another smile. Jahrra swallowed and tried again, doing a much better job this time.

"I, I'm so sorry," she managed lamely, stammering slightly in embarrassment.

After gaping like a suffocating fish for a few seconds, she continued, "I was mesmerized by your collection of plants, they're quite amazing."

Jahrra tried to smile, but realized it was a weak effort. She bit her bottom lip instead and allowed her gaze to falter, watching her hand sink into the black soil beside her instead.

"Ah yes," croaked the ancient woman, sounding not at all offended. "I've worked many hours keeping it happy."

"I'm terribly sorry to intrude," Jahrra repeated abashedly. She wondered why the woman hadn't yet questioned why a young girl had been trespassing and poking around in her yard.

She continued on, her face growing hot, "My classmates challenged me to come to the Belloughs. I had no idea anyone really lived here or I wouldn't have been so intrusive."

The old woman looked at Jahrra with her head cocked slightly to the side, as if trying to read her mind.

Jahrra suddenly wished she was a turtle so she could retreat within her shell, but unfortunately she didn't have that luxury.

After a few more moments of her scrutinizing stare, the woman spoke more quietly, "Most people avoid this part of Oescienne, so there was no way you could know anyone lived here. But I'm sure you've heard stories of a monster or a hag, and thus wished to see for yourself if such tales were true?"

The woman's golden eyes twinkled, revealing a startling youthfulness, and Jahrra turned from pink to crimson. The old woman was exactly right, of course. Yes, Jahrra had ideas of a vile creature lurking in the caves, but she'd never stopped to think that there just might be someone living here trying to avoid the very outsiders who persecuted them.

Jahrra sat in uncomfortable silence, ignoring the dampness soaking through her clothes.

It was only a short while before the old woman spoke once again, "No worries lass," she rasped. "I rarely receive company, and now you can tell your friends you've come face to face with the Witch of the Wreing. Come, you can't sit in the mud forever."

Jahrra looked up suddenly, forgetting her apprehension and before she could stop herself, she blurted, "Are you really a witch?"

The woman, who had her gnarled hand held out to give Jahrra a hand up, exploded in raucous laughter, lightening the atmosphere just a bit. Jahrra shrank farther into the mud.

"Well, the answer to that question really depends on who you ask," the woman said when she had regained her breath. "To some I am a witch; to others I'm a hag. To most I'm just a crazy old woman."

She gave a jagged smile, pulling up the timorous girl who'd finally taken her rough hand. Jahrra was surprised at how easily the woman yanked her up.

"My name is Archedenaeh, but you can call me Denaeh. I'm a Mystic and I've been awaiting your arrival for some time now."

Jahrra gaped at her, pausing in the middle of her effort to wipe off as much of the mud clinging to her backside as she could.

Once she found her voice, she stammered, "How, how did you know I was coming?"

"Like I said, I'm a Mystic."

Jahrra stood in the middle of the little clearing, her eyes wide with surprise. A million questions ran through her head, but this time she thought before speaking. In the calmest voice she could muster, she queried, "What exactly is a Mystic? Is it like a fortune teller?"

The woman laughed once again, clearly amused by these naïve questions. Normally, Jahrra would've been annoyed by all the laughter at her expense, but she could tell that the woman's amusement wasn't malicious in the least. Jahrra, slightly discomfited by her lack of knowledge, returned her focus to the ground, staring at a tiny golden mushroom that had strayed from the main crop.

The woman finished her fit of laughter and answered as she wiped a tear from the corner of her eye.

"It is not."

Jahrra braved a glance at the Mystic. She simply stood there grinning, the gleam of laughter lingering in her eyes.

Taking a deep breath, Jahrra pushed on. "What's the difference, then, between a fortune teller and a Mystic?" And before she could allow the woman any more awkward pauses, quickly added, "And where do oracles come in? And if you are a Mystic, why do people say you're a witch?"

The old woman looked pleased at these questions despite the urgency in which they were asked and simply answered serenely, "A fortune teller does mostly guess work, interpreting cards or signs they believe have significance. A fortune teller speaks in half-truths because they don't have all of the facts and essentially don't know the future. A fortune teller often only wishes to make a profit and will find a way to tell the listener what they want to hear, usually something vague that could be applied to any fortunate or unfortunate event in a person's life."

The old woman, standing hunched over with the tips of her knobby fingers pressed together, paused and looked at Jahrra to make sure she was following. Jahrra rubbed her arm and smiled in encouragement.

"A Mystic is a step above that," the woman continued, "interpreting the spiritual signals they receive from the world around them. A Mystic tells you the part of your future they can see, but emphasizes that they can only see a small portion. Most of it is up to that particular person and what they make of it. A Mystic will feed off of what spiritual essence a person possesses and will try and make an assessment of that information.

"An Oracle, on the other hand, is a being that actually knows the past, present and future. They speak in riddles because they know the absolute truth will drive any living being mad. An Oracle will tell you enough to help you through a rough patch, but will seldom give you more."

The old woman drew her sleeve-draped arms behind her back and began to slowly pace in front of Jahrra before continuing, "There are many fortunetellers in this world, fewer Mystics, and unfortunately, only two of the five Oracles of Ethöes remain in existence."

Jahrra was fascinated and completely enraptured with Denaeh's explanation. Hroombra would never tell her this much if she ever asked him.

She took advantage of this woman's willingness to answer her questions and asked a few more, "How does someone become a fortuneteller or a Mystic? And could you tell me more about the Oracles? Why are there only two left?"

Denaeh smiled again and released a small chuckle. "Fortunetellers are everyday people who require little training compared to Mystics. Mystics require extensive training and are changed significantly before they are qualified. Mystics also require a pre-existing gift toward the art of reading the future, and they must be magical."

Jahrra moved her mouth to form a question, but the old woman held up a withered hand to stop her. "The Oracles were created by the goddess Ethöes and are considered highly sacred.

Originally there were five, like I said, but two were killed during the rise and fall of the god Ciarrohn, and another was killed by the Crimson King, Cierryon. The Oracles are the supreme power when it comes to inquiries of the future, but Mystics have exceptional powers as well."

Suddenly, a branch snapped in the distance and Jahrra instinctively glanced in the direction the sound came from. As soon as she returned her eyes to Archedenaeh, she gasped in shock and took a quick step back, almost tripping over a decaying log. Instead of the old, haggard elderly woman that had been telling her all about Mystics and Oracles, she was looking at a young, beautiful woman standing exactly in her spot.

When she grinned, Jahrra noticed she had the same smile (but with several more teeth), the same glittering topaz eyes, and the same vibrant red hair that the older woman had.

In a much younger and more melodic voice, she said, "We Mystics also have a special power. We have the ability to take on three stages of life; infancy, youth and old age, but I rarely find use for infancy."

She said this as if instantaneously changing from an old woman to a young one were as natural as breathing. Her smile and eyes held laughter once again and before Jahrra's very eyes she melted back into the old woman, once more taking on the hunched posture and weathered features of age.

"Will that do for now, Jahrra?"

Jahrra started, not at the rough change in Denaeh's voice, but at the sound of her own name being spoken.

"You know my name."

It was more a statement than a question.

"Oh, yes lass, I know much about you. You are twelve years of age, I believe, the tallest in your age group at school, and you are unlike all of the other children you know, in more ways than you think. But don't bother to ask how or why I know these things, because now is not the time for you to know."

Jahrra had a sudden image of Hroombra telling a portion of one of his stories, and she began to wonder why this Mystic, living in the middle of the Wreing Florenn isolated from all of civilization, could know so much about her. But if Denaeh was what she claimed, Jahrra guessed she could tell anything about anyone who wandered into her swamp.

*This feels dangerous,* said a small voice in her head. Jahrra twitched and pushed the voice aside as she tried to think. *This is crazy!* the voice insisted, *You don't know this woman! Make some excuse and get out of there!* But an overwhelming blanket of calm and safety muffled her blaring conscience. She suddenly felt at ease and was able to get back to her own thoughts.

Jahrra gazed into the mysterious, golden eyes of the old woman as she tried to determine her intentions. *She could definitely be an ally when it comes to the twins,* she thought shrewdly, *but is all this kindness just a façade? Could she really be evil and simply be waiting to gain my trust, like the witches in all the old stories?*

Jahrra pondered these thoughts for a while, but in the end decided that the Mystic Archedenaeh wasn't dangerous in the least. *She's probably just glad to be talking to someone else after all her years of isolation.* Jahrra smiled once again, wondering if during all this time the woman had been reading her mind.

"Tell me about your garden," Jahrra said cheerfully, trying to cover her conspiratorial thoughts.

"I thought you'd never ask!" Denaeh beamed, turning once again into her younger, more vibrant self and leading Jahrra through the patches of mushrooms and clumps of grasses and vines.

Once she'd completely done away with her lingering hesitance, Jahrra spoke freely and easily with Denaeh. She found it comforting to talk with the Mystic, and soon she was telling her own story about her life and her friends and school. Denaeh listened carefully, nodding in the right places and smiling when Jahrra's story needed encouragement.

Although Denaeh seemed to be intrigued by Jahrra's stories, the Mystic wasn't paying particularly close attention to what the girl was saying. Not that she was insensitive to Jahrra's troubles, however. Denaeh merely needed to assess the girl, to figure out what she was made of. *Yes,* the Mystic thought to herself as her eyes glittered, making Jahrra believe she was smiling in response to her description of Kiniahn Kroi, *you are special indeed . . .*

". . . and then he pulled me down from the face of the waterfall, just like that, and I fell almost thirty feet!"

Jahrra's enthusiastic tale broke past Denaeh's thoughts, and the Mystic realized that she would have to think about the future later. Right now she needed to befriend this young girl, gain her undying trust and loyalty, and make sure she had some kind of influence on her life from this point on.

Jahrra paused, giving the Mystic an odd look. After a few moments, she continued on with her story, forgetting that her new friend had seemed to lose focus for awhile.

"Anyhow, we went back to their house, and Gieaun, Scede and I were able to spend the whole evening in the kitchens with all of the cooks and maids. It was the best Solstice Eve I've ever had. And can you believe it? I didn't even want to go!"

Archedenaeh grinned broadly over the small fire she had kindled beside her garden and added, "Yes, Jahrra, you'll learn in life that many of the things you wish against turn out to be the best things that ever happen to you."

Jahrra smiled at this. She liked this strange woman and at the same time wondered if Hroombra was aware of her presence in the forest. But her mentor would have told her by now, wouldn't he? He wouldn't stress how dangerous the Wreing Florenn was if he knew about Denaeh. Jahrra sighed wistfully. The Mystic was so much easier to talk to than the other adults she knew, and was so much more willing to answer her endless questions.

While Jahrra was reflecting on her sudden good fortune, a strange, crackling call cut through the thick air and a big, dark bird flew out of the mist, swooping down onto Denaeh's shoulder.

"Whoa!" Jahrra exclaimed, falling to the ground in surprise.

The strange bird grumbled and fluffed up his feathers while Denaeh laughed, absent-mindedly stroking its glossy wings. Jahrra quickly rolled back into a sitting position, gawking openly at the odd bird. It looked like a raven, but it was larger with shorter legs. She stood up slowly, brushing herself off for a second time and approached Denaeh cautiously. She let out a low sigh when she realized the bird wasn't black but a deep, dark blue color with silky feathers all around its neck, legs and back. Its neck feathers were streaked with a creamy yellow color, and the feathers on its back and legs were the same.

The bird made another strange cawing noise and Jahrra noticed that it had some sort of seed or acorn lodged in its glossy beak.

"Very well, Mílíhn, plant it on the edge of the mushroom patch," Denaeh said to the bird, smiling and smoothing its silky feathers.

The raven-like bird fluttered off of her shoulder and glided to the other side of the garden. It landed rather awkwardly, hopping to a stop, and quickly shoved the seed into the soil, using its beak to cover it back up with black soil.

"What on Ethöes was that?" Jahrra queried breathlessly.

"Ah," Denaeh said, smiling broadly, "that is my bird, Mílíhn. He's a korehv."

"What's a korehv?" Jahrra asked, still stunned, wondering if she could find it in any of Hroombra's books.

"A korehv is a bird native to Felldreim similar to ravens and crows. They're also highly intelligent and are prone to collecting seeds and other useful objects, so you can see why he and I are so compatible."

Mílíhn croaked contentedly and flew back to his master's shoulder. He fluffed up his feathers and shook, dropping one large wing feather as he did so. Denaeh reached out and plucked it from the air before it hit the ground. She turned the feather in her fingers, examining it. Then she held it out to Jahrra.

"A gift from the both of us, it will bring you luck."

Jahrra took the feather speechlessly, as if she were being offered a rare gem. She looked at it for a while, the shimmering blue color none like she'd ever seen.

"Thank you," she finally said, tucking it away safely into a pocket inside her vest.

"He keeps me company in this lonely place," Denaeh continued calmly after a short silence.

Mílíhn was now cocking his head to the side, observing Jahrra with one black, glossy eye. He let out a low, grumbling noise, causing Jahrra to flinch.

"That means he approves of you," the Mystic said, grinning and scratching behind the bird's neck.

"Oh, well, I like him too," Jahrra replied sheepishly.

Once the shock of Mílíhn's arrival wore off, Jahrra and Denaeh spent most of half an hour admiring the Mystic's exotic garden. Not only did she have every kind of mushroom that grew in Oescienne, but she grew many wild herbs and plants and spices as well, all useful in helping with different ailments.

"Now, this kind of mushroom," she said, leaning down and pulling up a dark purple one, "is very good at curing headaches. And this herb," she continued, plucking the leaves off of a green and white plant, "helps to ease the stomach."

Jahrra got out her journal and sketched and listed all of the different plants and fungi that Denaeh had growing in her garden. While Jahrra drew, the Mystic weeded, pulling at tough and stubborn plants that seemed to bring the whole earth up with them when she finally loosened them.

"Ugh, awful things these weeds, if only my other plants were so determined to stay alive," she said, and then to end the silence that had been emanating from the girl sketching next to her she added, "So, Jahrra, tell me more about yourself. What do you do with your friends other than get into trouble with your classmates?"

Denaeh flashed Jahrra a teasing grin, but the girl's head had flown up and her eyes had grown as large as apples.

"Oh no!" she said suddenly, shutting her journal with violence.

"What is it?" Denaeh asked, afraid she'd said something to offend her guest.

Jahrra saw the worried look on Denaeh's face and adjusted her tone. "No, nothing is wrong. It's just that I forgot. My friends will be worried about me. They're probably thinking I'm dead or captured! I'm sorry, but I have to go now."

"Oh, is that all?" Denaeh said, grinning impishly as she dusted off her soil-stained hands.

Jahrra scrambled to her feet in her haste, but stopped before moving any farther. She put her hand to her forehead and groaned.

"What now?" Denaeh asked, looking puzzled.

"Nothing, it's just . . ." Jahrra began.

Denaeh raised her eyebrows and Jahrra sighed. "Well, you know my classmates dared me to come here, but the thing is I have to prove that I came all the way to the Belloughs. But I have no idea how to prove something like that!"

Jahrra then told the Mystic everything, about the challenge, about her stupidity in falling for the twins' ruse, and especially about Lake Ossar.

"You see, only if I bring back some proof will they stay away from Lake Ossar for good. It was the only place I could go to get away from them."

Jahrra sighed deeply and slouched back to the ground, her legs crossed and her shoulders slumped. What was the point in going back if she had failed? She could bring back one of Denaeh's mushrooms, if the Mystic would let her, but what would that prove? It was no use; she had nothing to show for her accomplishment. She almost wished now that Denaeh had been a witch intent on eating her.

Denaeh gazed down at Jahrra, her lips pursed in scrutiny. She drew one hand up to her chin and her young face took on a pensive look. Jahrra didn't notice when the Mystic's thoughtful stance relaxed, but when she finally looked up at the young woman, she was beaming brightly at her.

"What?" Jahrra asked, confused by the Mystic's sudden joy.

"Jahrra, how good are you at acting?"

That was an odd question, considering the circumstances. But Jahrra simply shrugged. "I guess I'm alright at it, I've never really acted before. Why?"

"Well," Denaeh grinned, her golden eyes sparking with mischief, "I have an idea . . ."

# -Chapter Twenty-Two-

# What Goes Around Comes Around

"Eydeth! Just let us go! What if she's hurt or needs our help?"

The only thing that consumed Scede more than his anger was his fear, but Eydeth and his sister just smirked.

"I said she had to do it alone or no deal," he purred.

"It's been nearly four hours!" Scede screamed, his face turning red. "Surely that's long enough! And I don't care anymore, the deal is off!"

Scede stalked off to where Bhun and Aimhe were tied to a sapling, but Eydeth's voice called over the crowd of students still waiting around to learn Jahrra's fate.

"Oh, no you don't. She got herself into this and she can get herself out. No help from her loser friends!"

Scede turned around and glared back at the other boy. Eydeth had called upon his thugs and they were now standing in

a semi-circle, blocking off the trail Jahrra had taken earlier that morning.

"You think we're bad now, wait and see what happens to you at school if you try to go after your stupid friend."

Ellysian got up from the giant log she'd been sitting on and moved to stand next to her brother. A few more reluctant girls, who were often seen following her around, joined her. Scede looked over at Gieaun, leaning against a eucalyptus tree so she wouldn't fall over. Ever since Jahrra had disappeared into the woods that morning, she'd grown more and more tense and nervous. Now she was just barely holding on to the little sanity she had left.

Scede secretly cursed his friend for going through with this stupid dare and hoped more than anything that she'd just twisted an ankle or had managed to get lost. He refused to believe she was in any real danger, but he wasn't about to take any chances. Throwing one last glare of hatred in Eydeth's general direction, Scede snatched up Bhun's reins and hopped into the saddle.

"You'd better move unless you want to get trampled!" he shouted to the crowd blocking the path. He meant every word.

Scede looked down at his sister and she stared back, grim faced, but nodded. She hoisted herself up and staggered over to Aimhe who was staring after Bhun in a perplexed manner. Gieaun used an old tree stump to get into the saddle and soon drew her horse up next to her brother's.

"Now, are you going to move or not?" Scede demanded.

"What's the use in going in after her?" Eydeth said, trying to keep the twinge of fear from his voice. "If the witch hasn't captured her then she has most likely died of fright. In fact, that's probably what has happened to her. She saw an old gnarled tree and thought it was the witch and died on the spot! She would be just dumb enough to do something like that!"

The crowd tossed around a light, nervous chuckle, more to pass the time than for any other reason. They'd been standing around for hours, waiting for either Jahrra to return triumphant or for someone to finally decide she wasn't coming back at all. A few people had left and a few had come back, but little else had happened since Jahrra's brave disappearance into the Wreing Florenn. Everyone was ready for a little action, and now that Scede and Gieaun were up on their horses, it looked like something was finally going to happen.

"Have it your way," Scede said coldly. "Gieaun?"

Gieaun nodded once, gravely, and as the two prepared themselves to charge at the stubborn crowd, a loud, grating cry split the air. Everyone froze, gasping and ducking as a great black creature came flying out of the woods.

"What the . . . ?!""

Scede jerked to the side as a large raven swooped between him and Gieaun. Gieaun screamed, spooking Bhun and Aimhe even more. The horses stomped their feet and whinnied in terror.

The sound of several people shouting and scattering made Scede turn his head. Bhun was still trying to bolt, but Scede had control of him. A crashing sounded over the screaming group of students and Scede almost fell out of the saddle when he saw what it was.

"Run! Get out of here, RUN!!!!!!"

"JAHRRA!?" Gieaun screamed.

"Gieaun, Scede, everybody, RUN, NOW!!!!!"

She looked like a wild animal on top of Phrym, her hair flying free of its braid, her shirt and pants covered in mud. There was plant debris stuck under the saddle and Phrym's flanks were damp with sweat. Jahrra's eyes were dark, her face was pale and her jaw was tense with fear.

Everyone stopped their scurrying long enough to ogle at the bedraggled girl who'd flown out of the trees, but then something else happened. A fierce, wicked cackle split the stressed atmosphere. Everyone shivered and darted their panicked eyes back towards the wood where the horrible sound had come from.

"RUN!" Jahrra shrieked again, kicking her heels into Phrym's sides, causing him to whinny in protest before bolting forward.

And then, before anyone else could move, a dark, hunched figure dressed in a ragged cloak darted between the two largest trees only fifty yards away. If Jahrra's panicked voice and face hadn't made her classmates move, the sight of the Witch of the Wreing did.

Ellysian was the first to scream, followed by her brother. If Gieaun and Scede hadn't been so frightened, they would have laughed at them. The twins hurtled past everyone else, running at full speed to where they had tied their jumpy horses. After that, it was utter chaos. People were screeching and crying and clawing to get away from the forest's edge. Gieaun and Scede just sat on top of their own nervous horses, staring numbly in shock. Jahrra's voice finally broke them from their strange trance.

"C'mon!" she rasped. "It's the Witch of the Wreing! Let's go, now!"

Jahrra forced Phrym into a full trot, with Gieaun and Scede right on her heels. Scede's heart was beating out of his chest and Gieaun looked as pale as death, but they kept up with Jahrra as she and Phrym tore across the fields in the direction of the stables above the Castle Guard Ruin. By the time they got there, Gieaun was close to fainting and Scede was shaking violently. Jahrra, however, looked as calm as Lake Ossar on a windless day.

Once he caught his breath and found his voice, Scede gasped, "What *happened* back there?! Jahrra, how are you even still *alive?*"

Gieaun had to cover her mouth to keep from getting sick.

Jahrra took a deep breath, the fear that had dominated her eyes long gone. She glanced down the slope at the Ruin to make sure Hroombra hadn't seen them. She had a lot to explain and she wasn't ready to let her guardian in on what she'd been doing today.

"You have to promise not to be angry," she finally said.

"Angry?" Gieaun whispered. "How could we be angry, you're alive! The witch almost had you, but you escaped!"

Jahrra dropped her eyes and fiddled with Phrym's reins guiltily. She took a deep breath and released it.

"There is no witch."

"What!" Scede barked. "Did you not see that, *thing*, chasing you!?"

"She's not a witch."

"Alright, hag then. Jahrra, that wasn't your imagination this time, it was real. We all saw it, right Gieaun?"

Gieaun gave a short nod, looking sick again.

"No, she's real," Jahrra continued carefully. "Only she's not a hag, or a witch. She's a Mystic and her name is Archedenaeh."

Both Gieaun and Scede stared at her looking completely aghast. It was a while before either of them spoke and Jahrra had to fight hard not to squirm as she waited.

"*What?*" Scede managed.

Jahrra gritted her teeth and looked both of them in the eye. "I'm going to tell you what happened, but you have to promise not to tell anyone, alright?"

They both nodded, looking more confused than frightened now. They all slid from their horses, their legs still wobbly from their ordeal. As the three horses lowered their heads to eat field dandelions, Jahrra closed her eyes and began her tale. She told them how she had found Denaeh's garden and how the woman had surprised her. She told them about how she was a Mystic and knew who Jahrra was before she introduced herself. She told them about Mílíhn and the acorn and even about how Denaeh could transform from an old woman into a young woman in the blink of an eye. Then she told them about their plan.

"You see, I told Denaeh all about the dare and how I had to bring back proof to Eydeth. Then she got this idea. Why not pretend like she really was the witch? Why not act like I had gone into the Belloughs and angered her, and then have her chase me all the way back here? Wouldn't that be proof enough?"

Jahrra was afraid to look up. Not once had Gieaun or Scede interrupted her. She had no idea what they could be thinking right now. *Probably really angry with me for terrifying the wits out of them.* She braved a peek and met Scede's hard expression, impossible to read. She glanced over at Gieaun and found the same look on her face.

"I, I'm sorry," she attempted. "I didn't want to scare you two, but it was the only way to make sure our plan worked. And look at it this way, now we can have Lake Ossar back!"

"Who cares about Lake Ossar!" Scede shot venomously. Jahrra cringed, shrinking against Phrym's shoulder. "Jahrra, we thought you were dead! In fact, we were about to come in after you!"

Jahrra had never seen Scede so angry, and Gieaun's silent observance was even worse. Scede marched over to a gopher mound and kicked it fiercely, sending a cloud of sand into the air, startling the horses. Jahrra just stood silently, afraid to move from Phrym's side. Scede kept kicking at the gopher mound until it was leveled to the ground. By the time he was finished, he was panting and shaking. Jahrra wanted to go over and talk to him, but she was afraid he would lash out at her. Instead, Gieaun abandoned her place next to a grazing Aimhe and walked over to her friend, looking her up and down. Jahrra flinched, waiting for her tirade.

"Your hair looks terrible," she said quietly. "Did it get that way on its own or was that all part of the act?"

Jahrra's jaw dropped. Of all the things she was waiting to hear, that wasn't one of them. Gieaun's voice wasn't angry or frightened, but calm.

"Aren't you mad at me?" she asked.

Gieaun contemplated this. "Yes, but I'm more relieved that the witch, or whatever she is, didn't kill you."

Jahrra sighed deeply and smiled. She was so glad at least one of her friends didn't want to pummel her.

"Come on, Scede. You're going to forgive Jahrra, right?"

Scede glared over at them, but it didn't take long before his face softened and his anger passed. He walked over to his sister and his friend, grumbling the whole way.

He looked up at Jahrra, still not completely done with being angry at her, and said, "I guess so. But you owe us big time for scaring us like that."

Jahrra grinned. "Oh, don't worry, I know."

Gieaun let out a tiny yelp and threw her arms around Jahrra and Scede.

"Gieaun! What are you doing?!" Scede muffled past his sister's hair.

Jahrra simply gave in and hugged both her friends right back. Scede squirmed.

"Girls!" he grumbled, rolling his eyes.

Gieaun finally released Jahrra and her brother and held them at arms' length. Her green eyes were bright and she smiled widely.

"Well, it isn't noon yet. We have the whole day ahead of us, what should we do?"

Jahrra shot a wry glance at Scede who returned a smug grin. "I know. Let's go to Wood's End Ranch and pack a picnic. I happen to know of a nice little island that *won't* be visited by a certain brother and sister today."

Gieaun squealed in glee and Scede laughed out loud. They snatched up their horses' reins, jumped in the saddle and turned them up the dirt road leading south and eventually to Lake Ossar.

As they lazed on their tattered quilt spread over the soggy earth of Reed Island, Jahrra, Gieaun and Scede talked and laughed until they had stitches in their sides and tears in their eyes. Jahrra was overjoyed at the twins' reaction to her trick and Gieaun and Scede were fascinated by Jahrra's description of Denaeh and her garden.

"I still can't believe it worked! It seemed impossible when Denaeh suggested it," Jahrra admitted, trying to keep her eyelids from drooping.

"Trust me, it worked!" Scede insisted. "I'll be surprised if the twins ever leave their house again!"

Jahrra smiled, hoping what Scede said was true. Her eyes drooped again, but she forced them to stay open. She heard one of her friends yawn next to her and decided it was no use fighting her fatigue. She had been up early and had spent half the day scared to death, so she might as well give in to a short nap. She only knew she was sleeping when she sat up and found herself in a cool orchard cloaked in mist.

Jahrra sighed and smiled, knowing that she would soon see the stranger who stalked these dreams so often. The last time she'd seen him in her dreams was several years ago, right after the death of her parents. Jahrra frowned, hoping her dream wouldn't suddenly turn into one of the nightmares she'd experienced during that awful time.

A faint glowing light began to unfurl near the eastern edge of the orchard, so Jahrra knew her friend was coming soon. *Friend?* She rolled this idea around in her mind, wondering why it hadn't occurred to her before. *Well, I guess he is my friend, whoever he is.* She stood up, feeling strangely stiff and groggy, and moved toward the inviting light. The hooded figure hadn't shown up yet, but Jahrra knew it was only a matter of time. She trudged through the thick, dew-drenched grass, but before she reached the place where the hooded man would inevitably arrive, something moved in the corner of her eye.

She shot her head around and gasped when she saw a golden unicorn standing only twenty feet away from her. He was beautiful, more beautiful than the one she had seen in the meadow of the Wreing Florenn. He pricked his ears forward when he saw Jahrra looking at him and released a cry, a chiming, melodic whinny. Jahrra immediately forgot about the green cloaked stranger and cautiously approached the unicorn, fascinated by his metallic coat.

The unicorn let her pet him for a while but then turned and trotted out of the orchard. Jahrra quickly followed, entranced by this amazing animal. She walked easily through the forest surrounding the copse of fruit trees, moving downhill, always downhill. She struggled a little with the underbrush and had to push aside low hanging branches, but the unicorn always stayed in sight, not yet disappearing into the thick mist.

Finally, after several heart-racing minutes, the unicorn stopped dead in his tracks and stared down over a drop in the land. Jahrra slid next to him and focused her eyes on what he was seeing. She gasped. Below them was the Belloughs, Denaeh's garden and the cave she called home in plain view. A tendril of smoke curled from a small chimney in the hillside, but Jahrra sensed no movement from the cave or the surrounding trees.

Jahrra glanced at the unicorn, his pale eyes locking with hers. Suddenly, she felt happy and carefree, like she weighed no more than a feather. The unicorn slowly edged forward, and she gladly followed, not wanting to be torn from the blissful feeling the magical creature was emanating.

Jahrra was sure she would've followed this animal into a forest fire if he wished to lead her there, but suddenly something seemed to pull at her mind. It wasn't unpleasant, but it threatened to release her from the unicorn's trance. *No,* she thought, *he wants me to go down there, I must go.* But the force that pulled on her mind wouldn't relent. It gently surrounded her thoughts and lightly pushed the giddy feeling away. Jahrra gasped as the last thread of joyous peace was ripped from her mind. She clutched her head and took deep breaths as common sense returned to her.

What had she been doing, straying away from her safe orchard? Wasn't it dangerous to go wandering around in dreams, even ones this familiar? Jahrra shook her head, wondering if she was even still asleep. When she looked up from her crouched position, she knew that she was. She was still deep in the woods, far away from her orchard, but there, just in front of her was the tall, enigmatic figure she had grown to rely on. He gazed down at her, as always, from the shadow of his hood. She couldn't see his eyes, but she could feel them locked with her own. His arms were crossed and his back rigid, but she didn't feel threatened by him at all.

He stood aside and held out an arm as if inviting her to walk ahead of him. Jahrra nodded and slowly got back on her feet, rocking slightly from the dizzy after effects of the unicorn's influence on her. She stumbled forward, taking longer than she thought to get back to the orchard. Her hooded friend stayed right behind her, always keeping the same distance, and when they got back to the place where she had woken up in this dream, he nodded his head and she obediently lay back down upon the mattress of soft weeds.

Before she drifted off to join the world of the conscious, Jahrra asked him a question, her voice sounding strange in this otherworld, "You didn't want me to go with the unicorn, did you?"

He nodded, keeping his arms crossed and not saying a word. Jahrra swallowed.

"Why?"

But all he did was drop his arm in a welcoming gesture, signaling to her that now was the time to wake up.

Jahrra nodded and hunkered down into the thick grass. She didn't want to wake up yet; she had too much to think about and this was just the place to do some deep thinking. She thought about her new friend, Denaeh, and wondered if the strange path of this dream had anything to do with her. The Mystic was eccentric, Jahrra had to admit, but she liked the woman and felt that she could be a source of comfort and advice.

Jahrra thought about Hroombra and Jaax, wondering if two dragons could really know what was best for her. They were a mystery to her; Hroombra and his secrets, and Jaax and his mysterious life outside of Oescienne. Jahrra frowned mentally when she thought of the enigma that was the Tanaan dragon Raejaaxorix. She wondered about his mood swings and the way he looked at her, like he was always trying to figure out what she was, and she wondered about his mysterious friends, Viornen and Yaraa.

Jahrra loved her new trainers, but who were they really? Why did she have to keep their lessons a secret? And why did she have to keep the dragons' language a secret as well? Hroombra and Jaax had told her it could be dangerous if she told others about Kruelt, but if it were truly dangerous, why teach her at all? She knew there had to be more to it than what they claimed, but when would she be old enough to know the truth?

Jahrra sighed and buried her face in the fragrant meadow grasses, wondering if the hooded figure was still standing guard over her. She struggled to settle her mind and was surprised to finally feel her rackety thoughts calming and subsiding. Slowly, every muscle in her body relaxed and before she knew it she was listening to Scede's soft snoring, Gieaun's sleepy murmuring, and the gentle lap of water. Jahrra grinned, eyes still closed. There were several voices ringing over Lake Ossar that afternoon, but not one of them belonged to Eydeth or Ellysian.

# -Epilogue-
# Letters from Afar

Hroombra gazed languidly through the small window perched above the ledge in his study. The golden stalks of dying flowers and grasses nodded their heads lazily as the sun touched down over the azure ocean. Summer was coming to a close, and soon the long warm days would grow short, heating up one last time in the middle of autumn before succumbing to winter's chill.

The old dragon breathed in sharply through his nostrils and released a slow, heated breath. He could hardly believe all the time that had passed since Jaax had first brought Jahrra here those dozen odd years ago. A chuckle fought its way free of the dragon's throat. *Of course I can believe the quick passage of time, what is twelve years to me? What is a hundred, or even a thousand?* He'd seen so much time pass it was almost unnecessary for him to keep the history books the elves had written up for him.

What was the point in looking through them if he already knew, from personal experience, what had happened?

But they were for Jahrra to learn from, for there were things that had happened in the past, terrible things that the historians hadn't known to write down. Things that he'd seen happen and had allowed to happen, things that Jahrra shouldn't know about, at least not yet.

Hroombra drew another breath and then glanced back at his desk. As usual, it was cluttered with age stained scrolls and creased maps. Beside these familiar items lay several white pages, newer paper just arrived earlier that week. *Letters from the beautiful city of Lidien, and some from Nimbronia,* he mused. They'd been written with magic, the writer using the same technique he himself had used once to draw up the Kruelt alphabet for Jahrra.

*Magic that would be much easier to obtain within the mystical province of Felldreim,* the old dragon reminded himself. These particular letters hid a variety of emotions, if one read between the lines, and an abundance of information, some good, some not so good. These letters concerned Jahrra, the chosen one, the savior of the world, and they had all been written by the dragon Raejaaxorix.

Hroombra cast one last lingering look over the hushing fields and silent forest before settling himself comfortably behind his desk. He found his dragons' spectacles and managed to situate them between his snout and eyes and began to study the letters again. It was safe for him to review this information now, not only was it written in Kruelt (a language Jahrra still had trouble with), but Jahrra herself was gone for the weekend on another camping trip with her two best friends. No need to worry about her stumbling upon any information that she was too young to bear. Hroombra cleared his mind and started reading.

The first letter had been dated more than a month ago, and began with a curt but respectful tone:

*Hroombra,*

*Ever since leaving Oescienne the last time I visited, I've been tempted to take a trip east to gather what information I can. Not just to Rhiim or even the western expanses of Terre Moeserre, but all the way to Dhonoara Valley and perhaps beyond. I feel that this may be a risk worth taking because before long, Jahrra will be of age and what we have been waiting for and have prepared for will surely be upon us. I have not been beyond Terre Moeserre in over a hundred years, and much might have changed since then. Naturally, I wanted your opinion before undertaking such an odyssey.*

*For now I will resign myself to my usual task of scouting the more secluded areas of Torinn, Felldreim and Rhiim, searching for both enemies and allies alike. Much time has passed since I've recruited the help of others, and I'm hoping they'll be more willing to help our cause this time around. Just two weeks ago I found a small community nestled in the Kouriohnt Mountains, a place I had passed over before maybe fifty years earlier. The locals were elfin, perhaps even Resai, but they did not fear me and they spoke displeasingly of the Crimson King. A good sign, even if they weren't ready to jump up and storm the king's city right then and there. I told them who I was and that I would keep in touch. They seemed pleased to know that someone was watching out for them. Of course, I told them nothing of Jahrra.*

*I found a few more small settlements, nothing larger than a few hundred residents, and a good number of them were fearful of dragons so I didn't even land. Before coming to Lidien, where I am currently residing, I flew into Crie. Aydehn and his wife Thenya were pleased to see me. They seemed spirited enough, very glad to hear that Jahrra was doing well in Oescienne, disheartened to hear of the death of her parents but approving of your taking her in. Every time I stop by the tiny village they harass me about seeing her again. Someday I think I'll have to bring her there, even if it is just to show her where she came from.*

*A month has passed since I came to Lidien and I will be leaving before the week is ended. I have looked at many of the schools they have here, and have narrowed my choices down to three. They are all excellent and will provide Jahrra with everything she needs when she is old enough to attend one of them.*

*I will end my letter on a positive note: everywhere I go I feel less and less of the oppression that seemed to grip the land not twenty five years ago. It is almost as if the land itself senses Jahrra's presence and is passing it on to those souls living upon it. It is a good feeling and it gives me hope.*

*Sincerely,*

*Raejaaxorix*

Hroombra let his eyes linger over the last few sentences for several minutes. *It gives me hope too,* the old dragon thought. He felt joyful, peaceful and happy. Not only was it a good sign that Jaax had found more possible allies in the inevitable war against Cierryon, but the younger dragon felt hopeful. This wasn't just good, this was downright wonderful.

Hroombra smiled a true, heartfelt smile. For so long Jaax fought the possibility of the prophecy coming true. And why wouldn't he? Holding out hope for hundreds of years? Almost anyone would grow jaded and weary of clinging on to hope for so long, it was exhausting. Hroombra was only able to manage it because he was already old when the prophecy was born and he'd grown accustomed to the necessity of patience. He could wait a hundred thousand years for diamonds to form if he wished and not feel burdened at all.

Jaax however, like most Tanaan dragons, had inherited that human trait along with so many others: impatience, determination and stubbornness. No wonder Jaax and Jahrra ground so harshly against one another. Hroombra lost his smile at that sudden thought. He knew there would be more trouble between the two in the future. Jahrra wasn't getting any less headstrong and Jaax wasn't one to lose a fight. *But that's a long way away,* Hroombra reminded himself, narrowing his gaze to dive into the next letter.

*Hroombra,*

*I am in Nimbronia now. It took me several months to get here since I stopped off in Cahrdyarein along the way. I never meant to spend any time in that strange elfin city, but a late blizzard trapped me in the Hrunahn Footmountains and I had no choice but to wait it out. What I found, however, astounded me. The elves of these footmountains know much about the Crimson King and his past grievances. I was surprised, for you know as well as I do that very few people of this land know the truth behind the Tyrant's ascension to the throne.*

*Once I informed them of who I was and what my mission entailed, they showed me their city. They tell me the stone they use for their buildings is unique to the region, formed deep in the earth and later tempered on the frozen peaks. I was impressed by their society and their concern for this world, and I am more than happy to inform you that they have agreed whole-heartedly to join our cause.*

*I must confess, I nearly informed them of Jahrra's existence, but I avoided that temptation. After all, their adopted leader is younger than I am, and I know little of their history. I did tell them that the future looked hopeful, from what I have gathered from the surrounding provinces, and that I was finding more and more support for our purpose.*

*After leaving Cahrdyarein I headed straight for Nimbronia. In fact, I arrived only a half hour ago and haven't even had time to see the king. I plan on speaking with him soon but thought you would like to hear my news about Cahrdyarein first. I'll follow this letter with another as soon as I find the time.*

> *Sincerely,*
>
> *Raejaaxorix*

Hroombra grinned, his smile reaching his eyes. He imagined Jaax standing next to the king of the Creecemind, and the picture was something comparable to that of a small housecat standing beside a wolf. Despite the dragon king's immense size, Hroombra doubted Jaax would let this intimidate him. He could see the smaller dragon now, standing in the enormous frozen halls of Nimbronia, looking the king directly in the eye with the same cool indifference that he gave everyone else.

Hroombra sighed and moved to look at the next letter, dreading both its brevity and its informal heading. There was usually only one reason not to address a letter personally, that reason being there was a chance it might get intercepted by the wrong person. The first two letters had been quite positive so Hroombra feared that this final correspondence might contain bad news.

*Dear Reader,*

*I have spoken with his majesty and unfortunately have met with some bad news. He has informed me that his spies have noticed suspicious groups of people moving along the southern border. I immediately left the region to witness this for myself, and I fear that what he told me was true. I have seen with my own eyes the threat lingering on the southern border, your northern border, and so I felt it necessary to check elsewhere.*

*The news from the eastern rim is the same. Large troops of men seem to be congregating outside of the province, looking for weak links in the chain, places that can easily be entered. Furthermore, small camps and even military bases have sprung up in a few places, all positioned in such a way as to make them hard to spot from the air, and I cannot help but suspect an eventual invasion. As far as I know, the border has not been breached, but I fear it won't be long.*

# The Legend of Oescienne – The Finding

*His majesty has promised to deploy patrols to the northern border, something I am eternally grateful for, but I must find a way to secure the south and the east. I will write again as soon as I can, until then, keep your senses broad and your heart close.*

This letter wasn't signed, but Hroombra knew who had sent it. A shiver ran down his long spine and he felt a sudden fear grip his old bones. He read the last line again, lingering on the words *keep your senses broad and your heart close*. Jahrra was his heart; that was the code word for her in letters such as these.

But Jahrra wasn't close. She was somewhere camping with her friends. Hroombra's eyes darted to the date of the letter, only a few weeks ago. Could whoever was trying to sneak into Oescienne have done so by now? *No, Jaax would have returned if they were even close to invading. We still have time . . .*

Hroombra shivered against the evening air trickling in through the window. *Jahrra is fine,* he assured himself, *she'll be back tomorrow.*

The old dragon finally convinced himself not to worry about Jahrra anymore, but he couldn't rid his mind of what Jaax's last letter claimed. The Crimson King was no longer dormant. The search for Jahrra had begun, whether the Tyrant had gotten word of her birth or not, he was no longer sitting in his wretched fortress waiting for her to come to him.

"So now the world changes," Hroombra whispered into the encroaching twilight. "So now it begins."

# Pronunciation Guide

Aimhe – AIM-ee
Aldalis – AL-di-lees
Aldehren – AL-der-en
Archedenaeh – ARK-uh-di-nay-uh
Baherhb – BARB
Bhun – BOON
Ciarrohn – CHI-ron
Cierryon – CHAIR-ee-on
Dharedth – DARE-edth
Dhonoara – DEN-or-uh
Edyadth – ED-ee-adth
Ellysian – EL-lis-ee-en
Elornn – EE-lorn
Ethöes – ETH-oh-es
Eydeth – AY-deth
Felldreim – FELL-dreem
Gieaun – JOON
Hroombramantu – HROOM-bruh-mon-too
Jahrra – JARE-uh
Kiniahn Kroi – KIN-ee-an KROY
Kruelt – KROOLT
Lensterans – LENS-ter-ans
Magehn – MA-jen
Nesnan – NESH-nan
Nuun Esse – NOON ESS
Oescienne – AW-see-en
Oorn – OH-orn
Ossar – OH-sar
Phrym – FRIM
Raejaaxorix – RAY-jax-or-iks
Raenyan – REN-yun
Resai – RESH-eye
Samibi – SAM-ee-bee
Scede – SADE
Semequin – SEM-ek-win
Sobledthe – SO-bledth
Srithe – SREE-the
Strohm – STROME
Tanaan – TAN-en
Thorbet – TOR-bet
Viornen – VEE-or-nin
Wreing Florenn – WRAING flor-EN
Yaraa – YAR-uh

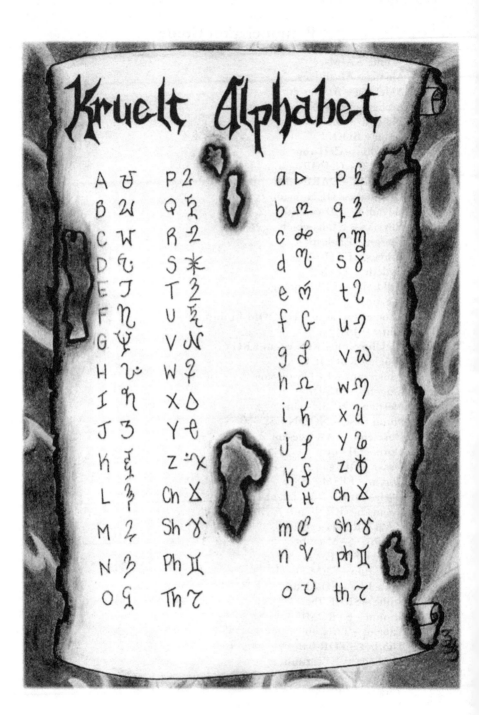

# ACKNOWLEDGMENTS

Many thanks to all those people who have supported me on this long and rocky road to publication:

To Sister Mary, who first taught me the intricate inner workings of the English language.

To Frank Wies, for his help with getting the cover for my first novel just right.

To all of the children and families of St. Patrick's School, for their undying inspiration, support and encouragement; for making sure I never gave up.

To my fellow author friend Rachel, who knew what I was going through and provided much support, both moral and literary.

And finally, a very special thanks to Suni Mills and her sixth grade class, for providing the light at the end of the tunnel.

JEJ

## ABOUT THE AUTHOR

Jenna Elizabeth Johnson grew up and still resides on the Central Coast of California, a place she finds as magical and enchanting as the worlds she creates.

Jenna received a BA in Art Practice with a minor in Celtic Studies from the University of California at Berkeley. It was during her time in college that she decided to begin her first novel, *The Legend of Oescienne - The Finding*. Reading such works as *Beowulf*, *The Mabinogi* and *The Second Battle of Maige Tuired* in her Scandinavian and Celtic Studies courses finally inspired her to start writing down her own tales of adventure and fantasy.

Jenna also enjoys creating the maps and some of the artwork for her various worlds. Besides writing and drawing, she is often found reading, gardening, camping, hiking, bird watching, and practicing long sword fighting and archery using a long bow. She also loves getting feedback from readers, so feel free to send her a message any time.

**Jenna Elizabeth Johnson can be contacted at**
**authorjejohnson@gmail.com**

# Other books by this author:

## The Legend of Oescienne Series
The Finding (Book One)
The Beginning (Book Two)
The Awakening (Book Three)
The Ascending (Book Four)
Tales of Oescienne - A Short Story Collection

## The Otherworld Series
### Meghan's POV
Faelorehn (Book One)
Dolmarehn (Book Two)
Luathara (Book Three)
### Cade's POV
Ehríad - A Novella of the Otherworld (Book Four)
Ghalien – A Novel of the Otherworld (Book Five)
### Robyn's POV
Lorehnin – A Novel of the Otherworld (Book Six)
Caelíhn – A Novel of the Otherworld (Book Seven)
### Cade's and Meghan's POV
Faeléahn – A Novella of the Otherworld (Book Eight)
### Standalone Novel
Faeborne - A Novel of the Otherworld (Book Nine)
### Aiden's POV
Faebound – A Novelal of the Otherworld (Book Ten)
### More Otherworld Stories
Faescorned - A Tale of the Otherworld (available in the *Once Upon A Curse* anthology)
Soot and Stone – A Fae Tale of the Otherworld (available in the *Once Upon A Kiss* anthology)
Flame and Form – A Novella of the Otherworld (available in the *A Plague of Dragons* anthology)

Made in the USA
Coppell, TX
01 October 2023

22268071R00298